FOR
Jim Pary.

WATER
DAMAGE

Daniel Ciller

WATER DAMAGE

A TALE OF NEW MEXICO, NEW YORK,
AND DAWNING TERROR IN AMERICA

SEQUEL TO
STATEHOOD OF AFFAIRS

DANIEL R. CILLIS, PhD

WATER DAMAGE
A Tale of New Mexico, New York, and Dawning Terror in America

Copyright © 2015 Daniel R. Cillis, PhD

All rights reserved. No part of this book may be used or reproduced by any means, graphic, electronic, or mechanical, including photocopying, recording, taping or by any information storage retrieval system without the written permission of the publisher except in the case of brief quotations embodied in critical articles and reviews.

Certain characters in this work are historical figures, and certain events portrayed did take place. However, this is a work of fiction. All of the other characters, names, and events as well as all places, incidents, organizations, and dialogue in this novel are either the products of the author's imagination or are used fictitiously.

iUniverse books may be ordered through booksellers or by contacting:

iUniverse
1663 Liberty Drive
Bloomington, IN 47403
www.iuniverse.com
1-800-Authors (1-800-288-4677)

Because of the dynamic nature of the Internet, any web addresses or links contained in this book may have changed since publication and may no longer be valid. The views expressed in this work are solely those of the author and do not necessarily reflect the views of the publisher, and the publisher hereby disclaims any responsibility for them.

Any people depicted in stock imagery provided by Thinkstock are models, and such images are being used for illustrative purposes only. Certain stock imagery © Thinkstock.

ISBN: 978-1-4917-5682-9 (sc)
ISBN: 978-1-4917-5681-2 (e)

Library of Congress Control Number: 2015901320

Print information available on the last page.

iUniverse rev. date: 3/19/2015

CONTENTS

PREFACE

*W*ater Damage, the sequel to *Statehood of Affairs,* continues the stories of Adobe Centori, Mad Mady Blaylock, John Murphy, Gabriella Zena and Jennifer Prower. In *Statehood of Affairs* set 1911, New Mexico was at the center of an international conspiracy that threatened its proposed statehood. The unjust commitment of a woman to an insane asylum reveals a plot to find a missing document, Article X of the Treaty of Mesilla—the Revert Document.

If the document emerges before Arizona and New Mexico can attain statehood, Mexico could recover the lost territories and change history. Tensions rise as the U.S. and Mexico pursue the document to control the territories, thereby putting the nations on a collision course toward war.

Adobe Centori, a hero of the Spanish-American War, is a New Mexico statehood delegate. Affairs of the heart complicate affairs of state as women representing a range of political views compound Centori's challenges. His strongest opponent is Gabriella Zena—*La Guerillera*. They share true love, but not the same side of the border.

In *Water Damage,* set in 1912, the story begins in New Mexico, but this time takes a New York turn. From New Mexico to New York, the trail leading to anarchists, secret agents and saboteurs is filled with intrigue and danger. In this story, Centori seeks redemption for his Revert Document decisions only to become involved in a greater conspiracy involving the dawning of organized terror in America. The story unfolds as the U.S. violates the Treaty of Mesilla and the Revert Document. That old government paper, partially destroyed by rain, once again threatens the political order between the U.S. and Mexico.

Environmental water damage can be slow or fast. Similarly, the impact of the Revert Document on international relations can slowly lead to damage. Sabotage, on the other hand, can be fast and lead to damage as an instrument of Germany's plan for the coming Great War.

DRAMATIS PERSONAE

Adoloreto "Adobe" Centori—Circle C Ranch owner, New Mexico sheriff

General Ramiro Vega—Mexican Army commander

Colonel Diego Venada—Mexican Army officer

Josiah Spooner— American Scream co-conspirator

Lysander Warren—American Scream co-conspirator

Martini di Arma di Taggia—Knickerbocker Hotel bartender

Charity Clarkson—Centori's New York lady friend

Lucy Hayward—American Scream co-conspirator

Emma Parsons—American Scream co-conspirator

John Murphy—Intelligence liaison to President Taft, friend of Centori

Gabriella Zena—Spiritual object of Centori's affection

Jennifer Prower—Publisher *Valtura Journal*, Centori's New Mexico lady friend

Henry McGillivray—federal agent

Jack Haughey—NYPD officer

A.P. Baker—Circle C Ranch foreman

Elizabeth "Mad Mady" Blaylock—owner Mad Mady's Saloon, friend of Centori

Felicity Brimwell—Prower's friend

Siegfried Seiler—German operative

Count Helmut von Riesenfelder—German ambassador to Mexico, Secret Service intelligence liaison to Berlin

José Victoriano Huerta Márquez—President of Mexico

Francisco Greigos—Circle C cowboy

Bernhard Bachmeier—German operative and saboteur

Dr. Luis Salazar—Professor of Geology, University of Mexico

Henry Parker—Circle C cowboy

Pedro Quesada—Circle C cowboy

Rhinelander Waldan—NYPD commissioner

Rocco Grandinetto—NYPD officer

Coyote—humorous and dangerous wild dog and cultural hero

PROLOGUE

GREAT DIVIDE

MAY 1912

An army of Mexican revolutionaries led by General Ramiro Vega is moving north from the Mexican border—and deeper into New Mexico. For several days, 200 fast-riding horsemen have traveled through a majestic land creating large dust clouds in their wake.

Now, the riders pass through vast mountain ranges that are divided by harsh desert basins, yet the open perilous land must be crossed. The resolve of the men, who are invading a sovereign nation, remains high. The army relentlessly pushes into the Southwest region of the new state, fixated on an American town and on a strategic raid.

Vega and his men are within 20 miles of their destination. The target is Stratford, New Mexico, a place poised to become famous across the country. In January, 1912, a gold discovery increased the town's activity along with the population. By some accounts, this gold strike could be the biggest in U.S. history and Vega's raid will have an equal if not greater impact on the town. Invading the U.S. is a bold plan with international implications extending from New Mexico to major cities in Europe. Although unknown to the invading Mexican army, this daring attack could change the course of the coming Great War.

The army continues north with a heightened sense of danger inherent in the hidden spirit of the desert. Then, a sandstorm begins. At first, dust devils dance around creating more of an annoyance than a danger. This storm quickly becomes a violent wailing wind that swirls surging sheets of sand. The massive dust formations obscure the landscape and the distant mountains. In fighting the violent storm, Vega believes they are moving off course. Suddenly, the sandstorm clears—as quickly as it appeared—revealing the first view of Stratford in the distance.

Stratford is located in Grant County near Silver City, east of the Great Divide—the mountain and water point that separates the east from the west. Extending from the Bering Strait to the Strait of Magellan, the Great Divide separates the watershed that flows to the Pacific Ocean from the watershed that flows to the Atlantic Ocean. Yet, there is no greater divide than the political divide distancing Mexico from the U.S., which once again could lead to a military struggle over the Southwest.

Most of Vega's men wear high-peaked sombreros and carry pistols and a dozen men have kerosene cans tied to their saddles. All of Vega's men carry rifles and bandoleers. The army needs provisions, munitions and money to continue a war against internal enemies. Although war supplies are an important factor, Vega has his eye on another purpose. He halts his cavalcade on a high mesa; he believes it is a good position for the attack.

"Hemos llegado bastante lejos." (We have gone far enough.) Vega instructs Colonel Diego Venada, his second in command.

"*Sí, General, esta es una buena posición.*" (Yes, General, this is a good position.) Venada replies.

Both leaders are veteran fighters with battle scars as testimony to their bravery. They are the same age of 36 years, but Vega appears older; Venada appears stronger. The experienced men are not strangers to war, but invading the United States is unprecedented. The uncertainty of the mission produces anxiety within the men.

"*Vamos a parar aqui y prepararnos para el ataque.*" (We will stop here and prepare for the attack.) Vega says evenly. "*Tráeme los informes de nuestros hombres en Stratford.*" (Get me the reports from our men in Stratford.)

"*De inmediato.*" Venada says sharply.

During the last few days, people in Stratford have noticed a number of strangers on the town's dusty main street. They were near the Avon Hotel, Assay Office, Stratford Saloon and the Gold Mine Superintendent's house. The strangers are spies gathering information in preparation for the raid. At the military camp, Vega waits for them with doubts about the mission.

The colonel returns: "*Los hombres estan llegando tarde.*" (The men are late.)

Vega ignores the problem: "*Diego, ¿por qué estoy de acuerdo con esto, todo para la gloria del presidente?*" (Diego, why did I agree to this, all for the president's glory?)

"*Usted tiene mi lealtad, si no mi acuerdo.*" (You have my loyalty if not my agreement.)

"*Esa es la única cosa de que estoy seguro.*" (That is the only thing I am sure about.)

"*Te seguiré en Stratford o de vuelta a México.*" (I will follow you into Stratford or back into Mexico.)

Vega looks at Venada in silence and then says, "*Gracias, yo dí mi palabra al presidente.*" (Thank you. I gave my word to the president.)

"A continuación vamos a completar la misión." (Then we will complete the mission.)

"Tráeme los informes en el momento en que los tiene." (Bring me the reports the minute you have them.)

Venada nods, mounts his horse, and gallops away.

Vega decides to inspect the men instead of his thoughts and walks with two aides. When Vega and his staff are seen moving around camp, shouts of "Viva Vega!" are heard from the Mexican combatants. This is alarming to Vega given the secret mission.

"Do not call my name here!" Vega shouts and turns to Venada. "We must not be identified as the invaders. You had orders about this."

"The orders were issued."

"Then why do they resist?"

"I suppose they love you too much."

Vega shakes his head and says, "Where are our men with the reports?"

"It is quiet down there, General. I am sure everything is alright."

"No matter, they were under orders to return this past hour."

"Shall I send in more men?"

"No. There are probably too many now. When they return, we will have their reports and wait for pre-dawn. Walk with me." After a few paces, Vega continues, "We will divide the men into two columns and enter the town from two directions."

"From both the north side and the south side of Main Street," Venada confirms.

"Yes. Let's review the map." The men enter Vega's command post tent where the general spreads out a sketch map of Stratford on a portable table.

"These are the points where we will sweep into the town from both directions. Here, at the head of Main Street near the Avon Hotel, you will enter the town with your men."

"Yes, General."

"This building," Vega points to the Gold Mine Superintendent's house and office, "is most important. You will capture the building by storm. Send six highly reliable men to the building. Four of the men will kill anyone who resists and will take every document in the office. They will leave the field of battle immediately with the papers, and return to camp to wait for me."

"And the other two men?"

"They will kill anyone who pursues the men with the documents. You must support them until they are out of town—leaving the same way they entered. If I do not return, they are to deliver the papers to Huerta. Are my orders clear?"

"Clear, General Vega."

"You must be wondering about the four university students."

"Yes, all of the men are wondering."

"They are studying geology with Professor Salazar at *La Universidad Nacional Autónoma de México.*"

Venada eagerly waits for more as Vega continues, "On the south end of town, we can see the head frame of the gold mine. A party of 20 fighters and the geology students will be detached to the mine. The four students will enter the mine; the fighters will remain at the entrance."

The colonel, who is not pleased about the mission in the mine, slightly shakes his head. Vega ignores him and continues, "A defensive line will be set up to protect the students while they work and aid in their retreat if needed. Then I enter the town on Main Street from the south. I will lead the main body of my command into town to link with you at the hotel. When I arrive at the Avon Hotel, I will reverse our direction and we will all continue south past the mines. We will meet at the campsite to regroup. If that is not possible, we continue south to Mexico."

"Are these orders perfectly clear, Venada?"

"Perfectly, General Vega."

"Good. Once again, it is imperative that your men shout, '*Viva Zapata*' during the raid."

"The men will wonder about such an order."

"Issue the order. I think you understand the reason for the deception."

"Yes. Do you think the Americans will be so easily fooled?"

"I don't know."

"So we are expected to conduct two unusual assignments within the attack."

"We are expected to follow the plan." He unties the rawhide strings of a saddlebag, removes the contents and says, "Take this pouch."

Venada accepts. "You must drop this pouch in the town the moment you are near the gold mine office. Do not forget to do so. Have the pouch in your hand ready to drop the moment the firing starts."

The men stare down at Stratford. In a dreadfully poignant way Vega says, "This is not my idea, Diego."

"Few things are for soldiers."

"We have planned all. If our men fail, we fail—and all will be over for us."

"That is what I am thinking, General."

PART ONE

CHARITY ENDS AT HOME

CHAPTER 1

CRIME OF THE CENTURY

OCTOBER 1910

I t was not an earthquake. It was dynamite.

Swedish chemist, industrialist and engineer, Alfred Nobel had discovered a way for highly volatile nitroglycerin to be safely handled. The new mixture was dynamite. Nobel's construction work during the mid-nineteenth century inspired his research for new methods of blasting rock.

In the early morning of October 1, 1910, another use for Nobel's creation emerged. On that day, dynamite exploded at the three-story *Los Angeles Times* building. The booming detonation destroyed the building along with the adjacent printing press structure, killing 20 people and injuring dozens of others. The explosion caused the three floors to collapse, demolished the heating plant and gas mains and created an inferno of death. The dynamiting was an ominous foreboding of things to come for America. The *Los Angeles Times* called the bombers murderers and called the bombing the crime of the century.

Men from the International Association of Bridge and Structural Iron Workers were accused of the bombing. In the past, the Iron Workers had resisted the open shop movement in Los Angeles and fought back aggressively. Months after the bombing, John and James McNamara were arrested; the brothers confessed to the crime in December, 1911. Two other men involved in the bombing conspiracy avoided arrest.

⁓⁓

Thirteen months later, the *Los Angeles Times* bombing faded in the minds of most people across America. This is not true for two men who travel in an exclusive Pullman—the blast repercussion echoes in their minds and throughout their journey across America. They are on a California Limited train car, surrounded by fine carpets, woodwork and furniture, and are heading to the Chicago rail hub. The men are ordinary in appearance and, at first glance, remarkably similar in their suits with waistcoats, cuffed and creased trousers and wing-collared shirts with bow ties. They are of average height and weight with brown hair and light colored eyes. Yet, Josiah Spooner is older and often appears angrier than Lysander Warren who wears a worried expression most of the time. Both are co-conspirators in the *Los Angeles Times* bombing—and they have formed an organization called America Scream.

Although they are physically nondescript, there is nothing nondescript about their plans. The conductor, who walks by with newspapers, freezes the men for a moment. Then Warren laments to Spooner, "I am sorry the McNamara brothers were arrested. It's a setback for the radical unions; we need them."

"It was the risk they accepted. About 25 years ago, the execution of the Haymarket Martyrs started a change within the large unions; they will continue the fight," Spooner responds.

"In part, but many could stop short of our vision."

"Consider that unions will become more fanatically opposed to capitalist economies as companies take larger pieces of cake and leave smaller pieces for workers. They know that capitalists who seem to create value are actually stealing from the workers. The McNamara brothers were arrested, but we survived to fight another day," Mr. Spooner instructs.

"Yes, I know. I am still sorry that people were killed. No one was supposed to be killed. We all have been accused of crimes," counters Warren.

A look of dislike crosses Spooner's austere features. "Consider the terror the unions have endured from employers—and from the government. Many would argue that what happened was justified. Lysander, those who point to our crimes know nothing of poverty, of oppression, and of exploitation."

The conversation is quickly halted by the sound of a door opening.

"Chicago is next, Chicago's Union Station!" The conductor shouts.

After the other door opens and closes, Spooner continues, "Many workers are close to being destitute; most are one paycheck away from begging."

"Josiah, we are nonetheless called criminals."

Rage rises up within Spooner like a tide. He points passionately at Warren and says, "We are not criminals. Who are the criminals? Is it those who force strikes? Is it those who use violent police against workers? Is it those who jail workers while their families go hungry? Are *they* not the criminals?"

"Yes, but will the public consider your position? Do we fight crime with more crime?" Warren calmly responds.

Concerned about attracting attention, Spooner constrains his gestures and says, "Don't you mean *our* position?"

"Yes, *our* position…since the arrest, I have been feeling uneasy."

"I understand. Fear not, the public will support worker rights and why we fight crimes against humanity."

"I am aware of the reasons for our actions. A man cannot allow another man to walk over him. Those views have moved our cause, but the people who died were newspaper workers," he pauses, "not criminals."

Spooner glares but replies with serenity, "Such are the fortunes of war."

"It was a dastardly deed to most and hard to justify, but war?"

Abruptly, Spooner defends, "Yes, to protect workers and injured workers against the industrial onslaught and against the revolting compensation system."

Warren narrows his eyes and remains silent as Spooner goes on. "Greed and control are the lifeblood of the powerful ruling class and the ruthless institutions serve as their way to dominate."

"Do you know that many Americans believe that capitalist wealth is not evidence of theft?" Warren asks.

Ignoring the question, Spooner says, "The answer is to transfer power to the people who created wealth for the capitalists. When that fails, the answer is attacking the system and that means war!"

The Los Angeles bombing was an overture to the orchestrated plans of American Scream. With grim stillness, Warren stares into the darkened train window and considers, *What happens if we destroy the system?*

Twenty minutes later, the train arrives in Chicago's Union Station. The men carry their small bags to the connecting track and board the Broadway Limited, the Pennsylvania Railroad's premier passenger train, for a 20-hour ride to their destination.

Entering a wood-paneled observation car, they sit across from each other on large, upholstered bench seats. Next to a table with fresh flower bouquets, they place their bags that are filled with blasting caps and alarm clocks.

"All aboard!"

The two men turn toward the small window and the trainman beyond.

"All aboard for Fort Wayne, Harrisburg, Philadelphia, Newark and New York!"

CHAPTER 2

SIDEWALKS OF NEW YORK

APRIL 1912

N ew Mexico Statehood Delegate Aldoloreto "Adobe"
Centori's defining time is not achieving statehood. Rather,
it is a state of mind consumed by romantic restlessness that began
in Cuba during the Spanish-American War. At times even great
disappointments can become opportunities, and sometimes people
go home to reorder their lives. Native New Yorker Adobe Centori
is going home.

Last year was an extraordinary period in his life, a time of the
long awaited New Mexico state constitution leading to statehood.
Territorial politics and the state of affairs with Mexico were energized
by sentiments, mayhem and the threat of war. As the complex and
dangerous year drew to a close, he actively rose to the challenge of
the time. There was more to his actions—beyond the importance of
statehood—than met the eye. During New Mexico's last territorial
days, he embodied the qualities of integrity and courage more than
he ever talked about them; adversity introduces a man to himself.

Forty-five-year-old Centori is slender, square-shouldered, square-jawed and handsome. His face carries none of the emotions that weigh on his heart, but his eyes have less soul. Of average height and steady temperament, he carries himself as a man in control. He is skilled in speaking Spanish and more than skilled in speaking to women.

After the Spanish-American War, Centori received the Congressional Medal of Honor. By any measure, he was an able politician adept in keeping himself suitable to those who favored statehood and to those who did not. As owner of the Circle C Ranch in Valtura, New Mexico, he is a good businessman, and as the sheriff of Corona County, he is an effective lawman.

Centori did not go to Washington as a New Mexico senator. The territorial governor's implied promise was broken. No matter, he was a respected statesman who contributed to the framing of New Mexico's Constitution and for delivering an inspiring statehood address in Valtura. After delivering that speech, the crowd thunderously applauded and cheered as some women waved handkerchiefs and some men waved hats.

The inherent qualities within his various roles are sometimes in conflict. Nevertheless, he has been successful in integrating the confrontational and diplomatic aspects of his professions. On the whole, he is consistent with moments of prominence.

On January 6, 1912, Delegate Centori witnessed President Taft sign the New Mexico Statehood Bill in Washington. Centori handed Taft a quill from an eagle in New Mexico. The president signed the proclamation and said, "New Mexico's long struggle for statehood is finally over." On that day, the Dow Jones Industrial Average, including General Electric, U.S. Rubber and U.S. Steel, was 82.36. Federal spending was $690 million with a $3 million surplus—and Centori decided to return to New York.

Several weeks later at the Circle C Ranch, Centori announced his intentions to go to New York and marvel over 20th century architecture. He acquits himself well, so most of the people in Valtura believed his story.

Unparalleled changes have occurred in Centori's life. Now, to change his environment he rides the train to New York. The rhythm of the rails eclipses his senses, his lonesomeness abates and his relentless cowboy lament fades. The native New Yorker prepares to change roles again. He turns to the window and to the speeding scenery and reflects upon his return. *In many ways my time in New Mexico was like a long trip. That trip has ended… it is good to start anew.*

The train decreases speed as it enters the tunnel. The conductor shouts, "New York, final destination, Pennsylvania Station, New York." Not even a minute later, the train decelerates and Centori buttons his coat; the train's slow crawl turns into a stop. He has arrived in New York's Pennsylvania Station on West 34th Street.

Carrying a duffel bag, he speeds along with the other passengers in the colossal concourse; a hall crowded with people moving to and from platforms and trains. Reminiscent of the Roman Baths of Caracalla, the station is a Beaux-Arts masterpiece, an epic introduction to New York. Wearing a three-piece suit, a wing-collared shirt and a tan cowboy hat, he enters Gotham as a king enters a palace.

On the streets of New York at twilight, Centori draws a deep breath of the cool evening air as his steel blue eyes widen. The city noise hits him in an exhilarating way. His cowboy hat attracts the attention of two "coppers" for a moment. He tips his hat and they nod in return.

Broadway is full of life. New York's commercial and cosmopolitan environments had developed since the turn of the century; a change that Centori welcomed. The city blocks are crowded with people;

WATER DAMAGE | 11

streets are filled with Hansoms, Broughams, Fords and Auburns. *This sure is different from the traffic around Valtura Plaza,* he observes.

Adobe Centori had something missing; now he is as solid as the New York bedrock on which he stands. Walking north and passing a saloon, he recognizes a song from his youth as the music flows outside to the street. The tune, a slow waltz about New York life during the 1890s, is called *The Sidewalks of New York.*

At times he struggles against sentimentality, seeking to avoid feelings as a basis of truth. This time he stops, listens and reminisces about his days as a child in New York.

East Side, West Side, all around the town
The tots sang ring-around-Rosie, London Bridge is falling down

Bounding on to a horse drawn streetcar, Centori sees benches lining both sides under the windows. An empty seat in the front looks inviting; he sits and rides along the smooth embedded steel tracks. With bells clanging, two weary white horses pull the streetcar. The white letters below the windows read BROADWAY. The music of iron-shod hoofs merge with bouncing harnesses; clip-clop and jingle are in rhythm.

A father and his young son around eight years of age are sitting on the opposite bench. Noticing the cowboy hat, the boy calls out with excitement. "Hey mister, are you from Texas?"

"No." Centori smiles, "I'm from New Mexico."

"I'm sorry, Sir," the father says.

"Why? He is a fine boy with a quick wit."

"Thank you."

At the next stop, the father and son stand. The boy calls out again, "Goodbye, mister."

Centori smiles again. "Goodbye, young fellow."

Traveling up Broadway he finds the rows of stooped, narrow brownstone houses on the side streets somewhat changed in color. Yet, the reddish brown sandstones that had weathered into a chocolate color are still familiar and comforting. Abruptly, the crowded streetcar feels unsettling and he is completely unprepared for what is next.

An exotic looking woman with straight black hair and large circular dark eyes is sitting in the rear of the streetcar. Instinctively, Centori turns and stares at her; a cold chill runs down his spine. She has an uncanny resemblance to Gabriella Zena. The woman he loved and lost remains impressed in his thoughts. He thinks of her not all the time, but most of the time. When he remembers her, loving reminiscences are quickly replaced by the painful memories. He simply suppresses the conflicting recollections when Gabriella enters his mind.

New York is 1,800 miles from New Mexico, far enough for the impact of environment on personality to change. Even so, pivotal moments can remain pressed in the hearts of people and transcend physical distance. Often in the human mind time stands still. The conductor calls out, "Times Square." The passengers move quickly and Centori turns away from the woman. When the scramble abates, the beautiful woman with black hair is gone. The distraction caused him to almost miss his stop.

In the middle of Times Square, Centori's eyes are at once drawn to the tall Times Building, the new focal point of the area. In 1904, *The New York Times* moved into a new skyscraper on 42nd Street at Longacre Square. The next year, the area was renamed "Times Square." On December 31, 1907, a ball signifying the start of the New Year was slowly dropped from the top of the Times Building. The event has continued for the last five years and seems likely to be ongoing.

Walking in Times Square, where carriage and delivery conveyances fill up the streets, he sees *Taming of the Shrew* playing at the Broadway Theater and soon after *Ben Hur* at the New Amsterdam Theater. The play is based on a book by former New Mexico territorial Governor Lew Wallace.

Centori passes a policeman on horseback who is managing his prancing horse. "That is a fine looking mount, officer."

"You look like you know horses," the policeman shouts.

"A little," he says with a smile.

His interest is divided between sightseeing and finding his destination: the newest Times Square hotel. The opulent Knickerbocker Hotel is on the southeast corner of Broadway and West 42nd Street.

Melville said, 'Life's a voyage that's homeward bound.' Adobe Centori, part tourist and all native—is home.

CHAPTER 3

KNICKERBOCKER HOTEL

TIMES SQUARE

The Knickerbocker Hotel is an outstanding 15-story structure with more than 550 rooms. The Beaux-Arts building is made of red brick with terra cotta details and a mansard roof. In the basement lobby and barroom, the hotel has its own subway entrance where a single door leads to the Interborough Rapid Transit station at Times Square.

Centori enters the opulently furnished and ornamented main lobby and pauses to view the painting of Father Knickerbocker. *I could have the time of my life here, or at least have a chance to sort out my life.*

"Hello, I am Adobe Centori," he says as he reaches the front desk.

"Welcome to the Knickerbocker, Mr. Centori," pronounces the spectacled clerk.

"Thank you," he says while signing the register.

"New Mexico! Welcome to the USA."

"Well, actually it is," he pauses, "thank you."

"We will have your bag sent to your room."

"No need. I'm okay."

In the elevator, as the only rider, he nods at the operator and requests, "Eight, please." Then, he watches the arrow indicate the floors. When it stops at eight, the cage opens; he steps out and finds room 808.

An hour later, Centori returns to the lobby. The Knickerbocker Hotel contains part of the Manhattan social scene; the bar is crowded with refined people. Centori finds and scans the grand room that boasts abundant mahogany, leather, polished brass and a long, ornately carved bar. Behind the bar are shelves filled with abundant liquor bottles; most notable to him is the array of Jameson Irish Whiskey. The barroom decorations consist of large paintings, including Maxfield Parrish's 'Old King Cole,' especially created for John Jacob Astor's new hotel.

Seeing a pathway, he moves with a slight strut of a cavalryman and passes several people. Some of them nod; some of them are annoyed. An older woman, who is *almost* pretty, offers a broad smile. He smiles in return. The cowboy hat generates interest at first, and then the crowd settles into uninterested glances. Most did not pay him the least amount of attention. It is a less than friendly place; just as well, he favors his own company right now.

Although bartender Martini di Arma di Taggia is known to have created a new drink of gin and dry vermouth, Centori approaches him and says, "Jameson with ice."

"Yes, Sir."

As Centori waits for his drink of choice, he notices a Remington painting, the dramatic *U.S. Cavalry Charge*, hung on the wall opposite the bar.

Hmm… I have been in New York less than an hour and another reminder of Cuba…that painting would look great hanging in the Circle C, he thinks.

The bartender returns with a glass of Jameson 12 year reserve, called 1780 for the year the brand was founded in Dublin.

Centori accepts with sincere appreciation. "Thank you."

The 1780 goes down smooth and fast.

Martini sees the empty glass. "Another Jameson," he spiritedly states.

"Yes, Sir."

Centori takes his second drink to a table and removes his cowboy hat. He immediately notices a young lady with blonde hair, blue eyes and Nordic features who is sitting at the next table. Her understated beauty is not instantly outstanding. *She seems to be smiling at me, but I could be imagining,* he thinks.

First impressions are important, especially in a formal New York setting. The New Mexican calls upon his New Yorker decorum while admiring her Merry Widow hat. Centori detects that she is slyly observing him. When he turns to catch her eye, she looks towards her glass.

She is fashionable and indeed dressed for an effect. As many young women have done, she replaced the Edwardian "S" shape dress with a straightened silhouette dress. The wide-brimmed hat with chiffon and feathers casts a shadow over her face creating an indistinct facial expression. In this light, her vacant face is remarkably reminiscent of the Georges Braque painting, *Tête de Femme*. Centori, the optimist, perceives a slight smile. The young lady removes her hat to offer a fleeting smile; his perception becomes reality.

The glances at each other continue as he admires her fashionable bob hairstyle. The bottom of her hair meets and frames the bottom of her face. Some consider the new short style to be rebellious. He considers it to be alluring.

She clearly observes his handsome face and notices his blue eyes. Paying special attention to his posture, he ventures, "Good evening, Miss."

He waits for a reply. It does not take long, "How do you do?" she says with confidence within a high-pitched voice.

"I'm Adobe Centori."

"I'm pleased to meet you, Mr. Centori. I am Charity Clarkson," she says seductively.

Although Charity's words speak of class, her delivery vaguely betrays. She seeks to distinguish herself by adhering to certain forms of speech and style of dressing as shown in magazines. Nonetheless, she is seen as a social climber at best.

Charity sips her *Crème de Violette* cordial, a drink with a floral aroma and a sweet taste. He takes a bigger sip of his not so sweet Jameson while noticing another glass on her table. She may not be alone.

"This hotel is quite a place," he smiles.

"People say so, but I am less pleased."

"I see…guess I am overly impressed having arrived from New Mexico."

With a wide smile, Charity inelegantly says, "I would never have guessed."

He peeks at his big cowboy hat on the chair post and replies, "It may shock you to learn that I was born and raised in New York."

"But now you live in a foreign country."

He suppresses his surprise, thinks about it and says, "Miss Clarkson, New Mexico is *not* a foreign country. It's a new U.S. state that borders Colorado."

"You don't say," she replies while viewing his squared-jawed good looks.

"Yes, in fact we obtained statehood in January," Centori informs. "And we have been part of the U.S. since 1846. It was a long struggle to statehood, ending with President Taft's signature."

Charity's eyes widen. "Oh, how do you know so much about the matter?"

"As a New Mexico statehood delegate, I was there!"

The dramatic statement had not been lost on her. She is impressed but does not respond for a moment. "Please tell me what life is like in Mexico."

"*New* Mexico. Life is simple and complete way out west." He lies. "New Mexico has the most beautiful views in the world." He tells the truth. "The mountain ranges, blue skies and vast open spaces all create a wonderful natural environment. After a rare rain, the sky shows a double rainbow. One reflects the other; one is more vibrant than the other."

"You create a lovely vision of such natural beauty; it sounds romantic."

"It can be very romantic."

"What do you do in Mexico?"

"Okay, you win. I run a cattle ranch called the Circle C...in *New* Mexico."

"Circle C, you *are* a real cowboy," she exclaims and glances at his Stetson.

"Yes, a cattle ranch, a business that allows this fine hotel to serve fine steaks."

"Tell me about your ranch."

"It's a hacienda-style ranch house, surrounded by a mixture of beautiful high-desert plants and good views of the mountains."

"Oh my, a serene and dignified place I am sure." They make eye contact and exchange succinct smiles before she says, "You are not like the usual stuffed shirts around here." *And possibly the most handsome man I have ever seen,* she thinks.

He considers her words in his mind. "They all look sophisticated and discerning."

Charity stays silent for a time and reacts, "Yes, they all appear to be ladies and gentlemen who are well aware of Manhattan etiquette, but few of the men are gentlemen. I often struggle with that."

The conversation turn is startling, sparking his interest. *I wonder how much a struggle that would be.*

"Some say I am less than salubrious and engage in shocking behavior."

"Shocking behavior?"

"Yes, entering a bar alone is the least of it," she declares and signals for another drink. "Others say I can resist anything except excitement."

"People can be judgmental."

"Yes, I am judged and found wanting. My way does not lead to their expectations."

"It only matters if you believe what they think."

"Never you mind, I harbor no self-pity. If they say shocking, I say I am good at it. Narrow is their gate and straight is their path. The women can be worse than the men; when you are down they push you down further. Oh...I know it sounds complicated."

"You make complicated interesting," he says with an inviting smile.

"Thank you. I admire a proper gentleman," she says with an even bigger smile.

They lock eyes and he imagines kissing her.

She takes a sip. "What brings you to New York?"

"As I said, this is my home town."

"What really brings you to New York?"

"Well, it is sort of a lengthy tale."

"People who love and lose will live to love another day."

"What?"

"There is something wrong about your love story."

"What? I have not even mentioned any love story, Miss Clarkson."

Ignoring, she goes on, "You seem like Adam, cast out of the charmed garden without your virtue."

He leans forward and repeats, "Miss Clarkson…"

Charity shows her teeth, white as clouds on a blue sky and snaps, "Never you mind."

The subject and his anger are gone but she remains and continues. "How long will you stay in New York?"

"For the foreseeable future, I guess."

"No one can see the future," she quips. "When I came here from Connecticut it seemed unlikely that I would be accepted in polite society. I had to strengthen my resolve to make New York my home."

Again she waves for a drink, prompting him to wonder how many she has had and if someone would return to the other glass.

"I was born into a family with little money. I had an uncertain future. My family said the road to ruin leads to New York with no way back. They were struggling and too optimistic about our fortunes."

"Perhaps they were making the best out of a bad situation."

"No matter, I had no compunction about leaving," she slurs slightly and asks, "Was that selfish?"

"We all make decisions," he quickly answers.

"Other girls in my situation became parlor maids. I did not."

"You seem to have made your own luck."

"The secret of luck is to never trust it," she offers.

The conversation ends with the arrival of Charity's male companion. They are strangers again. He reluctantly returns to his glass and thinks, *Perhaps she is not as pretty as I thought. She is nothing to write home about anyway.*

Although he told himself she did not matter, his waning interest waxes with disappointment. He had enjoyed the time; now he gives his drink full attention.

Given his history with Gabriella Zena and the potential future with Jennifer Prower, he is surprised that he liked her. Yet, he always had a propensity to admire the pretty women he encounters—ready to know them.

The human journey is complex with twists of fate, false starts and unexpected detours. For Centori, who has a hard time ignoring a challenge, life is a welcome mystery with a fate he sometimes predicts. Although expectations—if not his ambition—about women are reduced, he anticipates a positive return to New York. He drains his glass, grabs his Stetson, quits the bar and shakes off Charity, convinced that New York will not disappoint.

It is a calm night with many not-so-calm New Yorkers filling the dazzling streets of Times Square. The buildings obscure the moon and stars but he has a clear mind. Standing outside the hotel, he smiles at two passing women walking together. His eye for beauty prompts natural *not* calculating charm.

Centori looks up at the New York night. *This is a far cry from New Mexico's night sky with the city lights blocking stars from view,* he observes. *But New York's bright lights have their own fascination.* At the Circle C he would stare at the universe and identify the constellations. It is a glorious view—out of this world.

Down to earth, he reflects on his arrival in the Great Metropolis, *New York feels much different from the last time I was here. New York has changed. I guess I have changed as well. The days in New Mexico following statehood were identical and the nights seemed endless; it is good to be home again.*

Centori arrived in New York alone, yet as Cicero said, he is never less alone than when he is alone.

CHAPTER 4

WITHIN THE LAW

It could be attributed to accumulated stress stemming from the Revert Document affair or exhaustion from a lack of sleep during the last few months. Perhaps it was from the difficulties of long distance train travel. Whatever the cause, Centori slept for 15 hours. The restorative respite paved the way for a new day, a better day.

He decides to take a late breakfast in the hotel restaurant where silver trays of hams, pheasant and pressed beef are presented on a long table. Another table holds dishes of melon, nectarines, raspberries, pitchers of cold water and lemonade, pots of coffee and Chinese tea.

Entering the big room, with a book in hand, he is immediately greeted, "Good morning, Mr. Centori."

"Good morning, coffee please. Black!" he answers while escorted to a corner table now arrayed with pink carnations, toast racks, scones, honey and marmalade. Slowly his uneasiness about the past is replaced with a sense of comfort from being home. He reflects on the song from the opera *Clari: Or the Maid of Milan* and recalls some of the words.

Which seek thro' the world, is ne'er met elsewhere.
Home! Home!
Sweet, sweet home!
There's no place like home.

The most welcomed carafe arrives at Centori's table. He sits back to enjoy the coffee and to think about the day. Soon after, he draws discrete looks from patrons and selectively acknowledges the attention. Following breakfast, he moves into the lobby. A heavily carved hat rack is positioned in the middle of the entrance hall; he places his hat on the wood stand and sits on a chair next to a side table. After a few minutes of watching people move about the hotel, he settles into the chair with his novel: *The Hound of the Baskervilles* by Arthur Conan Doyle.

After spending the next few hours with the adventures found within the pages of his book, Centori is ready to start his New York adventure. He walks around Times Square and sees a Broadway show with a familiar name. Subsequently, he is in the audience at the Eltinge 42nd Street theatre.

Centori awaits the curtain to rise, ready for the matinee performance of *Within the Law*. In the play, the shop girl Mary is unjustly convicted of theft and during her prison time she plots revenge. Her accuser's son is targeted for extortion but falls in love with Mary.

In the end, the real thieves are punished and love wins. Walking out of the theatre, Centori muses, *Mary could have been named Mad Mary. Perhaps Mad Mady's Territorial Insane Asylum ordeal in New Mexico could be a good play on Broadway.*

CHAPTER 5

❦

ROMEO Y JULIETA

Back at the Knickerbocker, Centori is more than ready for a fine New York supper. At most of the tables in the lavish hotel dining room, the ladies and gentlemen are keenly engaged in eating and drinking and are surrounded by tapestries and a beamed ceiling reminiscent of Chateau de Fontainebleau. Light chamber music flows about the room from a distance.

Centori examines the room filled with the affluent, the powerful, or both. The Knickerbocker provides a stylish setting for New York society to express their elite identity and for the nouveaux riche to find social positions. All are enjoying a glittery evening; many are too busy with witty banter and classy hilarity to notice the unassuming cowboy enter.

"May I help you, Sir?" asks the maître d'hôtel.

"I would like a table, please," he says over noisy laughter.

"Yes, Sir, right this way."

Carrying his hat, Centori follows the maître d' to a corner table and sits with his back to a wall. A waiter in a white coat takes his order. "Jameson."

As an opera lover, he hopes to see Enrico Caruso who is a hotel resident known to take meals at the restaurant. He looks around the room and keeps an eye out for the Great Caruso.

After the first drink, Centori orders a fine dinner of puree of tomatoes, red-head duck, boiled potatoes, flageolet salad and diplomatique pudding in wine sauce. Summoning his polite dining manners he enjoys an expensive New York feast of $4.75. The peace of mind came free of charge—there were no reminders of Cuba.

Given the large three-story restaurant with seating for 2,000, he did not see Caruso among the crowd. However, sitting at a table several yards away is Mayor William Jay Gaynor and other leading Tammany Hall politicians. Two years ago the mayor was a victim of an assassination attempt. Although he survived the gunshot by a former city employee, the bullet remains lodged in his throat. Centori sees an important aura around the table but does not recognize the mayor.

After the evening meal, he returns to the lobby and to the same chair. He places his hat on the rack, reaches for a cigar and signals for an ash tray. At the Circle C, he smokes fine cigars with close friends. Other times, he smokes alone with his thoughts, a pleasure that recharges his spirits. A busy hotel in Times Square is a different story. He sits down and examines the fine textured wrapper leaf on the *Romeo y Julieta* and toasts the head of the Cuban brand.

Centori takes a long first puff, closes his eyes forgetting his environment for a second. Then he picks up a stack of New York newspapers on a side table. Scanning the headlines, he sees an article in *The New York Sun* that describes a new Navy ship. Looking away from the news story, he sadly thinks, *This reminds me of the voyage from Tampa Bay to Havana and the long return voyage without Gabriella.* Returning to the newspaper he learns that the U.S. Navy battleship, the USS *New York,* is scheduled to launch in October.

Construction of the *New York* started on September 11, 1911, in the Brooklyn Navy Yard.

Picking up *The New York World*, Centori recalls that long time publisher Joseph Pulitzer died last year. He reads that in national politics, former President Theodore Roosevelt will challenge William Taft for the Republican nomination for President. *Another reminder of Cuba. I came home to forget about things for a while. Well, I like both men, TR from the Cuban expedition and Taft for signing the statehood bill. TR was a good president and not a bad cowboy either. Guess TR has my vote again.* He draws on his corona shaped cigar and contemplates the coming presidential election, *Woodrow Wilson could run too; that would be something—the first southern president since the Civil War.*

A headline in *The New York Herald Tribune* reports that the recently completed RMS *Titanic* sailed from Belfast for sea trials before its maiden voyage. The massive ship is scheduled to arrive in New York on April 16th and dock at Chelsea Piers.

Although still enjoying the full flavor of the dark maduro leaf, he finds archaeologist Hiram Bingham's article about Machu Picchu to be a grim reminder of Chaco Canyon. Machu Picchu, a 15th-century Inca site in Peru, is almost 8,000 feet above sea level. The City of the Incas is similar to Chaco Canyon as a significant cultural site of an old civilization. In 1911, Bingham gave Machu Picchu international awareness. He ignores the article and turns to a more agreeable headline:

Alaska to Become U.S. Territory

So Alaska will be an organized, incorporated U.S. territory. Good luck to Alaskans. Hope they will not wait as long as New Mexicans did for statehood, if they want it at all, he ponders. Folding his newspaper he looks around, *Still no Caruso or Charity for that matter.*

For the first time since Chaco Canyon he is relaxed. The fine dinner contributed to a sense of serenity with a good measure of comfort provided by the *Romeo y Julieta* cigar. Then again, his new found inner peace could be the result of the streetcar encounter. Perhaps that woman only resembled Gabriella Zena—perhaps it was Gabriella's final goodbye. Either way, the beautiful woman is gone forever, nothing more to do except enjoy the tranquility. Though, moments of satisfaction are ephemeral like the cigar smoke itself.

CHAPTER 6

❦

RAIN DAMAGE

A few days later and a few miles south of Times Square, dark clouds move over New York Harbor with the chance of a storm increasing. In the Long Room of Fraunces Tavern, at 54 Pearl Street near Broad Street, four plain looking patrons are meeting; they are sitting near a plaque commemorating the American Revolution.

Fraunces Tavern played a prominent role at the end of the American Revolution. After the British evacuated New York, the tavern hosted a dinner for General Washington and his men. It was the scene of Washington's farewell address to the officers of the Continental Army:

> 'With a heart full of love and gratitude I now take leave of you.
> I most devoutly wish that your latter days may be as prosperous
> and happy as your former ones have been glorious and honorable.'

In that same room, Spooner, Warren and two women speak about issues that will affect the latter days of New Yorkers. The two men, recent arrivals to New York, are wearing dark suits. Spooner has been emboldened by the Los Angeles incident and the escape across the country. Now, he may have to adapt to the different political attitudes that are represented at the table.

Warren somewhat struggles with his political style since Los Angeles, but his vision and ambition remain the same. For him, it is a matter of sustained effort. Spooner is concerned that Warren's resolve has, at times, wavered since that early morning in Los Angeles. Both women, in unadorned black dresses with long sleeves, are under wide brim hats that cast shadows upon their faces.

Outside the tavern, more dark clouds appear like molten lava over the harbor. The rain steadily increases and beats against the windows as the faction continues their discussion. The rain arrives with a strong display of the wrath of nature while inside the tavern, the coming wrath of man is formulated.

Digressing from the operational phase, their political philosophy is expressed with and without justification. Their voices are calm as if they were discussing the weather and not a gathering political storm.

"Americans are naturally suspicious of federal authority and will accept the premise that government is best which governs least," says Warren.

Lucy Haywood, the woman sitting across from Warren, says, "You should be more aware of the strengths and weaknesses in that political movement."

She is a member of the Socialist party and she seeks to salvage traditional American democracy within the new industrial order of democratic socialism; she has written in support of national strikes of key industries.

Haywood goes on, "A government that governs least is encouraged by the political philosophy found in the Declaration of Independence. The highly valued American rights and liberties fuel that suspicion and can bring government closer to citizens' expectations."

"That irony will help our cause," says Emma Parsons, the second women who is older than Haywood but still pretty.

She is a Socialist Party member who embraces broader political change. Parsons, an essayist, writes about poverty and the anguish of industrial conditions. She is in conflict with Haywood and she advocates non-democratic state socialism, although both women aim at growing greed as a primary target.

Parsons adds, "Lucy, you are a dreamer. Production for profit must be stopped, *not* reduced. Only state socialism can fully control economic demand and value on utility—and stop the accumulation of capital."

Spooner, with his back against the wall announces, "You are both misguided. Cooperative management of the economy or a state-controlled economy just replaces one form of corruption with another. You say that capitalism creates concentrations of power for those who exploit the 'free-market' and your answer is stronger socialism."

"Yes, I would agree that government regulation beyond stronger unions and workers' councils are needed," Haywood says.

"Lucy, that is not enough," Parsons declares. "The public needs more protection and that means that government is best when it governs the most."

"So you both believe government regulation will promote, *not* suppress, the general welfare?" Spooner asks.

Parsons reflects on the question. "Yes, I do. Would you agree that the Pure Food and Drug Act improved conditions for the general welfare?"

"Would *you* agree that Roosevelt's law expanded government powers?" Spooner counters.

"It was not Roosevelt; it was Sinclair's book that revealed the horrid conditions in the meat-packing industry." Parsons replies, "He was a private citizen and he incited a movement that created the law."

"I agree, the government acted against this evil that caused sickness and death, based on a book, not violence." Warren adds to the mix.

Spooner glares Warren into silence; Parsons continues, "Sinclair caused an outcry and Mr. Roosevelt called upon Congress to help the general welfare."

"Can a book separate the general and the special interest?" Not waiting for an answer, Spooner continues, "Do you believe that books representing the general welfare can work against self-serving corporations who prevent economic equality?"

Hayward chimes in, "Sinclair exposed corrupt inspectors, but he did little about economic fairness. National wealth should be divided equitably so all have a fairer share—that means democratic socialism."

Spooner bitterly replies, "Miss Hayward, you can say that excessive private property must be re-distributed, but that doesn't encourage state reduction—government is best which governs not at all."

"You reject the state completely and call for a stateless society," retorts Parsons. "That can be dangerous—remember Hobbes said that in an anarchistic state of nature life would be solitary, poor, nasty, brutish and short."

"Human life would be subject to arbitrary and tyrannical edicts!" Absolute government is the only alternative?" Spooner asks.

"Yes, if the only alternative is a terrifying anarchy!"

"Wait," Haywood says while holding up her hand. She is right, without political law and order it would be as Hobbs said, 'war of all against all.' Yet, democratic socialism is supported by Locke and his social contract theory."

Spooner takes a deep breath and says, "Government works for itself, not the people. Government carries on for its own purpose. That's why I seek a stateless society, anarchy!" Spooner exclaims. "That is why American Scream exists."

"That is why *you* exist," Parsons shouts. "Who will make the hard moral decisions in your stateless society?"

"That is not easy to answer," Spooner admits. "Moral problems in any form of society can be complex."

"Ah, and moral issues are not 'moral' because you say so or because they go against your stateless standards. They are moral because they hurt other people in ways that they cannot control."

"Government action results in help to some people and harm to others. This combination of good and bad makes moral problems hard to resolve," Spooner concedes.

"So how do you decide, in a stateless society, which people will be better off as a result of a moral position and which people will be worse off?" Parsons asks.

With no good answer he looks at Haywood who says, "Mr. Spooner, anarchy is less likely to be accepted than socialism."

"Ladies, are you open enough to see that capitalists and governments excessively accumulate wealth created by the labor of others? Perhaps you know that hundreds of striking workers were killed and brutalized by police."

"I have written many essays on such issues, Mr. Spooner," Parsons declares.

"Then you know that the working man cannot fight Plutocratic tyrants and their armed guards, strike breakers and company spies. And do not forget the fatal accidents in the mines and factories—strikes are not enough, anarchy is necessary to combat the integral injustice of powerful capitalism."

"Regardless, no government at all can be worse than the disease you hope to cure."

His brow furrows, "Ha, then how do you expect to advance your socialist cause? Distributing wealth that someone else created is gross ignorance of a position that many Americans support—free market capitalism."

"You wish to destroy, not reform the economic system." Parsons states.

Spooner stares. "Yes, because all state power inherently is bad; we must eliminate all types of government. Even if you create your socialist dictatorship, an omnipotent government is dangerous. Government becomes controlled by corrupt power-hungry men who are clever in using the population for their interests."

"Mr. Spooner, if I may say, you seem confused as to which devil you seek to defeat. Is it corporate or government fiends?" Parsons asks.

"There is only one devil, with two heads. Anarchy is abhorrent to both business and government. Anarchy would grind down the power of the ruling classes and their oppressive control of the people. In this so-called democracy, the government is an instrument of the wealthy and powerful to the detriment of the people. That is the state of affairs in America. Anarchy is the cure for tyranny."

The various strategies at the table stem from the difficulties in defining the appropriate role of government and citizens in the modern 20th century. Indeed, the new century ushered in increased industrialization, urbanization and immigration—and increased social unrest, labor struggles and anti-capitalist agitation in the U.S. The increased activity from communists, socialists and anarchists give voice to a scream for change. While various groups differ in goals, their methods form an anti-American strategic alliance.

Nearby in Battery Park, wildly high winds reduce mighty trees to mere piles of wood stock. Crashing trees and dangling branches dominate the landscape outside the tavern and trump the imagination.

Within the tavern, they are determined to achieve their ultimate goal of making social, political, and economic history: the time to change America forever is now. The men and women at the tavern represent a new confederation of groups that are affiliated with the organization called American Scream.

CHAPTER 7

❧

STILL WATERS RUN DEEP

The next afternoon with the storm gone, Centori walks north from Times Square to Central Park. Twenty minutes later, he arrives at the Merchants' Gate entrance at Columbus Circle. At the gate, the Spanish-American War veteran sees the construction site for the USS *Maine* National Monument.

In 1898, the USS *Maine* exploded and sank in Havana Harbor. Although the cause of the disaster was unclear, it led the U.S. into the war. The memorial is expected to be completed next year. Centori immediately reflects on the first time he saw the beautiful Gabriella in Havana. Her black hair was straight, long and wrapped in a band bearing the words *Cuba Libre*.

He returns to Times Square and decides to see two short films. First, he views *Water Nymph*, directed by Max Sennett. It is a Keystone comedy that did not disappoint. Then in a nearby theater he saw, *The Female of the Species* directed by D. W. Griffith and with 'America's Sweetheart,' Mary Pickford.

That evening, Centori is back at the hotel bar; he unbuttons his jacket and draws a silver watch from his vest pocket. At the same time, John Murphy rides the rails on the Congressional Express from Washington, fast approaching New York. Centori and Murphy served together in the Spanish-America War and recently worked within the Revert Document affair to prevent a war with Mexico.

Standing at the bar, Centori scans the room checking for his old army friend. Murphy, who is on the evening train, reaches Grand Central Terminal. Thirty minutes later, a wiry, self-confident man, arrives at the Knickerbocker on time at 9:00 p.m. The former captain of the New Mexico Rangers enters the bar. His flat, wide-brimmed hat and sagging mustache are unmistakable to Centori; his city clothes are not. John Murphy carries a briefcase and a broad smile to the bar. It has been several months since last they met and resolved the Revert Document problem—for better or for worse.

"Adobe!"

"Murph!"

The cowboys in eastern suits smile broadly. The two men shake hands; they are brothers, not in blood, but in bond.

"Good to see you Adobe," Murphy says in his familiar baritone voice.

"Same here, Murph."

"How are you?"

"I'm fine. It's good to be home, but New York has really changed."

"Well, New York is a far cry from New Mexico."

"Isn't that the truth," Centori agrees. "And how about this fancy bar?" he continues while waving his hand around the sophisticated room.

"This place sure is not Mad Mady's Saloon." Murphy agrees as he points to the large painting of 'Old King Cole' behind the bar.

"It's not even her sister's place, what did Santa Fe Sharon call it?"

"It was Chéz Beau Sharon!"

Both men laugh, drawing slight attention from the bartender. Then Centori becomes less buoyant. "Mademoiselle Sharon would be funny, if she were not so deadly. Murph, I was surprised to get your telegraph. Why are you in New York?"

"I'll get to that. In the meantime, shall we drink to New Mexico statehood?" He doesn't wait for an answer; he waves and orders.

"Yes, statehood was long overdue," Centori says flatly.

They have two pints of a champagne cup at $1.50 per pint. After the toast, they walk across the room to a burning fireplace with an assemblage of large leather chairs.

"Murph, I have a couple of fine cigars."

"I was counting on that. I'll buy the whiskey," Murphy offers while Centori waves for a bottle.

Moments after they settle into the chairs the waiter interrupts, "For you and for your friend, Mr. Centori?"

"Yes, that's right."

Centori snips the ends off two Cuban cigars. Murphy pours two glasses of Irish whiskey, straight up. The filled crystal glasses shimmer in front of the blazing fire.

"To old friends," Centori announces. "And as the Irish poet said, all the saints had a past and all the sinners have a future."

Murphy looks puzzled at the toast, glasses click and they light up.

Both men take a puff on the big and choice cigars. On the exhale, Murphy says, "I understand you have a new love interest in Valtura."

"You do?" He nods and concedes, "Probably."

"If I didn't know better, I would say it was Mady Blaylock."

"No, she is too busy running her saloon. Besides, I suspect she could be as erratic as her sister Sharon."

"It's none of my business, but a man would search a long time to find a better woman than Mady."

"Not interested," he says through a cloud of smoke.

"After the trouble last year, I thought you would be together."

"Mady? Her temper is mercurial and sometimes her conversations are harsh. We would probably end up too often in disagreement."

"Why would you disagree with her?"

"Don't know but I'm sure she would show me," he says smiling. "Anyway, romance is behind me."

"Sure, Pard, *right* behind you." He takes another puff of the cigar. "So, who is she?"

He takes an equally long puff. "Her name is Jennifer Prower."

"She must be new in Valtura."

"Yes, she is and a recent arrival in New Mexico, from Troy, New York. We met on statehood day, at night on the plaza. She runs the *Valtura Journal*."

"It didn't take long for the newspaper to have new management. Probably didn't take long for you to fall under her spell."

After a moment of silence he says, "Jennifer purchased and lives in the colonel's house."

"It seems that she has become an important part of the town rather quickly. Are you in love?"

"Well, the greatest moment of my life was when she came into my life."

"You are in love again."

"Is there anything else in the world?"

"Ha! Not for you. You would sacrifice anything for romance."

"Perhaps I should have."

"Sorry, I didn't mean anything."

"I know," he nods slowly.

"How are you doing with that?"

"I thought I saw Gabriella on a streetcar."

"Hmm, that must have been disturbing. She is gone but not forgotten. How well do you know Jennifer?" Murph inquires. There is more in his voice than in his words.

WATER DAMAGE | 39

Centori looks uneasy with the question and inquires, "What are you getting at Murph?"

Attempting humor he says, "Nothing, except there is always a woman involved, one of the most interesting things in life."

"I suppose. Empires have been destroyed over women." He reflects on Gabriella whom he thinks about too often, *La Guerrillera was motivated by a noble cause with dignified self-possession.*

"What about you, Murph?"

"There is one disenchanted woman in Washington, not much to say for now. What about the future with Miss Prower?"

"Only a fool would answer that question."

CHAPTER 8

WATER DAMAGED

Many whiskeys and war stories later, Centori and Murphy find themselves past midnight. They remain at the fireplace relaxed in leather chairs. After draining the latest drink, Murphy proudly proclaims, "On July 4th, the 48-star American flag will become official with two new stars."

"Yes, heralding Arizona and New Mexico's equal status with the other states. It should be a big Independence Day celebration."

Murphy smiles, "The official flag is just a formality. By then all the statehood celebrations will have faded."

"Faded," Centori repeats. "Perhaps, but it is still a special Fourth of July. The new states will officially continue in perpetuity."

Murphy stops smiling and stares with concern. "We hope so."

"The last time you sounded that serious, we were racing to Chaco Canyon to prevent a war."

"I guess it's just my line of work."

"Ha-ha. What exactly is that line of work, Murph?"

"Are you gentlemen all right?" the waiter inquires.

"Yes," Murphy answers. He welcomed the interruption to no avail.

"So, what about your line of work," Centori presses.

"I am the Captain of the New Mexico Rangers!"

"You are a long way from riding the range. I suppose you are chasing cattle rustlers in Central Park," Centori jokes.

"You are a long way from New Mexico yourself," Murphy says somewhat defensively.

He does not respond immediately. "You never said what you did after the army and before you started to ride with the rangers."

"We can talk about that another time."

"That's what you said in New Mexico." Murphy did not comment and he continues, "The workings of Washington are a mystery, but I do remember a chain of command."

"If you value our friendship, do not ask again."

Centori is in check. "Okay, but I'm sure President Taft would be available to John Murphy."

"Never met him. As I recall you did meet him at the White House statehood signing ceremony. Look, you won't know until this matter is over."

"I don't think I will ever know."

Their eyes lock for a second. "I won't tell you about certain things, but I will tell you about our concerns."

Full of interest, Centori pours another glass of whiskey and stares across the table. Murphy suddenly stands, then casually looks around and sinks back into his overstuffed chair. He leans toward Centori. "The Circle C Ranch holds a relevant piece of history, understand?"

Centori does not reply. Murphy stares meditatively and waits.

"We had an interest in that piece of history," Centori understates. "Don't know what you are up to Murph, but I can guess."

"I am sure you can. There is renewed interest in as you say that piece of history. This time Washington's inertia is less than what we dealt with last year."

Centori thought about the comment but he doesn't have enough facts to draw a conclusion. He does, however, possess an old water-damaged government document. "You remember the things we experienced last year?"

"Yes, of course. It's the most heard story among the New Mexico Rangers who were involved."

"Then all is settled."

"Except that there are certain questions about that water-damaged paper." Murphy pauses for effect. "That document makes statehood illegitimate."

He waits a moment for more. "Murph, I don't know about that."

"I do."

"How can that be possible after all we went through last year?"

"There is an unsettled state of affairs, causing political forces to become restless about Arizona and New Mexico—I can't change facts."

"Because you're convinced you are right," he says with derision in his voice.

"Look, the two border territories illegally obtained statehood."

"You are not serious."

"Never more so—the U.S. is in violation of the Revert Document."

With feigned casualness Centori says, "The Revert Document, I was wondering how long it would take you to say those words."

"I am not the only one saying those words."

"Murph, history can be rewritten or reshaped; attempts are made to fill the past with opinion," he urges.

"But ultimately the truth is revealed."

"Well…it doesn't matter; it's all settled law now. The Statehood bill was signed, universally received and established." When Murphy is still, Centori continues, "And as you said, on July 4th, the 48-star American flag will become official."

"The truth matters, so near is a falsehood to truth that a wise man would do well not to trust the narrow edge."

"Now you refer to Cicero to make your point? Come on Murph, what's going on?"

"I refer to the Revert Document to make my point. You remember the deadline."

Going through the implications in his mind, Centori blinks absorbing the deadline. "December 31, 1911. If the border territories do not obtain statehood by the deadline, those territories would revert to Mexico." He thinks about his own words. "Oh my God, New Mexico statehood day was on January 6."

"Exactly, so on January 1, 1912, New Mexico legally reverted to Mexico." Murphy pauses then continues, "Arizona statehood was not until February 14, 1912."

"So you think the border territories reverted to Old Mexico?"

"Yes."

"Maybe in legal theory," Centori exclaims.

"In legal fact, the Revert Document was in effect," Murphy softly counters. "We can't change that deadline."

Both men reflect on the near empty glasses. Centori visually dismayed says, "It was all based on Mexico finding the Revert Document. That did not happen, so no legal facts."

"Can we be certain that Mexico will never find the Revert Document?"

"We both read the document. There is no provision on time limits if the agreement was violated. Mexico can present the Revert Document to a world court now or a hundred years from now."

"That sounds unlikely."

"Does it really? That's interesting, coming from a man who has an original manuscript copy. Listen, they could try to take back the border territories by force."

"Let them try."

"Adobe, they would not try it alone."

"Germany again."

"Yes, of course."

Murphy looks for an indication in Centori's face; clearly he has made a decision. They extinguish their cigars; the Revert Document also must be extinguished.

CHAPTER 9

ICE DAMAGE

APRIL 15, 1912

In the early morning of April 15, 1912, the RMS *Titanic* crashed into an iceberg. There was nothing partial about the subsequent disaster or the mountain of doom. The steamship was violently slashed causing catastrophic water damage.

In a short time, the unsinkable ship sank two miles to the North Atlantic Ocean floor; it was her maiden voyage. More than 1,500 passengers and crew never arrived in New York—the iceberg sent them to a sub-aquatic grave.

On April 10, the *Titanic* departed Southampton, stopped at Cherbourg, France, and Queenstown, Ireland, and then headed across the Atlantic to New York. Four days later and 400 miles south of Newfoundland, the ship hit the iceberg on her starboard side, slowly filling her with water.

Evacuation in lifeboats began and then hours later the *Titanic* broke apart and sank with more than 1,000 people still aboard.

When the RMS *Carpathia* arrived at the scene, the crew was able to take aboard about 700 survivors.

The world was shocked by the death toll and failures of the White Star Line company. Days later, a list of victims is posted in many public squares. There were 832 people who perished at sea including some of New York society's most prominent members: John Jacob Astor IV, Benjamin Guggenheim and Isidor and Ida Straus.

Chapter 10

Revert Document Redux

Among the late night patrons still in the Knickerbocker barroom are Centori and Murphy who continue to consume whiskey despite reaching their limit. Murphy's army training had taught him to act; his intelligence training taught him patience. He is ready to reveal the purpose of his New York visit—the Revert Document must remain lost to history.

Murphy takes a final sip of whiskey. "Let's go up to the rooftop. We need fresh air."

"Can we do that?" Centori asks.

"We can. The view will be great."

He follows Murphy's lead and a few minutes later, they are leaning over the short rooftop wall admiring the view of Times Square below and New York beyond.

"Amazing view; people cannot have a care in the world looking at the sparkling gem of Times Square," Centori declares.

Looking down to the bright lights of Broadway, Murphy starts the confidential conversation. "Adobe, that water-damaged document must never be found by Mexico or any other country in the world."

"That problem seems like a million miles away from up here."

"Yes, but it is only a few thousand miles away."

"Guess I knew the truth all along. U.S. history is distorted and misrepresented. Here we go again."

"We are unsure of how many people know that Arizona and New Mexico statehood is illegal."

"Illegal in theory, but the U.S. could be on the wrong side of history."

"Yes, and that's why I am in New York to see you," Murphy admits.

"New York *is* closer to Washington than New Mexico."

"How did you know I was in Washington?"

He pauses briefly to examine his unlighted cigar. "I didn't."

"Perhaps I can share a little with a brother in arms."

"Murph, I could not be less interested."

"Sure, as you guessed I am part of something new in U.S. history."

"That sounds important."

"Important and interesting. Let me back up. We were part of a history in the Spanish-American War."

"Yes, a major foreign expedition."

"There's more to it than that. As you probably know, the U.S. had practically no intelligence operations at the start of the Civil War."

"True enough. Lincoln knew nothing about the South's military efforts; he used amateurs to collect information about troop movements and fortifications," Centori adds.

"Correct, but then Allen Pinkerton's intelligence organization worked with and reported to union generals. They discovered important information, but often failed in communication. After the war, Uncle Sam started to create an organized, professional intelligence operation. Then in '85, President Cleveland put military attachés in foreign countries to collect information." Murphy stops for a moment and then keeps on. "That takes us to our time in Cuba."

Suddenly, Centori looks rather haunted.

"I mean our soldiering during the war."

He didn't answer.

"We were the first American soldiers to benefit from intelligence operations in war time."

"What benefit? Taking heavy fire in San Juan? That did not seem beneficial," he observes.

Murphy shows a slight smile. "Uncle Sam attained important intelligence about Spain's military readiness. The expedition was guided by men with insight of the enemy. It was imperfect knowledge, but as you recall, Cuba was a short affair."

"Yes it was; I understand your government duties go well beyond the rangers—as I surmised."

"You should know that Lieutenant Montero is now captain of the New Mexico Rangers."

"I am not surprised; he is a good man." Centori feels an adventurous sensation as he asserts, "Who exactly is interested in the Revert Document and will any foreign government press the issue?"

It is clear from Murphy's expression that no more secrets would be shared today. "Who else besides yourself knows about your keepsake at the Circle C?"

"I showed A.P."

"Anyone else?"

"No."

"Not even Jennifer Prower?" He takes a moment and his eyes move reflectively away. "I said no, Murph." His glance silences the questioner.

Centori folds his arms, narrows his eyes and considers Murphy's interest in Jennifer, *I have high hopes for Jennifer, but is she a woman I can trust?*

The Revert Document had destroyed the love of his life, rendering him conflicted about his service to America. He runs his hands through his hair with a sigh and inclines forward, "Murph, I did my part for the U.S. and paid dearly."

"Yes, I am painfully aware. You don't owe the country anything, but you are sentimental about the document; you must completely destroy it this time and any trace of its existence."

"It means more to me than politics," he stares.

The Revert Document is an odd memory of love, Murphy thinks but says, "I know, I was with you in Chaco Canyon. What you did was pure of purpose and just in its implementation."

"Was it right? Mexico was entitled to the border territories."

"It is too late for doubt. It is too late for second guessing; consider the territories to be the spoils of war. Adobe, with Gabriella it was the most selfless act imaginable. What happened at Chaco would test the strongest souls."

"But did I make the wrong decision?" Centori persists.

"She was fighting for Mexico's future and nothing would have stopped her, not even you."

"I suppose that is true," he answers distantly. "Murph what about now? You insist that there is legal fact beyond theory."

"Yes, now more practical than ever, given the deadline violation."

"Are you asking me as a government agent or as a friend?"

"What's the difference," Murphy is less than sensitive. Then he says, "Destroy the document; despite your experience in Chaco Canyon, we do not want to relive those last territorial days."

Centori feels a sense of outrage at the imposition as he replies sharply, "The U.S. has violated Article X of the Treaty of Mesilla— the Revert Document."

"That's right."

Murphy's stone face prompts him to stop protesting. He nods with a neutral face but his loyalty is naturally reasserted. "Ok, Murph, I will destroy it, but there could be other copies."

"We know, but it's a start and it could be enough."

"Where does this leave Uncle Sam?"

"Probably somewhere outside of international law."

The Revert Document is more than an odd memory of Gabriella. Centori has a profound ambivalence about the whole affair: how justice was denied to Mexico and how he deprived himself of Gabriella. He will never be entirely sure of his reasons for these actions surrounding the Revert Document affair.

The reasons why one decision is made over an alternate decision can be difficult, even impossible, to define. In any case, he made a decision, and the consequences are ongoing. A light rain begins to fall; the men stare down at Times Square without a word and with the matter settled.

A few moments later Murphy turns to Centori. "One other thing; do you know a town called Stratford, New Mexico?"

"Yes, it's a mining town near Silver City; it could be an insignificant ghost town now."

"Sometimes things are significant if connected to something else."

"Are you going to give me another history lesson?"

"No, not now." but a gold strike has changed things."

Centori wants more information but says with a cheerless smile, "Murph, you saved my life at Chaco; I never thanked you for what you did."

"We both know that's not needed."

"Just the same, you saved my life."

"We don't know that for sure." Murphy puts his arm around his heartbroken friend. "Pard, the only thing for sure is that we need another drink."

Darkness steals over Centori. "I'm not sure about that, but I am sure that you are a true friend."

That scene from the crucial Chaco Canyon moment comes to Murphy. *The hard rain continued and Centori fell to the ground horrified, wailing over Gabriella's lifeless body in the depths below. Murphy grabs him around the shoulders, fearing he will follow her by accident—or intention.*

He wonders if the place that destroyed Gabriella's body may have destroyed Centori's soul.

CHAPTER 11

୰◇◇◇

LOST ANGEL

After an eventful meeting with Murphy, Centori is stretched out on the bed in room 808, reflecting on the Revert Document warning and finding sleep to be elusive. The specter of second guessing his Chaco Canyon decision haunts him; he turns over the details of those last fateful moments in his mind. *If I gave her the document, she would not have fallen and she would be alive today.* These thoughts, coupled with too many drinks, affect his state of mind.

Finally, his mind starts to slow down, he enters a daydream state, still aware of Chaco Canyon. The street sounds of horses and motorcars are enhanced, but his alertness is more internal. The shock of her death is receding or at least he thinks so. Bursts of brain activity are followed by deep sleep that provides a gateway to mind and soul, and then a total shutdown before entering the most fascinating stage of sleep. His dreamscape returns to Chaco Canyon and the end of Gabriella.

In his haze he sees her energy drained. *One second…two, then three. For an instant, she appears to defy gravity and float in the air. She grasps the silver cross and without a word of farewell…*abruptly he bolts up with a shriek. His own primal scream wakes him in time to avoid the ultimate horror of seeing her fall to her death, but now she could be resurrected. She is standing at the foot of the bed; his chest feels hollow.

He stares in shocked doubt, barely projects words, "You do not exist."

"I am not flesh and blood, but I do exist."

"Why are you here? Why do you come back?"

"I love you, always, *mi corazón.*"

"I cried my heart out for you—how do I love a ghost?"

"We can be close in a different manner."

"Are you a lost angel? One who cannot rest?"

"I have always known my way, but rest eludes me."

"Gabriella, I never wished to hurt you," he pleads.

Her eyes flash with fire, "You did more than hurt me; you killed me."

In the history of the world, there had never been more hurtful words spoken. During her last moments, when she stopped struggling against the inevitable, he thought her eyes said as much, but it was not true.

Stunned, his hands clench so that his knuckles turn white. He rapidly blinks, trying to push her away and embrace her at the same time. A rush of relief washes over him; it was a nightmare. Then a second rush of awareness overcomes him. It was not a bad dream; it was a bad memory of the horrible and guilty reality of Chaco Canyon, just a few months ago.

He jumps out of bed and looks around the room for Gabriella. Perhaps his mind tricked him, making him see a woman that was not there. Perhaps he projected her image based on his knowledge and experiences with her. Whether she was an optical illusion or a not, his fear is realized. He would never be free of the past.

Centori welcomes a sleepless state of mind; it is an improvement to waking in the night stricken by the terror of Gabriella's demise. Finally, exhaustion forces him back to sleep.

CHAPTER 12

SPARTAN BREAKFAST

The next morning Centori wakes up with disturbing thoughts of Gabriella's last moments at Chaco Canyon and her appearance last night. *I was not a perfect man, but I loved her with all my heart.* His feet slowly hit the floor with restive expectancy about his New York adventure. With little energy to recall the Chaco Canyon event, he looks out the eighth floor window; New York canyons ease the troubling feelings. Again, he had dreamt of her; it was vague but her Spanish accent and beautiful voice rang true.

Returning to the hotel restaurant with the morning newspapers, he is immediately greeted, "Good morning, Mr. Centori."

"Good morning."

"Coffee? Black?"

"Yes," he answers while escorted to a corner table.

Opening the pages of *The Morning Telegraph* he recognizes a writer, Bat Masterson. The famous western adventurer is now a New York sports writer, editor and columnist. Although the *Telegraph* focuses on horse-racing, an article about the new baseball season concerns the Washington team. The Senators led by phenomenal pitcher Walter Johnson should dominate the American League, but Boston is predicted to win the pennant. *Well, good luck to the Red Sox in their brand new Fenway Park. I'll pick the New York Giants to meet Boston in the World Series.*

He finishes his first cup and reaches for a scone and honey. Then he sees an article on the summer Olympics in Stockholm that describes Jim Thorpe's likeliness to win gold medals for the pentathlon and decathlon. The paper makes a similar prognostication about a stallion named 'Worth' in next month's Kentucky Derby. *A stallion named Worth. I wonder how a stallion named Patriot is doing back at the Circle C.*

Moving from horses to horse power, Joe Dawson and his American-manufactured, four-cylinder National will enter the Indianapolis 500-mile race. *An average speed of 78 mph, that's impressive,* he thought while turning to an article about Heavyweight Champion Jack Johnson who will defend his title against Jim Flynn in New Mexico. *Wonder how A.P. is doing at the Circle C and if Mad Mady misses me. I am sure Jennifer misses me.*

"Mr. Centori?" A hotel man with an envelope on a silver tray politely inquires.

"Yes, I am Adobe Centori."

The dapper hotel man says, "This telegram arrived for you."

"Thank you," he says and curiously unfolds the paper.

> Hope you are enjoying NY Stop
> Writing a story of your trip Stop
> All is well in Valtura Stop
> Dare I say missing you, Don't Stop
> Jennifer

He pours a second cup as he smiles at her forwardness, one of her many favorable attributes. Jennifer Prower arrived in Valtura a week after statehood and quickly developed a special friendship with Centori. Her note shares feelings, but she knows things she does not share.

Placing the paper in his vest pocket he reflects, *Jennifer, what a beauty... I miss her, then why did I come home, or why did I leave home?* He writes an answer but tears it up. *Her telegraph is...*

"Oh my, that is a Spartan breakfast," says a familiar soprano voice.

Surprised, he looks up at a beaming Charity Clarkson.

"And you take your coffee black, too."

"Yes," he musters while standing up. *She certainly spends time in this hotel.* "How did you find me? What are you doing here so early?"

"Why do you have so many questions? Can you just be happy to see me?"

"I am happy to see you."

Finding him less distant than the first encounter, she replies, "Good."

He is also happy to see her outfit. Charity wears a navy blue ankle-length shirt with a white shirtwaist.

He smiles and says, "I like your dress, it is very pretty."

"Thank you. Will you ever ask a lady to sit down?"

"Of course, please sit down."

"I have a better idea. Do you like that coffee?"

"Well enough, yet it is not cowboy coffee."

"Okay cowboy, if you are unhappy with that cup, I want to show you something."

With effort he restrains his interest. "Show me something?"

She smiles and says, "Yes, I can show you the best coffee in New York."

He met her gaze but didn't answer. Although his world crumbled at Chaco Canyon, he intends to explore a new world. Charity finds him to be a gentleman yet somehow reckless. She also finds him to be exceedingly attractive.

"Come with me."

"Best coffee?"

"An interesting new place too; I do not spend all my time on the Ladies' Mile or at social tea. First empty your cup of the old; then you will be able to accept a new brew." She is attuned with strong empathy, "Perhaps you are in New York to pour out old stale feelings to make way for a new fresh feeling."

His empty smile lasted a moment. She searches his face for a sign that will allow her to connect. He is, more often than not, defensive, but now appears to be weakening, almost vulnerable.

Leveling a sympathetic gaze she pushes further, "Your truth is stranger than you admit."

"What are you saying? What do you know about it?"

"More questions," she smiles. "Perhaps, I understand your feelings because I have had a similar experience."

"Is that so?"

"Yes, some people are aware of the thoughts, emotions and experiences of others."

"Charity, I am not aware of things unspoken."

"Adobe, you need to have a measure of empathy first."

Charity is becoming more attractive and interesting, but there is Jennifer. This could be…no, this is a crossroad. "Did you say something about better coffee?"

"Yes, I did."

He offers his arm; she takes it with a haughty look, then a smile. Charity's discontent is cloaked by a physical vigor and exuberance of spirit. Centori tends to lead with his heart that is not cloaked at all.

CHAPTER 13

EXCELLENT AT THE TASK

They agreed to meet at the Pabst Grand Circle Hotel and Restaurant on Columbus Circle. Spooner and Warren wait alone; the two men sit with mugs of beer, transfixed on the trouble in society. They discuss current socioeconomic and political environments as they wait for a perceived solution to such problems. Spooner, more radical and revolutionary than Warren, has the talent to inspire others to commit acts of terror.

Warren looks around the room and observes, "Lucy and Emma are late."   "Perhaps we don't need them."

"What? They have been part of the planning."

"Yes, and now we progress to the next step—with the help of someone else."

"Someone else?"

"She is well-funded and will provide the money we need for this plan."

"We could do without the help; the wider the network, the greater the risk."

"She is organized and can supply explosives at the level we need. We shall work with her."

"Her?"

Spooner drains his beer mug and rants, "We will work with her because the people are held up, held down and robbed by government and capitalists. The government has so governed the people that it is no easy matter; we are inspected, expected, examined, reprimanded, summoned, commanded and compelled," he quickly takes a deep breath and goes on, "until all that we are supposed to do is provide a never-ending supply of time and an inexhaustible supply of labor for little money."

Warren considers Spooner's mental stability before saying, "That was somewhat long winded. We can expect a long reaction from the government and from the press after we execute our plan."

"I am sure of that. You can be sure that we will be cursed, abused, and lied about until they are simply tired or we are simply dead," Spooner adds.

"That is likely."

"I can honestly tell you that we won't stop our plan. The only reason I am hanging on to life is simply to see what the hell is coming next," Spooner declares.

"We should leave New York immediately after the attack."

"No, we will remain in New York after the attack. We have only begun and our new friends wish to operate here."

"Given the magnitude of the attack, it would not be wise to stay here. The police will be relentless in finding us."

"We will be relentless in avoiding them. Besides, we did not run away from Los Angeles so soon after that attack."

"I am not so sure about this."

"She gave me an address and a key to a house in Queens that will provide a retreat for us, far from Manhattan and the scene of the attack."

"Your new friend will be involved after this plan is performed?" Warren questions.

"Yes. They are experienced in the use of dynamite and we will need more and in larger quantities than we can procure. Perhaps hundreds of pounds of a new high explosive grade to destroy bigger targets."

"I assume she represents a larger group."

"I have an idea, but I am unsure of the network," Spooner lies.

"That sounds dangerous. Are they reliable?"

"Their reliability should be good enough for anyone," Spooner says, "and they are excellent at the task."

"I would like meet her."

"That is impossible at the moment; she not in New York."

"How did you find this woman?"

"I did not. She found me."

Warren looks around the room again. Parsons and Hayward arrive late.

CHAPTER 14

HORN AND HARDART

There is no roadmap for Adobe and Charity as they stagger forward in search of definition, but now they stride through the excitement of Times Square. The cultural center with theatres, music halls, upscale hotels and electrified advertisements on buildings has certainly changed since Centori's boyhood.

Although he did not realize at first, Charity is a woman of substance, a woman possibly worth his time. They move through crowds of hurrying pedestrians, under their diverse hats. His big Stetson and her Merry Widow turn more than a few heads—they are a rare act.

A few days after the Titanic disaster, crowds in New York flooded the streets around newspaper offices to see bulletins. In Times Square, *The New York Times* attracted the largest crowds. A list of victims was posted on the wall of the Times Building.

The cheerful couple stops at the Times Building to read the names of the passengers lost at sea. Centori scans the notable names; his stomach tightens when his eyes come to rest on the name Jennifer Prower of Troy, New York.

"What is wrong?" Charity quickly asks.

"Nothing, I thought I recognized a name that appeared on the list."

She is unconvinced, but offers, "Okay, follow me."

He follows without a word, *Jennifer Prower of Troy is running the Valtura Journal and living in a fine house—something is not right.*

Five minutes later, Charity stops in front of a stained glass façade and points, "This is the new Horn and Hardart Automat and it is a marvel!"

Inside, he takes in the marble floors and elaborate carved ceilings that provide an affluent environment for the not so affluent New Yorkers.

"What do you think about the Automat?"

"What?" he manages while still distracted by the notion of Jennifer. Then, observing the walls of little glass doors containing various food products he offers, "It would be hard to image a more democratic setting."

"I thought you would find this place amusing."

"Shall we have one of those ham sandwiches?" he offers while pointing.

"Yes," she beams. "That is *not* a Spartan breakfast."

He drops nickels in slots; opens little glass doors to compartments and stares straight ahead without moving. *Jennifer's name on the victims list could be the iceberg's tip.*

"Adobe!" she yells out. "What's wrong?"

"Oh, sorry," he pulls out two sandwiches and escorts Charity to a table.

"Now let's see about the coffee," he moves to the fresh-drip brewed coffee that pours from silver spigots. He fills two cups and returns.

Sitting across from Charity, he enjoys the closeness and the liveliness of many shop girls on their lunch break but falls into silence.

"Adobe, you seem distracted; I thought you would like this place."

"I do."

Trying not to pay attention to the shop girls, he sips the brew. One of the girls glances at him with interest.

"How is the coffee?" she says with friskiness.

It is certainly no cowboy coffee, he thinks before declaring, "Excellent, you were right; very good and quite different from boiled cowboy coffee."

"Said to be the best in New York!" she adds.

He takes another sip of the marginally good coffee. "You know the new Woolworth Building is said to be the best building in New York. I have read about the construction advancements and plan to visit downtown at sunrise."

"People say the building is wonderful."

"Since I have been away, New York construction has been remarkable," he correctly observes. "During my youth, walls supported buildings and wall thickness increased in relation to height."

"Really," she says flatly.

Forcing Jennifer from his mind, he replies, "Yes, new steel-frame construction that supports the building's weight eliminated the need for thick walls. Now exterior walls drape from the frame. Improvements in analyzing structural stresses have been fantastic."

"You seem to know much about New York for a cowboy."

Centori hears this with no surprise; he blinks and shrugs. "New techniques in elevators, producing steel and concrete reinforcement have driven skyscraper growth, and, as I said, I was born on this island."

"Perhaps you will stay on this island."

"I look forward to going back to New Mexico; Circle C is my home now, I have friends there."

"And now you have a friend here," she says dramatically.

"And a good sandwich," he deflects.

"So what are you planning for this day?"

"I will walk in Central Park. I remember the calliope music at the carousel; as a child I would ride wooden horses and dream of riding real horses on an open range."

"And your dream came true."

"Yes, it did," he says smiling.

Abruptly, Charity announces, "I must be going now."

First impressions are not always lasting. He is more receptive to Charity who seems different in a different setting. "Shall I escort you?"

"Not necessary; I am capable of being on my own."

No doubt about that, he thinks. "Perhaps I will see you again."

After a polite interval of time she says, "As I said, no one can predict the future."

She walks out; he watches her gait until she is gone from sight. Alone, he glances at the shop girls and finishes the 'best coffee in New York.' Soon after he leaves too. He walks east toward Central Park and thinks of Jennifer. *Perhaps she is too much of an unknown; that list of Titanic victims included a woman named Jennifer Prower of Troy, New York. There must be a reasonable explanation.*

He walks northeast and enters Central Park at the Artisans' Gate on 59th Street and 7th Avenue continuing north toward the carousel. In the distance the steam organ music plays a familiar tune:

Boys and girls together, me and Mamie O'Rourke
Tripped the light fantastic on the sidewalks of New York

The song blends with the sounds of children laughing and shouting under a bright sun; the joyful scene is a welcomed sight. After a time at the merry-go-round he enjoys a lively walk to the Central Park Zoo.

At the zoo, he finds a certain cruelty to caging animals, unlike the freedom of New Mexico wildlife including black bears, cougars, wolves, deer and coyotes. Time to move along, north to the Bethesda Terrace that overlooks a lake. Here he spends a thoughtful moment on the terrace reading the names of lovers scratched in the stone balcony. *What name would I write here? Adobe and…?*

He descends the Bethesda Fountain steps to the lower level. At a bench near the fountain, he settles down and finds the sounds of the rushing water peaceful.

In the middle of the fountain pool is an eight-foot statue of a winged woman known as the *Angel of the Waters*. Below are smaller cherubs called Temperance, Purity, Health and Peace.

Centori looks up at the tall statue and wonders, *Is she a lost angel? Is she lost at sea?*

CHAPTER 15

TROLLEY RIDE

The next morning after a better night of sleep, Centori walks through the hotel lobby. "Good morning, Mr. Centori," says a familiar hotel worker. He tips his big hat, and then takes coffee before taking the Broadway Trolley. As the sun rises, he leaves the hotel and jumps aboard the trolley; the clang of the bell prompts the horses to move forward. This time he travels south on the Broadway tracks to downtown New York, home to City Hall and the financial district.

The crowds are less unsettling and the tracks smoother than the first trip. Instinctively he searches the streetcar: she is not here. Gabriella Zena—her name conjures an image of a tragic love affair that began in Cuba and ended in New Mexico. She lived as a kind-hearted woman when contented, and an aggressive wildcat when frustrated.

He remembers how fate had dealt him that hand, how she died, choosing her duty to Mexico over her self-interest. How he tried to convince her that Mexico was not well represented by its government; how implementing the Revert Document would have been an international disaster.

At the next stop, two men board the trolley speaking an Italian dialect he recognizes from his youth, followed by two other men speaking Yiddish. For a moment he is distracted by the cacophony of languages. Astonishingly it happens again. It appears as if Gabriella is in rear of the streetcar. Then a heart stopping moment—she stands and effortlessly moves through the crowd. He is frozen in fascination. No other passenger seems to notice this haunting and striking woman.

In life she was a spirited and strong woman, now she is more spirit but just as strong. Her head moves slightly, long black hair dances in the air.

With eyes wide and fixed, her monotone voice in a Spanish accent whispers, "*Mi corazón.*"

Staring in disbelief he can barely speak. "I am not dreaming this time, but you are not real."

The passengers who are closest stare, wondering if the man with the cowboy hat is talking to himself.

"I am as real as you are real."

He shakes his head in denial.

"Why do you not believe in me?"

His words are barely audible. "Should I dare to believe in you?"

"We drink from the same cup, *mi amor.*"

His face is pale. "That cup is gone," he says in a pain-filled voice.

"It is not. How can it be gone?"

The trolley slows and he loses his footing for a second. "How can I be sure of you?"

A faint smile offers a hint and then she whispers, "Because you love me."

She was quick from smile to fury. Now tears course down her beautiful face.

"Gabriella, I do love you, but why are you here?"

"Adobe! You look like you saw a ghost!"

Oblivious to her presence, he rapidly turns and sees Charity. "What?" He turns again and Gabriella is gone.

"What did you say?"

"I said you look like you saw a ghost."

"Perhaps I have," *or I'm not in control of my senses.* "Charity, what are you doing here?"

"It's a public streetcar, don't look so surprised. Besides, I thought you would be expecting me."

"When did you get on?"

"Same time as you; I was right next to you," she answers with confusion. "Did you not smile at me?"

Although unsure about the time sequence, he welcomes the distraction and ignores the odd emergence of Charity. "Yes, of course, good morning to you."

"Are you going downtown to see the marvelous Woolworth Building?"

"That's right."

"I have not yet seen it."

"Perhaps I misunderstood," he says.

"You told me you were going at sunrise; I can see the building alone."

Next time ask, he thinks but says, "No, let's see the building together."

Charity was determined to involve herself with him and a day of whirlwind activity. She feels cheerful, able to reject the depression that comes and goes without notice. He feels cheerful about the turn of events.

Twenty minutes later, the trolley enters *Ladies' Mile* that extends up Broadway to Madison Square. This retail center contains Beaux Arts, Romanesque Revival and Queen Anne buildings that house Lord and Taylor, B. Altman, Best & Co. and Bergdorf Goodman. The fashionable department stores within a high class area provide a safe place for women to shop without men.

The Fuller Building is the focal point of *Ladies' Mile*. In Neo-Renaissance palazzo style, the skyscraper is groundbreaking and one of the tallest buildings in New York. Located on a triangular block formed by Broadway, Fifth Avenue and East 22nd Street, it resembles a flatiron for clothes.

As the trolley passes the Flatiron Building, a woman on the tip of the triangular corner stares vacantly. The ride continues past the building. On the corner, the woman remains fixed now looking toward him. He stares back. *Oh no, not again.* She fades into the background as the trolley clip-clops and jingles its way downtown. *Am I seeing a ray of hope or the end of earth?* A relatively uneventful ride follows the appearance of a dark-haired woman at the Flatiron Building.

Continuing south on Broadway, they pass Union Square. After the fall of Fort Sumter in 1861, the park was scene to a historic patriotic rally. The equestrian statue of Washington was draped with an American flag with hundreds of thousands of New Yorkers surrounding it expressing support for the union.

"We had several hundred people at Valtura Plaza for our statehood celebration, but in Union Square at the start of the Civil War, about a quarter of a million people came here."

"How do you know that?"

"My father told me; he was here. He was one of them."

Some ten minutes later, as the workhorses pull the trolley south, Cooper Union for the Advancement of Science and Art comes into view at Astor Place.

"Do you see that building, the Cooper Union?"

"Yes, what famous event happened there?" Charity jokes.

"As a matter of fact, Abraham Lincoln delivered a dramatic speech before his election. It was in the Great Hall where he challenged the spread of slavery in federal territories—including New Mexico."

"And you know this because your father was at the address."

"Well, yes he was, but even if he were not, it was a historical address. The speech helped Lincoln win the Republican nomination for president. Other presidents have used the Great Hall. Grant, Taft and Roosevelt gave historic addresses here."

"Sounds like *you* want to be president."

"Ha-ha, no I do not, but I have met Roosevelt and Taft."

"Now that is impressive."

The streetcar rides past Grand Street. "I was born a few blocks from here on Mulberry Street, in Little Italy."

"Oh, let's go there on the way back," Charity beams.

"I would like that. I could show you the tenement where I was born. We can go to an Italian restaurant."

"Okay, cowboy, I'm with you."

CHAPTER 16

SKYSCRAPER

The Broadway Trolley arrives at City Hall Park. Leaving the horse car with more agility than his first ride, Centori helps Charity down the steps and gazes upward, *The buildings are closer together than I remember and there is less sunlight.*

Walking to the park and standing in front of the grand French Renaissance building, he offers, "I recall that City Hall opened in 1812, another centennial."

"What?"

"Oh, nothing."

Entering the building, where the architectural style changes, they absorb the American-Georgian design. In the Governor's room, he says in a hushed tone, "I believe President Lincoln's coffin was placed here."

"Is that right?"

Centori looks up at the rotunda dome and turns to her. "I remember this ceiling and this room. President Grant was lying in state here. I was 15 years old; my father took me to say farewell."

"Is that right?" Charity evenly replies again.

"Yes. His military leadership did not serve well in civilian government. His administration was mired in scandal; a great general who was not a great president."

"Yet he was honored here."

"Grant ended the Civil War. He was not dishonest; he was only ignorant of the corruption."

"Well, I don't know much about that, but I do know who is buried in Grant's tomb!"

"Okay, Charity, let's go."

They leave City Hall, head to Broadway and turn south. They walk closely together until Centori stops in his tracks and confronts a commanding structure.

"What is it Adobe?"

"Oh—well this is spectacular!" It was a firsthand look at the new 20th century for him.

The skyscraper's steel-frame ascends toward the heavens from a foundation of reinforced concrete pillars starting from solid bedrock. Located on Broadway between Park Place and Barclay Street, the Woolworth Building causes people to come to a standstill and look toward the sky. That is exactly what Adobe and Charity do as they stand across Broadway.

Then they cross Broadway, dodging the carriages and pedestrians, and stop in front of the colossal building. He looks up and fixes an astonished stare at the top of the new corporate headquarters—a skyscraper 790 feet in the air.

"It certainly is tall. I heard this building is the tallest in the world," Charity says.

"I am sure of that; the Woolworth Building surpasses the Metropolitan Life Insurance Tower on Madison and East 23rd, but the number of stories is not the only measure of greatness."

"Really?"

"Oh, yes. Think of the admiration this skyscraper elicits more than economic prestige; it attracts attention as a beautiful and powerful corporate headquarters," he declares.

"Yes, indeed, I can see that Adobe," she breathlessly says as someone who knows about beauty and publicity. "It looks like a Cathedral; some people call it the Cathedral of Commerce."

"Charity, this is a remarkably expressive building. Look at the graceful structure and slim tower proportions that allow light to reach the street."

"Can we go inside?"

"Yes," he says while still looking up and bumping into a pedestrian.

Entering the ornate marble lobby, they marvel over the vaulted ceiling, mosaics, and stained-glass and bronze furnishings.

"Oh my, what breathtaking beauty. I am so glad you invited me here."

Smiling he replies, "I believe the sculpted caricatures include Woolworth himself; they are intriguing."

"Yes, they are." She points to the *Labor* and *Commerce* murals on the mezzanine which overlook sculpted plaster. "I like those paintings."

Eager to ride the new high-speed elevator to 57 stories above New York, he informs, "This building is braced for wind resistance; we should brace for a ride to the top of the built world. Follow me."

"Okay, cowboy, let's ride up!"

The express elevator is fast and level; halfway through the ascent, the other riders exit leaving Adobe and Charity alone for the final lift. A first elevator ride can capture anyone's imagination. She smiles nervously as she rapidly ascends. He focuses inwardly, imagining being far from home but not and far from himself. *After more than ten years in New Mexico, coming home to New York seems a strange and a welcome relief…there have been so many changes.*

"Sir?"

He turns to the well-dressed elevator operator, "Yes…?"

"This is the 57th floor observation deck."

"Thank you."

They step out of the elevator and attract some attention from the small crowd but no one can compete with the wondrous observation of New York.

"This is quite exciting," she says. "What a spectacular view of the city and the rivers."

"Yes, I have not been this high in the air since Fajita Butte in Chaco …"

Then unexpectedly she adds, "Oh my, the view and being here with you is special. I am happy we met."

She let that slip out; he let it pass for an instant. Then he kisses her cheek in plain sight of the other visitors and says, "From the top of Sandia Mountains, the natural views are great. But this is quite a different view, from a built environment."

Recovering from the surprise kiss, she observes, "You have been away for a long time."

I have been away for a long time…way too long.

The building is almost twice as high as Fajita Butte in Chaco Canyon, the place that ended Gabriella's life. It is a bright, sunny day, but compelled by a daydream, he is transported back in time. He hears then listens to hard rainfall.

"Move away from the edge!"

"Give me the Revert Document!"

Abruptly, a high-pitched coyote cry jars Gabriella, causing a catastrophic slide on the slippery rocks. She falls over the ledge, but manages to grasp a few jagged rocks. Frantically, she looks for a foothold but there is none. It is a sheer drop of over two hundred feet.

The rainstorm turns violent. She desperately tries to secure her right hand to the wet rocks. He desperately tries to secure his grip on her left hand. His grip is failing. Blood flows as the sharp rocks rip at their hands; the rain quickly washes it away.

"*Hold on!*"

One second…two, then three. She grasps the silver cross that hangs around her neck and without a word of farewell falls to her certain death. It was his nightmare in broad daylight.

"Adobe," he hears a faint call of his name that pulls him back to the present. Returning from the past and ending his daydream, he is in a Gothic castle in the sky with arches, spires, flying buttresses and gargoyles, a fantasy palace, a place of dreams. In the reflection of the glass window an image appears. At first he thinks it is Charity's mirror image. It is not. Then his head slips back to Chaco Canyon.

"*Am I dreaming?*"

"*No, you are not.*"

"*This cannot be true.*"

Gabriella moves, her head erect and stares into his eyes, "*It can be, there is another world out there. You struggle to see it,*" *she forces a smile.*

"*There's no truth in you.*"

"*Is there not? I know who you are, ¿no es verdad? Why did we suffer from the defects of your virtue,*" *her voice has a bitter sound in reaction to a betrayal.*

"*What do you want with me?*"

"*Mi corazón, you have summoned me.*"

"Adobe!" Charity demands. "What are you doing?"

He snaps back to the present, "Nothing."

Looking at him expectantly she presses, "Or everything."

The daydreaming detached him from his surroundings, blurred his reality and created a mild dissociation.

"It's nothing; perhaps I am a little light-headed from the elevator ride."

"Sure, what were you thinking or dreaming about?"

"It is a long story."

"Adobe, in case you have not noticed, I am ready for a long story."

"It's nothing," he says swiftly. "What is done cannot be undone, it is dead."

"The past is never dead, but it can be reconciled."

"Reliving the past is pointless. Make the most of the moment."

"We can make the most of our day, but you are hiding something bad. It is unclear to me but I believe someone is skulking and ready to hurt you."

"For now I'll say remember the lesson, forget the details."

"You should also remember that you cannot satisfy a dream of a lifetime with a dream."

Was that a dream or a hallucination?

A man can forget the terrible episodes of his life for a time and then something can trigger the memory in alarming precision.

⁓

On the street again, they walk slowly, each with their own thoughts. Charity is nonplussed and impatiently waits for an explanation. It does not happen. She enjoyed seeing the building, but she was disappointed with his behavior.

Centori wonders, *Why does Gabriella speak to me? Does she wish to have me understand her feelings about the Revert Document? What good would it do? It is too late for that, too late for us. Maybe I need to say I have painful second thoughts about the document. Maybe she would understand me, but it is all so impossible. Was it a sentimental fantasy or a moment of madness?*

It may not have been either option. Sometimes anguish can paint a picture in a person's mind.

"I feel like you are haunted by ghosts," Charity boldly says again.

There is only one ghost. "Charity, come closer; know me better."

She stirs and swiftly says, "I will come closer, but I don't think I will know you better."

The Trolley ride back to Times Square was without words; Adobe and Charity sat in silence, next to each other. There was no sighting of Gabriella and no Italian restaurant: the dinner in Little Italy long forgotten.

CHAPTER 17

DARK HORSE

That evening, in room 808 of the Knickerbocker Hotel, Centori finds the night sounds of the city disquieting and the absence of Charity disappointing. He re-reads Jennifer's telegram looking for additional meanings; none are evident. The street noise sounds as if it is just outside his window. Although they are the sounds of his childhood, he had become accustomed to the coyote calls in the distance. The iconic howl of the wide open spaces is a far cry from the sidewalks of New York.

Sometimes coyotes are better judges of people than people, he considers. *At first I had dismissed Charity as nothing more than a New York distraction. Then she improved with each passing moment, more interesting, more sexually attractive and now a beautiful American flower with high spirits. Her habit of appearing suddenly without as much as a word of warning is somehow charming.* The sound of knocking interrupts his thoughts. The door opens—it is Charity. She steps inside and closes the door.

Ironically he says, "Please come in."

She wears a day dress with a raised waistline, layered skirts and a broad smile. "Ha-ha, you should lock your door Adobe, the city can be perilous," she chirps.

His surge of surprise fades under the implied promise. With a rakish grin he says, "Are you dangerous?"

"I am not armed, Sir. But I know when to move from discussion to decision," she says in an entrancing way.

"I thought you made your decision when we said good night."

"I did no such thing."

"And now?"

"I am sure your imagination is vivid."

"You are in danger of losing your virtue."

"I am no longer in possession of that misunderstood quality."

He thinks for a moment, detects sweet perfume and moves with restive energy, "Yet, you are dangerous."

"Is that what you expect?"

"If you are like the beautiful sirens who enchanted sailors to shipwreck on the rocks, then yes."

Charity did not reply; rather she moves two steps closer. Centori stands his ground then sees Jennifer's telegram and suddenly turns cold without any allusion of regret.

"Am I not slim and glamorous enough for you?"

He notices a beautiful diamond pendant on a black ribbon decorating her slim and glamorous body. *That necklace looks expensive* he thinks. It is expensive; the pendant was purchased at the Lord & Taylor store.

"Charity, you know I will be gone in a few weeks," *and there could be no future for us.* He looks slightly worried.

"You are here now with me."

She retreats a step, his body relaxes for a moment before returning to the dilemma. Then his mind continues to race, *Why am I so uneasy?*

Charity interrupts the awkward silence, "Are you still obsessed with an old memory?"

Her words hang in the air. He stands in silence.

"A penny for your thoughts?" she offers.

He says nothing aloud, but thinks, *I have better options than Charity, or I thought I did,* and then: "You are a woman on whom nothing is lost."

"Never you mind, sometimes we act on faith."

"Let's sit down."

"Thank you. I told you, there are things wrong about your love story. There are things you must forget *or* tell me about. Do not take your secret to the grave."

A grave, an unmarked grave in a far away, forgotten place is my secret.

"Do not continue to live in a hard world," Charity advises.

"The world is hard."

"Quite right, but do not give up that easily and don't fight old battles."

"It is easy for you."

"Perhaps I expect less. Perhaps I am not afraid."

"Or you get what you tolerate."

"What does that mean?"

"Some study their mistakes; there are lessons to learn."

"I have learned that you have a path forward because your ties to women are strong, because you take time to create trust and respect. The pain of the past cannot be allowed to make you bitter about the present."

"I don't waste time blaming others." *It is not just the past holding me up, there is Jennifer.*

"Your despair is not engraved on your face, but I can still see it. Do you want to talk about her?"

She sees his face harden. "Not even a little. Please do not go too far."

"You are a dark horse, but you need me."

He returns the comment with a smile, "And you are quite the hellion." *What do I do now? Charity is a fine looking woman and there is no time to argue with myself.*

"Adobe, this is your homecoming. Go back to your past, better self. It is as simple and complicated as that."

"I have no home here," *I wonder if you* do. "We are in a hotel room."

Her face glows. His face is still, but his thoughts are turbulent, *Jennifer seems given to deception in the way she sometimes does not meet my eyes. Besides, she may leave Valtura as mysteriously as she arrived.*

He stares and continues to stall. Charity, who has learned how to control a situation, says, "You live your life like a chess game always moves ahead. It is your move now."

Move where? To the outskirts of Eden? Jennifer is beautiful and offers many things, except her body. This thought defeats his last line of defense; the only emotion he has left is physical desire. At the same time, Charity's well-shaped and seductive mouth implores or demands a kiss.

He stands and looks out the window. "I am happy to be back in New York."

"I am equally happy."

He touches her face and kisses her. The kiss is slow, careful and inevitable. Charity returns the kiss and takes a breath of air before she arches her lithe body against him. He quickly presses against her slim and sexy form; the waves of desire follow.

Her fair cheeks readily flush as she jokes, "Now let's see how a cowboy from Mexico loves a woman."

Ignoring her scandalous words he laughs. "That's *New* Mexico!"

Although thoughts and counter thoughts clutter his mind, he pulls her closer. He looks down at her face and her ever increasing beauty.

Charity removes her close-fitting bodice; with the upper part of her dress gone her soft breasts are revealed. His eyes move over her body; he appreciates the view yet thinks, *This could be a mistake.* Nevertheless, he kisses her with more passion. His eyes dip downward as he touches her curvy and feminine bottom. "Charity?"

"Yes, and with you 'yes' is my favorite word," her soprano voice purrs with passion. "It is a fine word and a grand proposal."

"You fall into my arms, yet you know nothing of me."

"It is impossible to know a person, especially a man," she counters with a fatuous smile. Then she whispers, "Sometimes love offered within any context should be accepted in disregard to the danger of consequences."

He has done so before; he has no further words. She watches him as she unclothes herself, her lower dress, her blouse, her stockings and her undergarments. Uncharacteristically, she turns in an attempt at modesty and closes her eyes for a moment, though she had abandoned any such pretense long since.

Another kiss stirs a longer, wilder kiss. Charity conjures her mania below the surface, ready to express love frantically and vigorously.

"Put your arms around me darling. Kiss my lips until I blush. Keep your arms around me, do not let me go; gracious how I love it so."

The sounds of the New York streets echo from below, but other sounds fill the room—they are complete lovers.

〰️

Once again the sounds of the city streets dominate. The lovers are in bed and now quiet, thinking about an uncertain future. Charity moves slowly toward the window seat. She sits naked and views moonlit Times Square. For the first time, she was intimate with a man she could love. He was a tender lover, so different from the other men she had known.

Centori sits up from the disheveled bed and stares at her naked beauty. A few moments of silence follow. Apprehensively, he thinks, *Charity is the first woman since El Paso, with Gabriella. I thought Jennifer would be my next lover. God, what about Jennifer? I guess east is east and west is west.*

"I suppose showing up here was not at all proper," Charity surprisingly explores.

"To hell with propriety," he answers with humor. "Just don't stop surprising me."

"Would it surprise you if you loved me?"

"Yes. Do you think I love you?"

"You did not say so, sometimes it's hard to distinguish."

"Do not bother to make that distinction at all."

"Adobe, the way you acted on the observation deck. I have held my tongue, unsure what to say, but my God! What was that you were doing?"

It was an extremely private moment but he offers, "It was hardly an uplifting experience."

"What caused you to drift away?"

"You are taking us down a dangerous road."

"I think you like danger. What is trapped in your heart?"

Centori feels trapped in his bed and changes the subject. "Charity, that man in the bar; how would he feel about us?"

"Never you mind. He would not care in the least, I am sure."

"Who is he?" he asks as a matter of fact.

"He is an Italian; a financial wizard."

"What is his name?"

"Charles Ponzetti."

"Never heard of him."

"Oh, you will; he is making money, a lot of money for his investors. A man like you may find Charles to be highly profitable for you."

"A man like me?"

"Never you mind."

Their hands join as if a long affectionate history exists between them.

"Charity, how do you feel? Are you happy?"

A shadow passes her face; dissatisfaction engraves her voice, "I have never been happy, though I show a happy face. I tend to see the possibility of failure."

"That is the inherent price of an adventurous life, but there is also the possibility of success."

"I suppose so."

"So you have been happy?"

Speaking in a whisper, "Yes, I have been happy some of the time. I am happy now."

CHAPTER 18

ROMAN GODDESS

The romantic rendezvous in room 808 extended into the morning and surprised both Adobe and Charity. He thought she was a woman who takes more than she gives. Last night disproved his theory. At sunrise, she leaves the room alone, wearing the same day dress as yesterday. He will follow.

Her posture is upright as she struts into the breakfast room for the entire world as if she were Gertrude Vanderbilt. There is nothing inelegant about Charity Clarkson on this day. She takes a seat and savors the first cup of coffee.

After a respectable ten minutes, he enters the breakfast room and slowly approaches. "Good morning, Miss Clarkson. How are you today?"

"Adobe, I can tell you how I am, Sir," she gushes. "You are the best time I ever had," she whispers.

He pours coffee for himself, refills her cup and responds to the admiration in her voice. "I am happy to be back in New York and happy to meet you."

"It was a lovely evening—without ruin, guilt or shame," she laughs. A flash of seriousness follows, "No trace of you ever treating me with condescension or social distance."

"It was indeed a good night and we could have a good day."

"Mr. Centori, perhaps you are being a little presumptuous," she says, lowering her voice as the staff keeps a discreet distance.

"You think so, after our time together yesterday—and last night? Okay, perhaps I am," he retreats.

"Never you mind; yesterday should not be all that passes between us. What New York adventure are you keen on today?"

"Libertas."

"What? Who?"

"The Roman Goddess with a torch held high to the sky. I was 16 years old when that robed figure arrived in New York harbor, a fascinating sight. Charity, would you like to visit the Statue of Liberty?"

"I would like very much to accompany you. Miss Libertas will be even more fascinating to you with me along."

"Good. Now how about getting some breakfast?"

She smiles in the affirmative and changes the subject. "I thought we could do something before visiting the statue. I would like you to meet Mr. Ponzetti. He was in the bar with me on the night we met."

"Why?"

"Well, I am sort of a sales agent for him."

"What are you selling?"

"Financial investments; people are making plenty of money with him. I have nothing to invest, but I do make a little money working for him. He can make you a rich man. I mean more than you are now, of course."

"I have all the high finance I need running the Circle C Ranch."

"I am paid for merely making introductions and it would be on our way to Battery Park."

"All for you, Charity."

CHAPTER 19

CENTRAL PARK GATEWAY

I t is not quite 10:00 am. Warren and Spooner stand at Central Park South and Fifth Avenue with no one aware of their destructive intentions. A group of ruffians loudly approach, Warren and Spooner move to the front of the Plaza Hotel, near the construction site of a new plaza. The Central Park entrance footprint, two semicircles inspired by Paris' Place de la Concorde, is already visible.

"When will we have all that is needed?" Warren asks.

"This very night, I am assured, all that is needed," Spooner informs. "We must have 100 pounds of dynamite, 500 pounds of heavy cast-iron sash weights and a timer-set detonator."

"And they are reliable bomb builders?"

"Yes, of course, I believe even better than our friends in Los Angeles. We can expect to receive a valuable education in the art and science of high explosives."

"There always seems as if there is one last thing do," Spooner observes and continues. "You will meet the contacts here at midnight as agreed."

Warren looks at his pocket watch, "Yes."

"Then expect them at noon and listen for the words 'she sent us' from one of the contacts."

"One last thing. It will be a horrifying demonstration."

"It will be culmination of our plan. Good day, Mr. Warren."

"We will be denounced as terrorists, more so than Los Angeles."

"Good day!"

At noon near the Central Park Zoo, Warren is in place for the rendezvous. They arrive on a horse drawn wagon. Two men in overcoats and bowler hats are on time. One comes off the wagon and says with a German accent and through his cigarette smoke, "Mr. Warren?"

"Yes."

"You are expecting us?"

"Perhaps."

"She sent us."

"Yes, then I am expecting you. Have you constructed a package to be placed on this wagon and to be delivered to us?"

"Indeed we have done so and will do so. You have a reliable delivery man? One who can deliver the package in broad daylight?"

"Yes, and he has insisted on a reliable timer," Warren replies. "That is imperative!"

"Of course."

Warren looks over his shoulder and says, "Are you sure that the fully equipped wagon will arrive at the designated time and designated location?"

"Within ten minutes, early or late."

"Then you are confident that all is prepared?"

"There is nothing left unplanned. Take note of this wagon, you will receive at the designated time and location."

"Always seems as if there is one last thing do," Warren observes.

CHAPTER 20

⌒∞⌒

GRAND CIRCLE

The high windows catch the morning light in Mr. Ponzetti's office that contains a safe, a metal file and multiple ledger cases. The self-proclaimed financial wizard sits at a roll-top desk filled with memoranda as they enter.

He stands and offers a sweaty hand, "Mr. Centori! I am pleased to meet you, I am Charles Ponzetti."

"Mr. Ponzetti."

"Miss Clarkson has told me you are visiting New York."

"Yes, that's right."

Centori dismisses him at a glance as his expression changes from neutral to one of concern; it is a change born of experience.

Ponzetti goes on, "I trust you are having a good time in New York."

"I am."

"Centori. Lei è italiano?" (Centori. Are you Italian?)

"I nonni erano da Potenza." (My grandparents were from Potenza.)

"*Io sono nato a Parma, nella regione Emilia-Romagna.*" (I was born in Parma, in the Emilia-Romagna region.)

"Si, lo so, fra Milano e Firenze." (I know, between Milan and Florence.)

"Italians such as Columbus and Caboto have contributed much to the America and Amerigo Vespucci gave his name to the U.S."

"That was just the beginning, Centori replies, "Filippo Mazzei's equality of man thesis is incorporated into the Declaration of Independence and William Paca *signed* the Declaration of Independence. Constantino Brumidi, the American Michelangelo, painted the rotunda of the Capitol."

"You are well informed about the Italians," Ponzetti flatters.

Charity, riveted on the conversation, chimes in, "He is well informed about many things."

"I am learning that. The Americans have given the Italians a mixed welcome to this country. Yet, there is a great monument at Grand Circle celebrating the 400th anniversary of Columbus coming to the new world."

"Some are calling it Columbus Circle now. It may have been more of an Italian effort than American," Centori states.

"How so?"

"*Il Progresso*, the Italian newspaper in New York, raised funds for the construction of the marble statue of Columbus. My father donated back then. Look, as interesting as this conversation is, we have plans for today."

"Certainly, I am sure that you know that A.P. Giannini founded the Bank of Italy in San Francisco, which leads me to the purpose of our meeting—high finance. Mr. Centori, your grandparents were Italians and now you seem to be a prosperous American living in Mexico."

"That's *New* Mexico," he corrects with rancor.

He returns Ponzetti's scrutiny with a look of disinterest and turns toward Charity.

"Oh, and a cattle baron too, I understand," Ponzetti says.

Centori flashes a glance at Charity. "You do?"

"Perhaps you have heard about my powerful financial strategy."

"No, not really."

"Allow me to explain a financial deal for someone successful and who desires to become more so."

"I can deliver to you 100% profit within 90 days with a form of arbitrage."

"That sounds like an idea for many people, but I don't think so."

"Mr. Centori, many of my clients have become very rich."

"No, thanks."

"But you have not yet heard any details."

"I have heard enough."

"You could be missing a great opportunity."

"I'll take that risk."

"At least let me explain my financial business"

"The answer is no."

"You should think about my proposition."

"I have. Now I am leaving. Charity?"

"Mr. Centori?" Ponzetti implores.

"Look, mister," he replies sternly.

"Perhaps I have made an honest mistake," Ponzetti says.

"I may make one myself. Good afternoon."

The cowboy is not as blind as Ponzetti's prejudice had suggested.

On the street, Charity and Adobe walk to the Trolley in silence until she stops to confront him. "Why were you so rude?"

"I don't like him," he says without preamble. "Besides, I showed enough reserve, but he was too eager and self-promoting."

"Do you think him evil?"

"I never attribute to wickedness that which ineptitude explains. How well do you know him?"

Charity gasps, "What do you mean?"

"I don't trust him. How well do you know him?"

"Not very well, I suppose. But many know that he is a respected financier; are you afraid of being rich?"

"No, but he should be afraid of the law *and me*. I suspect he is a fancy snake oil salesman who underestimated me, since I am from *Mexico*."

She sighs, "How could you know that?"

"There is something just not right about your friend. Now can we drop the subject and enjoy the day together?"

"Many New Yorkers have invested with him and made money."

With a tense exhausted look he replies, "Until the well goes dry. I have known men like him; they should be marked to warn the world."

"Never you mind. Shall we get back on the streetcar?"

"Yes, and then the ferry to Bedloe's Island. I have not been on a boat since Cuba."

"What's that?" Charity asks.

Centori drifts back to Havana Bay at the end of the war in Cuba.

"Murph, she's late and this ship will not wait."

"Don't worry; she agreed to travel to Tampa Bay with you."

The ship's horn blew; no sign of Gabriella.

"Flores para la venta."

"Chico, aquí, ahorita."

He grabbed the flowers and boarded the troop ship. Leaning over the rail he strained to see her in the crowd. She was not there. The final horn blew and the ship departed. He released the flowers to the harbor. The ship had a schedule, grief does not.

"Hey, cowboy!"

"Oh, let's forget Lady Liberty; there is another statue I would like to see."

"What about all that Roman Goddess talk that got you all in a dither?"

"It is not the best day for a boat ride."

"The sun could not shine more brilliantly."

"Let's go to the U.S. Sub-Treasury Building."

"I thought you didn't like this city's high finance."

Why does she know Ponzetti? Was the meeting well designed? he thinks, then continues, "The Sub-Treasury is located on the corner of Wall Street and Nassau Street—the site where the old Federal Hall Building once stood a*nd* Washington took his oath of office on the balcony."

"Another history lesson," Charity says half joking.

"And an art lesson too. An impressive statue of Washington marks the spot of the first inauguration."

"You are full of surprises."

CHAPTER 21

WALL STREET

At Trinity Church, Adobe and Charity turn left on Broadway onto Wall Street. They move slowly down the busy and narrow street that has many colorful corporate banners flying along with American and New York flags.

"I hope the day is living up to your expectations," Centori inquires.

"Yes, I am enjoying this day, quite right."

Charity enjoys all that the day offers: his company, his interests and especially having her hand drawn under his arm. She cannot think of anyone else with whom she would rather share such a New York adventure.

From a distance of 20 yards away, he halts on the crowded sidewalk and points upward to a Greek revival building that was once Federal Hall, "That is the U.S. Sub-Treasury. That pedestal and the monumental statue of George Washington on front steps are dramatic!"

"I have seen the statue before but with you it seems like the first time, Charity says." Then with a wistful look in her blue eyes she adds, "I am having the best time."

"Thanks for the warning," he jokes to lighten the moment. "Washington is about 12 feet high. Look at him reaching forward and the way the cape flows."

They walk directly across towards The House of Morgan at 23 Wall Street. "The façade is suggestive of a vault," he points out.

"Mr. Morgan has much to protect."

"His clients have much to protect as well."

Continuing on Wall Street toward Broad Street, they stop at the New York Stock Exchange, a Roman inspired structure with a dramatic colonnade.

"Charity, that glass curtain wall behind the colonnade provides light for the trading floor."

"That's interesting. You enjoy impressing a woman with your knowledge."

"You impress me. Speaking of impressive women, shall we walk to Battery Park and see the Statue of Liberty?"

"I thought I was the only woman who impresses you, and you said it was a bad day for a boat ride?"

"Things change."

"Oh, really?"

"Never you mind," he mimics.

"Ha-ha. Okay, cowboy, let's go."

The strong sun beams down and through the narrow streets, packed with lunchtime workers in the heart of the Financial District. As Adobe and Charity step away from the Stock Exchange, a mild breeze lifts Charity's wide hat brim slightly. A horse-drawn wagon crosses their path; they stop as the wagon moves toward the Morgan Bank.

The driver and the wagon continue forward through the crowd. Centori notices that the struggling horse is pulling a heavy load. Then the wagon stops near the U.S. Assay Office across from the Morgan Bank.

Standing on the Financial District's busiest corner, Centori has a sudden, strange sense of impending doom. When the driver abandons the wagon and speedily disappears into the crowd, Centori becomes concerned. He instinctively scans the crowd as they start to walk again, then he stops in midstride; his senses sharpening. Something is wrong and he is powerless to stop the world from changing forever.

Each second increases his alertness, his strength and his focus. Charity missteps and is propelled a few steps forward. She turns around with a fatuous smile and taunts, "What are you waiting for, cowboy? Too crowded? Miss the wide open spaces?"

"Charity, wait!"

"Don't worry, they are just messengers, clerks, stenographers and brokers—not wild west outlaws of *New* Mexico!"

Those were the last happy words ever spoken by Charity Clarkson on this earth. Darkness overcomes him within the sunlight; she smiles playfully, steps away and signals him to follow.

His pulse quickens. "Charity, wait, come back."

She is a few yards ahead but difficult to see in the crowd. With intense and rising anxiety his mind races, *Be alert, be on guard, be prepared. But where is she? Something's wrong. He turns his head right, left, right. All the women's hats look the same. What color is her hat?*

Charity is lost in the crowd. In an instant, Centori's sense of urgency and dread are overwhelming; his adrenaline surges, his blood rushes throughout his body. The approaching dragon cannot be slain. One second, two seconds, then he screams, "CHARITY!" One second later a great blast violently knocks him down, his ears ring. His eyes see stars explode as the wagon explodes. He cannot hear, but sees the blast send a shrapnel barrage into the crowd in all directions, tearing into flesh and killing scores of people.

Centori struggles to his feet and sees that the thunderous timer-set detonation blasts the horse and wagon beyond recognition then yields to massive smoke clouds and a hail of window glass flying. After a few seconds of strange silence, screams begin—just as Centori regains his hearing. Seconds after the explosion, an apocalypse wall of burning hot air, dust and debris containing unimaginable missiles consumes the heart of Wall Street.

About to be engulfed from all directions, Centori automatically hits the concrete ground to avoid the hellish energy and waits for the inevitable heavy infantry fire…Captain Centori looks for Sergeant Murphy and screams, *Murph, Murph, MURPH.* The 6th U.S. Cavalry brothers-in-arms lead two batteries of Gatling guns close to the Spanish lines. No Murphy, no heavy fire. *This is not Cuba. Oh my God, this is New York.*

Centori, battle tested in war, is nonetheless shocked. The old soldier, breathing hard, looks up, rises and quickly checks his wounds, bloody but not deadly. With the adrenaline still surging, he tries to control his body. *Calm down. Think straight. Where is Charity?* Amidst the chaos, he sees what a terror attack can produce: an ultimate catastrophe with people running panic-stricken through the narrow streets. Bloody bodies stagger in every direction; the walking dead shell shocked. A cascade of falling glass crashes to the ground as smoke billows from the wagon wreckage. The shocking scene is Dante-esque. At the speed of light, his dazed mind flashes on an eerie poem from his youth:

Phantoms, ghouls and hideous freakish fiends,
Battled virtuous and righteous souls, to win at any means.
Ravens and church bells dueled above as
witches flew in frenzied flight,
Mesmerized he watched in awe as the spirits clashed all night.

A split second later he returns to the carnage—as real as his time in combat—and clears his stricken mind, *Where is she?* Scanning the scale of the damage he desperately searches, *For God's sake, where is she?* She is down.

Centori moves through the stunned crowd surrounded by the moans of the wounded and men and women with severe injuries. One hundred pounds of dynamite packed with cast iron slugs increased the destructive power of the attack. *Where is she?* She is lying in the street close to the curb and close to death.

He sees Charity. Her body is riveted with cast-iron slugs; there is so much blood. She is terribly pale. It is painfully obvious, she has not much time.

"Charity," he summons his voice, placing his jacket under her head.

"What happened? Help me, it hurts so much," she moans.

There is no mistaking the horror in his eyes, "I don't know. Just don't move." *Please, dear God, do not let this woman die.*

"Adobe, I can't move," she cries.

His head turns frantically; his eyes move over the war-torn scene searching for help.

"Wait, don't go, please…" she whispers.

"I am with you now."

"I wanted to stand with you, stand by you," she intones gravely.

"You have," he says while taking her hand.

She moans and nods slowly, "You are kind to me, one of the few," her faint voice shakes.

"Charity."

Her eyes fill with tears. "In some ways we are alike."

"I know that we are."

On his knees and looking into her eyes, he looks away in guilt; he brought her to this place, to her death.

"Don't blame yourself for…you are a perfect gentleman," she says with tears coursing down her cheek.

But he does blame himself. Staring at the doomed woman, a familiar feeling runs down his spine. His heart beats hard, and his mind bursts to Gabriella's death scene. He quickly looks around for help as she murmurs, "Any plans for us are fatefully changed forever. I am…stay with me now."

Ripping his gaze from her, he scans the surrounding pandemonium. Citizens, acting as rescuers, are working feverishly attending to wounded. The first police officers arrive, rushing to perform first aid and taking automobiles as emergency vehicles to evacuate people.

He turns back to Charity who whispers, "You are the most honorable man I have ever known."

She is devastated, desolate and powerless to move and now powerless to breathe. There is nothing more to say, nothing more she can say…her faint voice expires.

Consumed with rage, Centori throws his fists up and screams, "NOOO!" His ferocity shatters the chaos for a second. He lovingly and protectively rocks Charity in his arms. Instantly diverted from the horrid drama unfolding, he hears a recognizable voice with a Spanish accent.

"*Mi corazón, I am with you.*"

"*Why are you here now? This is a different situation,*" he moans in compounded pain.

"*Yes, but my feelings are unchanged.*"

"*Then you are here to witness another great failure.*"

"*No, I am here to call you to be resolute in faith and strength in this time. I know your pain and suffering.*"

"*You should have loved me more, Gabriella.*"

"*More? I have given you all my heart.*"

"Then better...loved me better. Our time in Cuba was a great love story. Then in New Mexico your love changed to fury. The tragic end in Chaco Canyon was bitter, abrupt and unsettled. How much of you is fantasy, how much is real?"

"Mister, mister, there's nothing more to do for her. Help us with those that have a chance," a copper orders.

Centori answers with a chilling look while holding Charity's lifeless body. The copper calls out again, "Come on, time is of the essence."

With his power and self-possession returning, Centori's mind begins to focus on the sprawled bodies expressing a violent death. He inhales deeply, rubs his face and yells, "Lead the way, officer."

Noticing Centori's head is stained with dust, sweat and blood the officer asks, "Are you alright?"

"Just scratches."

"That's a bloody shirt. Let's get some bandages."

CHAPTER 22

RATTLESNAKES

After three hours of deciding the priority of treatment, transport and destination of the victims, Centori and the policeman rest on the steps of Federal Hall, in the shadow of Washington's statue. There were scores in need of help; many were beyond help. Both men are exhausted from the ordeal.

They sit in silence for a time until the policeman says, "You did good work today; you were strong and decisive."

"Good to be strong, better to be lucky, Officer."

"I guess so. Sorry about your lady friend."

He nods.

"What was her name?"

"Charity."

"She didn't deserve this ending. She was innocent."

"No one deserved this; all the victims were innocent."

"I know."

"She would have been proud of the way you helped so many people."

Centori drops his head in silence.

"You showed a policeman's character today."

"I am Sheriff of Corona County in New Mexico."

"You don't say; may I know your name?"

"I'm Adobe Centori. Call me Adobe."

"Officer Jack Haughey, NYPD. Call me Jack."

"It was an honor to work side by side with you today."

"Same here Jack."

"New Mexico, that's way out west."

"Born and raised in New York."

"I had a feeling."

"This does not look like an accident, the timing, this place, crowded at lunchtime. The attack seems aimed at the Morgan people."

"Or the system Morgan represents. You are right, it was no accident. This is unlike anything I experienced in war; this horrible slaughter was inflicted on civilians."

"But it doesn't make sense. Why was this done?"

Crestfallen, Centori responds, "Detective work will determine that, but I will not get entangled in the motives that fueled this monstrous act."

"You are right. Those criminals should not be taken seriously enough the wonder why—only to wonder how we get them to the gallows. Their reasons will be revealed and could be justified by some in the public."

"Jack, the motives of those responsible can be learned, their purpose deciphered, but I can only see this act, this carnage." Centori stares ahead and in a flat tone continues. "All the parts of cars, trucks and horses everywhere; bodies and parts of bodies spread all over the streets."

"No one here will ever forget this day," Haughey says.

Centori lowers his head and rubs his eyes. "I have shot rattlesnakes on my ranch in New Mexico, killed them in my horse barn and on the open range. I shoot rattlers because they aim to kill me. I don't wonder why rattlers kill, they just do. So, I kill them. I don't care to understand those who wielded this destruction and death on innocent Wall Street workers because nothing can justify the inhumanity of this terror attack."

⟨≈⟩

At sundown, Officer Jack Haughey is in the downtown police station. Adobe Centori is in the Knickerbocker Hotel and Charity Clarkson is in the morgue. Charity and Adobe had fought each other's darkness, only to arrive in a worse place.

The Wall Street bombing is New York's worst disaster since the Triangle Shirtwaist Factory fire that killed 146 young women. The factory fire was the worst industrial accident in New York history, but the Wall Street disaster was no accident.

It happened in a crowded public place, designed to increase casualties among financial workers. It was far more deadly than the Los Angeles Times bombing. This time the target was the Morgan building. The attack caused more than $2 million in damage to the strong stone building.

The location of the attack suggested that the bomb was detonated by radical anti-capitalists. Then, the next day revealed a warning note found in a post office box on Broadway. The political message was signed American Scream. The philosophy in the note is clear: the state is immoral in the affairs of social relations. Government enforcement will create coercion, authority and violence against the public. American Scream stands for a stateless society. Anarchy justified its destructive means of expression.

Undaunted by the explosion, the New York Stock Exchange board of governors declared that Wall Street would be open for business the next day, and it was opened. Investigators identified the victims in the hope of finding the driver of the wagon but they did not. An examination of what was left of the horse showed that he was newly shod. The attending blacksmith could not help the police. Detective work continues; Charity's life does not.

Part Two

Venus Rising

Chapter 23

⟋∞⟍

State of New Mexico

May 1912

In the days following the bombing, Centori stayed in his hotel room alone and utterly cold. He spent most of the time gripped by the Wall Street wreckage and by the wreckage in his mind. He deliberated that fateful day over and over; wondering what he had done wrong, if he could have done anything differently.

In due course, he gathered his strength for the long journey back to New Mexico. He had a narrow escape in New York, if it was an escape at all. A guardian angel may have saved his life; he thought it was an archangel. From Pennsylvania Station he rode the rails across the country and arrived in New Mexico—depressed and exhausted.

Centori had returned to the new state of New Mexico less than a week ago. Although securely entrenched at the Circle C Ranch, he remains torn apart by the shocking Wall Street explosion and the death of Charity. The tempo and the scale of New Mexico are vastly different from New York, changes he welcomed. There are other differences in Valtura that he will not welcome.

The Circle C, located in Corona County near Valtura, is one of the largest cattle spreads in New Mexico. The distinguished Spanish colonial ranch house is of adobe brick construction. Made of clay, straw and pebbles, the structurally strong bricks are naturally suited for New Mexico's hot summers and cold winters. The house has a portal of colonnade vigas, projected roof vigas, antique doors, large windows and a grand view of the Sandia Mountains.

Centori built the Circle C for himself, with the hope that Gabriella would one day share the dream house. It never happened. She never came and he never invited another woman. Most people found that hard to understand, but no more than Centori himself. All that could change with Jennifer Prower, despite the list of Titanic victims.

Wearing his big tan hat, dark red shirt, denim pants and old expensive boots, he stands in the front portal with the echo of the Wall Street blast still in his head. The emotionally drained man continues his habit of having cowboy coffee while viewing the sunrise. All the same, he would weather the storm—he always does.

As the sun clears the mountains, Centori returns to the kitchen to pour a second cup. The inside of the house has thick plaster walls, beautiful Saltillo floor tiles and southwest-style woodwork with exposed ceiling vigas. Entering the library he sits on a leather wing chair situated on an earth-toned Navajo rug. He kicks the ottoman away and vacantly finishes the coffee. A moment later, he sets down his cup and stares at a New York map hung behind the desk. New York was an extraordinary misadventure that had done no good for him.

Scanning the floor to ceiling bookshelves, he tries to rally for today's dedication while the New York experience clouds his brain. Charity's death and the Wall Street bombing were profoundly traumatic. The terrorist attack had awakened a past that is always in the back of his mind. That crucial day with Charity had forced him to re-examine the tragic tale at Chaco Canyon. Gabriella's death was distant, almost abstract, as she disappeared under the crushing rockslide. In contrast, the explosion in the heart of financial district was close and concrete—Charity died in his arms.

"Good morning, Boss. You have any more coffee?"

He welcomed the interruption. "Sure, let's go into the kitchen."

Almost ten years older than Centori, A.P. Baker entered the library with his usual optimism and his honorable personality. Since the colonel's death, A.P. has assumed the role of prime confidante. That aspect naturally developed, stemming from years of friendship. He is a trusted cowboy and the Circle C foreman who provides imaginative ideas for running the ranch. A.P. also offers sage personal advice.

Blaming himself for Gabriella's death, Centori had fallen apart and his state of mind created a threat to the running of the Circle C. He had always been able to harmonize a team and operate as a hands-on ranch owner, but after Chaco Canyon he spent an inordinate amount of time brooding. Sometimes, for only a moment, he appeared without a shadow of a hope of recovering from his great loss.

A.P. never saw a man so entirely overwhelmed with grief; he was cheerful and had tried to help, but Centori was seldom free of depression. Then A.P. suggested the New York trip.

In the kitchen, he pours, but seems lost in thought.

A.P. takes off his hat and runs his hands through his gray hair. "A penny for them, Boss."

He remembers Charity saying that. "That's about all they are worth." He hands over a cup.

"Thanks, Boss. Big day in town today."

"That's right."

"You haven't seen Mad Mady since returning."

"No, not yet."

"She has been worried about you." A.P. savors the coffee. "She asks about you whenever a Circle C cowboy goes to town."

"I am sure I'll see her today."

"Yes, everyone on the plaza will be there today. The colonel would be proud of what you did for the plaza in his memory."

He nods his head in the affirmative. "But perhaps not so proud of what happened in New York. A.P., the woman in New York I mentioned…"

"The woman you were with at the bombing, you said she was killed."

"Yes, an acquaintance, only an acquaintance."

A.P. raises his eyebrows. *I didn't ask,* he thinks.

"I feel as though I invited Charity to her death."

"You know as well as I do that you can't blame yourself."

"I tried to stop her from advancing toward that hell on wheels, but failed."

"Look, Boss, you always had good instincts, but those incarnate fiends who caused the explosion are to blame, plain and simple."

"Maybe the bombers are to blame—maybe I am. I thought it was me."

"You thought wrong."

"It was devastatingly destructive."

"The newspaper said the bombers had a political agenda."

"Yes, an agenda of violence. It started as a peaceful day; then it exploded into grotesque savagery. The financial center of New York became a choking war zone—buildings damaged, property destroyed, people killed. Clausewitz said that war is the continuation of policy by other means, meant to be fought on a battlefield. Those people in New York were noncombatants, civilians who got hurt and had to bear the burden. Wall Street is not a battlefield."

"Isn't it? I mean for those bombers."

Centori stares for a second. "I can't help to think that the Wall Street attack is a precursor to another attack. They have achieved their objectives—to kill on a large scale and to terrorize the public. However, there is something muddled about this whole affair, and the way Charity died in my arms."

He firmly places the cup down. "A.P., there is something about the two tragic deaths."

"What?"

"Gabriella and Charity died in dreadful ways. Up to this point, I have been trying to figure out why Gabriella died that way. But I realize that the issue was not *why* she died. Rather, the issue is *who* killed her."

"I am not sure what you mean, Boss."

"At Chaco, there was no one to blame for Gabriella's death, no clear responsibility; too many factors and too many conflicts. There were many parties involved in the Revert Document conspiracy, Germans, Mexicans, New Mexicans and hard cases."

I thought he blamed his patriotism, A.P. thinks, but would never say.

"All the parties were seeking the Revert Document but not necessarily her death. That was not the case in New York—killing was their purpose. They meant to kill and kill anyone they could."

"It sure seemed that way."

"They aimed to destroy; the blame is clear."

"Crystal clear, Boss. As I said, it falls on the people who caused the explosion."

"A note was found near Wall Street after the attack. It was signed American Scream. The message states that they are taking credit for the bombing."

"Then American Scream, whatever the hell that is, killed Charity."

"That's right. The note described the evils of capitalism and how private property rights and profit crush workers and how government supports those problems."

"I don't know about that. If workers are not oppressed, they could improve their lots without violence and there is not much government here in the wide open spaces."

"I have judged their morality and I don't care about their opposition to capital creation or government. The question is what to do next for Charity."

A.P. smiles and pats him on the shoulder. "That's a question for another day."

"It's too late to get justice for Gabriella, but not for Charity."

"Boss, right now let's think of the colonel."

He nods. "Yes, of course, the colonel."

"Colonel Santos was like a father to you."

"Yes, he was that indeed," Centori says and tightens his lips.

"Look, tough times don't last. Tough people do."

"Thanks."

"It's just the truth."

"Let's go," Centori grabs his bandana from his back pocket and they exit the house; A.P. walks faster than his friend to the horse barn. Patriot, the old warhorse, sees his rider and offers a neigh sound with his head high.

As they saddle up Centori turns to A.P., "Do you believe in ghosts?"

After a moment A.P. replies, "I think Jesus said 'allow the dead to bury their own dead.'"

Puzzled, he mounts Patriot and A.P. handles Mars for the six-mile ride to Valtura. Since returning to New Mexico, Centori has been unwilling to ride the range, but not today.

CHAPTER 24

VALTURA, NEW MEXICO

An hour after leaving the Circle C, Centori and A.P. stop on a low hill that overlooks Valtura. A.P. observes, "Valtura Plaza is more of a rectangle than a square, Boss."

"Yes, it is. Will anyone criticize the new name?"

Both men continue the ride toward the plaza that is surrounded by Spanish Colonial and adobe brick buildings; many are covered with earth tone stucco. There have been changes in Valtura since statehood. Several new mission style homes are under construction on East Corona Street. *El Dorado*, a moving picture theater near the plaza, is expected to open this summer. A new structure is rising on West Corona Street and Coyote Road as a hotel.

Passing Junction Street, the site selected for a rail station, Centori is reminded that Governor Jackson's friends were expected to finance the rail project. Construction of an extension from the station to town, scheduled to begin last month, has not started. The Valtura Rail Station remains a flag stop five miles from the plaza.

"A.P., the lack of a rail extension to town is disappointing. New Mexico has joined the union but Valtura has not joined the 20th century."

"A rail station near the plaza would bring new business."

"It seems that Jackson's views on Valtura's economic development have changed since his re-election."

"It seems so."

"Despite that, Boss, we are experiencing progress; thanks to investment from other sources we have more activity around the plaza. The town will get a picture show on National Street; the Crown Hotel will be five stories in territorial style with a stucco and brick roofline."

"It will rival the Plaza Hotel in Las Vegas."

"That's right, Boss."

They ride on to Corona Street, which extends through the plaza's north side, towards the red brick county courthouse and the adobe brick sheriff's office.

"There it is—the new Santos Square," A.P. says while pointing.

Both men view the new square. "It looks great, Boss, you should be proud."

"Thanks, A.P."

The street continues east toward the mountains. On the west plaza, the First National Bank of Santa Fe and post office can be found. Nearby is the telegraph office. The entire south plaza between First and Second Streets is the home of Mad Mady's Saloon. The Union Hotel and the *Valtura Journal* are located on the east plaza. Arriving at the north plaza, the riders stop at the sheriff's office and the time worn sign:

A. Centori, Sheriff,
Corona County
New Mexico Territory

WATER DAMAGE | 117

Hmm, New Mexico Territory, I'll have to change that sign. My name will stay since I am not going to Washington.

New Mexico became a state, but Centori did not become a senator; that honor went to Thomas Benton Catron and to Albert B. Fall. He accepts this outcome, but remembers the governor's implied promise. No matter, he is sheriff of Corona County—a position he earned from the voters.

He points at the sign. "A.P., I guess we need to drop the word territory."

"I am sure you can find some county funds for that."

Centori laughs and dismounts. A.P. looks down from Mars. "I need to see a lady and escort her to the dedication."

"Things have changed around there."

With a big smile A.P. says, "See you later, Boss."

The sheriff dismounts, enters the two-room office, and looks at his desk that is covered with books and piles of papers. The office looks the same way as it did on the day he departed, except for a coat of dust over everything. *Thought I asked Buster to see to things while I was gone.*

He removes and places his gun belt over a chair and sits behind a roll-top desk; not sure what to do next. *I must confront Jennifer about the Titanic list of victims. She could have a common name but I will confront her. I wonder if she knows that I have returned.* He stands at a front window and looks at the *Valtura Journal* office. *Is Jennifer there now? I could confront her, or wait until after the dedication. I should see Mady; this paperwork can wait.* So can his indecision about Jennifer.

Across the plaza on National Street is Mad Mady's Saloon. Since his return, Mady has been waiting to see him. Today's dedication will provide the chance, and she will not have to wait until noon.

Elizabeth Mad Mady Blaylock, is an attractive 35 year old woman with a good mind and good body. The former New Yorker stands at five feet, five inches, with dark hair and hazel eyes. She is attracted to the charismatic Centori and is the author of ongoing romantic tension.

There is something wild about Mady just below the surface. She often represses certain feelings about the emotionally elusive Centori. Despite her invitations, they are able to maintain closeness without intimacy. In the past, Mady wondered if he holds a different interpretation of courtly love. Now, she questions if he is as romantically despondent as he appears, especially with his new love interest.

Mad Mady's Saloon has a long bar and a chandelier suspended from the second-story stamped tin ceiling. There are many mahogany tables, plush chairs, curtains and rugs. Oil paintings in gold gilt frames and gas fixtures are on red walls. Upstairs, dreary small rooms with sparse furnishings house perfumed and painted women.

Five minutes later, Centori quits the office and walks across the plaza to the saloon. As always true in the mornings, the aroma of coffee brewing is in the saloon air. An attractive woman with a slender shape in a dark dress is behind the bar reading the *Valtura Journal*. She is young and pretty with bold brown eyes, straight brown hair and straight white teeth.

Mady sits at her private corner table surrounded by vacant tables. She is wearing blue pants, a red shirt and a blue vest. Centori pulls his gaze away from the pretty woman and continues to Mady's table.

"Good Morning, Mady." *I wonder if she knows about my ordeal.*

Mady is startled and her eyes brighten as she stands up. "Adobe! Welcome back! We missed you, I missed you."

"Good to be back, Mady."

"Is it true? Were you at the site of that horrible New York bombing?"

"Yes, it is true."

"Oh my God, are you alright?"

"Tolerable."

She gives him a hug; he glances at the attractive woman behind the bar who is disconcerted by Mady's outburst.

"I have been gone from New York so long that I don't know anyone, but you were right there. The newspaper said it was no accident."

"It was not."

"But why would anyone do such a terrible thing?"

"It is hard to make sense of their reasons, but nothing can justify what they did there. It was beyond evil; it was an insane act."

Mady nods in agreement and waves for coffee. "Sit with me."

The woman behind the bar looks up and folds her newspaper. They shuffle the chairs at Mady's table; he steals another look at the new woman who is preparing to serve. *She is quite lovely.*

"I thought you were staying in Times Square. Why were you at Wall Street?"

"It's a long story."

"When you use that phrase, it usually means a woman."

He stares in admission, "I heard that rumor. Don't believe it."

She does not press the issue. The new woman serves coffee without a word while outside in the plaza people begin to gather.

He grasps his cup and asks, "So how are you, Mady? Are things back to normal here at the saloon?"

"Sure, anything would be normal after the Territorial Insane Asylum!"

"I know and I am sorry you had that trouble."

"Trouble, that's putting it mildly. It was not your fault Adobe. I blame my sister. Although you could have acted faster to get me the hell out of there, I hated that place."

"You took care of that in fine fashion with a daring escape as I recall."

"That's right; a woman can get restless waiting for a man."

"It was your sister's fault. What is the latest with Santa Fe Sharon?"

"My dear sister is still awaiting trial in U.S. District Court in Albuquerque. It sounds serious, does it not?"

"Her list of crimes is serious and could include murder and arson."

"Wait a minute, you said Carrie killed Berta."

"Yes, on your sister's behalf."

"There is no such charge in her indictment and there is no direct evidence connecting her to the Circle C stable fire."

"And don't forget that you prevented her from shooting me."

"You are welcome again but she only attempted to kill you."

"Still defending the indefensible; she killed that *hombre* in Santa Fe."

"There is no direct link to the Santa Fe shooting."

"One thing in her favor, the government will not pursue any charges relating to the Revert Document. The U.S. does not want that affair to be public. It is top secret, like who was responsible for sinking the USS *Maine*."

"What?"

"Never you mind. I mean never mind. Sharon could be in a position to negotiate with the government."

"Perhaps we could advise her."

"What? Why would you lift a finger to help her now?"

"I have to—because she is my sister."

With a sense of sorrow, he adds, "If you count her different personalities, you mean *sisters*."

Mady stares in disapproval. Yet, given that Sharon burned down the Circle C stable and attempted to kill Centori, the comment was generous.

"I will let you handle Sharon's problems. Besides, she has a strong sense of self-preservation."

Mady drops the subject as the crowd in the plaza continues to increase in numbers.

"Word on the plaza is that you have shown interest in that new woman who is running the *Journal*."

"You mean Jennifer Prower. I would be interested in any newcomer to Valtura."

"Ha, yes of course you would be. Then you may find it interesting that your Miss Prower disappeared the day after you left for New York."

"You don't know that."

"Everyone on Valtura Plaza knows that."

"Disappeared? You make it sound mysterious. I don't know what to say."

"You should say something to her—if she returns."

"Right now I need to talk on behalf of the colonel."

"Are you sure you are not too distracted by the Jennifer mystery?" Mady is humorless.

"I will manage to...some way." His eyes dart toward the bar and the new charming creature that attracts his interest.

"Sorry. Adobe, the plaza looks great. You should be happy."

Smiling again he replies, "I am happy about that, Mady. You are a good friend and a good listener but sometimes...the new woman behind the bar, who is she?"

"Felicity Brimwell."

Leaving the saloon, he slyly looks at Felicity with his peripheral vision and a spark of excitement. Her black dress shows her compact lithe body to perfection. Standing perfectly calm, she absorbs his interest while feeling uneasy.

Outside, he sees the plaza crowded with revelers. Walking on National Street in the direction of the newspaper office, he avoids well-wishers and stealthily enters the office—concerned about

Jennifer. He quickly enters and discovers that the *Valtura Journal* is managed by another newcomer.

"May I help you Sir?"

"I am Sheriff Centori."

"Good day. I am Bernhard Bachmeier, editor."

"Is that right? I am wondering about Miss Prower."

"Oh, she is away at the moment," he replies firmly.

"I know that, where did she go and when will she return?"

"I don't know where…is this inquiry official?"

"No. Why would it be?"

"She is expected to return by rail in two days. I will meet her at the station."

"Do you mind if I surprise her?"

"I suppose not. You are acquainted with Miss Prower I assume."

"Thank you for your time, Mr. Bachmeier."

"You are welcome," he replies. Then, under his breath, "she will be very surprised."

CHAPTER 25

STRATFORD, NEW MEXICO

I n 1548 a silver vein seven miles long was discovered in New Spain. The Conquistadors called it *veta madre,* mother lode. Last century, there were several gold discoveries in North America such as the California, Victorian and Klondike Gold strikes. Each time a large migration of excited miners rushed to a gold discovery. Although most found gold mining unprofitable, some people made large fortunes.

Gold or silver discoveries create permanent settlements and new towns. That is the case in Stratford, New Mexico, where silver strikes attracted thousands of immigrants during peak periods of mining operations. As the silver mines played out, many tired miners left Stratford. Now, a new generation of immigrants will soon hear about another discovery.

Stratford is more than 300 miles south of Valtura. Located in Hidalgo County and two miles south of Silver City, Stratford started as a water source for Indians, Spaniards, pioneers and wagon trains. In the 1850s, the town was known as Spanish Springs and became a stop for a stagecoach line *en route* to California.

After the Civil War, a silver discovery impelled John Marlowe, a bank president, to take control of Spanish Springs and of the mines. That 1870 silver mining speculation attracted adventurers, financiers and caused rapid but short-lived economic growth.

When the silver mined out, the population dropped to less than 100 miners and the town faced a dark future. Then, in 1880 Englishmen representing the Stratford Mining Company arrived. Mining engineer Charles Boleyn staked company silver claims and changed the town name to Stratford.

By the mid-1880s the town had some 200 people with three saloons and two hotels. Prosperity continued until the 'Panic of 1893' which caused an economic recession in the country; the silver mines closed, the population decreased and finally Stratford became a ghost town. However, five years ago, a few old mines started operating again and Stratford became alive when the railroad line connected to the main line in Silver City.

On January 1, 1912, the new year dawned on Stratford, as all the mornings did in the southern New Mexican town, with quiet, calm and sunlight. Then a prospector stormed through Main Street wildly waving and yelling, "Gold! Gold!" It was a cold Monday in January when prospector Virgil Turpin found a rocky outcrop of gold-bearing veins in a long lost mine. The Stratford gold rush began—so did the search for the mother lode. The new economic boom increased the population again; the hotels reopened including the Avon Hotel.

Originally, the Avon was a one-story mud and rock construction; a half story adobe brick addition has been added. The modest accommodation is appropriate for a mining camp but unsuitable for the recent woman guest who arrived a few days ago.

When she entered the Avon Hotel, people were astonished by her elegant beauty. She was overdressed, over gemmed and out of place in the lawless town with no church and no newspaper. She signed in under the name Jennifer Prower. In the service of her husband's associates, she has travelled to European cities and New York, but never to such a remote town as Stratford.

Today, she once again seeks her contact: a man wearing a clean white shirt and waiting in the common area. No contact, so she enters the bar. The raw mining barroom strikes at her sensibilities; the saloon is unnerving to a woman accustomed to fine environments. Swirling smoke invades her lungs as the stale beer and sweat offend her nose. The men who crowd the bar are unkempt miners in coarse clothing. Some of the men are better dressed and sit at tables; all of the women have painted faces and are wearing gaudy low-cut dresses that expose most of their flesh.

One red-haired woman emerges from a dim smoky corner, where old crones and dispirited doves are assembled, and sashays to Jennifer. "You look lost, honey,"

"Yes, I am," she replies uneasily.

Jennifer turns and briskly leaves the bar for the hotel common area and waits. Less than an hour later while sitting near the front desk, she is approached by a tall man who says, "*Rote Frau?*"

She is startled by a man who is wearing a white linen shirt and brown pants placed into black boots. "My name is Siegfried Seiler."

"Yes, I am *Rote Frau*. Why have you summoned me to this God forsaken place—without a decent hotel?"

"You are well compensated, so why do you question me?"

"Do you know who my husband is and what he can do?"

"I know of your husband, but I report directly to the count in Mexico City. *Rote Frau,* for now you will report directly to me."

"As you say, but I would be careful about taking too many liberties with me," she reluctantly nods in acceptance.

"Walk with me to the edge of town," Seiler demands. "You will understand what is at stake and I will explain why you have been assigned to Valtura."

CHAPTER 26

SANTOS SQUARE

I n life, Colonel Antonio Santos was a prominent Valtura citizen. Last year, he was a casualty of the Revert Document affair— caught in a death trap created by the international conspiracy. It was another emotional blow to Centori who inherited the colonel's antique weapons collection, expensive chess set, silver watch with an engraved coyote image and an amount of money. The weapons, chess set and watch are at the Circle C; most of the money was placed in a plaza beautification fund.

Over the past two months, the plaza has been improved with new red bricks, new cast-iron benches and new cottonwood trees. A plaque describing the colonel's life, affixed to the gazebo, will be unveiled today. Centori was the leader in changing the name of Valtura Plaza to Santos Square and today, he will dedicate the place at high noon.

It is 11:45 a.m. The plaza is filled with hundreds of people waiting for the event. Red, white and blue bunting decorates the gazebo along with the new state flag and the new American flag— with two additional stars.

Centori is engaging people outside of Mad Mady's Saloon. At high noon, he heads to the gazebo, bounds up the steps to the center while the crowd applauds and cheers enthusiastically. He waits a moment, visibly moved by the welcome. Then, a small brass band strikes up the Star Spangled Banner to start the dedication. Following the music, the crowd applauds again.

"Thank you for the warm welcome. Almost all of you know me; for those who do not, I am Adobe Centori, Sheriff of Corona County. I am fortunate to have known Colonel Antonio Santos; he is the reason we are here. Welcome and thank you for coming today. I extend a special welcome to Senator Thomas Benton Catron, one of the first senators from the new State of New Mexico!"

There is a brief moment but then the crowd claps politely; in sharp contrast. Adobe Centori was the people's choice for senator, but the decision and appointment was up to the governor. After the short interruption, the speaker continues, "I would like to take a moment to ask Padre Morales to invoke God's blessing on those here today and on those who helped re-build this plaza."

The *padre* offers his benediction as Centori recognizes an old man in the crowd who is dressed in black with unnatural eyes. Several minutes later as the benediction comes to a close, the old man fades away. He gathers himself before continuing. "We are proud of our new town center. As we dedicate this plaza to Colonel Santos, please take time to remember his strong dedication to our community. Every man has a story. The colonel has a remarkable one; just ask the people who knew him. His story lives on in this bronze plaque for all to read. He was a leader in war and a leader in peace, and was committed to public service. Born in Las Cruces when that town was part of Spain, he witnessed the changes in New Mexico as we moved from New Spain to Old Mexico and finally to the United States of America."

After a moment of unexpected applause, Centori continues, "If you were to talk to 25 people who knew the colonel, you would hear 25 different tales of his good life. We do not speak only of his life, but of his wishes to see our community thrive in the future. For more than 100 years, Valtura Plaza was the center of parties, holiday celebrations, church activities and even weddings. Now, this enriched square will be the focal point of the community for generations to come. So we continue that tradition with the colonel in mind as more happy memories are created. When we think of the colonel, we will remember his kindness which helped Valtura to grow and prosper not just in an economic way, but in a humanitarian way.

The dream to have this place hold the memory of the colonel has been fulfilled. I hereby declare that Colonel Antonio Santos Square be open for all the people of Valtura and for the new State of New Mexico!"

Wild applause explodes and fills the air with everyone expressing the excitement of the moment—all except one man. The man dressed in black has reappeared on the plaza and offers a reassuring smile that only Centori can see.

CHAPTER 27

STARK REALITY

Following the Santos Square dedication, the crowd slowly files into Mad Mady's Saloon. They fill every table in the large barroom, except Mady's table; the rest are three deep at the bar. All are anticipating the whiskey and the beer to flow.

Soon afterward, Centori walks into the loud room and finds almost every table taken. As people turn to congratulate him, the piano player bangs out a tune. Then a round of applause; Centori doffs his hat.

A large rectangle table holds trays of roasts, chickens and hams with quantities of tortillas arrayed on plates. Another table contains earthenware pitchers of lemonade and bowls of corn and chili peppers. He settles in at Mady's table, one of the few who can take the liberty.

Within minutes A.P. and his lady friend arrive. She wears a light brown blouse with dark brown embroidery and a solid brown skirt.

"Boss, this is Charlotte Morgan."

"Please call me Lotta," she quickly adds.

"This is Adobe Centori."

"Yes, of course. You were wonderful at the plaza, er square."

He stands and says, "Thanks, it is nice to know you Lotta."

"My pleasure, I am sure."

He nods at A.P. indicating approval of the handsome middle aged woman.

Mady makes her way through the crowd with Felicity, who is carrying a tray of bottles and glasses. The men stand up.

"Hello everyone, Jameson Irish Whiskey," Mady offers playfully.

As Felicity leaves, A.P. says, "Mady, you know Lotta."

"Yes. Hello."

"Miss Mady."

A.P. pours then Mady leads the toast, "To Santos Square!"

"Good job, Sheriff," Lotta adds.

"Adobe, your dedication was passionate, as if the colonel were present," Mady says with a smile.

"Thanks, Mady, maybe he was."

A.P. turns toward him. "Nice speech, Boss."

"Thanks."

Mady goes on, "Most of Valtura was there along with all of the people who work on the plaza, I mean square."

"Guess we all have to get use to that change," Lotta says.

Mady revises, "All who work on the *square* were there, all except the new newspaper woman."

Centori stares; A.P. and Lotta shift in their chairs. Mady adds, "So what about the new newspaper woman? It seems odd that she didn't cover the big story on the square."

"Perhaps she is more concerned about the politics of the entire state than of a local event."

"Still, Valtura is her town now and she runs a town newspaper."

"The *Valtura Journal* is the Corona County paper of record. In any case, I think we all should have another drink," Centori says.

"Adobe, we are not at odds over her; quite the opposite."

"What, then?"

A.P. takes a deep breath and leans back in his chair and glances at Lotta.

"I would think that we have mutual concerns about her," Mady opines.

"Do you have a personal objection about Jennifer?"

"If I did, I would not say so here," Mady snaps.

"I think Lotta and I will find a cigar," A.P. states.

Centori stands with the couple, then awkwardly says, "Good afternoon to you both." After the couple leaves, he braces for Mady's intrusion.

"As I was saying, we are not at odds over your latest love."

"Why did you bring it up now? And drive them away?"

"You sure didn't want to talk about her before."

"Didn't I?" he rapidly replies.

"Look, no one on the plaza knows anything about her; all we know is what she says about herself."

"I am sure she will be more forthcoming in time."

"It's not a secret that you seek that in time."

Another stare in defense against Mady's forwardness; it does not work.

"Okay, you give her the benefit of the doubt, but why are you blindly in love so fast?"

"Whoever loved, that loved not at first sight?"

"What? You do not find it the slightest bit interesting that Miss Prower disappeared after you left for New York?" Mady says with growing impatience. "That is quite the mystery."

"Why are you so suspicious of Jennifer?"

"There is much to be suspicious about. Adobe, I thought that the New York trip was to help you forget last year's hardship."

"Hardship?"

"I mean tragedy. But if Jennifer is your answer, why did you go to New York?"

He slams his open palm on the table, "Hold on to yourself, Mady."

"Friends talk this way."

"This is not the time, Mady. This *was* a celebration."

"There is something else…I have been reading accounts of the New York bombing."

"Yes."

"Those fellows who claimed responsibility; their bombast sounds an awful lot like something published in Valtura. On the day you left town, the *Journal* published a letter to the editor that you may find troubling. I saved the paper."

"Troubling?"

"Shall I give you the letter?"

"If I said no, would it do any good?"

"Here you are," Mady says with the newspaper folded to the letter page. From behind the bar Felicity Brimwell watches with more than causal interest.

Dear Editor,

Now that all the New Mexico statehood celebrations have begun to fade, it is important to remember that with government comes the potential for danger to the people. If a citizen is under a government, that citizen could expect to be controlled in many forms. The public will be regulated and commanded by men who have not the wisdom or moral right to do so. That citizen can expect to be taxed, prohibited and punished. What's more, the government will claim the general interest of the public as justification to control the public. If citizens resist they should expect to be repressed, judged and imprisoned. That is what citizens could expect from more government.

Mr. Stark Reality

Centori looks up with a blank look. Mady stares into his eyes: "And?"

"It is interesting."

"And radical."

"Yes, it seems a little radical."

"A little! Come on Adobe, is she *that* beautiful?" Mady squints in disdain.

"You are wasting time. Look, not all were in favor of statehood."

"You don't say."

"Look, Mady, Jennifer did not write this."

"Oh my goodness, but she *did* publish it."

"Enough. She is returning soon," he replies uneasily. "There's no point in arguing this further."

"So, you will take your chances with her?"

"What chances?"

"The closer you get to her, the less you will see."

"What is there to fear?"

"Would you care to know what the people in town are saying?"

"I am sure it is nothing that would interest me."

"It should interest you!"

"I will be meeting her train," his voice rises, "I am sure she will be fine."

"*If* she returns, well, I would not wish to waste your time," she says coldly.

"You think me a fool."

"No, I just think a little less of you."

His anger fades fast. "*Adios*, Mady." He stands and turns toward the door.

"Wait, there is something else. While you were gone, two fancy dressed men from south of the border were asking about Gabriella Zena."

He stops in his tracks and freezes for a moment. Then, he turns back to Mady with stone cold concern and asks quietly, "What?"

"Two Mexican officials paid me a visit while you were gone."

"Yes, but why did they come here about Gabriella?"

"She may have stayed here during Sharon's control. There was upstairs talk of a mysterious Mexican woman staying here."

"Assuming she was Gabriella."

"Those *hombres* seemed to think so."

"What did they want?"

"I am sure you will find out."

"Thanks for letting me know—and she was Cuban, not Mexican."

"I know and she must have been *some* kind of woman, but this Jennifer…"

"Mady, do you believe in ghosts?"

"New ghosts or old ghosts?"

Riding back to the Circle C on Patriot, Centori is preoccupied. *What Mady said about Jennifer is troubling. Could she be connected to such ideas?* Then there was that last thing Mady said about Gabriella. As Valtura fades into the horizon he considers: *Who were those men asking about her? Probably government agents from Mexico City; she was an ambassador's wife. They seem to know Gabriella spent time in Valtura, but do they know she went to Chaco Canyon? There is nothing to do about it now.*

CHAPTER 28

⌘

DESCANSE EN PAZ

Back in Valtura the next day, Centori leaves his Corona Street office and walks east toward the Sandia Mountains. It is a warm afternoon; the dark green mountains are in stark contrast against the blue sky. As he moves past Mission Road he sees the colonel's former house in the distance. The Victorian-era building, a half-mile from the square on fashionable East Corona Street, is now Jennifer's home.

A few moments later, Centori takes a long, slow look while passing the house; no sign of any life. For the first time he notices the intricate detail that had escaped his attention when the colonel lived there. Now, he examines the house that has deep eaves, ornamental brackets and gingerbread trim. The porch, the place of many challenging chess games, affords views of the mountains to the east and of the square to the west.

Approaching Valtura Heights and the foothills, his destination comes into view: Valtura cemetery. He walks through the cemetery's gate and passes timeworn tombstones; some of early Spanish colonists and soldiers that are centuries old. There are more recent tombstones of men who served with Roosevelt's Rough Riders in Cuba; he stops and acknowledges one of those graves. Centori has someone else in mind as he walks past row after row until he comes to a stop at a tombstone marked:

Antonio Santos

1830-1911

Descanse En Paz

Santos was drawn into the Revert Document conspiracy and was killed protecting Centori and the secret of the document. He swore to bring Santos' killer to justice but formal justice was denied. The murderer was killed by the conspirators.

Centori's faith in the colonel deepens during times of stress; his love is always present. He looks around to confirm that the cemetery is devoid of the living. *Hola, mi amigo, I believe that you came to see me at the square; now I am here. The new square, named in your honor, is a wonderful place. You gave your life for me. I will spend the rest of my life with that burden. I know you did it with a full heart and have no regrets. I did not bring your killer to justice as I swore, yet he has paid for his crime.*

You were gone before La Guerrillera came to Chaco to meet her death. I went home to New York to help forget that terrible day, but did not find peace. Instead, another woman died for knowing me. I never delivered justice for Gabriella, I am unsure how that could be done. In New York, there was a woman, her name was Charity. We spent a few good days together. Then she followed me to her rendezvous with death.

Green leaves fall from the surrounding trees. A gentle breeze begins. *She was at Wall Street because of me. I am sure she does not blame me, but I cannot shake the feeling…I am feeling more and more compelled to find her killers.*

It is too early in the year for leaves to fall, but the wind blows through the graveyard spreading leaves through the old tombstones. Centori stops his spiritual thoughts for a moment and looks around. He is still physically alone.

Colonel, I do not like being in the dark; I feel worthless. If answers can be found, I am prepared to search for those killers. Unlike Gabriella, someone was clearly responsible for Charity's death and someone should pay. Those terrorists should be sent to Dante's Inferno.

I miss you. I valued our friendship and was proud to know you did too. You were as much a father to me as my own father, in some ways more so. Colonel, what is a man supposed to do now?

Green leaves strangely stir on the ground again. A sensed presence causes Centori to turn quickly; no one there.

Vaya con Dios, mi hijo, he hears and turns again; it is the wind.

Descanse en paz, mi amigo.

He received an answer: there will be grave consequences for the terrorists who bombed Wall Street and killed Charity.

CHAPTER 29

VENUS OF VALTURA

I t is before the summer rains, the driest time in New Mexico. Although still early in the day, the sun beats down from a cloudless sky as Centori expects her to arrive soon. He stands next to a small building and under a corrugated metal roof that covers the entire station. His perspiration is quickly absorbed by the aridness, a welcomed feature of the high desert. If she returns, his life will not be the same.

The Valtura Rail Station lies 2,000 feet above the level of the sea, overlooked by mountains that are 3,000 feet high. This solemn silent land is a lonely place with nobody else in sight. The only sound, other than from the curious coyotes, is the new 48-star American flag which rhythmically whips in the wind. He reaches for his pocket watch and momentarily stares at the engraved coyote image before flipping it open. *The train is late.*

Centori's attitude toward women was formed in Havana and fine-tuned in the Southwest. More than a decade earlier in Cuba, he was let down while waiting for a woman. Now, he finds himself in a parallel situation, waiting for Jennifer Prower. *Where is that train? It is unsettling that she left Valtura without word immediately following my departure to New York. Where did her telegram originate?*

Time in the army makes an impression on a man's life; time in war increases that imprint, especially with the impact of a lost love. At present, clear decisions about Jennifer remain elusive. He takes off his hat and leans on a cast-iron support column. *Will she be on this train? She is financially invested in Valtura; perhaps in me too, probably less so.* Then a soaring hawk screams above interrupting his thoughts, "*kaah, kaah.*"

The large hawk with iron-colored areas on his shoulders dives down screaming, "*kaah, kaah.*" The powerful raptor ascends and is gone in an instant. *After what happened in New York, what do I say about Charity? Do I mention her at all? How could I not? Charity died in my arms, but that was not the first time in my arms. And there is the list of Titanic victims...do I confront her right away? Provided she returns at all. So many questions, I might be better off if she does not return.*

Shaking off the uncertainty, he reflects on the night of their first encounter when the stars and one planet seemed especially bright. *Jennifer opens the door to my soul and reaches my deepest emotions that have been, for so long, unengaged. She is like Venus to me—Venus of Valtura.* That night, her love name was instantly born. Now he waits to confront her about another name.

The approaching train interrupts his thoughts returning him to the present. He adjusts his hat and squares his shoulders, ready for the moment of truth. The train arrives at the flag stop; after a minute of huffing and puffing, a trainman exits from the railcar. Then a lady gracefully steps down and appears in a dark, tight-fitting high-collared dress. She knows that her appearance would be either threatening or tempting. It does not matter which, as long as it provides an advantage in dealing with men. The classic beauty is Jennifer Prower. There is only one poem that expresses his feeling and comes to his mind in a flash:

Grace was in all her steps, heaven in her eye,
In every gesture dignity and love—Milton

As her five-foot, six-inch, 120-pound figure moves, it is plain that she possesses certain elegance; a picturesque quality that he finds irresistible. Staring from under a large wide-brimmed hat with abundant reddish hair streaming, she sees him.

With a slight raspy and sweet voice she projects, "Sheriff Centori, this is a great surprise."

Although her throaty voice remains alluring, the instant their eyes meet he knew something had changed. All the same, Centori fills himself with the sight of her femininity. "Welcome back, Jennifer."

"Thank you. I am surprised and delighted to have you greet me."

"I am surprised you left town. How was your trip? Where did you go?" he eagerly asks.

She is briefly silent and then replies, "It was a fine trip. I was in Santa Fe covering the first state legislature."

"Is that right?"

"Yes, that's right." She shifts her curvaceous figure and says, "I imagine you met Mr. Bachmeier."

"Yes, I have. I noticed other new people on the plaza, square."

"Adobe, what about you? Why are you back from New York so soon? And that horrible attack on Wall Street!"

"I want to tell you something," he says, raising his voice over the spring winds.

Her lips tighten. "Tell me something."

Before he can answer, the train departs. The locomotive slowly rolls away, picks up speed and then disappears in the vast desert.

"I have never been to hell, but I have an idea."

"The New York bombing?"

"Yes."

Jennifer sees the Model T Ford and he opens the passenger door. After a brief noisy ride on a rough road, he shuts the motor and opens the conversation.

Twenty minutes later, they continue driving to Valtura. He told her every detail about the New York bombing—except the part about Charity. Depression about Charity's death is still with him, but not the razor-sharp grief of the days following the explosion. Tolerance, not acceptance, is sinking into his mind and so is Jennifer.

To his surprise, Jennifer knew an extraordinary amount of detail about the Wall Street attack. She is a good newspaper woman, he thought. He had not confronted her about the *Titanic*—he will keep that card close to his chest for now.

An hour later, they come to a halt in front of the classic Victorian house once home to Colonel Santos. There had been changes to the Victorian and the surrounding environment since Santos lived and died here. The house is now virtually invisible from the road. *Things are sure different here. Why did she have a ten foot wall built around the house? At least the colonel's cottonwood trees are still visible from the road.*

They drive through the new gate that looks indestructible and enter to the sounds of birds in the trees and in the air. Jennifer turns toward a distinctive sound and smiles at a tiny hummingbird rapidly beating its wings. Then a warm dry wind arrives; the breeze stirs the old cottonwood trees on the grounds. The porch appears more cheerful and the old chess stand is gone.

Entering the house, Centori notices that the chess stand was salvaged; a telephone rests on the old table. His heart sinks as he sees the spot where the colonel was killed late last year. He forces himself to stop thinking about the former crime scene.

Viewing the cherrywood tables, walls papered in light blue, oil paintings and silver pieces that have transformed the interior he thinks, *This is clearly Jennifer's house now.*

"You have certainly changed things."

"For the better, I hope."

"Yes, for the better," he says evenly.

"I love this house; it is such a charming Victorian. I know you were close with the previous owner."

"I knew Colonel Santos. I knew him well. You missed his dedication."

"I thought you were going to schedule the dedication when you returned to Valtura."

"I did."

"Well, the new Santos Square is a good-looking place, the colonel would be happy with the result. It is true that he died in this house?"

"Yes, but I prefer to think of him living in the house and the time we spent playing chess here."

"I understand, so you are no stranger here."

"It feels strange now, but I know this house."

"I hope that your time here will continue."

Marginally surprised by the comment, he offers no reply. She pivots from the uncomfortable silence, "Thank you for meeting me at the station."

Reluctant to leave her seductive orb, he ignores the comment. "I find this house interesting for past and for future reasons; the Circle C house has equal appeal."

"Thank you again; it has been a long ride back."

After a brief hesitation, he shakes his head in agreement. "It was my pleasure. I should be getting back to the ranch," he says hoping for an objection.

"Of course. Good night."

"*Adios*, Jennifer."

Out the door on the porch, he glances at the place where he played chess with the colonel. *I will be back here, and for more than a game of chess.*

Driving down East Corona Street, Centori braces from the cool night or from the cold reception from Jennifer. Several blocks later he is in the new square. A few seconds later, Patriot and his office come into his view.

He parks the Ford and mounts Patriot without entering the office. Then he rides out of town to the Circle C. Alone on the night trail, it hits him, *Why did she say long ride back from Santa Fe? The railroad to Santa Fe is not long at all...something is not right.*

⁂

Late that evening, Centori stands outside the Circle C house under a bright full moon, places a cigar in his teeth and checks the pocket watch. It is midnight.

The way Jennifer abruptly ended the conversation...I suppose she was tired, or tired of me. The Titanic question can wait for now. She may bring up the topic first.

No answers were obtained tonight. She obtained an implied invitation to the Circle C. He field strips the cigar and enters the house. Then, he slowly enters the bedroom, feeling closer to her. *To sleep, perchance to dream, dream of Jennifer.*

At the same time, Jennifer is reading a report she received in Stratford. It is a dossier on Centori and the Revert Document affair.

CHAPTER 30

⟡

THE ZÓCALO

MEXICO CITY

I t is 11:30 a.m. The main plaza in the heart of Mexico City, the *Zócalo,* contains the mid-day crowd. The average May temperature in the capital is 80 degrees. Today, the temperature is close to 90 degrees. No one pays much attention to the European Count who marches across the plaza toward the *Palacio Nacional.*

Within the walls of the *Palacio Nacional,* the new German ambassador to Mexico will meet the new president of Mexico. The leader of the German legation shows his credentials and enters the Patio of Honor with a small duffel bag and moves toward the president's external office.

"Please wait here, *Señor,*" announces the president's secretary.

"Thank you."

The secretary nods and walks away. The official is not used to being kept waiting but tolerates the situation. Count Helmut von Riesenfelder of Imperial Germany prepares to discuss the contents of the bag. He will offer a plausible story with maximum promise and with minimum details. The new president of Mexico, José Victoriano Huerta Márquez, was a military leader and was loyal to President Madero. Then the Revert Document failure, in part, encouraged him to overthrow Madero. After days of fighting between loyalists and rebels, Huerta won control of the government and ultimately had Madero killed.

"The president will see you now. Please follow me."

Riesenfelder, a young man of greater than average stature, is a well-educated and cultured man with blond hair and a dueling scar on his face.

"President Huerta, congratulations on achieving this important position."

"I can say the same for you, *Señor* Riesenfelder, and welcome to Mexico."

"Thank you for seeing me."

"You are most welcome, *Señor*," *he flatly replies while staring at the* duffel bag.

"*Your Palacio Nacional is of magnificent architecture, representing the rich history and the culture of Mexico.*"

"*I am sure you are not here to discuss history and culture.*"

"*That is half true;* there is much to discuss. Our countries have mutual concerns."

"Such discussions are better served by my foreign secretary speaking with you."

"Ordinarily that is true, but we have an extraordinary matter— one that can only be presented to you. I know you are a busy man and will get right to the point."

Riesenfelder's duffel, filled with hard-rock gold ore, crashes on the president's large conference table with authority. The sound startles the president and his assistant. Without ceremony, he carefully takes out the contents. "This gold ore was found near Stratford, New Mexico."

"That is interesting, *Señor* Riesenfelder, but why are you telling me this news?"

"This gold represents a small vein that leads to the mysterious mother lode deep in the ground or high in the mountain."

"That is impressive, but again why are you telling me?"

"Mexico's war with the U.S. cost your country most of the Southwest territory."

"That is widely known."

"Yet, the story of the gold discovery is less known. When the California Gold Rush began in January 1848, California was part of Mexico."

"Yes, *was* part of Mexico. There were thousands of *Californios* and just hundreds of Americans in California," the president sighs.

"President Huerta, the peace treaty was signed in February 1848—after the gold discovery."

"We believe that the U.S. government knew about the gold before the declaration of war against your country."

"That was never established."

"Correct, and it was never doubted."

"Two years prior to the war, U.S. Consul Thomas Larkin in Monterey informed U.S. Secretary of State Buchanan that California was rich in silver, copper, quicksilver, lead, coal and gold. That was established."

Growing impatient with the young diplomat, Huerta crosses his arms. Ignoring the signal, Riesenfelder goes on, "Subsequently, the U.S. declared war on Mexico over the Texas border dispute."

The running commentary causes the president's assistant, who is standing near the large entry doors, to cross his arms while the president throws up his hands. "*Señor* Riesenfelder, as you said, I am a busy man. Do you have a point?"

"Please indulge me; I will make my point in a moment. The Treaty of Guadalupe Hidalgo ended the war and required Mexico to give the U.S. ownership of New Mexico, Arizona, Nevada, Utah—and California."

"We are in no need of a history lesson and to relive the past injustices against our country."

Riesenfelder pauses for a second. "President Huerta, George Santayana wrote in *Life of Reason* that those who cannot remember the past are condemned to repeat it."

"You suggest we are unaware of the terrible past we have had with the U.S. or how we lost much of the Southwest. We remember all too well."

"Yes, of course you do. I wish not to offend you, only to explain a suspicious sequence of events that can have current international implications."

"Since you are fond of quotes, consider the American senator who said 'to the victor belong the spoils.'"

"A famous quote, but what if the spoils were illegally obtained?"

"I am sure that you understand the American southwest is lost. All the gold and any resource within those territories are lost with the hidden reasons lost to history."

"Would that be true if the reasons violated international law?"

"The truth is buried. The burial started when President Polk announced the gold discovery and thousands of Americans went to California."

"President Huerta, do you agree?"

Holding his hand up he continues, "Not exactly, but I acknowledge that the gold prompted Polk to encourage the settlement of California, accelerating the rush."

"Yes, he did! He wanted rapid development of the wealth and resources—and to make California part of the U.S. for all time."

"We do not disagree on the past, *Señor,* but I ask again why tell me this news? And why have you damaged my table with a bag of rocks?"

"My apology, but that bag of rocks could represent tens of millions of dollars in gold!"

"You are trying my patience."

"Here is my point. Similar to the California Gold Rush, the recent discovery in Stratford occurred while New Mexico was part of Old Mexico!"

"*Señor* Riesenfelder, you are mistaken. New Mexico has been part of the U.S. for a very long time, since the Treaty of Guadalupe Hidalgo."

"Are you sure?

"Of course, I am sure." The president's eyes are daggers.

"May I have a few private moments?"

"No!"

He recovers from the affront then: "Are you aware of the Revert Document?"

"*Ay, Dios mio.* That is your point! So you wish me to repeat the mistakes of my predecessor."

"No. Not necessarily, President Huerta. In the people's hearts and minds the Southwest has always been an inseparable part of Mexico."

"Yet those territories are separate and now part of the U.S."

"Mexico has been predisposed to get back the border territories; now there is an added incentive—a twist of fate that could be used for political advantage."

"Please, the Revert Document is missing; are you unaware that New Mexico obtained U.S. statehood in January?"

"We are indeed aware—New Mexico statehood day was January 6, 1912."

"Correct. So there is nothing more to discuss. We have wasted enough time engaging in rhetoric."

"There is nothing more to discuss, except the deadline."

Huerta stops. He is intrigued yet hesitant, prompting the calculating German to continue, "The deadline was December 31, 1911. If New Mexico failed to obtain statehood before then, the territory reverts to Mexico."

"You dream. *Señor*, you dream."

"It is no dream that from January 1 through January 5 of this year the document was in effect: New Mexico reverted to Mexico along with Arizona. That is a legal fact, not a dream."

"Will you join me for a drink, *Señor*?"

"Yes, of course, President Huerta."

CHAPTER 31

GOLDEN OPPORTUNITY

Huerta and Riesenfelder sit alone with drinks and a dream; the president's secretary stands outside the big doors.

"While you may have convinced me that New Mexico and Arizona legally reverted to Mexico in January, the U.S. has disdain for the truth."

"There are ways in which Mexico's interest can be served."

"Still, you expect me to follow in the failed footsteps of Madero!"

"Things have changed since Madero was in office."

"Yet, the U.S. will twist the law to their favor—or do worse."

"There are ways to use the deadline as an opportunity to negotiate with the Americans."

"Why would they care to do so? It could open the door for further U.S. expansion in Mexico."

"This is the 20th century; the U.S. and Mexico have been at peace for almost 70 years and we can provide protection if needed."

"Can you stop the U.S. from waging war against Mexico?"

"In Germany we stand for international legitimacy and a defense against American aggression."

"So you wish to be of service to our government in this affair."

"Germany and Mexico can have common cause to confront shared problems and isolate the U.S."

"Isolate the U.S. from Mexico or from Europe? You call not for international legitimacy but for instability and trouble with the *norteamericanos.*"

"Berlin will be an ally to Mexico," Riesenfelder states.

"I am sure of that. Is foreign intervention a German plan?" Huerta asks.

"Not as the main goal, President Huerta. International law depends on governments taking over the contract provisions from their predecessors. You are right about negotiation; they will not care to do so. That is why we will take the issue to the world court in The Hague."

"A court that is thousands of miles from our shores," Huerta says.

"The Permanent Court of Arbitration resolves disputes between nations on the world stage. It should not take a great deal of convincing; the evidence is clear and compelling—the U.S. violated the Revert Document agreement."

Huerta falls into silence. Riesenfelder sees another opening. "We are talking about an appropriate world order for the 20th century, an order where nations respect international borders. Not an order where agreements are broken."

The president remains quiet, waves away Riesenfelder's ideas and says, "Mexico lost the territories; they did not revert and now the gold strike is lost. We have been deprived of a mother lode. The California gold story is repeated, this time in New Mexico."

"That is a historical irony that does not have to stand," Riesenfelder continues, "with the return of New Mexico all of Mexico will economically prosper—especially with the gold strike in Stratford."

Huerta boldly states, "All that you say is true, but Germany is looking for an excuse for war here—then you can dominate Europe without U.S. support of France or England. Your predecessor was clear about supporting Mexico in a war against the U.S."

"And he has been removed. We do not seek war. The U.S. and Germany are big trading partners. It would not be economically sound to wage war against the Americans. President Huerta, I assure you that war between industrial countries would be pointless, conquest does not make sense."

"It is hard to believe that what you say is Germany's position."

"You can believe that economic interdependence means that war between trading partners would be economically injurious to the warring nations."

"So war is impossible?"

"No, but it is highly unlikely. What's more, the conquering nation will eventually leave the territory with the local population but still pay for occupation."

Riesenfelder makes his case with full knowledge of his government's territorial ambitions. "The integration of the European economies is significant; war would be a lost enterprise. I will concede that if the U.S. participates in a European war, German intelligence could have a presence in Mexico."

"You mean your government is not already fully established here?"

He disregards the question, "Mexico could become the center of our North American intelligence network."

"Whether we approve of that or not."

"We wish to become allies, President Huerta."

"An international intelligence route could extend from Mexico into the U.S."

With a look of resentful respect Huerta responds, "You will excuse me now; I have many things that require my attention."

"President Huerta, you would be given credit for recovering a great gold discovery. The Stratford silver days have yielded to gold; the strike could be greater than the California gold strike."

Huerta displays no indication of interest, "*Señor* Riesenfelder, Mexican relations with the U.S. have been strained for decades; you wish to use us for political purposes."

"President Huerta, this opportunity is beyond politics; the Sierra Nevada Mountains had a mother lode of hard-rock gold deposits about three miles wide and 120 miles long. The same could be true of Stratford," Riesenfelder says.

"You will excuse me now."

"The Mexican government could have complete control of the mother lode that could yield at least ten dollars and up to 40 million dollars!"

"Gold is only as good as those who are looking for it and we are not. You will excuse me now," Huerta repeats.

The meeting is over. Two heavy doors swing open, the president's assistant appears. Riesenfelder collects his ore and his composure.

"Thank you for your time President Huerta," the count says, having missed a golden opportunity. Walking down a wide corridor, the president leans to his assistant. "Get me General Vega."

CHAPTER 32

LETTERS TO THE EDITOR

The Circle C comes to life under the early morning sky. Centori, wearing a red cotton shirt and denim pants, stands in his boots and under the portal with coffee. New Mexican mornings in spring can be cool, sometimes cold. Today is pleasantly cool and offers another dramatic sunrise. Centori is half-way through his coffee when A.P. rides up to the portal.

He stays mounted and says, "Good morning, Boss."

"Good morning," he replies from under his big hat.

"Are you ready to ride the range? We need to talk about the spring roundup."

"Not now, perhaps tonight. I'm going into town."

"Official business?"

"Sort of…at the *Valtura Journal*."

"I see, that's the best business of all."

"I don't mind seeing Jennifer, if that's what you mean. I have some county business to attend to at the office, too."

"Whatever makes you happy, Boss."

"Well, from what little I saw, you seemed to enjoy Lotta's company."

"Yes, and that was not the first time we met. I didn't want to bring it up, but Mady has some strong opinions about Jennifer."

"She sure does."

"A man would be wise to be mindful of her."

"Mady or Jennifer?"

"Ha."

"Let's talk about that another time."

"Okay, Boss. *Adios* for now."

A.P. rides to meet a few cowboys on the range. Francisco Greigos walks by calling out in Spanish. Greigos, a top ranch hand, is from Tampico, Mexico, where he was a *vaquero*.

In New Spain, *vaqueros* were horsemen and cattle herders who drove cattle between the North American southwest and Mexico City. The American cowboy's rough, hard-working cattle skills are rooted in the Mexican vaquero. No one at the Circle C Ranch is a better cowboy.

Centori sends him a wave and calls back in Spanish. He finishes the coffee and crosses to the corral and stable yard to where Greigos is saddling up Patriot.

"*Muchas gracias, Francisco.*"

"*De nada, Jefe. Es un buen caballo. Aunque no es joven.*"

"*Es verdad. Viejo, pero fuerte.*"

Centori mounts up. "*Adios Francisco, hasta luego.*"

"*Adios.*"

A.P. rides up to Circle C cowboy Pedro Quesada who sits in the saddle and looks over a small herd of cattle.

"Good morning, A.P."

"Pedro."

"How is the boss today?" Quesada asks with concern.

"He seems to be in a good mood; he is off to town."

"Think of the Cuban woman, the colonel and the New York woman. How does he handle all that trouble?"

"He does," A.P. dryly says.

Centori arrives in Santos Square and goes directly to the newspaper office. Jennifer sees him arrive and opens the door, "Welcome to the new *Valtura Journal*, Adobe."

"Thank you," he replies while holding his hand up.

Wearing a white shirt, black skirt, leather vest, a bold buckle and high-button shoes, she asks, "Why are you in town so early?"

"I have some business."

"I see. I know you have already met Bernhard."

"Yes, I have," he says with a distrustful glance.

Jennifer addresses Bachmeier in German prompting him to go into the press room. She turns to Centori who is startled to hear her speak German. "You will see changes here and I dare say improvements."

"That was clear the moment I entered the room and saw you," he replies.

"I mean the management and operation of the newspaper," she smiles.

"Of course, you seem to have settled into your position as publisher and editor."

"I'm sure the people are glad to have the newspaper back so soon especially after the demise of Johan Morgenstern and his daughter."

"I agree. Valtura is the center of Corona County. We should have a growing newspaper; her name was Klara."

"Please come into my office," she offers.

He accepts and follows her to a side room where they both sit down.

"You agree that people are happy the newspaper is back, yet not all are happy about a woman running a newspaper or a woman in a position of authority."

I would be happy with you in any position, he jokes to himself.

"I take my work seriously. I studied journalism at the *École supérieure de journalisme.* It is a *Grande École* in Paris. In time people will come to respect my efforts."

"That sounds fine. I am sure you are right."

"Our printing press will be modernized and we will hire two reporters, one to cover Corona Country politics and the other for the new state legislature."

"I thought you were covering the state legislature."

"Oh, yes, at this time, I am."

"I'm sure the legislative agenda will increase now that we are a U.S. state."

"It already has and I intend to provide information to the people who can make better local and state decisions. This is a method to promote good government."

"The press can also be a powerful force to promote a negative political perspective."

Her smile ended as quickly as it came. "I am not sure what you mean."

"Your newspaper has taken a somewhat new direction, at least in the letters to the editor."

"You are referring to the letter from Mr. Stark Reality."

"Yes, that's right."

"His position seems somewhat extreme."

"The *Valtura Journal* welcomes commentaries on both sides of issues, but we do not necessarily agree with the positions taken by our readers."

He angled his head suspiciously. "Not even a little?"

Her beautiful eyes widen with her words, "As you may know, American newspapers always had such letters as a medium of exchange for political ideas and opinions."

"Jennifer, I am aware that issues are expressed through letters to the editor, but I believe that you, as editor, assess which issues are important for your readers."

"Look, there is a difference between the editorial section and the front page. I did not present his point of view as a headline. I do not practice that type of journalism."

"Letters to the editor can reflect the opinion of the newspaper."

"Why are you so cynical about journalism, or is it just me?"

He offers no answer. She goes on. "Yes, letters can reflect the opinion of the publisher, but newspapers can print opinions not associated with the publication."

"So Mr. Reality's opinions are not associated with the *Valtura Journal?*"

She warily answers, "No."

"Oscar Wilde said give a man a mask and he will tell the truth. Letters to the editor can provide political cover."

"I am not sure how to respond, but I am sure that you believe in First Amendment rights."

"Jennifer, the Constitution insists upon it and I completely support the Bill of Rights, but that type of free speech could lead to the use of violence for obtaining political goals."

"Why are you making a big deal of this letter?"

"Perhaps it is a big deal."

"Or perhaps you are not over the Wall Street bombing."

"I may never be over it, but since you brought up the bombing, I have a point judging from the note found near the explosion."

"A note?"

"Yes, claiming responsibility for the terrorism, signed American Scream."

Her eyes dip before she says, "American Scream is a colorful name."

"So is Stark Reality."

Deadly silence follows.

"Letters are protected under the First Amendment; it is not like yelling fire in a crowded room," she argues.

"True, but that letter could start a fire."

"Balance that with the value of an independent press in opposing government power or worse."

"Just like Stark Reality's opposition to Wall Street? Look, there are some restrictions to free speech."

"Was the letter libelous, obscene or seditious? No! I am sorry for your experience in New York, but this letter is not evidence of a crime."

"I didn't say that. Perhaps I am overreacting to the New York disaster."

"That's understandable, you had a terrible ordeal."

He does not push, rather he asks, "Do you have a copy of the *Journal* dated April 16, 1912?"

"Just a moment," she answers.

The seconds drag on until, "Here you are."

Holding up the paper he says, "This is a historical headline."

"Yes, another disastrous news story last month."

"The *Titanic* was supposed to dock at Chelsea Piers in New York, but as you know, the ship never arrived." Centori's tone is even, hoping to engage her further. "I read the list of the passengers who died in the Atlantic."

Jennifer stares blankly and waits for the inevitable.

"I wonder if you would tell me something."

"If I can."

"Why does this issue not have the *Titanic* victims listed?"

"We just ran the Associate Press story."

"I read many newspapers. They all carried the victims list."

She shrugs her shoulders. "Editorial prerogative, I suppose."

More silence.

"So you saw the list?"

In check, she says, "Yes, I have read the list."

"Then you know there was a Jennifer Prower listed as dead."

"Yes, I do know that."

"And she was from Troy, New York."

"That is quite a coincidence."

"I am not a big believer in coincidence; even if I did, this is too much to be credible."

"What do you want from me?"

"I want an explanation."

"I have none to give you!"

"That would make things difficult between us."

"Yet, it seems that you wish to continue to know me."

He is in check: "Because you are beautiful and you intrigue me."

"Both are good reasons that deserve a discussion and an explanation, but not here."

"Jennifer," *if that is your name,* "will you meet me at Mad Mady's Saloon around 5 p.m. today?"

"I'd rather not; I don't think Mady likes me very much."

"I am sure she likes you. She speaks highly of you."

"Just the same," she offers, "perhaps we can discuss it later, at my house."

With a heart wiser than his head, it is an easy sell. "Okay, Jennifer, this evening. I look forward to it. Good day to you."

A few moments later, Jennifer stares through a window, watching Centori stride across the square towards his office.

Bachmeier approaches and says, *"Ist es schwer für Sie?"*

Reprovingly, she snaps, "We should speak English here from now on."

"Are you finding this line of work terrible for you?"

"No, it is lively work, but you are terrible."

"What?"

"Why did you publish that letter?" she demands.

"I found it amusing and thought it would please your New York friends."

"It can only draw unwanted attention."

"It can also cover our true plans."

"Damn you, this was not necessary."

"I would be careful as to what you say next."

She stops, then instantly looks out the window in time to see Centori crossing Corona Street.

"Will he be a problem for us?"

Staring in a hostile way she answers, "I can handle Adobe Centori."

"We hope you can," he says with a concerned smile.

She snarls, "Don't smile at me; never smile at me!"

"I can comply with your wish," Bachmeier says before backing off.

Still watching Centori she wonders, *Will he turn around and look back at me?*

CHAPTER 33

A GREATER FOOL

After a day of working as county sheriff, Centori enters the Union Hotel at twilight and blankly nods at desk clerk James Clarke. Taken aback but not deterred, he says, "Good evening, Sheriff. Welcome back; your dedication speech at the square was excellent."

He nods again in appreciation without breaking stride and continues to the restaurant. In the dining room, he sits at a table with his back against the wall. The service as usual is fast. "Welcome back. What can I get you?"

"Green chili burrito."

"Right away, Sheriff."

"Jameson, too."

"Of course."

The waiter returns quickly with a glass and a bottle of Irish whiskey. While sipping the drink, he thinks of what Mady said. *She does not know the story behind Jennifer, but I guess I don't know either.*

Gazing over the glass and through the familiar diners, he sees a man he does not recognize enter the room. The stranger reaches for his pocket watch and Centori returns his attention to the drink.

Less than ten minutes later, the waiter returns with a plate. Centori welcomes a flour tortilla filled with beef, onion and tomato covered with hot green chili. The green chili burrito is surrounded by *frijoles* and *posole*.

"Thanks. So, a new person in town I see."

The waiter glances over. "Yes, we have a few; most visit the *Valtura Journal*, so I have heard."

"Is that right? What about that woman with the beautiful black hair who is alone?"

He quickly turns. "What woman?"

"Near the window with her back to us, *Oh my God.*" He braces against the table.

"What is it, Sheriff?"

He waves away the waiter and downs his drink.

"Are you alright?"

"Yes, yes, I thought that woman was someone else."

The waiter turns again, the table is vacant—no one there. "Are you sure you are alright?"

"Yes, I am sure."

"Let me know if you need anything."

A moment later, Mad Mady enters, as the waiter exits, and inelegantly sits down at his table.

"Would you like to sit down?"

"That's very funny."

"How are you, Mady?"

"Just fine. Are you avoiding me?"

"No, why?"

"You usually come to the saloon after leaving your office."

"I needed some chili," he says. *And to not see you yet,* he thinks.

"Sure. So how is Jennifer?"

"She is back in town; I am sure you know."

"What I don't know is how she reacted to Mr. Stark Reality."

"As predicted, she separates herself from the letter."

"And that satisfies you?"

"Mady, please drop it for now."

"For now? You are better at poker."

"I may regret telling you."

"What is it?"

"There is something more troubling than the letter."

The waiter breaks in, "What can I get you, Mady?"

"Just bring another glass."

"Right away."

"So, what is it?"

"Have you read the list of *Titanic* passengers who died in the Atlantic?"

"Yes, there were several important people who died."

"But not the whole list?"

"No."

"Well, I have." Mady impatiently stares. Centori, with a flash of regret for broaching the topic, takes a sip of whiskey.

"And?"

"There was a Jennifer Prower from Troy, New York, listed as dead."

"What! I knew it! There is something not right about that vamp."

"Easy, Mady."

"How did she explain this?"

"Here you are, Mady. Can I get you something else?"

"No, thanks," she quickly says.

"She has not explained, not yet."

"That doesn't disturb you?"

"No."

"Why not!?"

"I have my reasons."

"Ha! You have one reason. You are impressed with her body and not much of anything else, it seems."

"She will tell me later."

"Later, I am sure *that* satisfies you," she fires off. "Let me guess, at her house, correct?"

His expression reveals the answer.

"I see."

"I will get to the bottom of this in my own way."

"You always do, but is it your way or her way?"

"I don't know, mutual I guess."

"You think she is not using a fake name?"

"I will not make a supposition."

"It is plain to see."

"Could be."

"Ha, I would wager my saloon."

"I will keep an open mind and wait for an explanation."

Flabbergasted, Mady paraphrases, "A greater fool than Adobe Centori has never breathed the breath of life."

"Mady, you are taking advantage of my good nature."

"You mean foolish nature. What you lack in a plan you make up with a dream. You are blinded by love—confront her."

"Emerson said treat people as they are and they will remain the same; treat people as they *could* be and they will become what they *should* be."

"What? So you admit there is a problem and you are going to change her with the great Centori charm? Adobe, you should leave your eastern education behind; this is the Wild West!"

"That's it; I will get the answers in my way, is that clear? Because if it isn't, have someone else draw you a picture. I haven't got the time."

She downs her drink and stands to leave. "Don't bother to stand," she mocks. He did not.

"Don't sell that woman short, Adobe, Mady warns. "She knows more than she reveals."

Mady rushes out in a temper; gone in a flash. Alone again Centori scans the room looking for Gabriella with little hope. No success. Sometimes desire can paint a picture in a person's mind.

His thoughts turn to Jennifer. *She probably is using a false name, but I have given her a name too: Venus of Valtura. Damn, what am I doing?*

CHAPTER 34

FACE AND FIGURE

A t exactly eight o'clock, Centori departs the hotel after a satisfying Mexican dinner. He starts a familiar walk on East Corona Street to the familiar Victorian house. It is a cool evening with the springtime sun still fading. The western sky with a colorful sunset is at his back. The Sandia Mountains to the east, reflecting the sunset, are changing in color.

Walking past Mission Road, Centori sees a coyote near the church confidently crossing East Corona carrying an old grain sack in his teeth. Looking like a trickster, the coyote slows his pace. He stops in his tracks. *You again! What is in the damn sack—where are you going?* The coyote stares back in a detached and dismissive way.

The sleek and graceful *canis latrans,* or barking dog, is an enthralling animal given the similarity between coyote nature and human nature. Unlike most predators and like most people, the coyote is both social and solitary.

Coyotes are strong, flexible hunters. As good communicators, they adapt to changing environments allowing more opportunity for survival. Both the cowboy and the coyote continue at a faster pace. The Sandia Mountains change color again as the coyote fades from sight.

When Jennifer arrived in New York several years ago she took the name Prower and secured a sales position in the doll department at Macy's. After a year, she opened her own doll shop on the Ladies' Mile in Manhattan. Her shop served prosperous collectors of antique dolls but was financially unsuccessful. Curiously, she continued to have money for a high life style, travel, and recently, for purchasing a newspaper and a Victorian house. Once more, the mountains change color as the house comes into focus.

Dusk is fading, but it is not totally dark. At the house, his heart rate increases, he draws a deep breath, opens the front gate and feels a little flash of dread. *Success with Jennifer will be hard to define, beyond the obvious. The* Titanic *issue is harder to understand. I could find that Mady is wrong—or right about her.* His boots jangle on the porch steps alerting Jennifer. She opens the door with little eagerness. Like a masterpiece painting, her lovely body is framed in the doorway. "Good evening. Please come in."

He replies in a composed manner, "Thank you, Jennifer." In a flash he visually devours her slim waist and long legs that sweep through a dark blue dress with 3/4 sleeves. She wears a cross-draped bodice, light blue underskirt and ankle-length blue overskirt. Her irresistible face set in confidence and framed with reddish cascading hair complete the vision.

Seeking a clue, he stares at her, *Hmm, demeanor seems cold and detached; this is not a good sign.*

"Shall I pour drinks?"

Better. "Yes," he smiles and follows her into the parlor.

Pieces of antique furniture fill the room including a fine French settee. There is a silver candelabrum on a small table between two upholstered armchairs. On a smaller table across the room, two glasses and a bottle of José Cuervo Tequila sit on a fine silver tray.

"Allow me." He pours liberally and hands her a drink.

For a short time, there is only the sound of tequila pouring into glasses. Jennifer likes the directness of his deep blue eyes. He is not staring, but makes no attempt to hide his intense interest. However, there is a mask over her face that hides her true emotions.

"Here's to our return to Valtura," he toasts.

She smiles in return, they drink, "I am sorry for the tense moments earlier today," she offers.

His interest in inquiry vanishes at the moment, "Think no more about that; I would rather think of your beauty."

"Are you trying to make me blush?"

"I don't think that is possible."

"You make me feel that all is possible."

"I will settle for most things."

She smiles again, real or not, it thrills him to the core.

They continue to talk and laugh and not once does he bring up the *Titanic*.

Jennifer is a perfect image of a woman, beautiful in face and figure. The thought lovingly trumps all other concerns for him, at least at the moment.

"Right now, it takes all my strength to look away from you," he boldly proclaims.

"Why struggle?"

He leans in closer. Then he pours more tequila and waits for her. The awkward silence prompts her. "You asked about the name of a woman on the *Titanic*."

"Yes, I am rather curious."

With a staccato sound to her voice, she says, "I did not act surprised when you mentioned the *Titanic*, yet you saw something in my face."

"Yes, I did. Go on."

"So, you know there may be a secret, but it may not be my secret to tell."

"Jennifer, if that is your real name, who are you?"

Reacting to his bluntness, she proclaims, "My name is Jennifer."

"That's nice to know, Jennifer, but not Prower."

"Correct."

"So what is your name?"

"I needed a new name and wish not to speak of the old one."

"Why?"

"I was in a bad situation"

"I don't understand."

"I needed to leave that situation; that is all I am prepared to say at the moment."

While not the least satisfied, he places her beauty over principle and tries to accept her story—making no attempt to rationalize his decision. She finishes the drink and waits for him to refill the glass. He does so.

A few long seconds later, she says in a clearly different voice. "I can see that you are disappointed with my answer."

"Jennifer, perhaps I can help you."

"Adobe, I will do a better job of explaining that bad situation, just not now."

"When?" he persists, then pours more tequila.

"When I trust you," she answers.

"Yet you trust me enough for a rendezvous at your home."

"Okay, let's say when I completely trust you."

"Jennifer, you have a talent for avoiding the truth."

"Please…when you know what is at stake, you will understand. I don't know how to tell you now, but I will in time."

She flashes her large and long-lashed eyes: "Readiness is all we need at this time."

"So you know Shakespeare, but not how to tell me certain things."

She is puzzled for a moment. "What?"

"You seemed to have quoted Hamlet."

"Oh, perhaps I did."

"Since we are quoting, King Lear said nothing will come of nothing. If you say nothing you will receive nothing from me."

"Is that right?" she replies as if accepting a challenge; she knows he cannot resist her charm. "You said you struggle to take your eyes away from me."

"Yes, I have said so."

"Try closing your eyes."

"What?"

"Oh, my, I can see you are surprised by my request."

His thoughts drift toward embracing the beautiful creature. He attempts to refocus but loses control of the conversation and of seeking the *Titanic* truth. Besides, first things first and he is not too surprised to want more.

Concealing his anticipation he says, "Let's just say surprised."

"And interested, too; let us take hold of happiness at once. How often is happiness destroyed by preparation, foolish preparation?"

"Well spoken, Jennifer."

"Jane Austen said it first."

"You say it better."

"Thank you. Now close your eyes," she whispers. "When you open your eyes take a new look. I have been yours for the asking."

He opens his eyes and smiles in agreement, knowing this could be a mistake, but can lead to his heart's desire."

"Adobe, do you think meeting you after your statehood address was an accident? No. I watched you from afar and waited for the perfect moment to approach."

"You did not need a perfect moment to engage me."

172 | DANIEL R. CILLIS, PHD

Another alluring smile appears. "I expect you to know that a look, a few words are all that is needed for me to make that leap," the sorcerer says.

"I have been looking."

"Please excuse me for a few minutes."

"Yes, of course."

She smiles while leaving the parlor; the smile disappears the second she turns her back—darkness consumes her purpose. Watching her leave the parlor, he considers, *This will lead to greater closeness but not answers. She is hiding something, but she is also revealing something, something more appealing and irresistible.*

Despite the real or perceived perils of Jennifer, her beauty consumes all resistance. He represses the conflicting emotions and will know her pleasure. Besides, he imagined loving her before the dilemma surfaced.

In her bedroom, Jennifer takes a deep breath and draws the draperies. The colonel's wardrobe cabinet has been replaced by a built-in closet that is kept locked. Sitting on a chest of drawers near her elaborate bed is an old china doll dressed in faded silk with one arm missing leaving an empty sleeve. The straggled hair is under a ripped cap.

Opening the locked closet, she places the doll and Centori's dossier in a trunk and retrieves a robe. She moves to a polished brass mirror hung on a wall over a table and slowly but deliberately undresses; she admires her reflection after changing attire. Her room and her body are ready.

Bare-limbed and barefoot, the scantily clad Jennifer returns to the parlor. Her bosom and erect nipples dance against her sheer robe. Centori is no stranger to salacious female behavior, but Jennifer's sexual aggression is astounding.

Her white teeth glow as she holds her arms out, "Why so surprised? You want me, so come and get me," the temptress commands with a voice that had grown huskier.

Although silenced by her boldness, his response is lightning fast. He cannot find the strength to resist, even if he wanted to do so. No matter what her name, he accepts. Jennifer pauses at the threshold of the bedroom, kisses him on the lips and whispers in his ear. Holding hands, they enter the bedroom, and he finally finds his voice. "You are so beautiful, but I don't know your real name."

"You do know—my name is lover."

Under the robe her breasts move up and down at a faster rate. Standing at the foot of her bed, her arms encircle him as her robe becomes loose. Darkness closes down, but there is enough candlelight.

Jennifer's robe falls away; she stands splendidly naked. He stops, wishing this image to be lastingly etched in his memory.

Then his hands find her ribs and her breasts. He buries his face in her warm neck, close to her full and soft lips. She purses her mouth, "Kiss me now."

They collapse onto the bed, and he places himself on top of her. In a flash, his mouth presses Venus' irresistible lips. She pushes away and says, "Call me lover."

No more communication for now, at least not the verbal sort. In time, all of his desires are fulfilled. She was willing and passionate, more of an intense lover than a tender lover. Outside the window, stars appear and spangle the great vastness with jewels. Inside, Jennifer blows out the candles and goes off to sleep. She sleeps like an angel or perhaps more like an agent—a German agent.

Somehow Centori's pre-dawn walk back to the square seems longer. In any case, the distraction from the *Titanic* issue is short lived. He has an awful feeling that she has lied again and he chose to ignore it last night.

Passing the Mission Church he sees a coyote; it could be the same one. No matter, all coyotes can be instructive and inspirational. Alphas are bold leaders who pursue goals relentlessly; however, Centori did not pursue the truth.

When it comes to Jennifer it only takes an ember to keep his passion aflame. He turns back toward her house, although it is well beyond view from the square. *She remains a mystery. I did not get what I came for; perhaps I did.*

CHAPTER 35

ZENA ZEITGEIST

Back at the Circle C Ranch, Centori remains thoughtful about the romantic rendezvous with Jennifer, an experience that was not quite right. More significantly, the evening did not include an explanation of her identity. He could force the issue at the risk of ending further intimate involvement.

Sitting on a wing chair in the library in the predawn hour, the room feels unusually cold. He gazes at the large kiva fireplace in a corner and decides to make a fire. After checking the damper and the draft, he sets the tinder and kindling, and then adds two large logs. He strikes a match and lights the tinder.

Wandering to the Victrola, he plays *Nessun dorma* from Giacomo Puccini's *Turandot*. The opera is about a prince who dangerously falls in love at first sight with the beautiful princess. Soon after, the kiva fireplace bursts into a rapid blaze. He feels the warmth wash over him; he allows the powerful opera to consume him.

The opera moves him; he moves to the desk. Then he unlocks the bottom drawer and grasps a photo and an old water-damaged paper. The document led to Gabriella's death, but it gave them a precious short-lived reprise of their love affair. Murphy expects that the government document will be destroyed, Centori promised as much. He returns the Revert Document to the drawer.

The dancing flames quiet his emotions; lack of sleep alters his mind. Drifting to the tryst with Jennifer, he thinks about the unspoken. She appears in his mind preventing sleep; then he slowly arrives upon a dream. *Jennifer, who are you really? Who was the woman on the Titanic? What is your real name?*

Adobe, why am I here with you? Why do you consume me with questions?

I seek the simple truth about who you are…about us.

What contemptuous remarks; I have shared all with you.

You shared your body with me, but little more.

So you diminish the arms and legs that embraced you?

No, I do not.

Then what do you want from me?

Who are you?

Don't make things more complicated.

Jennifer, do you have something important to tell me?

I have told you what I can.

Perhaps you are going to kill me.

I have thought of killing you.

A loud bang causes him to jump, shattering his fantasy and his glass. "What the hell is that?"

All at once an enchanting scent fills in the darkened library. The scent is stronger than the burning cedar and pinon and has an intense familiarity—it is the unmistakable musk of Gabriella Zena. *I must be dreaming…again.*

Apprehensive, he walks toward the bookshelves to discover the source of the disturbance. He examines a book on the floor, *The Odyssey of Homer.* The large volume is opened to a passage called *Exploration of Circe's Island.* Circe, a sorceress, lures men with her nymph followers and with wine. Using metamorphic magic, she transforms men into animals.

Am I losing my mind? Is this some kind of warning?

Then he enters the realm of the fantastic. Having traversed the bookcase, she appears naturally, not ghostly; she is dressed in the clothes she died in at Chaco Canyon. Even in this form her beauty is striking. Too astonished for fear, he watches in stone silence.

I am convinced that I am mad.

Can you deny my presence?

Gabriella, I want to believe in you.

You have doubts. You are a dreamer, but I am not a dream.

How can I be sure of you?

Why are you drawn to a woman who does not exist in your world?

I am distressed.

You are revealing your vulnerability by calling me.

Gabriella, something in your eyes says you could be real.

Something in your eyes says you want me to be real.

You have been dead for many months.

Love can be stronger than life or death.

Not strong enough to save us from destruction.

I am haunted by my decision at Chaco; sometimes my regret is unbearable.

What is done is done; it is too late for us, not for you.

You mourn me, I know that, mi corazón, yet you take another lover.

Gabriella…

Say nothing, but now you must be aware of the danger of seduction.

Danger?

Why are you now drawn to a strange woman who has too many secrets, a woman who is lying to you?

Perhaps to forget about you.

You have replaced me and so soon.

No one could ever replace you.

Nada mas, I forgive you. I know you are lonely and there is room in your heart for another woman.

Never, you are the love of my life.

But it is true, I have always been honest with you…it caused our tragedy. Can you say the same for your new woman?

I don't know.

Don't you? She is different from me; know that before it is too late.

In life she was never quick to smile; now in death she is unsmiling and then invisible. Coyote cries shatter the enchantment, but not the warning. Pale and shaken, he staggers from the library to the bedroom, falls face down on the bed as the sun comes up. His attempt to forget is futile. The fire in the library kiva still burns as does Gabriella's image in his mind. Madness or not, he must determine if she is right.

CHAPTER 36

⌒∞⌒

HARD ROCK

President Huerta distrusts Ambassador Riesenfelder and is unconvinced about the significance of the gold strike in Stratford. He is even more skeptical about the Revert Document's chance in the world court. On the other hand, the possibility of controlling the largest gold reserves ever discovered in New Mexico remains compelling.

If Riesenfelder is right about the gold and about the world court, Huerta's power will be vastly increased and his tenuous presidency will be secured. Yet, trusting him could place him on the road to ruin. He must know the truth before committing resources and before risking his reputation. It is a quandary that requires expert intervention and close examination of the mine. He will err on the side of caution.

Professor Luis Salazar from *la Universidad Nacional Autónoma de México* (National Autonomous University of Mexico) has been summoned by President Huerta. The institution was founded in

1910 as an alternative to the Royal and Pontifical University of Mexico, a Roman Catholic institution.

Salazar was quick to answer the call and arrives at the *Zócalo* to meet Huerta.

"President Huerta, it is my pleasure to meet you," Salazar says.

"Thank you for coming; I know you are busy at the university."

"How can I be of service to you, President Huerta?"

"I wish to learn about gold.""I see, gold is scarce in the earth."

"Yes, of course. Where is it most likely to be found?"

"While scarce, gold is geologically found in lode deposits and in placer deposits. Gold dust or placer deposits could be discovered in streambeds, mixed with the sand and the gravel. The mineralizing solutions would start a search for the source of the precious metal. Panhandlers trace sands upstream to discover the place where the gold eroded from hard-rock: mother of the gold."

"Just tell me about hard rock gold."

"Yes, of course. It can be found in different kinds of rocks and in different geographical places. For hard rock gold, the goal is to find the lode deposits."

"In gold mines."

"Ah, hard rock gold mining seeks to extract the gold covered in rock, in veins or ores, not in gold fragments in sediment."

"Professor, how can we determine the value of hard rock gold?"

"You are referring to the grade of the ore. We must know the amount of pure gold to the ton: how many tons of ore to be processed to obtain an ounce of gold. The gold content of mineralized rocks, the yield, may not be economical to recover."

"And from this we can determine the size of the deposit?"

"Reliable estimates can be made as to the deposit's value."

"Professor Salazar, you have been most helpful."

"I am happy to do so, President Huerta."

"There is one other thing. Do you have strong adventurist students who are studying with you?"

"Yes, there are such students," he responds with curiosity.

"Professor Salazar, there can be opportunities for you and your students in national government. I am very loyal to those who show they are dependable."

"I believe you wish to confide in me; you wish to determine my trustworthiness."

"Yes, Professor, I do indeed; please sit down and have a drink with me."

CHAPTER 37

FOREIGN SECRETARY

Returning to Valtura the next day, Centori enters the telegraph office on the west side of the square. He appears humorless as his boots jangle on the old wooden floor. He surprises the clerk, Bill "Buster" Brown, a tall, thin young man who admires Centori.

"Sheriff, I heard your dedication speech, it was great!" Buster exclaims.

"Thanks, how are things in town?"

"All quiet while you were gone; we have a few new faces in town."

"New faces?"

"Yes, I may have an opinion about that, Mr. Centori."

"What is it?"

"I can't put my finger on it, but almost all visit the newspaper office and keep pretty quiet, unfriendly too."

"Unfriendly is not a crime."

"Sheriff, they all just seem suspicious."

"Thanks for the warning, Buster."

"It's probably nothing, but what about you? We all read the big news in New York. The *Valtura Journal* ran the Associated Press story about the Wall Street bombing."

"All the newspapers had dispatches; I read many accounts on the train ride home. It was a national story, probably an international story."

"Some folks say you were at the scene—at Wall Street."

"That's right; I was there."

"Oh my goodness, then it is true."

"Yes, all too true."

"What was it like; I mean it must have been terrible."

"The gates of hell, Buster."

"I am glad you are alright."

"Many were not, including a new friend."

"Sorry, Sheriff, I didn't know about that part."

"The AP story said that the bombing caused increased investigation into anarchism in America."

"I may increase my investigation."

"What's that?"

"Never mind, Buster. Please send this note to John Murphy in Washington...wait, in New York...send this message to both places today. Here are the locations."

"Sure thing."

"Thanks," he turns to leave.

"Sheriff!"

"Yes?"

"Welcome back to Valtura."

"Thanks, and as I said on statehood day, call me Adobe."

Crossing the square, he sees two well-dressed men standing in front of his office. Instinctively, he knows why they are here. The men turn in his direction and wait.

"*Señor* Centori?"

"Yes, I am Sheriff Centori."

"I am *Señor Peña* and this is *Señor Sánchez*. We represent his Excellency *Pedro Lascuráin* of the office of foreign relations in Mexico City. May we enter your office?"

"Yes, of course. You have traveled far; it must be important."

"It is of the utmost importance," *Peña* says with conviction.

Centori opens the door and enters first. The others follow. "Please sit down."

"We prefer to stand," *Peña* replies.

"As you wish," he says and circles around to the front of his desk.

"*Señor* Centori, we are here on behalf of Riccardo Marta. He is the Cuban Foreign Secretary to Mexico," *Sánchez* announces.

"Is that right?" he offers while trying to control his expression.

"That is right; his wife is Gabriella Zena Marta."

"I do not know why you are telling me this," he says with a cool poker face and a tight stomach.

"Ambassador Marta is concerned about his wife's situation," *Peña* adds.

Centori's face is frozen, then: "That is a personal problem, not an official one."

"It is official. The Ambassador's wife has disappeared in New Mexico. He has not seen or heard from her in months."

"Perhaps she wishes not to see him," he defensively says.

Now *Peña's* face freezes. "May I remind you that this is a serious matter?"

"Wait a minute; you are a guest in my office."

After an angry frown, *Peña* says, "This is a delicate affair for all concerned."

"I can see that. How can I help you?"

"We understand that you were with her in El Paso."

"El Paso? So what?"

"So, you do know her."

In check, he does not confirm or deny.

"Your country seems to know nothing about *Señora Marta*. All diplomatic channels between our countries have failed to provide any comfort to her husband. That is why we are here."

"What makes you think I can provide comfort to him?"

"Because you and another man left this town as did *Señora Marta*—at the same time."

"You are wrong; I never left Valtura with her."

"I did not say together, I said at the same time."

"How can you be sure?"

"She did not arrive in Valtura alone."

"Is that a fact?"

"It has been revealed to us that Chaco Canyon was the destination on the day she was last seen."

Centori begins to sweat. "Look, you say she entered but did not leave Chaco Canyon?" His mental lapse fills the room.

"No, you have said it; we believe that is correct."

"And you are sure of this?"

"We believe the reports," *Sánchez* says.

"And you have searched for her?"

"We have done so for some time—she has vanished."

"Chaco Canyon is a dangerous place," Centori submits.

"Are you suggesting something terrible has befallen her?"

"No, I am merely saying Chaco is risky."

"Yet you and your friend returned."

Centori looks at *Peña* and then *Sánchez* without a word.

"You returned but *Señora* Marta did not; she remains missing."

"I am sorry about that." Centori's face softens.

"For the first time, I believe you. *Señor* Centori, Ambassador Marta knows that we have little or no power on this side of the border."

"Power has nothing to do with it," Centori states.

"If a man has the power to relieve another man's suffering, he should do so."

"I am not sure what you wish from me."

It is an opportunity for *Peña*. "Can you simply tell us if Ambassador Marta will ever see his wife again?"

"I cannot answer that question."

"Cannot or will not?"

No answer. Centori's resolute eyes stare into his accuser's eyes. Two seconds later he says, "I can do no more for you, gents."

"You mean you will not do more," *Peña* replies with great disappointment.

"The hotel across the square serves a good meal. Tell them I sent you."

Sánchez opens the door and *Peña* looks at Centori, "I advise you to not come into Mexico. It would not be wise for you."

"That seems mighty unfriendly especially since you are standing on my side of the border."

"Friendliness has nothing to do with this. *Buenas tardes Señor.*"

Centori stayed in his office until the Mexican officials left the hotel restaurant and Valtura. Although he was vague with the officials, they received enough information to confirm Gabriella's death. The highly personal details of her demise will be lost to history, just like the Revert Document. He has found reasons for his mistakes with Gabriella; he even considers the reasons as truthful. Today, Mexican officials revealed another truth.

CHAPTER 38

EVERY INTENTION

Centori rides out of Valtura with the focus of his mind on the Mexican officials and their pointed Gabriella questions. Patriot, who knows the way to the Circle C, allows his rider to think about other things. The men from Old Mexico add to his distress about the New York cataclysm and the Jennifer mystery. Now he is consumed by the three issues in equal measure.

Six miles later, Centori arrives at the Circle C hoping not to see A.P. or any of the other cowboys. He immediately retreats to a secluded place that he holds in high regard, the Circle C library—his *sanctum sanctorum.* It is also a place where the Jameson is in good supply. He pours a large drink and sinks into a large chair.

Problem resolution remains elusive; the Jameson is not. He stares at the fireplace. He savors the whiskey. The world will have to take care of itself, at least for this night.

The next morning at the Circle C portal, A.P., Greigos and Quesada walk up to see Centori.

"Good morning, Boss," A.P. says.

"Mornin', Boys."

"Good morning. We need to talk about the roundup," Greigos says.

A.P. and Quesada nod in agreement.

"Guess I lost sight of that."

"We didn't want to bring it up right now, but we are a little late," A.P. adds.

"I know it's time. I trust that you all can do the job without me."

"What are you saying?"

"I'm not heading for the roundup."

"That would not be right. You love riding the range with the Circle C cowboys."

Greigos states, "We have a new hand to talk to, Henry Parker. He is a strong young man who is ready to be a cowboy."

"Good idea," A.P. agrees, "I will be along directly."

"Let's go inside," Centori says.

They step inside the house and into the Great Room, "Okay, Boss, what's going on?"

"I am planning to return to New York."

"Boss, are you mad? What for?"

"For Charity."

"You are not fooling me."

"I am not trying to, for Gabriella then. Probably for both of them."

"Okay, but what do you gain by returning to New York?"

"Remember Gabriella's death and how Charity died in my arms?"

"Yes, you keep saying; I am not entirely sure what you mean."

"No one is to blame for Gabriella's death, but it was American Scream who killed Charity. I was unable to do anything about Gabriella's death, but I *can* do something about Charity's death."

"Still, you should not go back to New York. It's a fool's errand."

"A.P."

"Look, Boss, you have had enough trouble in New York and consider the roundup."

"There is something else. A man can get over a broken heart in time, but how does a man ever get over killing another human being?"

"Come on Boss, we talked about this. You didn't kill anyone."

"It sure feels that way; she may think so."

"How could you possibly know that?"

"She told me so."

"What?"

"I am having dreams about Gabriella. I think they are dreams."

"Boss, you know I will back your play in any way you say, but we have not heard New York calling for your guns."

"No, they have not, but all the same I will get answers, resolution."

"That will take some doing."

"I know."

"Why not run the roundup and then go to New York?"

"Right before we saddled up for the dedication of the square, I said that the question is what to do *next*."

"So, now you have the answer?"

"Yes, find Charity's killers. Her murderers must pay for their actions. Fate has in a strange way given me a chance for redemption."

"Listen, Pard, is it fate that drives you and forces you to action?"

"I believe so."

"Yet your decision is not in your stars, but within yourself. You can decide not to go to New York. We know which way you go when the chips are down, but this is not your fight."

"A.P., they killed a woman who was with me; we were close."

"Yeah, I kind of figured that, but you are not a big city policeman or federal government agent."

"That never stopped me before."

"I know that; I know you can damn well take care of yourself. The few people who knew the Revert Document secret operation knew it too. You are the biggest unknown American hero; let those New York fellers handle this one."

"I already sent a message to John Murphy; I have a feeling he could be part of the manhunt."

"Will you at least wait until after the roundup has started?"

"A.P., I am leaving all ranch management to you while I am gone, including the roundup. The Circle C cowboys are more than ready to run things around here."

"Sure, but will you at least wait until you hear from Murph?"

"Yes, I can do that; I need to do that."

A.P. is determined to roundup Circle C branded cattle and to find and prepare unbranded calves for a Circle C mark. Centori is determined to take his police talents from the New Mexico mesa to the New York metropolis. Transformed to seek justice, he has every intention of finding Charity's killers and sending them to Hell.

CHAPTER 39

c⚭ɔ

WE HAVE WAYS

MEXICO CITY

Since Riesenfelder received the diplomatic dispatch from the *Zocalo*, he has been eager to see President Huerta; the message revealed an interest that could be politically exploited. The U.S. Southwest has a long and regretful history for Mexico. Now, the gold discovery in Stratford opens old wounds on the Mexican psyche. This controlling combination is not lost on Riesenfelder.

It is noon at the *Palacio Nacional* where the German ambassador to Mexico will meet the Mexican president again. Riesenfelder shows his credentials, enters the Patio of Honor, and then enters the president's office.

"Please wait here, *Señor*," announces the president's secretary.

"Thank you," he says without surprise.

The secretary walks away. Riesenfelder prepares for another chance to achieve his goal and he does not wait long.

"The president will see you now."

"President Huerta, I received your message with much interest."

"*Señor* Riesenfelder, I have thought much about our last meeting. There are many questions that remain."

"I am sure we can address those questions."

"You are sure because Germans have their ways?"

"We wish to address the concerns of your government and to improve the relations between our countries."

"Yes, of course. At our last meeting you spoke of how the Americans had violated an old treaty and about presenting our legal argument to the international court."

"Yes, all that is true."

"All true provided the document can be found. Do you have the Revert Document? No! Do you know where it is? No! Are you sure you will have it? No!"

"President Huerta, the Revert Document is not yet necessary."

"I will not make the same mistake as Madero!" the president repeats.

"Then I am puzzled as to why you summoned me."

"Again, as Santayana said, those who cannot remember the past are condemned to repeat it. Madero was a fool. Too many people were involved with his failed plan. He was consumed with finding the document to a fault, a fatal fault."

Riesenfelder is reassured that the president did not mention Germany's involvement with Madero. Huerta gazes out a window to the large plaza in front of the palace and turns back. "I wish to make it clear that the Mexican government will not take any official position—until you have the document."

"We will have the document," Riesenfelder shows dismay.

"You must understand that Mexico's international relations have often followed a poorly predictable path. Foreign affairs have hardened into conflict and too many times a chance for Mexico was lost."

"It would be wise to begin our summit meetings sooner rather than later."

"I think you will find the accounts of an army engaged in organizing and training interesting. We can describe how to build an army in size and strength and to prepare for activation," Riesenfelder boasts.

Huerta throws his fist on his desk. "Not now! And unless the paper is found—not ever!"

"Of course."

After a moment, "Forgive my manners. May I pour you a drink?"

"Yes, thank you."

"*Salud.*"

"To you, General. You have a reasonable position; your involvement shall be kept secret."

"Do you have any idea or plan to find the paper?"

"As you said, we have our ways. We know that the last known original copy was concealed in Chaco Canyon, New Mexico, by Mexican troops. We also know that an American was close to a member of that expedition."

"Provided that it was in Chaco Canyon and provided that the American somehow knows the whereabouts of the document."

"We believe that he knew the secret and found the paper."

"But you don't know he has the document."

"We do not know it; we believe it."

"If he did, why would he not destroy the paper—and destroy the indictment against his country?"

"Men can do foolish things, especially this American."

"If he destroyed the Revert Document, we could pay him to testify about the paper's existence."

"That is unlikely," Riesenfelder argues. He would not publicly betray his country. However, such an important and valuable document; it could be sold for a fortune—anonymously."

"What do you know about this American's integrity?"

"Enough."

"Enough to say he would sell out his country?"

"Every man has a price; perhaps we will find his price."

"That sounds somewhat slight."

"President Huerta, we have another plan in place as we speak."

"You seem to know much about this affair, but not all."

"It is our business to know much."

"I understand, but again your grand plan is contingent on finding the Revert Document. Even if you do, there are no assurances that the world will care; the U.S. will certainly not."

"As we have discussed, the world court that was produced by The Hague Peace Conference will hear our case."

"Can we be sure?"

"The court has been operating for almost 15 years; there are members of our government who, either through experience or knowledge, have information concerning appropriate channels with the world court."

"You failed to answer my question. Even if you are sure they will hear the case, Mexico will probably lose the court battle."

"That is possible, yet we could have a negotiated settlement relating to the gold."

"If the gold exists."

"There is gold in the Stratford mines, President Huerta."

"But how much is yet to be confirmed."

"Nevertheless, the U.S. has violated the Revert Document agreement. There is a strong chance for a settlement, which is more likely than the U.S. giving back a large part of their country."

"You mean *our* country. That is a good analysis, but again, we come back to the document."

"Beyond the document possibilities, an alliance with Berlin against the U.S. would help Mexico and your presidency."

Ignoring the forward remark, Huerta says, "An alliance with Berlin?"

"Yes, during the past few years the German army has been engaged in obtaining information, planning and completing land surveys."

"How very interesting, *Señor* Riesenfelder, for your country."

"To maintain your interest and to keep your government informed, a series of conferences and meetings can be held between our two countries."

"Why would we agree to such meetings?"

"To promote acquaintance among the various components of our governments; we will discuss topics of timely and national interest."

"National?" What nation do you refer to?"

"Allow me to explain. There are new directives for implementing an alliance for greater German sovereignty. Our policies should readily command the attention of all military men with ambition; the directives provide for prompt action."

"Once again, they are programs that are interesting for your country."

"Mexico, too. Germany is currently engaged in military reorganization and training our army to be activated in the near future."

"You fail to explain what this alliance will mean for the various countries."

"I am required to limit our discussions to information on the alliance of our two nations."

"Potential alliances; what can you tell me?"

"Are you aware of the Triple Alliance?"

"Let me guess the implication, the Triple Alliance will assist Mexico in regaining territory stolen by the U.S. in war."

"That is not entirely impossible," Riesenfelder understates.

"Mexico would be in a better bargaining position, at the least."

"Are your statements the official position of your government?"

"They are from authentic sources and can be checked for accuracy."

"I see. Please continue."

"When Kaiser Wilhelm I ascended to the throne, German relations with Great Britain and Russia began to decline. Germany became concerned about the potential of war on both the western and eastern fronts. As a defense, Italy, Austria-Hungary and Germany formed the Triple Alliance in 1882. Russia, France and Britain formed the Triple Entente as a counter."

"That is all fascinating. Since the Revert Document failure last year, Berlin has not been idle; the document remains part of your master plan or at least the idea does."

"We are confident that any conflict in Europe would be fast with a German victory. If Mexico provides help, we would be most appreciative."

"If you can produce the Revert Document, we will meet again. *Buenos dias, Señor* Riesenfelder."

Riesenfelder smiles in agreement, ending the meeting but starting a plan with major international implications that will have earth-shaking results.

CHAPTER 40

❦

THINGS START EARLY

Daybreak is behind the Sandia Mountains, on the horizon and across America to New York where Manhattan is already awake. Although the corner of Broad and Wall is back to normal, an indication of the Wall Street bombing can be found at the Morgan Building. Shrapnel scars, engraved into the granite cornerstone, will be there as long as the building stands.

The first light of dawn appears on the mountain peak. Moments later, Centori feels the first rays of sun on his closed eyes, hears the sounds of excited crows flying across the sky and smells a hint of fragrance. All the sensations cause his mind to elevate beyond consciousness to a perceived perfect morning. The sun streaks the eastern sky with shades of cool blue. First light strains into the large bedroom, illuminating her exquisite beauty.

The Circle C became whole when she arrived to create touches of decorative warmth and to add a certain spirit within an air of affection. He treasures waking next to her glowing presence and anticipating the day. She usually starts the morning brushing her silky black hair; they usually have a coffee and a kiss before riding the range together.

The beautiful sleeping woman shifts to a more inviting position; the increasing sunlight continues to magnify her loveliness. He moves closer, gazing as if she were a masterpiece painting. Intimacy is moments away; he is about to accept the Queen of Circle C.

Then out of a clear sky a distant noise causes him to stir. Seconds later the sound is closer; a horse on a path to the house approaches. He turns toward the window then looks back over his shoulder; there is an empty bed. Another dream of the mind—Gabriella's vision of beauty is gone again. There is nothing but a big unmade bed in the middle of the back wall.

The louder rhythm of hoof beats completes his return to reality and sinks his heart. Dawn is over and so is the dream. As he pulls on his pants and shirt, there is knocking on the main door. "Adobe," the visitor calls out. Answering the door with unrequited passion, he sees another vision of beauty. She is wearing black riding pants, high black boots and a blue cotton shirt. The stunning woman with a strong smile is Jennifer Prower.

"I hope this is a welcomed surprise and not a terrible shock."

"It is wonderful to see you; this unannounced and early visit is surprising."

"I thought you had invited me; you said I would find the Circle C appealing."

"Yes, sort of—of course I did, but why so early?"

"Well, I understand that things start early at the Circle C and I have a newspaper to publish."

Too suspicious to detect irony, he nods and offers, "Jennifer, please come inside."

Escorting her to the Great Room, he quickly tucks in his shirttails. "Please make yourself comfortable; I will be right back."

Jennifer looks around the large room that contains solid wood furniture and a massive floor to ceiling kiva fireplace. She has achieved in a few months what Mad Mady, or any woman, has not achieved in years. He returns fully dressed.

"This is a grand house; you must be very happy here."

"Happy enough; I built this place."

"You are a man of much substance. I have never known that more than right now."

"I wish I knew why."

"Because I see that this great house and all that you express here; you are indeed a man who loves architecture, art and the decorative arts."

"It will do. Shall we go to the kitchen for coffee?" he asks with certainty.

"Yes, thank you."

They walk to the kitchen; the sway of her hips is accentuated because he is looking. The bright New Mexico sunrise washes through the kitchen windows.

Centori grabs the coffee beans and grinder just as A.P. knocks and walks in through the front door and approaches the kitchen, "Everything okay, Boss?"

"Yes, this is Jennifer Prower from the *Valtura Journal.*"

A.P. nods and says, "Good morning, Miss Jennifer."

She smiles in return.

"Coffee?" He does not mean the invitation.

"No, thanks. I will get to getting," he awkwardly answers.

"Okay."

A.P. tips his hat and leaves.

"He seems quite protective of you."

"A.P. is a good friend and rich in character."

He reaches for the coffee pot and sets up the brew on a wood burning stove. "You are quite energetic this early in the morning," he says.

"So are the New Mexico and Old Mexico visual cultures that surround you."

"Yes, I love the southwest and this house; always been that way."

"Quite right, everything about the Circle C design shows your clear vision, yet the place does not bode well for you."

"Really?"

"Yes, it is clear that something is missing."

"That is a harsh observation. You sound pretty sure of yourself and about knowing me."

She moves close to him. "Knowing you is not so hard to do, especially after our evening at my house."

Somewhat startled he quickly says, "It was a very special time."

"Very special."

"So what did you mean about something missing?"

"You are an accomplished man, though not as accomplished as you think. We both know you would welcome the right woman at the Circle C."

She scans the large kitchen waiting for a reaction; it did not come. As she glances back, he puts out a pair of coffee mugs and asks, "So I am sure you could have gotten coffee at the plaza; I mean the square."

"I heard there is something special about Circle C cowboy coffee."

"Okay, Jennifer, why are you here so early?"

"I wish to invite you to write a letter to the editor."

He pours two cups and waits for more.

She smiles, lifts her coffee and takes a sip. "This is surprisingly excellent."

"No need for surprise. You can find a good cup of cowboy coffee here, but what about that letter?"

"Your letter would be in reaction to Stark Reality."

"I see."

"This will show you that I am open to opposing views and to you."

He takes another sip of coffee while taking in the comment. "I have thought of doing so; in fact wait here a moment."

He quickly goes to the library; she examines the room, searching for insights into his personality. Less than a minute later he returns with a book in hand.

"Have you read Cicero, the Roman Philosopher?" Not waiting for an answer, he goes on, "Since New York, I have been re-reading him and would like to publish his words. We can sign it the Ghost of Cicero."

"You do not wish your name attached?"

"No, it is about the message, not me. Besides, they are Cicero's words. If asked I will say it was my idea. Or I can sign it Centurion, a Roman army officer," he suggests. "Here, take a look at the passage."

'A nation can survive its fools, and even the ambitious. But it cannot survive treason from within. An enemy at the gates is less formidable, for he is known and carries his banner openly. But the traitor moves amongst those within the gate freely, his sly whispers rustling through all the alleys, heard in the very halls of government itself. For the traitor appears not a traitor; he speaks in accents familiar to his victims, and he wears their face and their arguments, he appeals to the baseness that lies deep in the hearts of all men. He rots the soul of a nation, he works secretly and unknown in the night to undermine the pillars of the city, he infects the body politic so that it can no longer resist. A murderer is less to fear.'

Jennifer carefully places the book down. "Quite a powerful piece."

"I thought so."

"Adobe, a man with your insight, record and talents should be naturally drawn to politics."

"Being a statehood delegate was enough politics for me."

"We could explore interests in the wider world, beyond Valtura."

"Our interests?"

"Yes, I can see that you agree. Together we could achieve political power; your charisma and experience and my power of the press. You could be governor of New Mexico!"

"Ha, I think you should be in the Territorial Insane Asylum. Guess I should say State Asylum now. So you are willing to publish the Cicero letter?"

"It is an interesting idea…yes, of course," she lies.

CHAPTER 41

THE MEXICAN AFFAIR

A fter a long journey from Mexico City, Siegfried Seiler arrived in Valtura. He spent the night in the Union Hotel. On Santos Square, he walks past Bill "Buster" Brown who stares at the newcomer. Seiler quickly looks away, enters the newspaper office and is greeted by Bernhard Bachmeier. "Herr Seiler, we were not expecting you."

"Herr Bachmeier, in our business we must be prepared for the unexpected."

Bachmeier sneers and asks, "Why are you here?"

"I am here to see *Rote Frau*."

"She has not yet arrived."

"Has *Rote Frau* made progress on the plan found in the Centori dossier?"

"I am sure that she has done so."

"You must confirm and continue to correspond with Mexico City and Berlin through agreed upon channels."

"You have traveled far for that message."

"I am travelling to New York. In time, you will be summoned to *Kleindeutschland*."

On East Corona Street, Seiler sits in the big house with the big fence and waits for *Rote Frau*. She has proceeded with the Mexican affair, but success remains elusive.

CHAPTER 42

WOLVES

C entori escorts his early morning guest to his library. He returns the book; she studies the room.

"Cicero's treason from within notion was evident in New York," he says to her surprise.

"I am not sure what you mean," she says while being sure of what he means.

"The Wall Street bombing was the act of Americans, not a foreign enemy—treason from within."

"Are you sure about that?"

"Remember, that gang is called American Scream."

"I see, there were no foreign powers involved."

"Perhaps you should take the book."

With a smile she says, "Thank you, I will enjoy reading it," she lies again. "Adobe, there is another reason why I came here."

"I had a feeling."

"I have re-lived being with you many times since our night."

"That is true for me too; it is never far from my mind."

"Our night has made me realize that certain things should pass between us."

"Certain things you say; but not all things you mean."

"I am saying that you wish to have a woman to share all."

She could be right, I don't know. "Is that so?"

"It is so; it will help you to reveal a secret you need to tell me."

"Let's sit down for a while."

"Thank you."

"Jennifer, if I had a secret, why would I need you to free me of the burden?"

"I didn't say it was a burden, but you need to tell a woman who is filled with caring and intimacy."

"I thought you were the one with a secret," Centori probes.

She evades and says, "I could assure your happiness; that is no secret."

"Jennifer, we had a wonderful evening together; I loved holding you, but let me ask again. Who are you?"

"Some things are only discovered by taking risks."

"How about taking me seriously? Tell me about your background. Most men would not accept you this way."

"Are you sure about that?"

He is not. "Tell me your real name."

After a long pause she says, "Previous to moving to New Mexico, I lived in New York."

"Yes, I know that, Jennifer."

Then a shorter pause, "I entered New York in '08 using a forged Swiss passport."

Centori's interest peaks as she goes on, "My husband, a Deutsche Bank executive, remained in Europe."

"Husband!"

"Wait, I had to leave him in a hurry."

"That is insipid and wicked at the same time, quite a trick."

"That is very cold of you."

"Probably."

At the top of her voice, she replies, "I was escaping his cruelty."

"Still, why change your name?"

"I needed another identity to escape a dangerous situation."

Recoiling from her outburst he says, "Please rein in your temper, Jennifer."

"Adobe, he was selfish leaving me in a state of suspense and tormented with desire. Then he became abusive."

"What did you do about it?" he asks with concern.

"Nothing, I just left him. No one would believe me; he was an important man and a successful finance minister. I was just a wife, who felt his wrath."

Although still skeptical he offers, "A man who makes war on women is not an important man; he is a small man."

"Now you understand the predicament I faced in Europe."

"Jennifer, I am sorry for that, but will you tell me your name?"

"I have, my name is Jennifer. You think me a hard woman; I resent you for thinking so. If I am hard it is with good reason."

"I may not believe you, but it may be true. You have a talent for lying to me and I think you like it."

"I have concealed things but never lied to you."

"Is that right, Miss Prower?"

"My name was changed in the face of the situation; they are powerful government people."

"You said it was a marriage issue and you did not indicate any such thing."

"So what do you want from me?"

"Do I have to say it again?"

"I have many doubts about things; try to understand."

"Mark Twain said, 'when in doubt tell the truth.'"

"My husband is a Deutsche Bank executive but he is also involved with high levels of government."

He rubs his eyes lightly. "Go on."

"One day he found me looking through his private papers—and became more violent than usual."

"I'm sorry you had that experience."

"I am worried that he will find me and extract his vengeance for leaving."

"Do not worry, Jennifer. That will never happen while I still draw a breath, and there are others that would back my play. Tell me more about the papers."

"I didn't know more; I didn't have time to read much. My husband thought I read enough for me to fear him."

"What do you think they were?"

After a pause she replies, "They may have been government reports."

"I figured that."

"I told you I did not read much."

"You must have some idea," he presses.

"They could be secret documentation regarding state policy."

"Regarding state policy or espionage?"

"I'm not sure," she nervously replies, wondering if she has said too much.

It is a razor's edge; she intends to feed enough to trap him, and no more.

"Adobe, I would rather talk about us than another man."

Her sophisticated presentation gains his empathy but not his complete trust. "Jennifer, perhaps I am sensitive to German issues. I really don't like those guys."

"I can understand that."

Wait a minute, she can?

"I also understand that you need to share your feelings with a woman who is filled with compassion and closeness."

"You could be right about that."

"Of course I am right and you will see that in time. I will engage you at different levels and in different ways. Those things will become known in time. Adobe, beyond romance you want a woman to be politically attuned to the world, to be strong, to be intelligent and imaginative."

"You forgot honest."

"Nowhere is your vanity more apparent than in the affairs of the heart."

"I think you can appreciate that quality. Jennifer, you are adverse to the truth."

"There are many truths; perhaps I have not shared them all. Nor have you, but sometimes we know secrets without being told."

"Is that right?"

"We must all try to forget the past, but it is not that easy."

"What do you know about it?"

"Enough."

"Please continue."

"I know that you have a secret involving a woman that invokes bad memories."

"Hold on. As a newcomer to Valtura, what do you know about my past anyway?"

"People talk on the plaza. Some say you are tortured about a lost love," she says while not mentioning Felicity, her spy in Mad Mady's Saloon.

"People talk to you? You are new in town."

"Well, I am a newspaper woman too."

"Sure."

"Your secret prevents you from seeking emotional exposure with a woman you respect and love."

He does not mind and admits, "It is not that easy for me."

"Stop spending time in an impossible love affair. It rarely occurs to you that it is your fault women are always at arm's length. You are seen as foolish for not inviting women to the Circle C, until now. I did not wait for a formal invitation because you needed me to force the issue, so I am here."

"You are taking many liberties at my expense."

"With good reason. Your vanity and an unresolved past blinds you to a full realization of romance. Knowing what you're thinking and understanding how you react to me and to the world are important. I can be solely dedicated to you as a woman to be trusted beyond doubt."

"That is what you expect me to believe?"

For good measure, Jennifer offers a gentle kiss, embrace and wicked look. Then hoof beats of an approaching horse clouds the conversation.

"When I say things start early at the Circle C, I didn't mean this thing," he says anxiously. She quickly fixes the slight disarray of her clothes and touches her hair.

Outside, A.P. rides up and slips from his saddle. Centori walks to the portal. "Sorry to interrupt, Boss." A.P. is tentative. "We need to talk with Francisco and Pedro."

"Miss Prower was just leaving. We all know that things start early in the ranching business."

A.P. tips his hat; he walks to the corral and rests his arms on the top rail.

"Goodbye, Jennifer. You were certainly interesting at this unfashionable hour."

"Unfashionable for whom? Good day, gentlemen."

Centori watches Jennifer and thinks, *next time warn me*. He did not mean it at all.

She gracefully swings back on her horse. Astride with strength and confidence, she wheels and directs the black mare into a canter. Horse and woman are an elegant and skillful image. Then she gallops off in the direction of Valtura, riding fast—as though wolves are chasing her.

Adobe and Jennifer are an improbable couple; too adversarial on the surface for romance. He acutely wants her; she may not want him at all.

Centori walks to a stand of cottonwood trees near the house to intercept Francisco and Pedro. "We all need to talk. Let's go to the house to have some chilies, eggs and tortillas."

"You are the boss, Boss."

Before Centori goes back inside, he waves to A.P. and notices a riotous bloom of white wild flowers that have appeared overnight. They are beautiful; they are weeds.

An hour later, Jennifer returns to her Victorian house. The house is concealed by a big fence. Siegfried Seiler is concealed inside the house.

Jennifer enters through the front door and is surprised and confronted by Seiler.

"What are you doing in my house?"

"A better question is what you are doing to help our cause?"

Seiler, who sits next to the telephone table, stands up. "Do you have what is required?"

"No, not yet."

"Riesenfelder is not a tolerant man. He is waiting for results. Each day increases our risk. You must complete the plan in the dossier and report to Riesenfelder as soon as you have done your job! The entire Mexican affair depends on you."

"You have made yourself quite clear, Herr Seiler."

"*Sehr gut. Auf wiedersehen.*"

CHAPTER 43

TO THE GRAVE

Since Huerta's takeover of power, he has struggled to maintain his position in the face of challenges from several factions including his strongest opponent: Zapata. This is the only issue to be discussed at the meeting with General Ramiro Vega. The two men who are equal in ego, not in power, sit across the conference table in the president's office.

"General Vega, thank you for coming."

"It is my pleasure, President Huerta."

"I would like to discuss an important plan; one that will be of great service to our country."

Vega's eyes widen as the president goes on, "What I am about to tell you must never be repeated. Do you agree never to speak of this meeting to anyone at any time?"

"Yes, I agree."

"Do you understand that this meeting and the words spoken are top secret? We must take it to the grave!"

"I understand all that you require."

"Good. You know we have enemies in Mexico."

"Yes, we have many."

"I am particularly concerned about Zapata. During the Revolution, his forces successfully contributed to the fall of President Díaz, and Madero was a fool for disavowing the Zapatistas," Huerta says.

"That strengthened Zapata's position and army; you are president now. Madero *was* a fool." Vega adds.

"Still, I am worried about Carranza, Villa, and most of all, Zapata. He is known to shoot down any *federales* that get in his way. We must destroy Zapata and his army—we can do so with the help of the Americans."

"What? That would be a great advantage but also a great task."

"You are a great general. We have an opportunity to discuss a plan to ensure the end of Zapata. For that plan to work we must have U.S. support."

"How do we obtain such support from President Taft?"

"Would you like a drink before we continue?"

"That is a good idea, or a bad idea. Yes, thank you."

The president pours the tequila and the general ponders.

"*Salud*, General."

"*Salud*, Mr. President." The drink did not go down smoothly for Vega. The same is true for the president's words. Vega has little choice at the moment and waits for more.

"You will remember when we were fighting our enemies and considered raiding Columbus, New Mexico, for needed supplies?"

"That is your plan to gain American support? They would not support us; they would seek to bury us." Vega downs another drink.

"It is part of my plan, General. Allow me to continue. We will execute the raid while concealing our involvement."

"What are you saying?"

"You will design a raid on an American town in a way to deceive."

Vega takes another drink as Huerta goes on. "It will appear that the raid was conducted by Zapata and not by us. The raid will pit the Americans against our enemy."

Visually shaken, Vega says, "President Huerta, while it is true that we could gain American support from such a bold plan, it is a very risky one."

"Perhaps not as much as you think. Americans are good at such things. This would be a kind of justice."

"How do you come to that conclusion?"

"The U.S. wanted Spain out of Cuba and sent the USS *Maine*. An explosion destroyed the ship, killing hundreds of sailors. The U.S. blamed Spain despite a lack of evidence and had a pretext to invade Cuba and expel Spain. General Vega, your men will appear as Zapatista revolutionaries to the Americans."

"What do you mean? How can we convince the Americans?" Vega nervously replies.

"Your men will shout 'Viva Zapata' during the raid."

"You are not serious. It sounds ridiculous." Vega protests.

"General, I am pleased that no one is here to witness your insults."

"My apologies, President Huerta; I do not see how this deception will be possible."

"There is something much more important than shouting his name. You will drop a document pouch containing orders and other papers, all properly signed by Zapata."

"Forged documents that adds a layer of trickery, but still not impenetrable. Do you believe that the Americans will be so fooled?"

"If you follow my orders, the forgery will be convincing—you must drop the pouch in the town, all is dependent on your action. Follow my orders and Zapata will be blamed for the raid. To the grave we take this plan."

"That could be sooner than later."

Huerta ignores the remark and continues, "The raid will inflame the American public opinion; the U.S. will support our government financially and will want me to remain in power."

"To help them pursue and crush Zapata?"

"Exactly."

Vega nods with little enthusiasm and says, "If the Americans believe he conducted the raid."

"One more thing, General, we will change the American town in question. Columbus was considered because of the closeness to the border."

Vega looks down but waits for more. "We will gain more if you move your troops north for about 50 miles. The border towns may expect a raid, but a town so far in the U.S. will certainly be unaware and undefended. It will also cause more anger in the U.S."

"My God, you wish me to lead a small army of men 50 miles north of the border?"

"I do not wish it, General, I expect you to do so." Vega frowns and says nothing. "I have plotted a trail through the desert that will conceal your movement for most of the journey."

"But we will be exposed as invaders."

"You will be exposed to coyotes and rattlesnakes. Your path is through uninhabited desert."

"For 50 miles!"

Huerta looks at him sharply and then, "Do you know about a legendary expedition led by a Colonel Alvarado who penetrated hundreds of miles into American territory?"

"I do not know of such a legend."

"Alvarado had a much smaller force and a much longer distance to enter Chaco Canyon in Northern New Mexico."

Vega stares blankly and offers no further resistance. The president takes another drink and continues, "There is more to the mission. You will be taking a small group of university geologists with your men."

"I do not understand."

"They will follow you to the town and will inspect a nearby gold mine."

"Inspecting mines! That is highly unusual for such a mission. May I remind you that my men will be quite busy?"

"Busy with the other part of the raid. While your men invade the town, the geologists will collect hard rock samples and inspect the quantity and quality of the vein of gold."

"You are asking too much of me."

"Perhaps, not enough. I will send geologists with your army. The raid provides an opportunity to verify certain assertions about the outcropping."

"I don't understand."

"All you need to understand is that your men will appear as soldiers of Bad Man Zapata. The raid will seem to be the work of my rival, will undermine him and we will gain American support for our government. It is a gamble, I admit but one we will take."

Resigned to the unwelcomed assignment, Vega asks, "You say the town is 70 miles north of the border."

"Yes, near Silver City."

"What is the name of the town?"

"Stratford, New Mexico."

CHAPTER 44

ROTE FRAU

Four days have passed without word from John Murphy. At twilight, Centori paces the library floor, anxious about the return to New York. *Where would I begin without Murph? There was Officer Jack Haughey of the NYPD. I could contact him, but why would the New York police welcome a New Mexico county sheriff?* He stands and takes a quick look outside. *She should be arriving soon.*

Jennifer is holding something back from Centori, but holds little back in providing service to Germany. Now on the trail from Valtura, she intends to provide a service to Adobe Centori. She has been informed about the Siegfried Seiler visit and planned her tactics for the next encounter. This time she called to arrange a Circle C visit.

Centori moves outside watching for a rider in the distance. Standing on the portal, he sees her approach on horseback; rider and horse move in one motion. It is clear that Jennifer Prower is an experienced equestrian; her intentions are unclear.

She comes into waving distance. He walks from under the portal and waits for her to dismount. "You appear comfortable in the saddle for a city slicker."

"I grew up in horse country," Jennifer lies, "in upstate New York."

"Welcome back to the Circle C Ranch."

"Thank you," she says while handing over the bridle reins. "This is a much better reception, I might add."

He tethers her horse and offers her a seat under the portal, "So upstate New York; I thought you said Europe."

"Do I sound like I have an accent? I am, however, well-travelled."

"Tell me, were your parents German?"

"No, why do you ask?"

"You spoke German to Bachmeier."

"It was easy for me to pick up German, living with my husband."

"It sounded as if you spoke perfect German."

"What? Why don't we sit for a while and watch the sunset?"

He backs off. "Yes, of course."

"Adobe, this is what I love most about New Mexico."

"The twilight and sunsets are transcendentally beautiful, as you are too."

"Are you trying to make me blush?"

"We both know that is not an easy task."

"Knowing each other has not been entirely easy."

"Despite our difficulties, you know how I feel about you."

"I know your feelings are mixed and you are not entirely satisfied with my explanation."

"Jennifer, I thought we could start fresh."

"Yes, if that is what you want."

He nods. "I would like to think that is what we *both* want. Look, we both have past problems that are hard to reconcile with the present."

"Thank you for understanding my difficulties. In time we can settle any differences we may have."

"Let me get a bottle and two glasses. Tequila?"

"Yes, I have become very fond of that drink from the blue agave plant, over the past year."

Centori returns with a tray. In the short time he was away, the light and beauty had changed, as it does so swiftly this time of day.

"Here's to a fresh start!"

"*Salud.*"

"Ha, you are becoming a New Mexican," *Salud to the first woman to be at the Circle C.*

The light changes again, creating more dramatic beauty of the mountains and of the heavens.

"I hope that now you fully understand the *Titanic* issue. I am sorry for that woman and for all the victims."

"Why did you take her name?"

"It was more of an impersonation than a name change. I though her classy world would be safe for me."

"Did you know her?"

"Remember, a fresh start; let's not speak of it again."

Darkness emerges as the sun disappears in the west. The sun will return as will his mistrust. "Jennifer, I love watching the night sky from the Circle C; now with you the stars are especially exquisite."

"It seems as if we could almost reach and touch the stars," she adds.

"The clearness of the universe, the peacefulness of the air and you combine to balance the mind and produce the most memorable moment."

"You are a poet too."

"Sure."

"Or is it the tequila?"

"It's just you."

"The moon in the southwest presents a far greater radiance than back East. Sometimes I can read by moonlight."

"Some call that a rustler's moon," he says before sipping more of his drink.

"Now that I can see it all, I am falling in love with New Mexico. The brightness of the milky-way makes all dreams seem possible here and that brilliant planet Venus."

"Venus!"

"Yes."

"Venus, named for the Roman Goddess of love and beauty, is next to Earth in the solar system as I am next to you."

Jennifer smiles in agreement. He presses his advantage. "Only the moon is brighter in the night sky."

"Yes, the planet is bright enough to cast a shadow and it is the brightest after sunset, as we can see now. Venus is bright enough to be called the evening star."

"You know much of Venus."

"Why so surprised, Adobe?"

"I'm not, you are a woman of superior substance, but I'll bet you do not know how special Venus is to me."

"Oh?"

"When I think of you, I think of Venus of Valtura."

"What?"

"That is my loving name for you."

"It sounds more generous than accurate. Who knows this besides you?"

"No one knows—now you know. So now I have shared a secret."

"Thank you, very charming."

"My pleasure, but some secrets are greater than others."

She ignores another attempt to probe into her background and squeezes his hand to remind him of the fresh start. He is willing to surrender to her charms, again. They continue their rendezvous into the library and into the evening.

Now bowls of apples and grapes add to the tequila and to the building passion. The Victor scratches out the aria, *La donna e mobile* from Giuseppe Verdi's opera *Rigoletto.* They are both inclined to move closer. Abruptly, Jennifer enters a trance-like state and says, "To touch and to be touched; to kiss and to be kissed, that is how I dream of you."

"You look especially pretty saying that," he says.

She runs a hand through her hair seductively. "Now you are seeing things my way; somewhat differently from our last time."

"Things could become even clearer."

"Indeed, we can embrace a spiritual love beyond our last encounter; then you will be ready to share all things with me. Reveal your private thoughts and our desire will become the only thing we can breathe or taste," she declares.

That was more than enough words. "You are a very desirable woman, Jennifer," he says peacefully, ready for her embrace.

She smiles as her nimble fingers work the buttons on her shirt; she sweeps it open. They withdraw to his bedroom, a place that had hosted, until now, only a ghost of a woman.

Centori thrusts his hands into Jennifer's lustrous long hair. His lips touch her cheek; his light breath causes her to move. When a prolonged kiss ends, he gently turns her around and hugs her from behind.

"I guess we will never see eye to eye," she quips.

He hesitates, "You strike me as having eyes in the back of your head."

Then, without warning, he lifts her skirt up. Now they are against the wall and next to a window; she feels her skirt rise up along her thighs, intensely responsive to his body pressed against hers.

She takes a quick look back, glances at him; their eyes meet for a second before he softly fondles her high breasts from behind. Then he firmly touches her slim hips and places his hands above her contours. As the waves of passion coil through her body, she releases a hoarse guttural sound. It is the genesis of their splendor; a certain fervor that produces an ardent upsurge in human nature.

Moving her hair away he kisses the back of her neck and slowly uncovers Jennifer; as her clothes fall away, Venus of Valtura is revealed. He views the stream of reddish blonde hair dancing over nakedness. *I love this beauty.*

Jennifer sways into him in a naturally occurring response. He pulls her against him. Seconds later, she anticipates his desires; he takes the naked beauty as she braces on the window shelf.

She turns her head slightly attempting to look back. He offers a strong physical reply that jolts her head upward; she sees the timbered ceiling before closing her eyes. When her eyes open, she steals a look through the window and sees the night sky. Her eyes continue to open and close at intervals and in tune with an ideal rhythm.

Jennifer, adept in political subterfuge, stole an identity, one that would open doors in New York. She arrived in the U.S. with two small capsules containing secret codes buried between her ample breasts and $750,000 in German treasury notes hidden in her baggage. She laundered the funds with German American businesses and distributed money to a network of agents as needed. Jennifer Prower, Venus of Valtura, has another name, more practical than endearing: *Rote Frau* (Red Woman).

CHAPTER 45

BEST LAID SCHEMES

Three hundred miles south of Valtura and the Circle C, General Vega and his army of horsemen are on the brink of raiding Stratford. His spies have returned from gathering information. The tactics have been reviewed time and again; the only thing left is to wait.

It is just before dawn; anticipation has prevented Vega from sleeping. He stares down at the quiet town from outside his command tent, thinking of the unsuspecting citizens. A wave of uncertainty consumes the general. He calls to the closest aide-de-camp, "I need to see Colonel Venada now."

Within a minute, the colonel arrives, "Yes, General."

"We have time for one last meeting before we attack."

"We have gone over and over the plan."

"Colonel Venada! We shall conduct a final review."

"General, our men have returned from town to confirm our suppositions. All of my captains are ready and so are the men."

"This could be the moment we remember—the chance to end this madness," Vega says.

"It is your decision, General."

Venada's wavering disturbs Vega and fuels his doubt. "I cannot return to Mexico without completing the mission—if I return at all. One more time, we invade from the north and from the south—separately and simultaneously."

"I understand, as do the men."

"Still, let's look at the map again."

Pointing at the map, he repeats, "Here are the points, you lead your men into town from the north. Then proceed to the gold mine office while firing to support the office invaders if necessary."

"Yes, General, We have gone over this already."

"We cannot be too well versed with our plans. Colonel, remember the office."

"I know, I know. Take every paper and shoot anyone who tries to stop our retreat. The men will take the documents to camp."

"Exactly. If I do not return, deliver the papers to the president."

"I understand, General. Forgive me, you seem anxious."

Vega, places his hands up and admits, "I am uncertain and feel uneasy about this mission."

"It is true; we are indeed entering unfamiliar territory."

Knowing the lesson of Prussian Field Marshal Moltke—no plan of operations extends with certainty beyond the first encounter with the enemy's main strength—adds to his anxiety. Also, he knows that any military raid is unpredictable, but U.S. soil increases the unknowable.

Vega deals with this unknown with redundancy of preparation, "I will approach the town from the south and stop at the mine and detach the geology party."

"Yes, General, as you have said. Then you lead your men to link with me at the hotel."

"Good, and at that time we will reverse and ride back to camp with your men."

"I understand your orders, General Vega."

"It is absolutely vital the men shout 'Viva Zapata' during the raid. Take this pouch and drop it near the hotel—the entire mission depends on you doing so. Remember you must drop the pouch!"

"Diego, we have planned all. Good luck to you."

Except that Vega has not planned all. It is an imperfect plan that lacks the crucial knowledge of a U.S. Cavalry troop garrisoned in nearby Silver City.

"General, I should think that this is my last campaign."

"Diego, you have served well. Not all battle scars are from bullets or shells. Some injuries are unseen and are emotional. We must know when our time is done."

The United States 6th Cavalry served in Cuba during the Spanish-American War. The 6th and other army units patrolled the Mexican border where they encountered raiders and smugglers. Now, the army maintains a southern presence to protect and defend border towns. *Vega* considered the U.S. army unlikely to be in Silver City given distance from the border; the cavalrymen are overlooked by his spies. The regiments are less than two miles away from Stratford, ready to defend America.

At 5:00 a.m., 200 men wait for Vega's command to attack Stratford. Seconds later: "The army will ADVANCE!" he shouts. They move out quickly and divide into two columns—Vega's men ride to the south and Venada's men ride to the north.

At full gallop, the divergent commands move toward Stratford from two directions. Vega points to a washed-out mining road and shouts his orders to the detachment. The students, led by José Cardinales, move nervously in their saddles. They negotiate through the road and toward the mine eager to engage in mineral exploration.

Vega reins his horse toward the town and the students reach and enter the mine. They will determine the magnitude and value of the ore—and must do so in a hurry. Twenty men form a defensive line at the mine entrance. Vega's horse pounds the road sensing the urgency. Riding low in the saddle, he continues to town with most of his command. At the same time, Venada's men enter from the north; now raiders are sweeping into town from both directions and catching everyone off guard.

"Viva Zapata," many raiders yell from the saddle while spraying bullets.

Cardinales and the other students move deeper in the mine and find sacks of gold ore, a basic forge, ore crusher and crudely-smelted gold bars. They fervidly begin digging and collect hard rock samples; then rumbling sounds force the students to stop working. Rocks and dust fall all around; coughing and confused the students turn toward the entrance.

A second rumbling causes them to seek cover in fear of a ceiling cave-in, but no shelter can be found as more rocks and dust fill the space. Abruptly, another rumbling forces the students down then a sound of the ceiling caving-in. Cardinales shakes his head, now disoriented, and rises to his knees in the near pitch black. He makes it to his feet and the students follow as less debris falls.

The students continue the mission, despite the danger. There is another rumbling ahead that crumbles a rock wall; the dust settles and the area brightens espousing a startling sight: *"Ay, Dios mio,"* Cardinales whispers.

Vega's men advance onto Main Street, some splash kerosene on buildings and put them to the torch. Mexican fighters fire their guns, set off explosions and burn several houses including the general store; the blaze illuminates the pre-dawn showing men and riderless horses running in all directions. The shooting and shouting increase as does the general confusion of the people in town. Yet, the townspeople quickly respond with Springfield rifles and shotguns running to secure points. Darkness makes finding targets difficult for the defenders while the attackers wound several defenders.

In Silver City, Captain Reed signals the troopers. The cavalrymen, who wear flat-brimmed campaign hats, khaki and olive drab breeches, shirts and puttees, move out in a hurry. Almost 200 strong soldiers on tough government horses rush to town.

"Secure the superintendent's office," Venada commands as they draw near. Other Stratford men take positions near the Avon and give enough fire to hold off the attackers from entering the office. More residents hurry outside seeking defensive locations. Others form a barricade across Main Street blocking the invaders from entering the superintendent's office. The defenders make every shot count and put up a persistent fight. Yet, the invaders are not discouraged and overrun the defense with sheer numbers.

Venada's men capture almost every file and every paper in the superintendent's office as Vega's men reach the Avon Hotel and join the fight. They immediately withdraw and ride hard through the town. The raiders begin to loot the town, capturing rifles, supplies and equipment. The coming daylight increases the accuracy of the defenders who now have a clear field of fire to target the invaders.

In the distance, the blaring sound of the bugle is heard over the chaos. With red-over-white guidons whipping in the wind, they dash to the sounds of the heaviest firing. The neatly dressed columns of disciplined, well-armed, U.S. soldiers charge into Stratford.

In the diffused morning light, regimental pennants show the number six of the U.S. 6th Cavalry. The thunder of galloping horses enters town with a large cloud of dust in their wake. The U.S. cavalrymen attract everyone in town; they are a welcomed sight for the besieged citizens, but not for the Mexicans. Everyone on Avon Street watches the cavalrymen stream forward and stop at Captain Reed's command. They regroup and then he shouts a command, "Charge!"

Reed and his troopers charge into town with guns blazing, hitting the raiders with almost every shot; the outnumbered men return fire with little effect. Vega sees the size of the army; he orders a retreat. Just before leaving town, Venada drops the pouch. Vega's full command rides south with the troopers in pursuit.

The cavalrymen shoot from the saddle and ride after the retreating invaders. The Mexican rear guard turns and opens fire at close range. The exposed but well-disciplined troopers drive back the rear guard and continue the pursuit. The charging cavalry exacts heavy losses on the retreating Mexicans with no Americans down.

Out of town, past the gold mine and in the open, the troopers fight another rear-guard action. The troopers smash through and chase the raiders south. After a mile south, the firing diminishes and stops. Reed commands the troopers to return to Stratford, convinced that the invaders would not come again.

The U.S. cavalrymen turn their mounts and retrace the trail to town—a trail that contains scores of dead men. In town, more raiders lay writhing and dying along with dozens of wounded civilians, some shot dead.

The military mission ends in defeat for Vega. Many of his men are dead and strewn about the streets of Stratford. It is a military rout but a political victory: Huerta will have the documents needed to assess the viability of the German plan while Zapata is blamed for the invasion.

CHAPTER 46

EPIC LOVE

C entori sits comfortably in the library with an unlighted cigar and Jennifer's company. He is in blue jeans, wool socks and a gray long sleeve undershirt. She sits a few feet away seductively wrapped in an Indian blanket. The passionate heat that has passed between them is gone, but an affectionate atmosphere continues. It seems quite right that they sit alone in the Circle C waiting for sunrise.

Then he becomes distracted with thoughts of another woman, *Jennifer can change my future, but she cannot change my past.* He forces himself to think of Jennifer and all of the beauty that is under the blanket. At that moment, he recalls her words, *she became very fond of tequila over the past year, but she has been in New Mexico far less than a year.* She interrupts the troubling thought. "Your Circle C is a haven of righteous simplicity."

He leans back in the big leather chair, "Not sure what that means, but I will take it as a compliment."

"As it was intended; in your wonderful Circle C, physical love can transcend to pure spiritual love, as I expected."

"Another compliment?"

"Of course. I can also compliment your curious love-making manner."

"Curious?"

"Yes, as if you had something against using your bed—or perhaps the bed was occupied."

"Sometimes passion cannot wait," he deflects.

"Hmm, more likely your past has altered the course of things."

"Not sure what that means, either. I am happy to invite you to my bed."

"Are you?"

"Yes, of course."

The loosely wrapped blanket reveals more flesh. "Yet we are here in your library."

"Jennifer, I am learning that you like to quarrel. What happened to a fresh start?""

"I am merely observing, so I can make confident judgments about you. I am learning that you are unsure about me."

"Well, if I am, it is with good reason."

"I see, have I not told you my story? Have I not explained?"

"You told me a story, yes."

"So you don't believe me." Her eyes close then open and she stares up at the ceiling.

"Are you a woman I can trust?" he said unemotionally.

She opens the blanket to reveal her naked body. "I have trusted you with all of me."

"Have you told me everything? Can you tell me everything?"

"You believed me enough to love me! Ha, but not enough to take me to your bed. The way you made love to me—in that unusual way. I never felt that way while standing up."

They both express amusement for a moment. "Adobe, I wish not to quarrel. Rather, to convince you that we should not live our lives to protect the past if it prevents the future."

"Our most recent past was not prevented. This very night contradicts your point."

She looks away at the speed of light then faces him just as fast. "Yes, we were intimate. Yet, I sensed a certain distance; a barrier between us. May I be frank with you?"

"You haven't been all along?"

Silent for a moment, she bites her lower lip. "Not loving me in your bed is more significant than you are willing to make known."

"You think so?"

"Yes, I do. I also think that the sources of your wealth are apparent, but you have barren riches and lack a marriage."

"Wait a minute, we all make choices," he says with a nervous smile.

"You may have had the inclination if not the talents for a successful choice and now you wonder about past decisions."

"Okay, Jennifer, it's too late for you to return home. You should stay here."

She rises up to her bare feet, causing the blanket to fall open as she yells, "I can make that choice on my own."

Naked, she brazenly walks toward him making every attempt to celebrate her body, "Perhaps I will stay."

"I hope you stay. In this light, in this room, you look amazingly beautiful."

"You certainly like to pressure a lady. That would have been better said last night, if we were in your bed."

"I suppose that is fair."

Before he can react, she covers herself, sits down and reveals another thought, "Love can induce a man to act foolishly and to build castles in the air."

"What's that?"

"I think you know what I am talking about." She stops, and then offers shocking words. "Did you make the right choice at Chaco Canyon?"

"What!? Who the hell are you?" *How could she possibly know about Chaco Canyon?* "What are you talking about?"

"Your guilt about the Revert Document and how it has filled you with despair."

"You are mad."

"And you know much about the whole affair."

"No, I try to stay away from government affairs. I asked you a question."

"I am a newspaper woman," she says with a stubborn mien. "Don't bother to deny."

"Ha, do you really own the *Valtura Journal*?"

No answer.

"Why do you mention Chaco?"

"You were there at a pivotal moment in time."

"And why do you think this?"

No answer.

"Be careful about speaking impulsively about my life, Jennifer."

"Impulsive, but not without consideration," she says with an insolent tone.

"Why so angry? Is there more at stake than your misinformed notion of my sorrowful personal affairs?"

"Don't you see that the Revert Document protects your past? You use the document as a flag of convenience."

"Forget that past. I am saying *today* that I want you; the rest does not matter. Don't you believe me?"

"I believe you mean it at the moment you say it—and only then. I fled my husband's hell, so I am careful about giving my heart."

"Hell, you say? Do you have any idea what happened in Chaco Canyon?"

"So you were there—with the Revert Document."

In check, he shouts, "Damn you. You are especially equipped to turn a conversation toward yourself."

"Adobe, I am with you now. That it is all the more reason to bury the past—and that symbolic document. You told me because you want to be free; that is my point."

"I am not sure what your point is."

"Make no mistake, Adobe, we both look out for number one, at least I am willing to admit it—but this does not preclude us from happiness."

No answer.

"I can see it in your face; you want to talk. Why do you resist?" Seeing his distress, she stops. "I am sure we can resolve this."

"Resolve what? And how do you know so much about Chaco?"

"I am not aware of the entire situation."

"Okay, Jennifer, you seem to know enough about that day, so you should know the document was destroyed."

"Is it really destroyed? Or do you keep it to keep her alive."

"Damn you! Why are you so interested in the document anyway?"

"Once you free yourself of the burden, you can completely join me and find true comfort in my arms. What's more, I am convinced you will then trust me and stop the incessant interrogation."

"Why are you so sure?"

"A man can have only one epic love of a lifetime."

CHAPTER 47

HIGH GRADE

President Huerta nervously paces in his *Palacio Nacional* office waiting for Professor Salazar. The morning visit from General Vega provided a mixed report. The U.S. Army's counter attack was a defeat for Vega's men, but the Americans have blamed Zapatista revolutionaries for the Stratford raid.

The documents stolen from Stratford and the hard rock ore were sent to Salazar for examination and assessment. Although Salazar is not late, the president remains anxious.

"President Huerta, it is a pleasure to see you again," Salazar.

"Professor Salazar, thank you for returning to the *Zocalo*. Please send my personal regards to your students."

"You are most welcome. President Huerta, we examined all the papers that you have obtained. The documents are remarkable."

"What do you mean?"

"First, if I may say so, remarkable that you had acquired them and remarkable that the Stratford strike is indeed rich. The mining papers and hard rock samples reveal that Stratford's gold mine contains high grade ore."

"The gold content is significant?"

"Highly significant—the amount of pure gold to the ton is astonishing."

"You can provide reliable estimates as to the deposit's value?"

"With confidence, we can provide estimates only."

"Yes, of course, but before you answer, remember I will be counting on your estimates. To what level is the deposit's value?"

"An extremely high level," Salazar states.

"As rich as the California strike?"

"I don't know, but it could be the biggest strike in U.S. history."

"Let's say in the history of North America. Please sit down, Professor. How can you be sure of such a bold statement?"

"Our students discovered what the Americans would have eventually found—the mother lode. There is much gold in Stratford, of this my students are sure. It is only a matter of time before this is widely known."

So Riesenfelder is correct. The discovery could be greater than the California gold strike. Huerta thinks and then says, "Thank you, professor, you must excuse me now."

"Of course."

"You and your students will be remembered for their help."

Two heavy doors open and the president's assistant escorts Salazar down a wide corridor. He promptly returns to the office and finds Huerta writing a note.

"Take this message to Count Helmut von Riesenfelder. After he reads it, return immediately to burn it in this fireplace. Do you understand?"

"Perfectly."

CHAPTER 48

LADY GODIVA

Jennifer and Adobe sit quietly in the Circle C library. The silence is deafening and seems interminable. A coyote cry breaks the tension and prompts her to say, "There seems to be some misunderstanding. Adobe, a ghost prevents us from fully realizing our romance and when I was not allowed in your bed—it hurt. You must destroy the document; only then you can bury the past. Do it for her."

"Do it for whom?"

"Gabriella, she wanted it for Mexico's history and culture. It was her last wish before you killed that Cuban woman."

"What? I did not kill her!"

"I don't believe you."

"It was an accident!"

"What's the difference; she is dead and you still have what she wanted. Fulfill her last wish and free yourself of the guilt."

The grief of Gabriella registers on his face. "Do not mistake regret for guilt."

"Do you regret cheating Mexico out of the border territories?"

"You are not interested in history or culture—just power. I am getting weary of this; I told you the paper was destroyed. Burned at Chaco Canyon," he could not be more unconvincing.

"I understand," she lies. "Destroy it in your own time."

He reluctantly nods. It is the wrong response.

"I will get dressed now," she teases with eyes and smile.

"No need for that; you look great."

"You would have me return to Valtura as Lady Godiva?"

"Why go at all?"

"Things start early at the *Valtura Journal* and, besides, I will not insist on using your bed this time."

Jennifer stands, drops the blanket to the floor and poses in her naked glory. Sexuality pours from her as she declares, "Did she look this good? Face it, Adobe, the queen is dead, long live the queen."

Alone in the library, Centori's sensual and survival instincts are in conflict. The internal struggle rages as he waits for Jennifer. At the desk, several minutes pass, hoping that she would return soon. He leans forward in his chair and considers the Revert Document, believing the delay tactic places her in check. It is a fateful decision that he will live to regret.

Jennifer returns fully dressed. "I will be leaving now. You should not delay this, the sooner the better. Will you do it now?"

"No." The answer is emphatic.

"I must ask you again. Will you destroy the barrier between us?"

"I will destroy the document in my own time."

"No, you must do it now."

"All of your beauty, all your loveliness, all of your fondness of a lover is pierced by your demand to destroy a piece a paper. I will do it my way. Is that clear? Because if it isn't, have someone else draw you a picture. I haven't got the time."

"I need the document now," she reveals.

"You need it?" His tone is hard. "Look, I did not like those who pursued it last year, and I am beginning not to like you very much either. What about putting my past behind me?"

"I mean we need it to…"

"Stop!" He draws closer, "I know, destroying the document will stop my bad memories."

Jennifer stares at him a moment and surveys the room as though looking for the document. Then she straightens her spine and says, "If I do not get that document, I will be killed!" she screams.

"How can I believe you?"

"Because it is true."

"Tell me what you know and why you are pressing the issue."

"It may be connected to those who know about dark theories of history."

"So that's it; are you working under orders from Germany. Your friends in Berlin will give you only information that promotes their interests."

"Such probing can be dangerous for you. You should believe me."

"Any dark theories are an illusion. You are under a spell of belief, or are you just following orders?"

"Spell of belief, ha, coming from you that is interesting. I fear for your sanity; you need the document for its own sake, as a source of power."

"You are misinformed; the document is worthless. Your friends are a little late. New Mexico is an American state."

"Just the same, let me worry about that. Now give me the Revert Document."

"It will be of no practical use to Germany, Mexico or any other nation."

"Don't you understand, if I don't produce the document, I am a dead woman. They will probably kill you on general principle."

"You said you were leaving," he coldly states.

He freezes; the woman he thinks he loves draws a pistol. "I am sorry for this, but I must have the document. Give it to me," she demands.

CHAPTER 49

AGENT PROVOCATEUR

The flash in Jennifer' face is sinister. Disbelief fills Centori's eyes and a sense of danger fills his head. Then crushing disappointment runs through his body.

"Why so shocked? You have been suspicious since I returned."

Looking down the barrel of her gun he says, "Mady was right; I am a fool about you. You are right, too, this is no moment of realization."

Resolutely, he shakes off the stress, "The height of your beauty is exceeded by the depth of your duplicity. I pointed my heart at you and you point a gun at my heart."

Her voice reveals the pressure she feels, "Ironic, but the world is full of folly and danger."

"And disappointment. Why do you need the document?"

"Nothing happens for one reason; the world is filled with chain reactions."

He swears under his breath and meets her eyes, "Betrayal is the only reason, and we add it to your list."

She feels her gun hand shudder. "I kept my word by not giving my word."

"Nice talk, darlin'; I trusted you, based on actions, not words."

"Liar, you never trusted me. Who is being betrayed now?"

"And what does that tell you?"

Jennifer appears more apprehensive than angry eliciting his empathy, "It tells me I will have no regrets."

"None at all? You amaze me. This illustrates your character, your poor state of mind and the immorality that characterizes your ways."

"Stop wasting time; stop stalling."

"Indeed, we have wasted time. You were doubtful all along, now your nature becomes inescapable."

"Give me the document!" she yells.

"First, you fall into my arms, and then you rave like a lunatic. Jennifer, you are going to rot in Hell for this play."

"I was born in Hell and I like it there," she vehemently replies. "Now, give it to me!"

"Do I appear to have lost my senses? Why would I give it to you?"

"This gun pointed at your chest."

"Jennifer, put the gun down. I will do it for you despite your motives; perhaps it will ease your obsession. The document would be useless to Germany anyway. I am with you now—that trumps the past."

She eases the pressure on the trigger. "It would not be in your interest to cross me."

"Unlike you, I am unfamiliar with treachery."

Centori reaches in his desk for the old water-damaged government document. "Here, it has caused enough trouble. I am glad to be rid of it, relieved in fact."

She drops her guard for a second. "I tried my best to love you, Jennifer. Consider this my last gesture of love."

"I am sorry for this, Adobe."

"Your qualities prevent remorse."

"That is not true."

"You have chosen the fatherland over me—that is an undeniable truth."

His perceived capitulation distracts her and the weight of the gun causes the weapon in her hand to drop several inches. Centori pounces like a mountain lion slapping the gun away with one hand, and pushing her down with the other.

He stands over her, looking down in disgust. She looks up, "Is this how a brave war hero treats a woman?"

"You threatened my life, so I would thank you not to comment."

"And you embrace violence against me; your truth is revealed. You are no gentleman."

"You are right. When any living creature threatens my life, I am no gentleman."

He helps her to stand up, "You think yourself strong and special, with inconspicuous superiority, but you are poisoned and bitter about the past, and your judgment of women has shown to be irregular and now aggressive."

"Stop talking. You don't give a damn about me and you have underestimated what the document means to the outside world."

"Perhaps, but to you it is an object of beauty, from an art museum or a precious jewel of your discontent."

"As far as you are concerned, the Revert Document affair is over."

"It continues because you risk yourself for some imperiled cause."

"I said it is over and so is our time together. You took advantage my affections. Your love was filled with cunning."

"If you think so, you are at liberty to leave me."

She steps forward and he demands, "Stay where you are." He opens the bottom drawer, moves Gabriella's photo aside and holds up the old government paper. Reaching for matches, he says, "I should have done this a long time ago."

He moves toward the fireplace, "It will be reduced to ashes—ruined just like our romance."

She turns and looks at the gun that was slapped away. "Don't do it, Jennifer. I will look the other way about that gun."

Even with a disheveled appearance, Jennifer remains beautiful in face and figure, a Venus who implores, "Don't burn it!" she screams.

"Mady said a greater fool than Adobe Centori had never breathed the breath of life. You took me for a fool."

"I had much to work with," she shouts.

"Perhaps that's true, but you must leave Valtura. Start with the Circle C. Leave that pistol on the floor. Take your treachery—and your broomstick."

"Damn you."

"No need to swear, no need for any words at all." He sets a paper on fire and tosses it into the fireplace.

"Damn you! You just killed me—you must like killing women!" She screams as the paper burns.

In a fit of rage, he jumps forward, grabs her shoulders and yells, "GET OUT!"

Jennifer Prower, an agent provocateur, leaves the Circle C without turning back. Centori stares into the fireplace and watches the telegram he received in New York from Jennifer disintegrate.

CHAPTER 50

ALL THAT GLITTERS

The geology reports from Stratford confirm Riesenfelder's assertion about the gold strike. Once again, it is alleged that the Americans have committed monumental theft against the Mexican people—the Stratford gold discovery occurred while New Mexico was part of Mexico.

President Huerta sent an urgent request to see Riesenfelder. The same day, he answers the request, eager to see Huerta. Instead of meeting at the palace, they will meet at *Castillo de Chapultepec*.

The castle, over 7,500 above sea level and on a sacred Aztec site, is a museum of Mexican history. Huerta, dressed down in disguise, hopes to make his own Mexican history. Riesenfelder rendezvous with him in a garden area that has an observatory, hoping not to be observed.

"Good day," Huerta says, before getting to the point, "I am ready to accept your proposal to take our case to the international court."

"Excellent."

"One factor remains. Have you recovered the document?"

CHAPTER 51

VENUS WANING

J ennifer stands passively at the front windows of her Victorian house on East Corona Street. The game is up; Centori could not be turned. In the end, his foolishness contained limitations, preventing her from pushing beyond what he perceived as justified.

She is in a contemplative mood as a light wind rattles the curtains, then blows her lavish reddish hair around her shoulders. The desert air is scented with sagebrush and wildflowers and the sky is entirely painted. She touches her choker, watches the deserted street and questions her political values and convictions. She is attracted to Centori; the westerner in a remote place who is strangely familiar to her. A loud knock on the front door startles Jennifer. She runs to answer; she expects to see Centori. It is Bernhard Bachmeier.

After the visit, Jennifer considers her next move. *A letter to him could work.* Jennifer goes to her notepaper and thinks for a moment before penning a note:

Dear Adobe,

I hope this finds you well and as happy as possible. Much has happened between us in a short period of time. Some of what occurred was expected and much unexpected. Mistakes were made, perhaps by both of us. Folly prevailed over fortitude; madness over empathy. I offer you a few words for what they are worth in your heart and mind.

You will notice that the gun I left behind was not loaded. Yet, it did have the intended impact without placing you in danger; I could never come to harm you in any way.

I wish to have more than memories about the times we were together sharing great passion. I know we have made each other happy; kissing, holding and loving. Please take this note as a declaration of regret and of my sincere wish to see you again. Let the world be damned. We can steal away from the political madness and...

Jennifer abruptly stops writing. She knows that the letter is useless. Whether real or fake, remorse will not work; Venus of Valtura has failed.

There is no future between them; she rips the unfinished letter two times and drops it in a basket. There is one last card to play. Jennifer will leave Valtura, but not before she places certain actions in motion. Shakespeare said, 'To thine own self be true.'

CHAPTER 52

RUSTLER'S MOON

I t is a rustler's moon over the Circle C Ranch tonight, enough light for Centori to read outside. Yet, he sits in the library reading the *Valtura Journal*. The frantic farewell confrontation with Jennifer has occupied him for the last few days.

He puts the newspaper down, picks up a Cuban cigar and ruminates over what he knows of Jennifer. *She has not published the Cicero letter. She did not obtain the Revert Document but has confirmed its location. Her relationship with Germany is probably ruined and she could be in danger. She should think about packing her bags and leaving Valtura. I should think about my trip to New York.* There are things that he does not know about her. Jennifer receives German funds that are channeled to agents in New York and to American Scream.

A.P. and a few cowboys, including Pedro Quesada and the recently hired Henry Parker, are sitting down to play cards in the bunkhouse. Francisco Greigos and most of the other ranch hands are in Mad Mady's Saloon—and under surveillance.

A.P. lights his cigar and starts to deal when Parker says, "High card deals, right Mr. Baker?"

"Ha, you are right Henry."

In rotation, each player takes a card off the top of the deck: jack, deuce, queen; A.P. draws the ace of spades.

"This could be your lucky night, Mr. Baker," Parkers smiles.

"We'll see, Henry," he replies through a whirl of cigar smoke.

A.P. shuffles and says to the cowboy on his right, "Cut the cards."

With a quick snap, A.P. sends the cards across the table, dealing out five to each player.

"Open for two dollars, Parker says."

"Out."

"Out."

"Call and raise two," A.P. answers.

"Sure that isn't more than you can handle, Mr. Baker?"

"Ha, don't worry Henry; bet them if you have them. How many?"

"I'll take two."

Before A.P. can deal the two cards, abrupt coyote cries cause him to turn. Back in the house, the yelps cause Centori to become uneasy. The coyotes are especially plaintive tonight, somewhat disturbing and definitely distracting. In the deepest part of his being he feels that things are not right. *Something is wrong, very wrong.*

Centori walks to the desk and pulls out a sepia photograph of Gabriella. It is the only photo of her in his possession, taken years before in Cuba. He places the photograph on the desk and opens an old brown envelope containing the Revert Document. His silhouette is visible from outside and framed in the window. The photograph drifts to the floor for no apparent reason. Startled, he bends down to retrieve Gabriella's image. The next second a hail of gun fire rips through the window destroying the glass, sending a shower of fragments across the library, tearing into the books and smashing into the shelves.

He crashes into a reading table sending objects flying. He hits the hard floor, spreads as flat as possible, bracing against another fire storm. A second hail storm of hot lead goes through the shattered window frame. He crawls toward the library door moving as fast as possible, minimizing his body as a target. Moving quickly he reaches up for his .36 caliber Navy Colt revolver. Then, the sound of a shootout is magnified in the still night driving the coyotes into a high-pitched frenzy.

Centori bursts out the front door with his revolver drawn ready to join the battle. With menace in the air, he runs to the sound of gunfire and to engage in the fight. He moves like a predator ready to fire the Colt. In seconds flat, A.P., three cowboys and five strangers come into view. Facing each other, the Circle C men and the strangers stand in the open, six-shooters blazing at close-range with equal speed and determination. Deafening noise and a ferocious fusillade fill the air; bullets slam against the outside library walls.

Two strangers fall, one dead instantly, one badly wounded and dying. A.P.—a pistol in each hand—is hit but stays up and continues firing. Despite his wound, he holds his ground and empties his gun. Quesada is hit in the chest and falls dead. Centori fires hitting another stranger in the front, the man stumbles back then sinks to the ground dead. The other two cowboys hit targets: four strangers down. The fifth stranger staggers toward Centori who quickly aims—the stranger falls dead at his feet before he can fire. The gunfire stops. It is over as fast as it began.

Then silence comes; it does not last long. Coyote calls shatter the stillness again while Centori, revolver still drawn, scans for further danger. Exhausted from the adrenaline expenditure, he inhales deeply and calms himself, preparing for more trouble. He checks the three strangers—all dead. He checks Quesada; no vital signs, then he sees A.P. on the ground.

Nausea shocks his stomach; air surges in and out of his lungs. "A.P.?"

"I think I am done for, Adobe."

Turning to the new cowboy, Centori demands, "What's your name son?"

"Henry Parker, Mr. Centori."

"Go into the house and call Doc, then take the fastest horse to town and find Francisco and the men, probably at Mad Mady's. Get them back to Circle C."

The new ranch hand freezes.

"Move it," he screams.

Parker runs to the house.

"It is too late, Boss. I know it, Henry knows it."

"Hold on, A.P."

Centori races into the house for towels and returns in seconds flat. Then he places a crumpled towel under A.P.'s head. Applying first aid training he learned in Cuba, he treats the chest wound.

"Who the hell were those men?" A.P. whispers.

"They were here for me, not you. This is my fault, A.P."

"Your war is my war, always been that way."

"Just the same, it's my fault."

"It has been an honor to know you, to work and live here at the Circle C."

"A.P."

"It's okay; I had more time than most men."

He ignores the comment and continues to apply pressure, "Save your breath."

"Wish we could have one more roundup together; guess I had my last one."

A.P. slowly and painfully raises his right hand, Centori takes it as the Circle C foreman gasps out his last breath, "Take good care, Pard. Keep a sharp eye; more trouble coming."

A.P. Baker is no more.

"NOOO!" With his knees and palms on the ground, Centori wails from the depths. The coyotes respond in kind, howling and echoing the pain that flows from him. Then a rare nighttime wind blows through the apocalyptic scene. A paper is extracted by the wind from a dead stranger's pocket. It blows into Centori's chest. The writing is in German.

His face freezes in grief and rage; mouth wide open, hands trembling at his ears—a silent scream. The other surviving cowboy runs toward him and screams, "Mr. Centori, Mr. Centori!"

⌒⋞⊙⌐⊃

Once again tragedy, not deliverance, calls. This time a field of dead men, including a good friend and great cowboy, are left in its path. A rustler's moon *and* an unlucky star were over the Circle C tonight. The only road to redemption, atoning for his part in the deaths of Gabriella, Charity—and now A.P., leads to New York.

CHAPTER 53

DARK AND DANGEROUS

All through the night, the Circle C cowboys took turns on guard duty; three men rode a perimeter around the house. When Francisco returned from Valtura, he quickly engaged the cowboys to cover the bodies of A.P. and Quesada and bring them into the bunk house. They dragged the attackers to the back of the bunk house, outside in the dust.

At first light with no sleep, Centori checks his Winchester and slides it back into the saddle holster and pats down Patriot. Slightly shaking with rage, he checks his Navy Colt, slides it back into his gun belt holster.

Francisco approaches, "All secure, nothing unusual during the night. I don't know if this is over or not."

"We will not let our guard down yet. Francisco, you are running Circle C now. You are the new foreman. Is that okay with you?"

"Yes, I will do my best."

"I know that is true."

"Thank you for your confidence."

"That's easy. I am going into town; I'll be back as soon as I can."

Centori mounts Patriot and prompts the stallion into a dead run. He knows the lay of the land well: every short cut and all possible ambush points. His acute awareness is put into play.

Although the handwritten note is in German, it is not hard evidence against Jennifer. It was unsigned; the few words indicated date and time. Nevertheless, Centori cannot discount her connection to the murder of A.P. and Quesada.

After sunrise and with Valtura in sight, Centori gently pulls back on the reins. He enters town and shifts his weight in the saddle. Then he rides directly to the house on East Corona Street and signals, "Whoa."

The front gate is unlocked and ajar. He ties Patriot to a cottonwood, runs to the front door and doesn't bother to knock; he kicks open the door with gun drawn. There is no one in the house. The parlor seems dark and dangerous. With his Navy Colt at the ready he enters the bedroom. An inspection of her bedroom shows that Jennifer left in a hurry. She is gone.

He holsters his gun and looks around. There are a few papers scattered in her closet, perhaps left in haste or perhaps on purpose. He gathers the papers, returns to the parlor, scans the room and sees the front door damage. *I am sorry for that, Colonel.*

Before leaving the house, he pours a drink to calm down. Outside, he stuffs the papers in his saddle bag, swings back on Patriot and heads to Mad Mady's Saloon.

Chapter 54

Dead Sure

Centori walks into Mad Mady's Saloon with dust and sweat and an air of maelstrom and tragedy surrounding him. Mady hurries across the large barroom the moment she sees him.

"Adobe! What happened last night?"

"Good morning, Mady."

"After the young cowboy rushed in here for Francisco and the other men, I didn't know what to think. What's going on?"

"Sit down," he says and she gulps.

"Just tell me what happened." Mady nervously demands.

"There was a gunfight at the Circle C last night."

Mady mutters, "Oh, no."

Centori begins to tell her about the shootout. He speaks in a matter of fact way—detached as if the gunfight happened to someone else or he was a witness reporting the event objectively. However, when the story turns to A.P. Baker, his eyes fill.

"It's A.P. and Quesada; bad news."

"How bad?" she finds her seat.

"Very bad. Both were killed last night."

"Oh my goodness," she grabs his hand.

He closes his eyes and rubs his face, "It was entirely my fault. Five bad cases fired into the library, hoping to kill me."

"Kill you? Why?"

"I believe they were after the Revert Document."

"That cursed paper again? I thought that was settled last year."

"So did I."

"What happened?"

"There was an assassination attempt on me. They fired through the window; somehow they missed. A.P. and the boys heard the shots and came out firing. Then I joined the fight."

"Who were the men?"

"A better question is who they represent."

"I am confused."

"Mady, there are few pieces to the puzzle that elude me. There seems to be a link between the document and Jennifer," he understates.

"Did you confront her?

"I tried to; I just came from her house."

"What happened to Jennifer?" Mady asks.

"Jennifer Prower is in the wind."

She understands at once, but she will not hit him when he is down.

"Mady."

"Yes."

"Quesada was a good cowboy; he was too young, A.P. was a good friend and, as a cowboy, none better."

"I know…I know."

"Look, I have some accountability to the county. I should get to my office."

"Let me know if you need anything."

It is close to midnight on Santos Square. Mady is concerned enough to watch Centori's office from outside her place. She notices the lights are on in the sheriff's office and decides to walk across the square. As she passes the closed newspaper office, she flashes a disapproving look.

Mady enters the office without knocking: "It is unusual for you to work this late. Are you are okay?"

"Since the shootout and killing of A.P., no, but now I'm starting to..." A moment later he says, "Mady, you should know something."

"What is it?"

"I am going back to New York."

"What for?"

"First, to meet Murph; he will arrive in New York from Washington."

"I hope this is not true."

He nods in the affirmative."

"And then?"

"I intend to find Charity's killers."

"The woman killed at the Wall Street explosion?"

"That's right."

"Are you sure about this?"

"Dead sure."

"I know that when you make a decision...it is plain to see you should take time at the Circle C. A.P.'s violent death hit you hard."

"I intend to find Charity's killers first."

"You should wait before going to New York, if you go at all."

After a long pause he says, "You must not tell anyone. One of the attackers was carrying a note written in German."

"What did the note say?"

"Nothing conclusive except it could indicate a connection to a German network of agents."

"Don't those guys ever stop? Now you are fighting Germans?"

"I said I will find Charity's killers; I will go wherever that takes me."

"You narrowly survived the shootout."

"At least the physical kind," he laments.

"Stay here with me for a while."

Poignantly, he says, "Mady, your concern always has been a part of our turbulent friendship. I appreciate that, but I am going to New York."

Accepting his position she asks, "You said a piece of the puzzle is missing. Could Jennifer be the missing piece?"

"Yes."

"I am not happy about being right."

Classy enough not to say the obvious, he just looks at her.

"I guess you can forget about her now."

"I have given up on her; half memories will stay with me."

"Really, how do you not hate her?"

"I thought she was someone else. In the end I was blind to the Marshall Swindle."

"What?"

"In chess, Frank Marshall allowed his queen to be captured, then won the game in a few moves, a trick. Jennifer appeared to stand down before she pulled out her gun."

"I see. Be careful in New York."

With a certain Spartan reserve, he replies, "I intend to do so; I never thought she was out for blood."

"I may have a small piece of the puzzle myself."

Centori stares and waits. "Felicity never showed today; she is gone with bag and baggage and without a word."

"Is that right? Any ideas?"

"No. She is, as you say, in the wind."

CHAPTER 55

COME HELL OR HIGH WATER

The aftermath of the shootout was traumatic for all Circle C cowboys. For Centori, saying farewell to A.P. Baker racked him with physical pain. Now the time is near for him to return to New York. He received a response from Murphy and arrangements are in place.

Packing his bags, he remembers the papers from Jennifer's house and dashes to his saddle bag. In the horse barn, he reads the papers to his bewilderment. *How could this be? This is crazy; we are almost 2,000 miles from Wall Street.* He re-reads the title of the pamphlet, *Amerikanischen Schrei.*

On the last night at the Circle C, he paces the floor of the library. Boarded windows have replaced the shattered glass; bullet holes are visible on the expanse of the bookcases. He stops intermittently to look out the window at the shootout scene—with a feeling of dread.

She is connected to the organization that bombed Wall Street. That is astonishing, but I believe it to be true.

Restless, he moves outside and sits facing the Sandia Mountains in the night; his mood is gloomy. He had attended to all of the ranch affairs including the impending roundup; the Circle C will be in good hands with the new foreman, Francisco Greigos. Nothing left to do but leave New Mexico and return to New York.

❧

At sunrise, Centori stands in the library, surveying the destruction. Then as he examines his desk, Greigos walks in to talk business.

"Good morning," Centori says while shuffling papers on his desk. "I am happy you will run the ranch while I am gone."

"I am honored to do so. I wish you luck in New York; may God be with you."

"Thank you, my Navy Colt will be with me, too."

"Yes, of course. That is good."

"Good luck with the roundup."

"It will not be so easy now, but we have good men to see it through."

"We have a good new leader too," Centori nods.

Greigos smiles, "We will all do our best."

❧

After discussing the roundup and other ranch business, Centroi reaches into his desk drawer and says, "I have one favor to ask of you."

"Yes, how can I help you?"

"This paper, bury it on Little Hill Top. If I do not return from New York, burn it and toss the ashes into the wind."

"You can burn it yourself when you return."

"Have a drink with me."

The new foreman says, "I will always have a drink with you."

"*Salud.*"

"*Salud.*"

The two men shake hands and grasp each other's shoulder.

"Farewell, Francisco."

"Adios, Adobe Centori."

Centori goes to the horse barn, walks down the sawdust and straw center lane and sees Patriot toss his head. He saddles up, mounts up and rides tall in the saddle. He takes his leave of the Circle C Ranch.

With the help of Murphy's comprehensive intelligence, he is confident of achieving success in New York. Francisco takes a shovel to the high point of the ranch and the first visible feature to appear at daybreak: Little Hill Top.

CHAPTER 56

CONTINENTAL DRIFT

Mexico City, the oldest capital city in the Americas, has been inhabited since the 14th century. Today the city has one less inhabitant. Count Helmut von Riesenfelder, the German ambassador to Mexico, said farewell to Mexico. His letter to the president begins:

Dear President Huerta:

For the last several months, I have had the honor of serving as Ambassador of Germany to Mexico. My short time here has included challenges and wonderful memories of the benevolence and hospitality of the Mexican people. I would like to express the happiness of the German people in establishing a strong partnership between our embassy and Mexico. Our embassy wishes to continually support a secure and prosperous Mexico.

The Revert Document affair was reopened in secrecy and it closed in secrecy. This strategy protected Riesenfelder and Huerta from the negative consequence of failure. In addition to his ambassador role, Riesenfelder was director of special operations in Mexico and intelligence liaison to the German Secret Service. Now that the Revert Document affair closed, he has been reassigned to New York and will become the director of operations in America: the top spymaster in the U.S.

The Andes, the longest mountain range in the world, extends through several South America countries. Professor Salazar and his four students will be studying geology further south in Argentina, Ecuador and Peru.

The new science of plate tectonics, that defines the Earth's extensive movement, will become the focus of their research. Salazar and his students will be well-compensated for studying the Earth's lithosphere and continental drift.

Moreover, they will study how plate motion causes earthquakes and volcanic activity. The assignment is likely to take several years.

CHAPTER 57

WATER UNDER THE BRIDGE

Few words are spoken between Adobe and Mady. With Jennifer gone, the chance to move closer dominates Mady's thoughts; but that chance may be slipping away. As they drive to the rail station in the Model T Ford, she becomes increasingly uncomfortable, consumed with the prospect of never being intimate with him, or never seeing him again. His last trip to New York was a retreat of sorts. This time, it will be a visit filled with danger, with his destiny in his own hands.

"Are you sure you will be able to drive this back to town?"

"Well, I will be more experienced once I return. Besides, I have Buster riding out with two horses if I am not back in a few hours."

They both grin and then fall back into the silence. Arriving at the station, she has a sense of apprehension. She realizes that his luck could run out in New York and wonders how many times he can narrowly escape death.

Stopping the Model T, Centori says, "You have been a good friend, Mady, ever since I arrived in Valtura. Did I say you are a fine looking woman?"

"I am sure you did not."

"Well, it is true."

"Thank you."

"I guess it's a long overdue compliment."

They step out of the Ford and he walks around to face her.

"The train should arrive soon, Mady."

"I know. I hope I am not being presumptuous, but would you like a goodbye kiss?"

"Yes, you are being presumptuous."

"Very funny," Mady playfully says with her hands resting on her hips.

Centori moves within inches of her; she stps forward and asks. "Do you have any objections?"

"No objections. I have long considered this."

"How many years have you contained this interest?"

"Probably since I arrived in Valtura."

Their bodies brush together. She reacts to the closeness. "Well?"

He smiles in response.

Mady declares, "It can be dangerous but you are no stranger to danger."

Adobe Centori kisses Mad Mady Blaylock for the first time. It is long overdue. She loops her arms around his neck. He touches the small of her back. They turn to the low sound of the approaching train in the distance and end the embrace; they stare at the train, separation minutes away. He steps back and, to her disappointment, pivots away from the moment. The train arrives at the flag stop huffing and puffing.

"This is it, Mady."

"Yes, last chance to come to your senses and stay...with me."

"Francisco Greigos is the new Circle C foreman."

The trainman exits from a railcar, separation seconds away. "When Francisco and the Circle C cowboys go to your place after the roundup, charge my account."

"Okay and the first round of drinks is on the house."

The train's whistle blows. Adobe looks into Mady's eyes, "Take care of yourself."

"Be careful in New York; stay close to Murph."

"Ha, or maybe he should stay close to me. Don't worry. I may be a fool about women but a sage about danger."

"I don't know about it, just come back to the sagebrush."

They embrace one last time and the whistle blows again. Centori climbs the first step of the railcar; before he takes the second step Mady calls, "Hey, Adobe Centori."

He turns, looks down and waits.

She smiles and shouts, "Give my regards to Broadway."

"I sure will, Mady. *Adios.*"

PART THREE

SABOTEUR

CHAPTER 58

❦

SAGAMORE: ALGONQUIN CHIEF

MAY 1912

N ative Americans called it *Paumonock*, the Dutch *Lange Eilandy* and the English *Long Island*. The 120-mile, fish-shaped island is the largest off the continental U.S. coast, with the Atlantic Ocean on the south and on the east coasts. The Long Island Sound is on the north shore and Manhattan Island is across the west shore. Near the north shore town of Oyster Bay is Sagamore Hill, home to former chief executive, Theodore Roosevelt.

In 1904, President Roosevelt promised not to run for a third term. Had he not promised this, he probably would have been reelected. Instead, William Taft became president in 1908. After a voter rebuke of the Republicans in the 1910 elections, Roosevelt became distant from his party. Unhappy with Taft's leadership in advancing his agenda, Roosevelt decided once again to become a presidential contender. He settled on Long Island in his country home preparing to regain the White House in the fall. This interval will continue for several weeks, leading up to the 1912 Republican National Convention in Chicago.

Roosevelt, the first American to win the Nobel Peace Prize, starts his peaceful day on the veranda breathing the cool air from the Long Island Sound. The grand porch under a grand green awning offers a wide view of the bay and of the sound. Roosevelt's mansion is perfectly situated on Sagamore Hill overlooking 100 acres of forest, tidal salt marsh and bay beach.

Near to the 23-room house, Mrs. Roosevelt maintains a large flower garden that shows her active interest in planting and in blooming of flowers. In the back of the house, there are fields of oats and timothy. Each night around 9:00 p.m., the estate is usually silent and calm; it is a time for Roosevelt to reflect on his special home becoming the summer White House again.

A high stone wall is between the Long Island Railroad station and Sagamore Hill with security men inside the gate. Although the public, including artists and newspaper cameramen, find it hard to get past the gate, John Murphy does not have that problem. Murphy and his associate Henry McGillivray approach in a black sedan motorcar. The two men are immediately confronted by security.

"John Murphy here to see Mr. Roosevelt," he declares.

"Yes, Sir, he is expecting you. Please leave your motorcar here and follow me."

McGillivray nods and Murphy walks toward the mansion with one of the security men. They enter a center hall with access to the dining room, kitchen, drawing room and the library.

"Mr. Roosevelt is waiting in the library."

"Thank you."

The potential presidential candidate is at a broad table with mail and morning newspapers arrayed. Standing near a shallow bay window, he reads through the headlines and frowns as Murphy is escorted into the well-furnished room.

"Mr. Murphy!"

"Mr. President."

"Welcome to Sagamore Hill! How is my favorite New Mexico ranger?"

"Just fine; how is my favorite president?"

"Fine, fine!"

"You have a beautiful place here."

"Thank you, John. My family is very happy here. We love the growing gardens and the blossom-spray of spring."

"Spring is a fine time of year."

"We are having a wonderful spring; seasons are spectacular here. We love winter with the snows and bare woods, the green dance of summer and the sharp fall winds."

"A place fit for a president!"

"A president without the White House is no president at all. As you know, I am hoping to return to Washington."

"You have my vote again."

"John, I thought you would like to ride a fine mount along the shaded roads of Sagamore Hill and through the quiet streets of Oyster Bay. You will find it a little different from the vast New Mexico mesas," he jokes.

"I have not been in a saddle since leaving Albuquerque."

"Given the Stratford raid, New Mexico could have used a good New Mexico ranger."

Murphy stares at Roosevelt.

"Yes, I read the report; the story will be in the newspapers soon," Roosevelt informs.

"You wish me to pursue Zapata?"

"No, an army expedition into Mexico already has begun; Taft made the decision after you left Washington."

"I see."

"Zapata will pay for his invasion of the U.S."

"It was a bold move on his part."

"It was a foolish move; Zapata and his men were routed."

"The raid shows a weakness in our southern border."

"Indeed it does. John, we have two new mounts; Audrey is a black mare and Roswell a bay hunter. Both were purchased in Virginia."

"That is fine horse country."

"Both horses are of strong action and spirit."

"It would be an honor to ride with you."

"Before we go…" He retrieves an envelope that lay on a tray and hands it to Murphy. "Please look at this."

Murphy slowly opens the envelope, removes the document and looks at Roosevelt. Then he reads the paper through once:

From: Washington (William H. Taft) May 1, 1912
To: New York (T. Roosevelt) # 027
Top Secret

Place John Murphy in full charge of directing
New York terror attack investigation.
He is to maintain close contact with our offices
to coordinate information gathering.
All offices are to offer all assistance available.
He is to travel wherever necessary to contact information officials.
He is to travel wherever necessary and to pursue this investigation.
Funds have been provided to assure freedom
of action in pursuing this work.
He is to enlist people and resources as necessary.
Investigation can be expanded to include all terror activities.
Pay attention to collecting intelligence material
under classification outlines in
Trans 22-4-12.

He reviews the document and in a clear voice says, "I understand."

"So, you accept?"

"Yes, Sir."

Murphy looks at the paper one more time before placing it into the envelope and then into his pocket.

"I knew you would. Although I had a falling out with Taft on some issues, we are working together on this attack. Of course, I plan to replace him."

"Of course."

"So, you will lead the federal investigation into the Wall Street bombing. The national implications are significant. Since Taft has endorsed my decision, you will have the full support of Washington."

"I will do my best, Mr. President."

"Of that I have no doubt, John. You did a good job with the Revert Document affair. Your reputation in Washington never has been better."

"Thank you, but I didn't work alone on that issue. My top secret report identified Adobe Centori as having a vital part in the affair."

"The New Mexican sheriff."

"Yes. He was with us in Cuba."

"A captain; I met him after San Juan Hill."

"Yes, and he deserves all the credit."

"You are a loyal friend to him. Unlike our time in Cuba, we are faced with a different enemy. McKinley's assassination may have been the action of one man, but it was symptomatic of a threat to our country. Since then, there have been other attacks, and too many railroad 'accidents' in this country."

"Now we have Wall Street."

"We will answer the terrible attack. When I was New York Police Commissioner," he pauses and redirects, "John, we are faced with an enemy within the U.S."

"That appears to be the case."

"As a boy I watched Lincoln's New York cortege from my window. I remember that he warned of such a destructive internal force."

"Yes, in his Lyceum address."

"Do you believe that democracy begets tyranny and in turn begets anarchy?"

"I would not like to think so, but anarchy can be a response to a failed democracy and to some a defense against tyranny."

"In any case, we must accept the fact that America is facing a new kind of threat—a different type of war."

"We will win that war," Murphy flatly states.

"Those who terrorized Wall Street must pay for their dreadful crimes," Roosevelt says with determination. "With you in charge of the investigation they *will* pay."

Murphy nods in the affirmative. Roosevelt, with a broad smile, offers, "Are you ready to ride?"

"Yes, Sir."

"I quite agree!"

Roosevelt has not come late to understanding the anarchist presence in the U.S. In 1901, Leon Czolgosz assassinated President McKinley in Buffalo, New York, propelling Vice President Roosevelt to the White House. Czolgosz, a former steel worker, became involved with the anarchist movement in America and President Roosevelt acknowledged the terrorist threat in the U.S. As a result, Congress passed immigration laws aimed at deporting anarchists.

Riding side by side on a country road, Roosevelt turns to Murphy, "Where are the New York Police in the Wall Street investigation? Who are the primary suspects?"

"An organization known as American Scream has claimed responsibility for the attack."

"The note found after the attack?"

"Yes. They are reviewing radical literature and subscription lists, looking for any affiliation with American Scream—and any active connection beyond readership. With the help of the postmaster, they are watching for any American Scream pamphlets sent through the mails."

"You will keep me directly informed of your progress during the investigation."

"Yes, Sir."

The two Spanish-American War veterans fall into silence, enjoying the view and the steady rhythm of the horses. Murphy recalls a part of that famous Lincoln speech, *'All the armies of Europe and Asia could not by force take a drink from the Ohio River. No, if destruction be our lot we must ourselves be its author and finisher. As a nation of free men we will live forever or die by suicide.'*

At the end of their meeting, Murphy returns to McGillivray who is waiting in the motorcar: "Where to next, Mr. Murphy?"

"New York."

CHAPTER 59

ST. LOUIS POST-DISPATCH

Centori's long train ride from New Mexico to St. Louis offered a chance to reflect on past decisions, good and bad, that are somehow connected and culminating with this trip. Mady's image at the flag stop has all but faded; she is another good reason to return as soon as possible. Her eastern refinement is somewhat reduced by the years in New Mexico; yet, her western manner is engaging. For now, he will focus on changing trains at Union Station in St Louis.

Centori moves along with the other passengers with his duffel. He arrives at the Grand Hall that features Romanesque arches, vaulted ceilings and a clock tower almost 300 feet high. In the busy hall, he immediately hears shouts and reverberations. "Extra, extra, read all about it."

Several newsboys in waiting rooms and ticketing offices are yelling. He cannot get near a newsboy; each one is surrounded by crowds eager for the big news.

"Extra, extra, read all about it!" Then he sees an opening, "Hey, son, newspaper here."

The newsboy hands over a copy and shouts, "Two cents, Mister."

He flips a buffalo head nickel, "Keep it."

"Thanks, Mister. Extra, extra..."

Centori places the duffel on a bench and quickly reads the headline:

Wall Street Bombers Arrested

He places the newspaper under his arm, picks up the duffel and heads for the eastbound train to New York. Suddenly, the urgency of returning there is reduced.

CHAPTER 60

KNICKERBOCKER COMEBACK

The last time, Centori entered New York with a sense of excitement; this time, he enters with a sense of profound purpose. The city has recovered from the Wall Street blast—Centori has not. He arrives at the hotel lobby wearing a three-piece suit and his cowboy hat; he glances at the now familiar Father Knickerbocker painting. The hotel staff recognizes the unmistakable big hat the instant he appears; the significance of his return is unknown.

"Welcome back to the Knickerbocker, Mr. Centori," says the front desk clerk.

"Thank you."

"We didn't expect you back so soon."

"I didn't either. Is 808 available?"

"Just a moment," he says. "Yes 808 is available, we will have your bag sent up."

"No need."

"Oh, that's right; enjoy your stay."

The clerk's eyes track his walk to the elevator.

Centori nods at the operator, "Hello, Jimmy, eight please."

"Mr. Centori, good to see you again. If you need anything be sure to let me know."

"I will do that, thanks."

The elevator cage opens and he finds room 808. The room floods his mind with images of Charity in his arms; he tries not to dwell on the memory too long. However, he can almost smell her perfume in the room, almost see her naked body on the bed.

Centori does not need directions to find the 'Old King Cole' bar. With his big Stetson, he walks in as a regular of the Manhattan social scene, as if he were entering Mad Mady's Saloon.

As usual, the bar is crowded with gentlemen. Centori senses eyes on his back, as though people recognize him. Finding a spot in the center of the bar, he orders: "Jameson Irish Whiskey."

With a wide smile, bartender Martini di Arma di Taggia says, "Mr. Centori, welcome back."

"Thank you."

He reaches for a bottle. "What brings you back to New York?"

"Business," he answers grimly and thinks *serious business*.

Facing the large 'Old King Cole' painting behind the bar, he studies the image until, "Here you are, Jameson with ice."

"That's a nice pour."

Martini smiles in return. After several minutes and several sips of whiskey, Centori surveys the room and turns toward a nearby table. He is taken back to the time he met Charity. It was natural for them to come together; unnatural for them to be torn apart.

There is no shortage of attractive women in New York or in the hotel. As time passes, a few women are sporadically drawn to his direction. He is tempted to return the attention. Instead, he drains his glass, drifts back to the first Charity encounter and how it all began with a glance.

"Hey, cowboy," Murphy takes Centori's thoughts to the present.

"Murph, it's good to see you."

"Good to see you too, however unexpected." They shake hands. "Are you sure you know what you are doing?"

"We will find out," he understates.

"Okay."

"I was sorry to read your telegram about A.P. and the other cowboy."

"It was a hell of a shootout."

"What happened?"

"I am trying to figure it out; I have an idea." He stalls by saying, "I read that the Wall Street bombers were arrested."

"Don't believe the newspapers."

"I was skeptical about the story."

Murphy orders a drink, then says, "The police are under great pressure to solve the case, so a few radical Italians were picked up."

"Italians have become unwelcome immigrants," Centori states.

"So were the Irish after the famine. The threat of arrest and deportation in radical circles loosened tongues and caused some finger pointing. The police have the wrong men; they are not our suspects."

"You sound sure."

"I am. Those men who were arrested are not responsible for the Wall Street explosion—they didn't do it."

"Will they be released?"

"The police will hold them as long as possible, then yes."

"Once again, you know more than you tell."

"Adobe, A.P. was a good man; I didn't know the other cowboy."

"His name was Quesada; they were both good men."

"Who killed them?"

"Four hard cases; they were shot to hell for their trouble. If anyone brings war to the Circle C there will be no survivors."

"What did they want?"

"Murph, I believe they were acting under orders from Jennifer Prower."

"Your new love interest?"

"Yes, you don't sound surprised."

"I'm not, but why do you think so?"

"You probably won't be surprised to learn that she was after the Revert Document. She may have sent them to finish the job."

"I thought you agreed to destroy that paper."

"I did agree," he sighs. "I was blind to your warning about Jennifer and ignored my inner warnings—it got people killed."

"I have never known you to break your word and certainly not with me. You are a man I trust."

"Trusted men can make mistakes."

"My request didn't matter to you; you persuaded yourself that she was a good woman."

"I was wrong."

"Dangerously wrong; dead wrong," Murphy admonishes.

Centori puts his palm up. "Okay. Have you ever been in love?"

"For a night at a time I guess, here and there. Look, I asked you as a friend. Now I ask you in an official capacity. That document does no good for any country or for any person. Maybe the U.S. stole the land from Mexico, but that is the tale of history. The Spanish stole the land from the Indians. The best we can do is not repeat mistakes. Even Colonel Santos agreed. Destroy it; tell me when the deed is done."

Centori makes eye contact and gives him an assenting nod. "She beguiled me to produce the document and planned to destroy me for it; then the shootout came. One of the hard cases had a note written in German."

"Did you get it translated?"

"No need; it was dates and times, but in German."

"There is no doubt that Jennifer is driven by politics and nationalism; she has important friends in Germany."

"There's more. I found a paper in her house that had *Amerikanischen Schrei* written on it; she is aware of American Scream and could be involved."

"We can talk about that later," he says without showing surprise. "Where is the document?"

"I get sick to my stomach to think she could be connected to the Wall Street bombing."

"Adobe, where is the Revert Document?"

"In good hands; it will be destroyed if I do not return to New Mexico."

"Or when you return," Murphy says with a slightly raised voice.

"The document will be burned, as sure as I am standing here."

"Okay."

"I was a damn fool; I still despair over the shootout."

"Mourn the loss of friends; don't hold yourself at fault. She protested and you became her target; those men pulled the trigger."

"I guess so; we have a few triggers of our own."

"That's right."

"You gents like another drink?" Martini asks.

"Yes, thanks," Centori answers. "I have seen the last of Jennifer, I'm sure."

"No—now she is the target."

"Murph, I met a woman right in this bar. We became friends and we were there together that day at Wall Street; her name was Charity."

"You witnessed the bombing?"

"Yes, I did."

Martini delivers another round of drinks.

"Are you okay?"

"I was thrown to the ground by the blast and banged up; many others were hurt far worse—or killed."

"You said her name *was* Charity?"

"Yes, I had an unsettling precognition about her the moment she stepped away from me. One moment the bells of Trinity Church were tolling, and the next, a large crater with smoke and rubble was on Wall and Broad Streets. Shocked lunchtime crowds ran away in every direction—and Charity was dead."

CHAPTER 61

RED FLOWERS

After Centori describes his ill-fated New York romance to Murphy, they sit in silence for a moment. Then Murphy says, "I am sorry you had to endure that tragedy, especially after Chaco Canyon. You have had more than enough trouble for one man."

"Charity was a fine woman. I liked her very much; sometimes she would encourage me to talk about my adventures and misadventures in this world. Then she had the worst of all calamities."

"You could be too personally involved with the case."

"No. The men and women who were hurt or killed in the blast were working people, clerks, messengers, secretaries and salesmen. They were bankers and brokers and maybe some veterans—men we may have served with in Cuba."

"Veterans were there, some hurt, some killed," Murphy confirms.

"I may have a personal stake, but I will find the men who terrorized New York."

"Okay."

"Murph, the attack felt like a warning, to show us how vulnerable we are in stopping other attacks."

"Your instincts are probably correct; we think this is the beginning. This case must be solved and another attack must be prevented."

"So, let's prevent it."

"About that, we have a meeting at police headquarters. In the morning, we will present a letter of introduction from the president, given to me by TR, to the NYPD."

"The president, hmm, you are in good company."

"Taft's letter gives us justification as federal agents to investigate the Wall Street case."

"Agents?"

"We have the full support of Washington; as far as they are concerned, you are a government agent."

"So the New York Police will welcome an Italian?"

"We will see how you do in the big city," Murphy jokes.

"Here we go again, off to save the world."

"We won't need our horses this time. Get some rest and meet me at Police Headquarters, 240 Centre Street at 9:00 a.m."

"In Little Italy."

"Listen, Adobe, that document must be destroyed once and for all," Murphy says with force.

That evening at the Knickerbocker Hotel, Centori retires to his room and writes a telegram to Francisco Greigos:

> This is about paper concealed as requested
> Upon receipt of this, burn paper.

Alone again in room 808, Centori feels liberated that the final chapter of the Revert Document saga has been written; the cursed document will be destroyed. Having adapted to the night sounds of the city, he quickly drifts off to sleep.

At 3:00 a.m. he jumps straight up in bed and stares. As he shakes off sleep he considers, *Here I am back in this room at a different time… such a different time…can we really measure the time and space between events, or are we left with our own perceptions…unreliable perceptions… can we objectively measure the gap of time between events…what am I thinking about?*

Perhaps you are thinking of me.

The unmistakable and charming musk of Gabriella Zena fills the air, before he sees her. She appears dressed in the clothes she wore for that special night in El Paso. It was their last romantic rendezvous. The understated white dress hemmed in embroidered red flowers celebrates her profound beauty.

I must be dreaming…again.

Mi corazón, I have said you are a dreamer; I am not a dream. You know why I am here.

Yes I do; that is what I fear the most.

Fear not, the time has come; a time to say a final farewell. Forget me not and accept a part of me in your mind forever. We are at a distance, but I will never go. Find a loving place in your mind, for that is where I will be.

Gabriella…

Grieve no more for me, remember your dreams and let not my shadow vanish from your mind. Farewell, mi corazón.

CHAPTER 62

❧❦❧

CENTRE STREET

At 8:00 a.m. the next morning, Centori wakes up relieved. After breakfast, he rides a trolley from Times Square to Little Italy. Murphy rides in his motorcar from his three-story brownstone in Gramercy Park to the same destination. Both men are travelling south on Broadway heading to New York City Police Headquarters located at 240 Centre Street. Opened in 1909, the monumental Beaux-Arts style structure, which sits on a triangular lot in Little Italy, contains a basement shooting range and a rooftop observation deck. *The New York Times* stated that 'the grand building fully contrasted with the surrounding little buildings and crooked streets.'

Centori arrives and finds Murphy waiting in front of the building.

"Good morning." Murphy's bearing is serious.

"Murph."

"This is the last chance to return to Circle C."

"No chance; let's meet these *hombres*."

Two policemen exit; all four men exchange nods. Murphy waits a second and says, "We should keep the Jennifer connection quiet, at least until we understand the entire situation."

"We should be less than honest with the local police?"

"We can be honest without full disclosure. Some files remain classified and sometimes sleuthing requires complete secrecy."

"I hope we do not overplay our hand."

"They have a head start on the investigation and can withhold anything they wish."

"I see."

"Are you ready to meet the police commissioner?"

"Not yet."

"What is it?"

"Murph, we have known each other for a very long time. I would like to know exactly what your government job is before we go inside."

"Okay, pard. It is not generally recognized. I am the head of the Military Intelligence Division, appointed by TR during his second term and reappointed by Taft."

"Not bad *bona fides*."

Three more policemen exit the building and walk past the federal agents, once again the men exchange nods.

Murphy says, "I thought you would approve. Also, I have a special liaison position to the Bureau of Investigation. If TR is elected in November, he may appoint me commander in chief of all intelligence departments, including the Secret Service and the Post Office Inspectors."

"Friendships forged in war are long lasting and trusting. We will have to get TR elected president of these United States."

"For now, I am a personal representative of President Taft."

"Even more impressive."

"Yes, and so here *we* are," Murphy says with a big smile. "Okay, let's go to work."

"Hold on."

"What now?"

"I think you forgot your cloak and dagger."

"Just the cloak; now let's go."

Murphy leads the way through the front doors of police headquarters and up a wide stone staircase to the second floor. At the top, they continue along a marble hall and confront a burly police sergeant standing in front of large double doors; he quickly ushers them inside to the commissioner's office.

Inside, six men sit around a long conference table; the stern assembly of policemen is all business. Centori and Murphy enter and see two police captains, Inspector John Cropsey, Deputy Commissioner of Detectives William Bingham, First Deputy Police Commissioner Francis MacKay and Police Commissioner Rhinelander Waldan. All the men, except the police commissioner, are wearing full police uniforms. The commissioner, who sits at the head of the table in a dapper suit, believes that Murphy holds an unclear position as an important special agent.

"Good morning, gentlemen," declares Commissioner Waldan with an expressionless face. "Let's bring this meeting to order. Welcome our guest Mr. John Murphy, a federal representative from Washington."

Centori surveys the room, only one of the police captains is looking at him. The rest of the men, including Murphy, focus on the PC.

"Commissioner, this is Adobe Centori, he is working with us."

"I don't know who you are Mr. Cento—or why you are here," the commissioner charges.

"My name is *Centori,* sheriff of Corona County, New Mexico."

"You came a long way to keep an eye on us."

"No, I came to help."

"The New York police need the help of a western lawman?"

"Commissioner," Murphy interrupts and points to Centori, "We served together in Cuba."

The commissioner who served as an infantry officer during the war replies, "Many of us have served."

"Mr. Centori received the Congressional Medal of Honor for action at San Juan Hill. He is much more than a highly capable western lawman."

The PC continues to scrutinize, but his opinion softens, "That is indeed impressive, Mr. Centori; courage is the first virtue."

All nod in agreement and Centori says, "Many served well in Cuba."

"Some say knowledge is the second virtue," Waldan continues. "We are faced with a much different situation than Cuba."

"This is not the first time we have worked on a government case," Murphy quickly adds. "The experience he has acquired and his judgment will be of great help to this investigation."

"That is overshadowed by protocol, Mr. Murphy. The NYPD has jurisdiction over bombings in our city; it doesn't require federal involvement."

"Beyond that supposition, the attack was on the financial heart of America and on the American people. The bomb exploded in front of the U.S. Assay office, damaging the Assay and the U.S. Sub-Treasury buildings. I am sure you are aware of the army battalion on Wall Street—sent by the Treasury department to protect government gold. The attack was on the American government; that makes it a national crime."

Silence fills the room. Then the commissioner says, "As the local police, we are investigating. Our men are in the process of examining thousands of pieces of potential evidence and interviewing hundreds of witnesses."

"Have there been any significant arrests in the case?"

"You must know of the recent arrests of well-known Italian anarchists. We did not have any tangible evidence; those men were released this morning. Any further arrests now would be hasty," he says with a glare.

Deputy Commissioner MacKay, a man with a high forehead who sits next to Waldan adds, "Many radical organizations claim not to be associated with the bombing. That shrinks the immediate suspect pool."

Centori thinks, *so arrest any Italian,* but says, "That does not eliminate them from suspicion."

"We did not say that," snaps Deputy Commissioner Bingham who sits opposite Cropsey. He continues the point. "Statements from radical groups profess reform over revolution and the use of peaceful methods to engender social change. Given a history of government reactions to violence and terrorism, it is an understandable statement that could be true."

"I understand," Murphy offers. "Commissioner, are you conducting surveillance of known radicals?"

"We have infiltrated anarchist coffeehouses and meeting halls and are tailing the usual suspects."

MacKay adds, "What's more, we are examining the victims and their backgrounds; we are visiting hospitals to question them."

Bingham interjects, "Detectives can describe the dynamite wagon. From the fragments, we see that it was a butter and egg delivery wagon. The horse pulling the wagon, or the parts of that horse, show that the animal was recently shod. We are visiting blacksmith shops and livery stables across the city for leads."

Inspector Cropsey pronounces, "What we know for sure is that a bomb exploded in a wagon that terrorized America's financial center. We have issued a public request for any witness to contact us."

"So you see, Mr. Murphy, the local police have been busy," Waldan declares. "Also, we have the undercover bomb squad investigating almost every scare."

"The Wall Street explosion was a stark message to the U.S. government; I have no doubt of the capability of the NYPD in this matter, gentlemen."

The PC takes a mental bow and goes on, "The note signed American Scream, found near the attack, is a name that is new to us and lacks credibility as an organization."

Centori speaks up, "Its members appear not to be new at their work and the attack did not lack credibility."

"As I said, the name is new to us."

"They could be a consolidation of different political fanatics coming together for a common purpose."

Murphy shifts in his chair and looks at Centori.

"You sound rather convinced of your opinion," the commissioner says without hiding his annoyance.

"Mr. Centori was at the Wall Street bombing," Murphy chimes in.

"That does not make one an expert on the matter. If this is a consolidation, why do the radical organizations claim no association, in any way, with the attack?"

Centori glances at Murphy, "Except for the note left at the scene, claiming responsibility for the attack—signed American Scream."

Murphy becomes more uncomfortable. Centori goes on, "That leads us back to identifying members of American Scream. I come to that without the requisite expertise."

The PC glares at Centori with daggers. "How do you know the organization exists at all?"

He pushes back, "My instincts tell me so."

"We don't work that way in the big city; this is not Texas, Mr. Centori."

His expression darkens, "That's New Mexico."

"Mr. Centori is a New Yorker, born a few blocks from here," Murphy proposes.

"All the same, this is highly irregular." Waldan throws up his hands. "I am not aware of Mr. Centori being part of any official investigation agency."

Murphy reaches into his inside breast pocket, "Look at this letter, Commissioner."

Waldan reads the paper from Taft, appointing Murphy and whomever he decides to enlist for this case.

"Why didn't you show me this before?"

"I think cooperation is better than coercion."

Offended, the commissioner stares. "I see."

With more credibility, Centori offers, "We have a crime scene note by American Scream."

"As I have said, every dangerous radical group—communists, socialists and anarchists—in the city denies involvement in a bomb plot."

MacKay adds, "Some assert it was an industrial accident caused by an automobile crashing into a dynamite wagon. Yet no construction companies report any missing wagons."

"It was a deliberate attack, not an accident," Centori states. "Consider the time and the place of the explosion."

One of the captains says, "We start without a clear idea of the identity of American Scream, if it is a new organization."

The other captain exclaims, "Deport revolutionary anarchists and bomb throwers—that would be a good place to start!"

"I see we have more than one cowboy at the table," Waldan jests. "No offense, Mr. Centori."

"None taken."

"There are too many possibilities, beyond the typical suspects, in identifying the leaders. We need to entertain new ideas to further the investigation," Waldan demands.

Murphy responds, "You all recall the Los Angeles bombing in 1910—not all the accomplices were caught."

"That is farfetched," Waldan counters.

"Perhaps, but it is a theory that is beyond the typical suspects."

"The union radicals in Los Angeles are interested in New York?"

"It would not be the first time a militant union became nationally active."

"The Los Angeles attack was done in the middle of the night, presumably to minimize the death toll. The Wall Street bombing was in the middle of the day for the opposite purpose: the bomb intended to cause mass killings."

"The only thing we know for sure is that the cause of both explosions was dynamite," Murphy admits, "However, they could have changed their purpose."

"If we identify the Los Angeles accomplices who are linked to the McNamara brothers, what do you propose?"

"Tell them to expect us," Centori impulsively blurts.

Murphy's face registers alarm. "Mr. Centori, it seems that you are indeed a cowboy," the commissioner smiles. "But I am sure you will embrace traditional police methods."

"We all will," Murphy says, "I will contact our agents in Los Angeles."

Waldan turns to Centori. "You were an eyewitness to the attack?"

"That's right, Commissioner Waldan."

"I see you emerged unscathed."

Ignoring the comment he says, "I worked with Officer Jack Haughey following the explosion. He is a good man. I would like him to join us."

"You want a beat policeman?" the commissioner asks.

Murphy all but touches the letter in his pocket. "We need the police manpower."

The commissioner stands. "Thank you, gentlemen, we all have our assignments. We will meet again in three days to review and discuss our progress."

In the middle of the chair shuffling and several side conversations, one of the police captains approaches Centori. "Federal government involvement with the traditional jobs of the local police is new for the commissioner."

"This is new to me too, Captain."

"Sure. So, the wild west must be exciting for you."

"Sometimes too exciting; it is a great place, a land of enchantment."

"Do you speak Mexican?"

Amused, Centori replies, "No, but I'm fluent in Spanish."

CHAPTER 63

DELMONICO'S RESTAURANT

O utside police headquarters, Murphy and Centori wait for
the black sedan.

"Welcome to New York politics in police work," Murphy laughs.

"He was an unfriendly commissioner. He seemed more against
me than against the facts of the case."

"You took all he gave and were more than equal to the task."

"They sure didn't hold out a welcoming hand. What arrogance."

"Forget it; I know a place that *will* hold out a welcoming hand.
Have you been to Delmonico's?"

"No, but I heard about the Delmonico steak."

"They are one of the best steaks, even for a cattle rancher
like you."

McGillivray drives up in front the building, stopping the
conversation.

In the back seat of the black sedan, Murphy turns to Centori.
"What about *Amerikanischen Schrei*?"

Centori pulls out a leaflet, "Here is the paper recovered in
Jennifer's bedroom.

"Bedroom, I thought you said in house."

"This paper would have helped my argument."

"Adobe, we do not like to share information until it is conclusive. Besides, the police *are* looking for American Scream members—despite the commissioner's attitude."

Murphy calls to the front seat, "Henry, get us a full translation of this leaflet."

"Okay."

They continue to drive south to the restaurant. Centori takes in all the traffic and all the New York life from his window.

"Are you missing New Mexico?" Murphy asks.

"Hmm, just wondering about the Circle C roundup."

"Wondering about Mad Mady, too?"

"There you go again," Centori laughs causing McGillivray to slightly turn his head around.

"Do you remember I mentioned Stratford, New Mexico, the last time we met?"

"Yes, the town near Silver City; you said there was a gold strike."

"That strike is panning out to be substantial."

"It will be good for New Mexico."

"Things are not so good for Stratford, at least not for now."

"What are you talking about?"

"There will be a story in the newspapers about it."

Centori takes a deep breath, "What happened down there?"

"Zapata led a few hundred horsemen into the town."

"What? It was an invasion."

"Yep."

"Were they after the gold?"

"They seemed to be after supplies and munitions. Fortunately, an army unit was close by in Silver City. The invaders were driven out by Captain Reed and his mounted troops."

"Reed, I met him once."

"He is a fine soldier. We have a report that a woman matching Jennifer's description was seen in Stratford around the time of your first New York trip."

"Nothing about her surprises me now. I was doubtful about her trip to Santa Fe. There were too many things that did not add up. So, Stratford, do you know for sure?"

"I know for sure that we will find her and shake the truth from her."

"I thought you would say that."

Ten minutes later, they arrive at Delmonico's Restaurant; McGillivray turns his head around. "I'll get the translation and return in two hours."

"No lunch?" Centori asks.

"No, thanks."

"I think he has lunch scheduled with a much better looking person."

"Oh, I understand."

"Adobe, of all people, I am sure you do! Say hello to her, Henry."

They exit the sedan, enter the elaborate dining room and are shown to a good table; they each order whiskey.

"Very fancy place, Murph."

"You should be used to it since you are staying at the Knickerbocker."

"It's a fine hotel."

"Have you seen any old friends or family in New York?"

"No, I planned to go to the old neighborhood with Charity but something got in the way."

The drinks arrive and they sit quietly before Murphy says, "Something changed in you after I mentioned Jennifer's trip to Stratford."

Centori drinks his whiskey and rubs his face. "You noticed."

"I did."

"Well, I certainly don't need more evidence about her wicked ways. Perhaps it is anger or something more complicated; I knew all along I was being used."

"Sometimes a man tries to bend the world to fit his idealistic view."

"Sure, a foolish man; she is beautiful and I allowed myself to entertain a fantasy."

"Now we will entertain her to solve this case," Murphy proposes.

The waiter returns and they order steaks and baked potatoes.

Changing the subject, Centori asks, "You mentioned contacting Los Angeles agents?"

"The co-conspirators, if there were any, have not been identified in the case. I made the point to see the commissioner's reaction."

"I thought we were all on the same side."

"We are. Perhaps I have been at this too long. The police have worked the case, including looking for lost dynamite wagons, interviewing known radicals and collecting eyewitness reports. Yet, they have a perplexing lack of evidence."

"They are looking in the wrong places."

"Their investigation should be wider. It is not just radicals attacking the capitalist system and terrorizing New York; we believe they are allied with the German government."

"So the police are focused on old internal enemies."

"Yes, we believe Germany provided the financing for the Wall Street explosion. As the police told us, some radial organizations avoid violence, but others do not. Those are probably the people who are aligned with the Germans."

"Where do we stand on terror plots now?"

"The extent of the German threat is not generally known to local police. They are looking for radicals, but they don't know, or will not admit, that Wall Street was part of something much wider in scope."

"And more sinister."

Twenty minutes and two drinks later, Centori examines his steak that is placed in front of him. Both men cut into their steak and have a bite. Centori lifts his knife and fork again and sees Murphy watching him. "What is it, Murph?"

"Is that the best steak you have ever had?"

"Ha, it is good," he says with a trace of a smile.

"Adobe, what I am about to say is top secret. German intelligence has started a program of terror against an unknowing U.S. This is a new kind of war and we can't be out maneuvered."

"I understand. It sounds like a major security issue."

"Yes, the likes of which have never been seen in this country. This threat is not fully understood by the police and the public is completely unaware. Let's talk about your shadowy newspaper woman."

"You mean Jennifer."

"Yes, you should know what we know," Murphy says while cutting into steak.

"It's about time."

"There have been military intelligence investigations…she is a German courier and financier."

"That sounds about right; I believe she paid those hard cases to shoot up the Circle C."

"You are probably right about her involvement, but there is more; she is an accomplice in the Wall Street plot."

Centori raises his eyebrows and takes a cut of his steak.

"I thought she can no longer surprise you; we need to interrogate her to get relevant information about her network of agents who have the organizational and technical skills to build sophisticated bombs. By the way, her real name is Jarvia Hoffmann. She was born in Norway to German parents."

"Jarvia, I thought her first name was…never mind."

"In German, *Jarvia* means 'skilled with a spear' but her last name is more significant—her husband is Erich Hoffmann of Imperial Germany. Hoffmann is a man of great wealth and the head of the German secret service in Berlin. She has money and power to recruit agents in the U.S., but not the power to select targets. Jarvia is plenty smart but not the mastermind; we have to identify the top German spy in New York. You sure can pick them, Adobe."

All Centori can do is shake his head and say, "So, she is a spy."

"Beyond spying, the aim of the German intelligence is to perform secret operations that will damage Germany's enemies—declared or not—and that means the U.S."

"Well, she has gone to ground."

"Don't worry, we will dig her up and then bury her again—after she leads us to the German ringleaders."

"After the shootout, she abandoned the colonel's house and Valtura in a hurry."

"We have not heard the last of Jarvia—she is on a mission."

"What more do you know about her?"

"After she left New York, we visited her apartment."

"She has a New York apartment?"

"Yes, on Park Avenue and 66th Street."

"Leave it to her to live on New York's classiest street, home to the rich and in *her* case, the infamous."

"We discovered hundreds of pages of financial information."

"Discovered?"

"We were suspicious of her doll shop and found she is using it to channel significant sums of money from Berlin into the U.S. She has accounts in a few New York banks and she still funds operatives—money to finance future bomb plots. We believe that she paid for the entire Wall Street operation before leaving New York."

"You kept all this information from me?"

"Murphy cuts his steak again and says, "We have an incomplete understanding of her network and lack hard evidence. Would you like to read the intelligence report?"

"Not now. She revealed enough in New Mexico—so have you. I knew she was more than a news gatherer at the *Valtura Journal*."

"Much more. We have codes of many operatives in the U.S.; we think her code name is *Rote Frau*."

"Red woman. Do you have any idea about their next move?"

"Nothing concrete. While the NYPD is focused on solving the Wall Street case, we must prevent another bombing."

"Are you sure they are planning another terror attack?"

"I am afraid so."

"She moves money and papers across the Atlantic to German agents who use American Scream to deflect attention away from them. As long as the police think the attackers are U.S. anarchists, the Germans feel safe."

"So, you were not fully open about this with the police."

"The NYPD seems unwilling to identify the real enemy. That could be an advantage for us against Germany—if they think we are not on their trail."

"Okay, so what is our next step?"

"We confront Jarvia and give her a chance to save her life."

"No deals. She is responsible for the death of A.P. and Quesada—Charity too!"

WATER DAMAGE | 305

"I understand that, but she will be responsible for the death of hundreds more if we do not stop her network. I told you, we think they are planning further terror attacks on New York. She can provide an opportunity to find the leaders."

"We still have to find her," Centori says.

"If Jarvia returns to her New York apartment, we will find her."

"First an explosion in New York, then an invasion on our southern border; you know, Murph, the U.S. is being pushed around," he says before taking another bite. "I think it is time we use that 'Big Stick' TR spoke about."

"I think you are right. We will need it because more attacks are coming."

They sit and reminisce about their army days in Cuba as they finish the last of a great steak. Then Centori says, "There is something troubling me about this coming war that many think is inevitable."

Murphy puts down his utensils and looks up. "What's that?"

"It's been 13 years since we fought in Cuba; in that time, weapons of war have developed and improved for their purpose. The new machine guns have highly destructive firepower. One gun could be equal to as much as 100 rifles. In Cuba, I think the U.S. lost fewer than 2,500 men."

"Yes, that is true."

"I fear that with the machine gun development, the losses would be shocking on all sides."

"That is true too; mankind has become much better at killing each other."

The waiter places a silver tray on the table.

"Are our actions preventing the U.S. from entering such a horrible war or are they getting us into a war?"

"I don't know Adobe; all we can do is push back."

"I know, I know."

"So, was I right about this place?"

"You were quite right! This was a great meal," Centori says while reaching for his billfold.

Murphy grabs the check. "This one is on Uncle Sam."

Back in the black sedan, McGillivray says, "Here is the *Amerikanischen Schrei* translation." Murphy grabs the file found in Jarvia's Valtura house.

"What is it, Murph?"

"Looks like an encoded list of contacts with ambiguous locations. Other information is coded as well."

"So we have learned little."

"Except that this confirms the link between Germany and American Scream."

CHAPTER 64

PLAIN CLOTHES

Officer Jack Haughey was called immediately after the high-level meeting to see the commissioner. Haughey is one of NYPD's best men. In 1900, he joined the force eager with honorable intentions to protect the public and work on the side of the law. After years of walking the beat in Manhattan precincts, he knows people and he knows criminals. The New York sidewalks have sharpened his police sense.

The next day, Haughey arrives at the commissioner's office concerned and puzzled. The police sergeant escorts him into the big office.

Waldan sees he is disconcerted and quickly says, "Please sit down, Officer Haughey. I know you are wondering why I called you here today."

"Yes, Commissioner Waldan."

"I will get right to the issue at hand. I have contacted your captain; you have been temporarily assigned to my office."

"I don't understand, Commissioner."

"This is about the Wall Street explosion. I know you were on the scene."

"I was. I did the best I could do."

"Yes, I have no doubt. You will be working on the Wall Street investigation. Federal agent John Murphy and his associate Adobe Centori…"

"Adobe Centori," Haughey says with surprise. "Sorry, Commissioner."

"As I was saying, Murphy and Centori have requested that you work with them for the Wall Street investigation."

"What? Why me?"

"They want a good man; they want you."

"Centori is in New York?"

"Yes. What do you think of that cowboy?"

"He is a good man; an honest man, a New Yorker too."

"What happened at Wall Street?"

"We worked together after the explosion. Centori was blown down in the blast and his lady friend was killed—yet he showed no signs of slowing down until we did all we could for the other victims."

"Well, he is impressed with you too. That is why he wants you for this job. He is staying at the Knickerbocker. You have been reassigned to Federal Agent Murphy. I know this comes as a surprise. Are you ready for this assignment?"

"Yes, Commissioner, I will do my best."

"I know you will. The cowboy is a little hasty; Murphy seems more restrained."

"I appreciate your confidence in me, Commissioner."

"Of course; I want you to report any significant progress made on the case and keep our communication confidential. Do you understand?"

"Yes, Sir."

"This assignment should help your career. Get up to Times Square and see Centori. If he is not in, wait for him."

"The Knickerbocker."

"Good luck, Haughey."

"Thank you, Commissioner."

"One last thing, leave your uniform at the station. You will be working in plain clothes."

CHAPTER 65

BROADWAY CENTRAL HOTEL

The Broadway Central Hotel opened at 673 Broadway in 1870 with great renown as the largest in the world. The eight-story, 400-room hotel is between Bleecker and Amity Streets near New York University. It features three fine dining rooms, fancy furnishings, an ornate lobby and a grand stairway. In one of its three fine restaurants, Warren and Spooner sit at a corner table. Warren looks toward the door and pulls out a pocket watch. "They are late."

"They are not coming," Spooner confidently replies.

"Why is that?"

"Because they were not invited and are no longer involved."

"I don't understand."

"I tried to tell you before. We must be rid of them. They are of no further use to American Scream."

"Josiah, what are you talking about?"

"Lucy and Emma are parlor radicals; they have no enthusiasm for our new direction."

"How can you be sure?"

"They vastly underestimated the impact of our last event, thinking it would be a symbolic attack against Wall Street, not a mass terror attack. Now they are fearful of being caught."

"But they were involved with the planning."

"Those parlor radicals did not load that wagon. Also, they believe that a society without laws is a society governed by factions and they will not abandon socialism…"

"To embrace anarchy."

"That's right. They do not fully understand what is needed to respond to social injustice. Revolutionary warfare requires more dynamite and we will answer with more dynamite."

"So you are convinced that they are unprepared for what is coming next."

"Yes. They have no desire for the destruction that is coming. Besides, our new friends would not approve of them."

"You have kept me in the dark about them for too long. I fear that the new destruction was not part of our original plan. Do you not trust me?"

"I do not trust them."

"What can you tell me?"

Spooner scans the room and lowers his voice. "I will prepare you for who is coming to meet us. Germany is concerned that the U.S. industrial strength and continental resources will support their enemy nations."

"We are a long way from Europe. The vast Atlantic Ocean should prevent any concerns."

"They want America to stay on this side of the ocean."

"The Americans are not inclined to be involved with European conflicts. So why are the Germans worried?"

"Perhaps not directly, but the U.S. is sending supply ships to Germany's potential enemies. They aim to stop war supply shipments that are intended to help England and France. We will discuss this further when she arrives."

Spooner watches the door and sees her approach with unwavering confidence. She is attractive of face and figure with long beautiful red hair, but work as a German agent in New Mexico has taken a toll.

"Good day, gentlemen."

Both men stand to attention to greet Jarvia Hoffmann.

"Frau Hoffmann." Spooner whispers. "This is Lysander Warren. Welcome back to New York."

"You have done well on Wall Street."

Spooner quickly nods. "Did you have a successful time away?"

Jarvia glances down. "Successful enough, but we are here to discuss the future."

"Yes, of course, we have much in common."

She rolls her eyes. "After this meeting, you shall see me no more."

"I understand."

"I wish to talk about the railroads," she says more as a demand than a request.

"Yes, of course," Spooner defers as Warren sits and listens.

"We are concerned about trains that are transporting war materiel for assemblage in plants and factories for shipment to Europe."

"That is beyond American Scream, Frau Hoffman."

"You were dissatisfied with the Wall Street affair?"

"No, but…"

"Perhaps we have misjudged you and your organization," she snarls. "Do I need to remind you of our agreement and that you are very well funded?"

"No."

Spooner braces for her wrath, but she is calm. "It would not be wise to make any further objections. Now, there is a bridge that is logistically significant as a passage from Canadian manufacturers to New York assembly plants. All details will be given to you. Meet Herr Seiler and Herr Bachmeier on the upper deck of the Staten Island ferry in two hours; they will approach you. They will be your operational contacts for this mission. Here is the boat number and their descriptions. Have I been clear?"

Both men nod affirmatively.

Two hours later, Spooner and Warren are confronted on board the ferry, "I am Herr Bachmeier. This is Herr Seiler; he will be your contact for all railroad events. Do you understand?"

"Yes," he answers while taking the apparent measure of the German agents.

Seiler instructs, "Read these papers very carefully and follow the instructions, then destroy all papers. It is imperative that the bomb explodes when the train is on the bridge. The bomb must be small enough to avoid detection but large enough to cause a derailment. Although the train will be carrying war materiel, the bridge itself is an important target; it will be difficult to remove the wreckage and further train traffic will be delayed."

"That will require a reliable detonator."

"We have reliability in our network; the detonator in the bomb will engage while the train is on the bridge."

It happened 300 miles to the northwest of New York City on a bridge over Canandaigua Outlet. A Lehigh Valley Railroad train wreck near Manchester, New York, was reported by telegraph. Twenty-nine people were killed and almost 100 people were injured as the train came off the rails and hit the trestle. Eastbound from Buffalo, train

13 included two locomotives, express car, mail, baggage, dining, parlor, coaches and terrified passengers.

Crumpled rail cars torn in half showed the intensity of the crash; some badly damaged cars fell down to the channel. Chaos prevailed as rescue workers raced to untangle cars and to extricate trapped people. One injured victim embodied the anguish of the wreck when he shouted, "What horror! My God, what horror!"

Men from the Department of Commerce & Labor interviewed the train crew, the passengers and the track inspectors. They examined the broken rail to determine the cause of failure; no manufacturing defects were revealed. Yet, investigators concluded that a defective rail caused the derailment and declared the incident an accident. There are some accidents that cannot be prevented, especially those that are not accidents. The saboteurs bombed the wrong train. It was not carrying war materiel—it was carrying passengers.

American Scream received additional orders from Seiler. A fire at the Kingsfield munitions factory in New Jersey destroyed more than one million high explosive artillery shells. The factory assembles shells, shrapnel and powder to supply Russia and France. In upstate New York, a fire and explosion destroyed a chemical munitions plant.

Chapter 66

Not a Moment too Soon

Centori spends the morning in his room with coffee and the military intelligence report. Reading about Jarvia Hoffman is fascinating and distressing at the same time. The more he reads, the more he feels like a fool. In his mind all of her physical beauty collapses into an amorphous mass of evil. *Is she a warrior or a criminal? It does not matter, she killed civilians.*

He places the report in his duffel and under the bed. He walks down eight flights of stairs into the lobby to summon a bellboy, "If someone calls, I will be back within the hour."

"Yes, Mr. Centori."

He walks to Times Square and then to the Horn and Hardart Automat. Inside, he drops nickels in a slot, opens a little glass door and pulls out a ham sandwich. He pours a coffee and smiles to himself, *the best in New York, Charity said. When this is all over, I should write her parents and tell them about the last few days of her life.*

The merriment of four young women at the next table causes him to smile again. *Perhaps they are talking about me,* he muses.

After finishing the sandwich and the coffee, he sits and watches the happy crowd and cannot find the strength to leave the simple happy environment. Yet, some minutes later, he finds the energy to return to the Knickerbocker lobby.

As he enters, he is met by Officer Jack Haughey.

"Adobe."

"Jack."

"Welcome back to New York."

"It's good to see you again."

"You are not surprised to see me. Yet, I was surprised to get a call from the commissioner."

"Hope you don't mind. I guess I should have asked you first."

"It's okay. I am ready to work with you. We saw firsthand what those criminals did to innocent people."

Haughey offers a narrow grin and says, "I have been a policeman for more than ten years and I have never seen anything as destructive as the Wall Street attack."

"We will do what we must. It's a little early in the day, but let me buy you a drink."

The two men sit dead center at the 'Old King Cole' bar.

"Jameson," says the bartender.

"Yes, and for my friend," Centori gestures toward Haughey.

"Same, thanks. Irish whiskey; you have good taste."

"Jack, the police are not fully aware of the extent of American Scream's intentions and capabilities."

Haughey looks around and then whispers, "The commissioner ordered me to report to him."

"I am not surprised."

The bartender set up the drinks, "Here you go, gents."

"We have another meeting with the commissioner in a few days. In the meantime, we will talk to John Murphy—a federal agent."

"Yes, the PC mentioned him."

"For now, here's to new friends."

The men take a sip of the Irish whiskey and reflect on the task ahead.

"So, Jack, are you a family man?"

"We have five children, all boys. What about you?"

"Mr. Centori?" a bellboy interrupts.

"Yes."

"We have a telephone call for you at the front desk."

Murphy informs him of reports about a train wreck, munitions factory fire and an explosion at a chemical munitions plant. He ends the conversation with, "Adobe, they did it despite strong security at the factories."

Centori returns to Haughey who asks, "What was that?"

"You have arrived—and not a moment too soon."

CHAPTER 67

KLEINDEUTSCHLAND

Distinguished aristocrat Count Helmut von Riesenfelder arrived in New York from Mexico City to run the spy network as intelligence liaison to the secret service in Berlin. He has taken a three-story brownstone on East 88th Street and East End Avenue in the Yorkville section of Manhattan. The German community calls the neighborhood *Kleindeutschland.*

Wasting no time on his first day in New York, Riesenfelder met community leaders in the afternoon. The discussions were conducted over beer and bratwurst with sweet mustard on a hard roll; Yorkville is a good place to be German. In the evening, he met with two prominent German naval officers at the Metropolitan Club, a private club formed by J.P. Morgan; a good place to be American.

In the parlor of his brownstone that night, Riesenfelder studies a detailed map of New York Harbor, one of the largest natural harbors in the world. It is located at the mouth of the Hudson River that flows into New York Bay and into the Atlantic Ocean.

The count puts the map aside and pours a glass of *schnaps*. After taking a sip, he reviews classified files prepared by high-ranking German officials. Germany seeks to destabilize the U.S. and to distract the Americans away from European affairs. The documents contain diplomatic codebooks and comprehensive espionage, sabotage and propaganda campaigns.

Opening another classified folder, Riesenfelder reads about commerce raiding, or *Handelskrieg*, that will be conducted on the Atlantic. Underwater boats, the *U-Boot*, will attack America's Merchant Marine ships. He places the folder down and considers, *The U Boot attacks will not be enough; the probability of destroying all Atlantic shipping is low. We must stop the flow of supplies at the source,* he thinks.

Taking another sip of *schnaps*, he reviews another classified file that contains manuals describing tradecraft methods. Then he writes a coded report to Berlin, confirming his arrival in New York and the German imperative—stop enemies from receiving U.S. munitions and supplies. He finishes his drink and writes a note to himself: meet Frau Hoffman. Finally, Riesenfelder prepares to retire, having done enough service for the fatherland for one day.

CHAPTER 68

TESTING THE WATER

The next day at 4:00 p.m., Riesenfelder waits at the German beer hall on Second Avenue. He sits at a table with a heavy, hand-painted beer stein with a metal lid. The *hofbrau* is loud with Bavarian music. Coincidentally, the music stops at the moment she arrives. *Rote Frau* takes her time walking to his table, where he stands at attention. "Welcome to New York, Herr Riesenfelder."

"Thank you, Frau Hoffman. Has Bachmeier arrived?"

"No. He will arrive within the week."

"He will be instrumental here in Yorkville. He will report to you as he did in New Mexico. I do not wish to meet him now."

"I understand."

"So, Frau Hoffman, are you enjoying this neighborhood?"

"Yes, it's almost like home."

"It is certainly more so than the southwest."

"Speaking of home, much has changed in Berlin."

"I understand, my husband tries to keep me informed."

"May I get you a beer?"

She smiles. "Yes, thank you."

He waves to the bartender and says to her, "Has your husband told you that Berlin considers war inevitable?"

No answer.

"I can see that he has not," he states, "but it is true."

"I am sure you are correct, Herr Riesenfelder."

"Indeed, and Berlin is concerned about the outcome of the next war."

"Of course."

"You do not fully understand—that is why I am here; that is why you are here."

"We must prevent failure in the coming conflict," she confirms.

"Yes, Frau Hoffman," he pauses for a moment. "Failure in the New Mexico affair seems to be overlooked by Berlin. Your husband is very influential."

Startled by his rudeness, she replies, "Perhaps we both failed in that affair, Herr Riesenfelder."

"That is a misguided statement."

"I am sure there is enough responsibility to go around."

Ignoring the comment, Riesenfelder states, "Frau Hoffman, tell me about the network you have established in New York."

Another heavy, hand-painted beer stein arrives. She waits a moment then answers, "It is well-financed and effective."

"Are they all German immigrants?"

"Yes."

"Have any of them approached you first?"

"No, I do not trust anyone who makes initial contact; that would be risky."

"That is a smart policy. You have created a capable and reliable network?"

"Yes. Having a large fund helps in that endeavor."

"I congratulate you on the munitions factory and chemical munitions plant attacks. Those events have helped our cause."

"Thank you," she says waiting for more.

"What I will tell you is highly classified; few people are aware of this plan."

She lifts her stein and prepares to listen.

"The Kaiser wishes to repeat the quick victory over the French in the coming war. In the 1870 war, innovations in our military system had strategic advantages."

"I am unfamiliar with that war."

"Yes, of course, young lady. Here's a history lesson for you: the Prussian general staff showed independent thinking and deployed highly effective mobilization systems in large battlefields. Army commanders reported directly to the Kaiser; the French chain of command was disorganized hurting their commanders' ability to communicate."

"That is interesting but I fail to see what you intend to do."

"As I said, innovations in the German military had advantages. We will continue to innovate."

"I see," she says before sipping her beer.

"The Kaiser wishes to conduct secret strikes against the U.S. that will prevent destruction to our men and our country."

"We have struck Wall Street."

Riesenfelder stares at her with contempt, "I am sure you know that is not sufficient. In the coming war, American made bullets will kill our men while a British blockade will stop supplies to Germany."

"That is a new path and inconsistent with the targets of American Scream."

"We must move forward with the Kaiser's plan," Riesenfelder insists. "We will select targets and finance the operations; they will comply. Keep them involved as long as possible."

"Yes, I will do so."

"Ultimately, we can operate without them. Remember, Frau Hoffman, we are to fulfill our orders. This goal has taken on great significance in Berlin. The U.S. must be prevented from producing or at least shipping ammunition to Europe."

Rote Frau looks at the pictures on the beer stein and takes a big gulp.

CHAPTER 69

CARL SCHURZ PARK

*R*ote *Frau* summoned Bachmeier to meet her at Carl Schurz Park. Near the German community of Yorkville and on the East River, the park is named for German-born Civil War General Carl Schurz. Standing between a bench and a rail that overlooks the river, they appear to be discussing ordinary topics.

She is wearing a tan dress and a wide-brimmed hat. Bachmeier's stiff straw hat with flat top and brim has a grosgrain ribbon around the crown; his black suit is unkempt. "This is most extraordinary. Frau Hoffmann. After leaving New Mexico we were not to meet each other again, especially in a public place."

Rote Frau bristles at his tone. "Do not use my name," she angrily orders. "We are invisible in plain sight, and what I need to tell requires an encounter."

"Where is Herr Riesenfelder?"

"You are the only man in the world who would not enjoy seeing me."

"But I understood that…"

"Riesenfelder avoids creating any pattern in his behavior; you will talk to me. Besides, I will continue to finance the attacks, so you will see me for the funds. Now, it is imperative that war materiel be stopped to save German soldiers in the coming war."

"I understand that very well."

"Your orders from Riesenfelder are clear. You are to explore the New York and New Jersey waterfronts, make detailed charts and record any movements of security guards. You will make contacts with any pro-German waterfront workers."

"That dangerous job will take time."

"Berlin expects results within two weeks. You will learn all you can about U.S. shipping of war supplies to our enemies: schedules, quantities and destinations."

Bachmeier appears anxious. "Yes, I understand."

"You will establish communication networks on the waterfront with German immigrants loyal to the fatherland."

"That will take time; I am new here, *Rote Frau.*"

"You must start now. Go to this address in Queens and to this location in the basement," she demands. "You will find a codebook with instructions that explain how to expand your network with American Scream."

"Will they cooperate with the new plan?"

"As long as we include capitalist targets, they will completely cooperate."

"Are they necessary at all?"

"Do you agree that they can distract the police from us?"

He nods and she smiles. "You will meet them in the beer hall on Second Avenue. Do you know the one?"

"Yes," he responds with concern.

"Are you losing your nerve, Bachmeier?"

"No, of course not!"

Rote Frau looks into his eyes, "Good, you must not...and you will know the planning and execution phases of the operation and you will coordinate the network as soon as possible."

She reaches into a smaller bag and orders, "Take this envelope. You will be prudent in the distribution of these funds, but use enough to get the job done."

Late that night, Bachmeier skulks around the New York waterfront. Comparing the intelligence gathering with his own inspection, he notes the guards on duty and the ships that appear to be loaded with munitions—especially the transport ships going to England and France. Then he retreats to a house in Corona, Queens.

CHAPTER 70

TROUBLED WATERS

L ess than two weeks following Riesenfelder's arrival in New York, strikes on facilities started. Although *Rote Frau* secretly finances the attacks, Bachmeier is the author of the terror. He is the personification of Germany's secret war in New York.

Reports of shipboard fires on merchant ships appear in the New York newspapers. The mysterious fires happen after the transports left New York Harbor; they were reported as accidents. The fires had the desired result of slowing shipments of war supplies to the Allies.

Commissioner Waldan called a second meeting at the big building on Centre Street. This time the PC's forum is in his private office. He is reading a pile of official reports; his desk is covered with newspapers including the *Shipping News*. Murphy, Centori and Haughey return to police headquarters and enter the office to find the commissioner sitting alone.

"Gentlemen, thank you for coming. It seems that things have escalated."

The PC appears changed, more determined to outwardly acknowledge the danger of state-sponsored terror and the mysterious explosions in the middle of the Atlantic Ocean. "Please sit down. Gentlemen, the waterfront has become a target; ships at sea as well. Fires and explosions on board ships heading to Europe are no accidents."

Murphy agrees and adds, "Those steamships were carrying munitions to England and France."

"No surprise there," Centori says.

The PC states, "We have increased security on the waterfront but with secret attacks, the odds are against us. Still, we must protect New York and the ships going to Europe. There is no doubt that we are dealing with an organized network of spies and saboteurs."

"You are right." Murphy says. *And about time*, he thinks while flashing a look at Centori.

"Why now? There is no war in Europe," Haughey asks.

Murphy quickly answers, "Not now, but this seems like some kind of preventive strike on the Allies."

"Hmm, regardless of logic, we need to know who is making bombs and who is behind the shipboard attacks," the PC says. "How do they do it? War supply shipments to Europe are secret."

"They should be top secret," Murphy says.

"What's more, we are facing a hard-nosed enemy that is ready and able to attack the U.S. with no known limit," Centori adds.

The PC stands and pounds his fist on the table. "New York is now subject to attacks of terror and the NYPD will take all the needed action to stop further attacks."

"But, who are the operatives? Who are the leaders?" Haughey softly asks.

"Our investigation is stalled," Waldan says.

"We are not stalled," Murphy replies.

"You think so?"

"Yes, Commissioner, this case is different from standard police work. A lot of people are working on this; we just have not gotten any solid leads that can crack this case. We have to explain how it is possible for saboteurs to gain unhindered access into supply ships."

"You are correct," Waldan says. "We have not identified the ringleaders but we continue the collection and preservation of evidence. We are conducting investigations and interrogations of suspects, but with limited information. They appear to be trained and experienced criminals."

"They are not criminals, Commissioner. They are terrorists." Murphy says.

"Thank you for coming."

Back in the sedan, Centori turns to Murphy, "I heard from the Circle C. That paper has turned to ash; that door is closed."

"Good, that is one thing off my mind, but the New York door is wide open."

Eighteen hundred miles away in New Mexico, Greigos had climbed Little Hill Top and unceremoniously set the Revert Document aflame. It rapidly burned with ashes spreading in the air; it is destroyed—once and for all time.

CHAPTER 71

BROOKLYN NAVY YARD

After the American Revolution, the Brooklyn waterfront produced merchant ships. In 1801, the U.S. government purchased the docks and 40 acres, and the site became a U.S. Navy shipyard. In 1890, the ill-fated USS *Maine* launched from the Brooklyn Navy Yard. The USS *New York* will launch from the Navy Yard in the fall.

Bachmeier and recent arrival Siegfried Seiler have been watching the Brooklyn Navy Yard for signs of weakness—they found a few. The next morning, an explosion in the Navy Yard destroyed a barge filled with munitions.

Encouraged by the Navy Yard explosion, Riesenfelder takes an evening ferry to Jersey City; he rides the ferry with the behavior of a tourist and the heart of a predator. On the New Jersey side of the Hudson River, he wanders and wonders. Then, in the distance, he sees a massive munitions depot with scores of transport ships—it is an auspicious discovery.

The next day, Riesenfelder sits in the Second Avenue beer hall with a less than notable Bachmeier. There is no need to whisper in the noisy *hofbrau*. The Germans drink from heavy beer steins.

After finishing their first beers, Bachmeier says, "I am honored that you wish to see me. That was not what I understood."

"That decision was professional; things have changed. We must now communicate directly."

Bachmeier drains his stein and waits.

"The waterfront operation is lacking."

"Herr Riesenfelder, I have been successful. We have recruited reliable and capable men from the docks, many loyal to the Kaiser," Bachmeier protests.

"All that is true."

"I assure you that our work will continue and remain a secret."

"I am not questioning your performance," Riesenfelder states. "Your men have done well but the attacks are erratic and their value momentary."

"Herr Riesenfelder, we have a highly-financed operation and…"

"Wait! The shipboard fires and explosions are simply not enough. U.S. war supply production is efficient with great capacity. Shipments to Europe are ongoing, preparing our enemies for war and will continue despite your work. Obstruction of U.S. munitions exports is completely inadequate. There are too many ships leaving the harbor to supply our enemies—too many to stop."

"Herr Riesenfelder, what are you suggesting?"

"We must think about the waterfront operation differently."

"What do you mean?"

"If we cannot stop shipping, we must seriously limit the enemies' capacity to supply their ships."

"I understand."

"Your work in Brooklyn destroyed large amounts of munitions. That excellent news was well received in Berlin, prompting the next phase of our campaign."

"What can I do?"

"Have you ever taken a ride on the Staten Island Ferry?"

CHAPTER 72

NOTCH IN TIME

Driving around Times Square, Murphy says, "Adobe, the Brooklyn Navy Yard explosion made us look very bad."

"It was worse for the people involved."

"Of course, I think it is time to take a firsthand look."

"What do you mean?"

"I know you are partial to Irish whiskey, but how about some German beer?"

Centori stares and waits.

"There is beer hall in Yorkville on Second Avenue that is under surveillance. It has been reported that German dock workers are showing up more frequently; I just have a hunch. Let's have German beer."

"Okay."

"Henry, please drive us uptown to Yorkville."

McGillivray hits the gas and drives uptown to Columbus Circle and then through Central Park to the East side and Yorkville. They exit the black sedan on a side street near the beer hall. McGillivray slowly drives away.

"We will enter separately; I will go in first. Take your big hat off and hold that Stetson down low."

"Ha-ha, good idea."

Murphy walks around the corner to Second Avenue, enters the *hofbrau* that specializes in beer—and revelry. The band plays Bavarian music as the bartender taps a new keg and another man refills a wooden bowl with large pretzels. The federal agent approaches the long bar and notices German words and painted murals that cover the walls. He can't read the signs but he knows it is the right neighborhood.

Two minutes later, Centori walks in as the bar "regulars" sing along with the German music.

"Feeling a little out of place?" Murphy asks.

Centori, looks around and smiles, "Yep, only one thing to do: let's have a beer."

The break in the music yields to the loud noise of the reveling patrons. The two federal agents sip their beers and try not to look conspicuous. Centori turns his head slightly and sees a back room with long, communal tables.

"Lively crowd," he acknowledges.

Murphy nods and sips his dark brew. Suddenly, a song breaks out in the back room; men at a communal table sing their rendition of *Soldiers in the Park* in German.

Too drunk for discretion, they loudly greet a man who enters from the back door. The new arrival holds up his hands to quiet the crowd and finds a seat at the table.

Speaking over the music and in German, he holds court at the table. The one-way conversation is brief and to the point. Soon after, the speaker stands to leave at the moment Centori looks in that direction. Their eyes meet. The German shows fear. Centori shows outrage. Both men freeze in place, one second, two seconds;

Bachmeier bursts out the back door. Without a word, Centori runs to the back room leaving a shocked Murphy behind.

Outside, Centori sees him running toward Lexington Avenue and breaks into a run. Dozens watch as he chases after Bachmeier who runs to the subway entrance and downstairs to the station—violently knocking over anyone in his way. Centori goes into the subway station able to keep him in sight. Pushing people out of the way, he jumps the turnstile and runs along the platform. In wild pursuit, Centori follows. The saboteur, cornered, quickly jumps on the tracks leading Centori into the tunnel. A subterranean pursuit follows. Now, in an underground chase, they run along the tracks in dim light. The next station is just ahead. The screeching sound of a train fills the tunnel behind them. Bachmeier makes it to the next station but no time for Centori. The train bears down. He sees a worker's safety alcove and jams his body into the shallow notch in the wall, narrowly avoiding death. The saboteur climbs onto the platform, returns to street level and walks slowly as the train roars by Centori, inches from his face, violently whipping his shirt. It is quiet. Centori remains frozen as if the train was still flashing by his body—breathing heavily with his heart pounding against his chest. Seconds later, he realizes he lost the fleeing Bachmeier and his cowboy hat.

McGillivray and Murphy are driving a few blocks near the beer hall looking for Centori, who is walking back from the 77th Street subway station. At Second Avenue and 80th Street, the black sedan pulls over.

"What the hell happened?" Murphy yells.

"Thought I saw someone I knew."

CHAPTER 73

THE NEW YORK AMERICAN

Two nights later in his Knickerbocker room, Centori is still disturbed about failing in the wild subway chase. He could have stopped Bachmeier and perhaps cracked the entire German network. Sleep finally overcomes his regret.

At midnight he is shaken by a loud blast—as were thousands of New Yorkers. He rushes to the eighth floor window to see an eerie light in the sky. He dresses and heads to the lobby. Workers and guests are buzzing about the explosion, trying to learn the cause of the blast and where it occurred.

Centori quickly approaches the front desk, "What happened?"

"Sounds like it came from Jersey; that's all we know."

The next morning as he enters the lobby, a newsboy in front of the hotel shouts, "Extra, Extra, read all about it, blast rocks harbor." The newsboy carries copies of *The New York American* with a big front page bulletin:

Big Munitions Explosion Rocks New York Harbor

Last night at midnight, small fires erupted on the pier that contains a munitions depot with over two million pounds of ammunition: shrapnel, black powder and dynamite. Fearing the explosion, some of the warehouse guards fled; others tried fighting the fires before summoning the fire department. A succession of small explosions followed. Then a terrifying blast destroyed the largest munitions shipping point in the U.S.

When most of the smoke cleared, the destruction to the depot, warehouses, railroads, barges and piers was exposed. The Brooklyn Bridge was shaken and thousands of window panes were shattered in New York and New Jersey buildings. Scores of people were killed and hundreds were injured. The munitions, stored in freight cars and barges within the Gotham Dock and Storage Company, were destined for shipment to England, France and Russia.

Centori finishes reading a newspaper account of the blast and stares ahead in disbelief. *What in the world is happening?*

He returns to the lobby, walks near the front desk and hears, "Mr. Centori, this telephone message arrived for you."

"Thank you."

He opens the small envelope; the message inside reads:

Battery Park 10:00 a.m.
N.Mex Ranger

Centori folds the note, turns back. "Please have any other messages sent to my room immediately."

"I am happy to do so."

"If I am not here, call police headquarters and ask for Jack Haughey of the commissioner's office."

"Yes, Sir, Mr. Centori."

CHAPTER 74

BATTERY PARK

Battery Park, at the southern point of Manhattan, faces New York Harbor. Gun batteries once occupied the site to protect the settlement in the 17th and 18th centuries. The park contains the old fort, Castle Clinton, a U.S. Coast Guard building and a view of the Statue of Liberty.

Presented to the U.S. from France in recognition of the American Revolution alliance, the Statue of Liberty stands on Bedloe's Island as a strong icon of freedom—unshaken for 25 years, until now. The inspiring face of America was shaken by the harbor explosion. Fragments of metal from the blast were widely dispersed—shrapnel damage rendering her torch unstable. After the initial explosion, smaller blasts endured for hours, all through the night. Small clouds of black smoke hover over the Jersey City dock and are visible from Battery Park.

Murphy is leaning on the railing staring at the disaster site across the water when a hatless Centori arrives. "What the hell happened out there?"

"We have some good ideas," Murphy replies.

"The blast nearly knocked me out of bed."

"Shock waves and noise from the explosions were heard along the Jersey shoreline, Staten Island, Brooklyn and as far as Philadelphia. This attack is bigger and more ambitious than the Navy Yard and the shipping fires—and certainty bigger than Wall Street."

"As the center of capitalism, the Wall Street attack was driven by economic grievances, but this…"

"Yes, this is military."

"Wall Street was only the beginning—as we suspected from the beginning."

"Yes, and Wall Street was done by internal enemies with the help of external enemies." Murphy points across the harbor. "That is a powerful attack on a military target. However, the goals of the attacks are connected—damage or destroy a common foe."

"The stakes, as expected, continue to rise. Each terror attack has been bigger than the last one with increased destruction. We have a far greater threat than American Scream."

"I am afraid so; the harbor bombing was a high skill professional effort, beyond the talent of bomb throwing anarchists."

"External and military."

"No doubt. Who benefits from the New Jersey explosion?" Murphy does not wait for an answer. "Consider that war materiel made in the east coast and assembled at the Jersey City munitions depot is earmarked for transport to Europe. Germany is served by the destruction of supplies to the Allies or anything that cripples America's war industry."

"This is the work of German saboteurs—dangerous saboteurs. Germany has declared a secret war against the U.S. Murph, that man I chased through the subway tunnel…I told you he worked with Jarvia in Valtura. Now I think he is the key saboteur."

"Bachmeier is high on our list."

"They have expanded their interest in the U.S. from our southern border to the east coast."

"With good reason; German army commanders created a Franco-German war plan *without* Russia as an eastern front threat. It calls for Germany to invade France from the German-Belgian border."

"The Germans could defeat the smaller French Army," Centori adds.

"Yes, but with Russia as an eastern enemy that is not probable since a two-front war reduces German forces in the West."

"And that makes the German war plan obsolete."

"Correct. So, German agents are determined to prevent delivery of munitions to France, to England and to Russia—countries likely to be Germany's enemies.

"It would get worse for Germany with U.S. involvement."

"In the event of war, the U.S. will side with France—that is what the Germans fear."

To that point, Centori says, "The U.S. is already involved by shipping munitions to Europe."

"We are involved…the harbor attack was an endeavor to fight back—an act of war."

"What do we do now?"

"The commissioner has men protecting the stock exchange and other key buildings; we don't see additional threats there. We have a man watching Jarvia's building around the clock. Her doorman is watching for us too."

"She is a leader of the German network of spies and saboteurs in New York and can lead us to Bachmeier and other key agents."

"Jarvia is our most important lead, but she is a phantom. Her trail from Valtura is cold."

"Let's hope she needs to come in from the cold and is homesick for Park Avenue. We need to find her and stop the attacks."

Centori stares away and says, "She is beautiful."

"What? Come on Adobe, forget Jarvia; she is the enemy now."

"No, I am talking about her," he points to the neoclassical realistic robed figure in the harbor.

The Statue of Liberty, designed by Frederic Auguste Bartholdi, holds a *tabula ansata* with the inscription July 4, 1776, and Centori's fascination.

"Yes, she is beautiful," Murphy says. He turns back to the black smoke over the dock and what is left of the Gotham Dock and Storage Company.

Aldoloreto 'Adobe' Centori's family was part of the first large group of Italian immigrants to America. When immigrants aboard steamships entered the harbor, the Statue of Liberty was their first look at America. After docking, first and second class passengers went ashore; steerage passengers went to Ellis Island by ferries.

On Ellis Island, immigrants entered the enormous air space of the Registry Room or Main Hall and marveled over the size and the arched windows. They looked up at a complex terra-cotta ceiling with thousands of self-supporting interlocking tiles almost 60 feet high.

As the large crowds of immigrants moved through the Registry Room, they gazed at the ceiling with a feeling of wonder. Centori reflects on family stories about the room and about inspiring starts to a better future. Many immigrants never forgot that magnificent ceiling—a gateway to their new home in America.

CHAPTER 75

COMMON ENEMY

Police Commissioner Waldan called a meeting immediately following the New York Harbor blast, this time in his private office. Centori, Murphy and Haughey sit in front of the commissioner's large desk, once used by former Police Commissioner Theodore Roosevelt, and wait for him to start.

"The official police position will be in today's papers. We consider the harbor explosion an accident until we know differently."

"An accident?" Centori stares.

Murphy glances at him. "He is right, Commissioner, this is no accident."

The PC's tone is different, more willing to admit what is becoming apparent. "Perhaps, but we wish not to alarm the public."

"Commissioner, Wall Street has already alarmed the public and the two explosions are connected," Murphy states.

"How do you know? What is the common denominator?"

"Jarvia Hoffmann," Centori says without hesitation.

"Who?"

"She is the German link to American Scream."

"That is your conclusion? What evidence do you have?"

"Take a look at this file," Murphy says before handing it to the PC. "American Scream is German in origin or supported by Germany—that is the connection between the Wall Street and the harbor explosions. Germany is hiding behind internal anarchists, so that the terror attacks point away from them."

Waldan glances at the report. "We are dealing with socialists, communists and anarchists. Now we add Germans to the mix?"

"Yes, they have conducted small attacks, each one increasing in destruction until this major attack," Murphy replies. "Also, Mr. Centori has successfully worked on a serious national issue involving Germany; do not discount his assessment."

This time Centori glances at Murphy. Haughey stares in silence, taking it all in.

"Mr. Murphy, perhaps you should focus on international affairs and leave New York to the NYPD," the PC says.

Murphy responds, "We are trying to tell you that New York is involved in international affairs. The goals of the two factions are different; class war versus world war. Yet, American Scream is a puppet of Berlin. As long as the money flows, the anarchists will do as instructed. They have dissimilar political perspectives, but they are all dynamiters with a common enemy—the United States."

"Commissioner, this would not be the first time that European conflicts entwine with American conflicts," Centori points out. "I know what I am talking about."

"I can attest to that. We are not as vulnerable as England or France. The Atlantic Ocean is wide enough to protect the U.S. from military invasion. However, some of the Germans in Yorkville may have loyalty to Berlin."

Haughey shifts in his chair as Murphy continues, "Most are loyal Americans. Many fought in the Civil War for the north and are not in love with the fatherland. However, there are Germans who were sent here to settle, take jobs, live among us and spy for the fatherland."

Haughey ventures an opinion, "Also, they could contact traditional German immigrants and try to corrupt them against America. There are thousands across the country."

"We are not dealing with domestic criminals—these people are out for blood, a lot of blood. It may be hard to believe that we have foreign agents here in New York. We must wake up to that fact," Murphy adds before taking a deep breath. "Please understand, that file has valuable information."

"I know you are right," the PC finally admits. "But how will you proceed without exposing us to charges of being belligerents against Germany? We cannot be compelled to enter a war. Do you have names and operational plans?"

"We have enough not to ignore Germany's secret war against Uncle Sam."

"No one is ignoring the danger, industrial accidents or not."

"Commissioner, we are fighting Germans, American sympathizers and the Kaiser's spies. Either way, it is most certainly the job of the federal government, but we need the help of the New York police."

Waldan slowly shakes his head in agreement and says, "We will protect New York."

"We need more men working undercover in Yorkville and more men to patrol the waterfront," Murphy states. "We need the new bomb squad to help find the men who make the explosive mixes. They will raise the stakes, so let's be a step ahead."

"Gentlemen, I don't need to tell you of the pressure I am getting from the mayor. I guess it comes with the job."

Officer Haughey nods.

"We will all do our jobs," Murphy promises.

Centori agrees. "We will do what it takes to stop the leaders of the German ring of spies and saboteurs."

"You need to find them first, Mr. Centori."

Turning to Murphy and Haughey he says, "Let's go."

"Good luck, gentlemen," the commissioner sincerely says.

The three men march downstairs and outside to stand in front of headquarters. They form a circle on Centre Street to converse. Murphy leads the talk, "We will continue to seek information to identify the members of American Scream."

"And German nationals in New York, besides Jarvia, who are linked to American Scream," Centori adds.

"That's right. Jack, can you recommend a policeman to work with us?" Murphy asks.

"Yes, Mr. Murphy, I can do that."

"After walking the beat, coppers are of a mind to protect New York and will have good instincts to help us rope in the German agents. And call me Murph, just as this cowboy does!"

They all laugh and walk to the black sedan parked on the side of the building. Murphy takes the front seat next to McGillivray; Centori and Haughey sit in the back seat. Murphy turns to the back seat. "There could be something more to the PC's resistance to acknowledging a secret war against the U.S."

"What's that?" Centori asks.

"American neutrality is creating big profits for U.S. industries, making many powerful people much richer."

"Hmm, the shipment of supplies to Europe is very profitable."

"That's right, and war with Germany could change that if the U.S. makes a quick end to the conflict. Wall Street capitalists have made generous loans to the Allies for the purchase of U.S. supplies; armament makers are making millions."

"All that does not sound very neutral," Haughey says.

"You have a point, but there are dominant forces that like things just the way they are."

"That sounds incredible," Centori says.

"So was the Revert Document."

"Revert what?" Haughey asks.

"Where to?" McGillivray asks.

Before Murphy can answer, a young policeman knocks on the window.

"Mr. Murphy, this message just arrived for you."

"Thank you, Officer.

A few seconds later, Centori asks, "What is it?"

"It's from the doorman at Jarvia's building. He has accepted delivery of several packages for her."

"So, she could be back in New York," Centori says.

"Or coming back soon; we have a man watching for a beautiful redhead from the Seventh Regiment Armory.

"Armory?"

CHAPTER 76

❧❧❧

MEINE LIEBE

JUNE, 1912

J arvia Hoffmann and a young, pretty woman with brown eyes and brown hair walk together on Park Avenue. The wide boulevard that runs north and south on the east side of Manhattan was originally called Fourth Avenue. The two women, who move north from Grand Central Terminal, are wearing dark dresses.

"I am happy you are here," Jarvia says in her deep seductive voice. "I thought you would never arrive."

"I had my difficulties finding my way here."

"Now that you are here, I am comforted," Jarvia admits.

Several minutes later they arrive at the corner of 66th Street and Park Avenue. Jarvia smiles, "This is my building; I live here."

"Very fancy place," she smiles too.

"I must leave you for a time; take my key and wait for me here."

"But Jennifer, I just arrived with much anticipation after a hard journey."

"I must leave; it is imperative that I do so," she snaps.

"Yes, of course."

"The doorman may question you. Tell him you are the new owner of my apartment—and be sure to flirt. You do know how to flirt with a man, don't you?"

"I will wait for you here."

"Our anticipation shall sustain us for now."

Eager to show more tenderness than wildness, Felicity whispers, "I have missed you."

"I have missed you. *Auf wiedersehen, meine liebe.*"

The doorman, busy receiving a package for Jarvia, does not question the young woman's entrance into the building and into the elevator.

Chapter 77

Champagne Cocktails

Count Helmut von Riesenfelder and Jarvia Hoffman meet again at the main entrance of the Plaza Hotel on Fifth Avenue. He arrives wearing a black double-breasted suit and admires her lacy, drop waist black dress. The French Renaissance hotel that opened five years earlier faces the nearly completed Grand Army Plaza. The plaza will commemorate the Grand Army of the Potomac, the Union Army during the Civil War.

"Frau Hoffman."

"Shall we?"

"Yes."

The count escorts her to the Champagne Porch, an outside restaurant overlooking Fifth Avenue. The place is located between the outdoor columns and the hotel itself. They are escorted to a table close to a column.

"It is nice to see you again, Frau Hoffmann. You are looking even more beautiful."

"Thank you."

"What would you like to drink?"

"I would like a champagne cocktail."

Riesenfelder orders; minutes later a fancy dressed waiter with white gloves returns with two drinks on a silver tray. *Rote Frau* is fond of champagne sweetened with a sugar cube, bitters and a lemon twist—a drink that she sorely missed while in New Mexico.

"Frau Hoffman, allow me to toast our great success in New York. The fatherland and your husband are proud of your work, an important effort in saving our brave soldiers once the war begins."

"Thank you, Herr Riesenfelder."

"We will continue with the overall strategy with some changes."

"Yes, I am sure of that."

"I have met Bachmeier and have taken his measure. You will contact him immediately and inform him of certain changes. I will not see him now."

"Tell me about these certain changes."

Riesenfelder smiles, "The good work in the harbor is our largest success to date."

"Yes, however, I am afraid the police will increase their activities in trying to identify our organization and our people; they are already crawling around the waterfronts asking questions."

"That is why we will change our campaign. Let the police concentrate on the waterfront; we will not return. Rather, we must think about an event that will shatter the confidence of the American people and prevent them from ever interfering with European affairs." Riesenfelder sips his drink. "Once we destroy the target, American resolve to enter the coming war will decrease—or at least the political leadership will seek reasons to remain isolationists."

"You must have identified a highly significant target."

"Our plan will eclipse all the other attacks—it is a plan with catastrophic consequences for New York and for the U.S."

"That is especially ominous and confident. What is your plan?"

He opens a map of Manhattan. "This is the target. We are making a bomb to take it to the ground—an explosion that will fiercely shake the building down to its foundation."

After a moment of shocked silence, she looks away from the map and says, "Herr Riesenfelder, is it believed that such a massive terror attack will convince America to stay out of European affairs?"

"Yes, the internal instability caused by the destruction of this target will also destroy their drive for interfering with Europe. They will stop helping our foes—stop killing our brave German soldiers!"

"Shatter the confidence of the American people, you say?"

"That is correct. You have objections?"

"Oh, yes."

"What is it?"

"You do not wish to know."

"Humor me, Frau Hoffman."

"First, you have just arrived in America and yet you presume to know the American character; you do not. Second, I have lived with the Americans; you have not."

"You have more than lived with the Americans, Frau Hoffman."

Angered by his indelicate comment, she replies, "I know more. Centori is an indication of the American character. You will not shatter their confidence. If you do this, the American resolve to fight in Europe will increase. They will come by day and come by night. It would be the end of Germany. Yes, Herr Riesenfelder, I have many objections."

"And we have our orders, Frau Hoffman. The Kaiser's plan can ensure a victory for us when the guns begin to fire.

Returning to Park Avenue, an uncertain Jarvia enters her building and draws a curious look from the doorman.

"Welcome back, Miss Prower."

She smiles past the doorman and rides the elevator to her apartment where Felicity Brimwell readily greets her. "I hope you will not be rushing off again."

"Not before morning, my dear. Shall I make us champagne cocktails?"

CHAPTER 78

GREATER TASK

Jarvia and Felicity leave the apartment separately the next morning. Felicity walks southwest. Jarvia walks northeast. She demanded another meeting with Bachmeier at Carl Schurz Park; this time at a different bench.

Bachmeier is late, having started the day at a house in Queens. The Corona house, used for planning and retreating, is considered safe by the network. It is away from the main chess board of Manhattan.

She is looking at the East River when he boorishly arrives. "Where is Herr Riesenfelder?"

"I told you before, he avoids creating patterns. I will tell you his orders."

He impolitely sits down on the bench; she follows. "We must assemble a large amount of TNT. To do that, you will procure small amounts in different places."

"What you are asking is very dangerous," he protests.

"If you think so, then prepare for what I say next!"

He stares in defiance and says nothing. She looks around the park before revealing the plan. "We are moving into another phase of our campaign, away from military targets. It is an imperative for Riesenfelder and other high-ranking officials in the secret service. The attack will be welcomed by Spooner as well."

"A civilian target?"

"Yes."

"Where?"

"It is a very important building in New York, a very big building."

"Can you tell me the building?"

"Yes, in time."

"I don't understand; we have been charged with destroying military targets."

"No longer, at least not until we finish this task."

"I am not sure…."

"I am losing my good humor. Berlin has approved this plan; shall I report your lack of cooperation?"

"I am not unwilling.

"Good."

"You are serious about this business?"

"Quiet serious."

"I am unsure of the purpose."

"The U.S. is financing loans for war supplies to our enemies. We must prevent this injustice against Germany. The destruction of this building can slow or stop that stream of money."

"I presume all necessary precautions will be taken."

"Yes."

"When will you tell the target?"

"Go to the Corona house. The details of the plan will be sent there. Yet, you can begin the process immediately."

"I understand."

"Your must recruit a TNT specialist with the technical skills to build a dynamite bomb big enough for the purpose. Also, we need information from structural engineers in bomb placement."

"We can meet the requirements."

"Good. So, you are up to the task?"

"Yes."

She hands him a fat envelope. He feels the heft, "It is a much greater amount this time."

"You have a much greater task. Inform your network in Yorkville."

"What do you mean?"

"Tell them to instruct trusted Germans to avoid downtown on the designated date—tell them as late as possible."

CHAPTER 79

BLACK WIDOW

The Seventh Regiment Armory occupies an entire block and is visible from Jarvia's apartment window across the avenue; Murphy's sedan is not. The medieval building was headquarters of the 7th New York Militia, an infantry regiment in the Union Army. McGillivray, Murphy and Centori sit in the motorcar that is parked in the shadows of the armory.

"Are you sure she is here?" Centori says nervously.

"I have hunch that she is back in New York."

"You do?"

"Yes, we can expect her to return here at some point."

"I want her to admit to her involvement in the Circle C shootout."

"We have no incriminating evidence; she is too good to leave a trace and you killed the attackers."

"What about the trip to Stratford."

"Adobe, we know enough but not enough to arrest her."

"What about her involvement with Wall Street?"

"The evidence is not strong enough. The law right now does not cover suspicion. We need to catch *Rote Frau* red-handed. Besides, continuing surveillance could lead to the sabotage ring; she may not talk if arrested. What you do with her after that is your business—if she survives."

Centori stares and says nothing.

"Let's go in and wait upstairs."

They leave McGillivray in the sedan and walk to the entrance of the elegant apartment building. Murphy nods at the doorman.

"Mr. Murphy, I am glad you got my message."

"Yes, packages are arriving for her."

"No! She is back!"

They run up the steps to the third floor and arrive at apartment 3E. Murphy pounds on the door. "Open up."

No answer.

"Wait here," Murphy says.

He returns with the doorman who has a key, drawing attention from a curious resident. The apartment is empty.

"Okay, no more mistakes, we wait here," Murphy says.

Almost an hour later, the former Venus of Valtura arrives on the third floor and turns a hall corner toward her apartment. She stops dead in her tracks.

Jarvia's mouth falls open.

Cold as ice, she stands frozen in place with a disbelieving stare, trying to process the trap. Centori looks at her, but not in the same way. "You look surprised to see me," he says with his Navy Colt in hand. Then his eyes move over her body, looking for a gun.

The shocked Jarvia feels a shiver of alarm. With a husky voice and wide eyes the fiery redhead demands, "What are you doing here?"

Murphy says, "We know who you are and what you do. If you do not help us, you will be profoundly sorry."

Staring down the business end of Murphy's 32 caliber Colt Revolver with a 4" barrel she growls, "Who are you?"

His face set in resolve; he touches her arm and says, "I am the person who can destroy you as easily as stepping on a black widow spider."

"I suggest you keep your damn hands off me!"

She looks at the door and Murphy says, "No one is in there; you are alone."

Turning back to Centori, she says, "All the way from New Mexico to see me? I am flattered."

"Don't be."

Murphy holsters his gun and says, "It would be in your best interest to help us. Tell me the names of those connected with the Wall Street bombing."

"I know nothing about that."

"What do you know about the Brooklyn Navy Yard and the Gotham Dock and Storage Company?"

"Nothing."

"When is the next New York attack?" Murphy demands.

"I don't know anything about any attacks. Don't you understand English?"

"Sure, as well as you understand German," Centori interjects.

"If you do not cooperate, you will spend the rest of your life in a U.S. prison," Murphy promises.

Trembling with rage she screams, "I have diplomatic immunity. I am a close associate of the Kaiser."

"I would not count on that. Give me the operatives in your network."

"No. There is nothing I can do for you."

"Then there is nothing I can do for you."

Jarvia looks at Centori for help based on his feelings, if they still exist.

Centori with his gun now at his side says, "Did you send armed men to the Circle C?"

Still concealing her fear, she says, "No."

"One of my best friends was killed! A young cowboy was killed too."

"I don't know what you are saying."

"So it was all a tragic misunderstanding?"

She sees no relief from her predicament and turns back to Murphy.

"What do you want from me?"

"Provide information that will stop the next attack."

"I don't know."

"Who are the leaders of American Scream?"

"How would I know that?"

"Where are the German spies and saboteurs?"

"He means besides you," Centori states.

She does not respond.

Murphy pulls out a set of iron handcuffs, "I have had enough."

"Turn around," Murphy orders.

"You have no reason to arrest me."

"We can determine that at the city jail, it is called the Tombs here."

No longer concealing fear, she looks at Centori again, but he is cold and offers no recourse.

"Wait! Perhaps I can provide some help."

"You will identify the ring of spies and saboteurs and their locations."

"I am not sure, but I have heard some talk about a secret house."

Playing along with her charade, Murphy says, "Go on."

"There may be a house across the river near Corona Plaza."

Centori questions, "Corona Plaza? Is that some kind of joke?"

Murphy turns to him and informs, "There is a village called Corona across the river in Queens, probably started after you left New York."

"Feeling sentimental about our time in New Mexico, Adobe?" she mocks.

He holsters his gun and replies, "No, just hoping you would not cooperate so we would throw you in prison."

"He's right. You will be in jail if you are not telling the truth," Murphy says before signaling through the window for McGillivray to come up.

"The house number is 34 off 42nd Avenue," she reluctantly says.

Centori steps closer and stares into Jarvia's eyes, "How could you do it?"

She laughs as Murphy pulls him away and signals through the window.

A few moments later, McGillivray arrives at the apartment.

"Henry, I will take the motorcar. Stay here, we will be back. Don't let her out of your sight."

"Okay, that is not so hard to do."

"Be careful—she bites," Centori grumbles.

Walking to the sedan Centori says. "Her cooperation does not help her situation."

"That's right…far from it."

CHAPTER 80

CORONA PLAZA

As they walk down three flights of steps, Murphy says to Centori, "Jack and our new man should be at the armory now." They cross Park Avenue and find Hughley and another man standing near the sedan. "John Murphy, Adobe Centori, this is Rocco Grandinetto."

After a round of handshakes, Hughley's recommendation says, "Good to know you men."

Grandinetto is a serious young man who was born in Italy. He came to America as a child and grew up in Little Italy. Murphy takes the driver seat, the two officers take the back seat and Centori rides 'shotgun.' "It will be quicker to take the El train from Grand Central Terminal," Murphy says.

They reach the terminal in five minutes. From there, they park the sedan and ride the new IRT subway line to Corona that becomes an elevated train in Queens and extends from the Queensboro Plaza station to the Alburtis Avenue-Corona Plaza station. The village was a late 19th century residential development by the Crown Building

Company. Italian immigrants called the new town the Italian and Spanish word for 'crown,' Corona.

The elevated train rolls into the Corona Plaza 103rd Street station with metal wheels screeching on metal rails; the men exit to the platform and down the steps. They walk on Alburtis Avenue toward a public school and public park with a lake in the middle. Turning on 42nd Avenue they look for house number 34. Centori and Haughey position themselves next to the front door; Murphy and Grandinetto are at the side door that leads to the cellar.

All enter at the same time—with force. Murphy and Grandinetto quickly scan the basement. "No one here," Murphy calls out. They run to the first floor where Centori reports, "No one here either. Jack, Rocco, wait here to cover our backs."

With guns drawn, Centori, and Murphy grab a heavy wooden banister and race up the staircase. They take the stairs two steps at a time to a short hallway with three doors.

The bathroom door is open—empty. The two other doors are closed. Centori kicks through one of them; it hurls open crashing against a wall. He rushes inside with his Navy Colt in front; no one is there. At the same moment, the second door slowly opens from the inside, light flows into the hall, illuminating a hand gripping a weapon. Murphy rapidly pushes through the door pushing the man back. Centori follows and hits the man low slamming him to the floor. The man, who is wearing a leather vest with a wet bit of sackcloth over his shoulder, groans with pain. Murphy grabs a little hammer from the man's belt and demands, "Who are you?"

"Sono l'uomo di ghiaccio."

"What?" Murphy yells.

"He is the iceman." Centori explains.

"There is an ice wagon parked near the public school," Haughey adds.

"Why are you here?"

"Allow me Mr. Murphy," Grandinetto says. He turns to the shaken man and speaks in Italian. "We are the police. Why are you here?"

"I told you I am the iceman. I deliver ice and keep this house supplied with beer."

"Where are the people who pay you?"

"They are never here when I come; they leave money in the icebox."

"You never met them?"

"One time only."

"Were they American?"

"No, German."

Grandinetto looks at Murphy and explains the conversation.

"Either Jarvia warned them or our timing is off," Murphy states. "Let him go."

After the iceman drives away in his wagon, they search desk drawers and closets on both floors but find nothing of value. "Let's go to the lower ground floor," Centori says.

In the cellar, they search and again come up empty. Murphy orders, "Okay, that's all. Let's get back to Jarvia."

"Wait a minute," Centori replies, "this house has a raised porch."

"What are you getting at?" Murphy asks.

Instead of answering, Centori reaches to the top of the cellar wall with his arm full extended. He bangs the wall with his gun butt, bang, bang, bang and crash—an imperceptible door is revealed. It covers a porch crawl space and opens to a secret storage area. "Grab a chair," Centori says.

A moment later, he steps on the chair and pulls himself up and into the dark crawl space. He struggles to retrieve a match from his pocket. Striking the match provides some light in the confined space.

"I see something," he yells down.

"What is it?" Murphy shouts back.

Instead of answering, Centori, hands him a small crate, "Take this box; there are others further back." Murphy opens the box to find a wireless telegraphy machine.

Centori hands down two other boxes to Grandinetto who takes off the covers to find notebooks, sheets of paper and books.

Haughey removes and examines a file from one of the boxes and exclaims, "It's all in German."

"If there was any doubt of international implications, it is gone now," Grandinetto says.

Murphy stares at Grandinetto and says, "This case was always about the Imperial German government. Let's go."

The four men rush back to Corona Plaza and the El bounding up the stairs to the train platform, resolute to confront Jarvia. Once again treachery is her tool. A track problem slows the IRT ride, adding more stress. At Grand Central, they waste no time and march up Park Avenue to 66th Street.

At 50th Street the men pass a young woman who is walking at a brisk pace. Centori notices her for an additional reason; she looks familiar. She gives a quick turn as if she recognizes him too.

No time for him to think about that now. They approach the armory and cross the street. At the center divider waiting for the motorcar traffic, it hits him. *That woman is Felicity from Mad Mady's Saloon.*

Centori breaks into a run and yells, "Let's get to the apartment, *pronto.*"

They run into the building, rush past the doorman and race up the stairs. They find the apartment door slightly ajar. It becomes instantly and astonishingly clear that the place is completely empty of furniture and any sign that Jarvia ever lived there. There is one object in the entire vacant apartment—Henry McGillivray's body—shot dead.

The shocked men stand in silence until, in a rare display of raw emotion, Murphy shouts, "I want her DEAD! DEAD! DEAD!"

Centori and Murphy are both driven to seek revenge on Jarvia. Although their emotional reaction to her murdering ways prompts retaliation, they know that impartial punishment is the answer. Jennifer Prower aka *Rote Frau* would be the first woman hanged in the U.S. since 1905—that would be justice for Jarvia.

Chapter 81

Catastrophic Consequences

June 13th

Murphy received the translation of the papers recovered in the Corona house. Centori, Haughey and Grandinetto sit at a table at the 'Old King Cole' bar eager to learn about the information they contained.

"Leaving the plans in the Corona house was careless, especially for such smart guys," Centori observes with sarcasm.

After the drinks arrive, Murphy arrives and joins the table; he is prepared to discuss the findings and interpretation.

"You look serious," Centori says.

"It is serious," Murphy answers as he sits. "A big attack plan is exposed. The papers contain plans for making a very powerful bomb."

"For what purpose...or target?" Grandinetto asks.

"That is ambiguous, but it is powerful enough to knock down a major structure."

"So the target is not clear?" Centori asks.

"Right, but the size of the potential explosion is disturbingly clear. They will assemble a very large amount of TNT." Murphy answers.

"When will they attack?" Haughey asks.

Murphy shakes his head and replies, "The papers do not indicate a date."

"If this plan is real, we have confirmation that Germany intends to carry out a major terrorist attack against the U.S.," Centori states.

"Yes. We just don't know the target or the time," Murphy adds.

Centori says, "It could be Wall Street again."

Murphy replies, "It could be any major building in New York. The Wall Street bombing is relatively small compared to the destruction indicated in the Corona house papers."

"Only the sabotage method is known," Haughey says.

"It is a method that suggests something big. Jack, have the department investigate any unusually large purchases of TNT," Murphy says.

"Sure. I will call the commissioner now."

"He will know shortly. A copy of the translation was sent to his office."

"They may have purchased small amounts of TNT in many places," Haughey adds.

"Good point."

"We still do not know the target," Grandinetto says.

"In most of the papers, written in a type of code, there is a repeated reference to propaganda by deed and to the *Kathedrale*," Murphy says.

"A cathedral; St. Patrick's Cathedral could be the target," Haughey states.

"I don't know, perhaps," Murphy says.

"Destroy St. Patrick's?" Centori questions, "It doesn't sound like a German target. They attack strategic and logistical targets."

"That's true. Germany wants to destroy U.S. munitions and supplies heading across the Atlantic that can be thrown against their army," Murphy agrees. "St. Patrick's is not consistent with previous attacks. But its destruction is consistent with achieving pure terror."

Grandinetto shakes his head with skepticism. "How can that be a German interest?"

"Germany funds American Scream," Murphy replies. "That could be the interest."

"If American Scream is responsible for the Los Angeles and Wall Street bombs, why would a church be next?" Centori asks.

"One theory is a continued attack on the pillars of American society," Murphy replies. "First the free press in Los Angeles and then commerce in New York. Now the church."

"If you are not safe in church, then you are not safe anywhere," Haughey observes.

"You think the target is St. Patrick's?" Centori inquires.

"It's a theory. The word *Kathedrale* is repeated. We should visit St Patrick's Cathedral," Murphy answers.

"The NYPD has placed extra security around St. Patrick's. There have been no reports of suspicious activity there," Grandinetto says.

"I know; let's see for ourselves."

Centori looks at Murphy, "I am sorry about Henry, sorry I didn't take time to know him better. Was he married?"

"No, he was a single man; she will pay for his murder."

Haughey and Grandinetto add their condolences.

"Murph, your theory about St. Patrick's…," Centori says. "Yes."

"If correct, the plan could have catastrophic consequences."

"Adobe, it would be a massive attack and a deliberate act of terror, something we have never seen before."

CHAPTER 82

TO THE GROUND

The distance between the Knickerbocker Hotel and the Plaza Hotel is less than a mile. Warren and Spooner stand near the Plaza Hotel, at Central Park South and Fifth Avenue, waiting for German saboteur, Bachmeier. They are ten blocks away from St. Patrick's Cathedral. It will be the final rendezvous before the plan takes action.

"Good day," Spooner grimly says to the arriving Bachmeier.

"We have the needed TNT. It has been carefully inserted into two suitcases to form one very powerful bomb. Our construction engineer has determined precisely where to place the bomb for the best chance to take down the building," Bachmeier informs.

"So, what do we do next?" Spooner asks.

"We will meet at Battery Park at 3:00 a.m. on the target day."

Warren says, "You know exactly where to hide the bomb?"

"Yes, I will tell you later."

"What about security?" Spooner questions.

"There are men who work there who are loyal to us; money increases that loyalty. They will look the other way and then will leave New York with a small fortune in cash. We will enter before dawn and plant the bomb with a timer-set detonator."

"What time?"

"I will tell you that later at the park. Be sure to leave a note signed by American Scream just like Wall Street."

"The Americans will know it was Germany."

"They will want to save face and blame a domestic foe to avoid a war, so let's give them that gift."

"That is quite a gift: the building will be taken to the ground," Spooner says.

"Your organization will achieve worldwide fame. Remember, Battery Park at 3:00 a.m. on the target day."

Warren and Spooner nod in agreement.

"One last thing; never return to the Corona house."

Bachmeier returns to Yorkville and to the Second Avenue *hofbrau*, which remains under surveillance. As usual, it is filled with Bavarian music. The bartender quickly nods at Bachmeier, who is disguised as a dock worker, as he enters.

He walks past the bar and moves to the communal tables in the back room. Speaking in German, he instructs, "I have but one minute to inform you."

"You must have a beer with us," the least drunk man says.

"No. Listen to me. All those who are loyal to the Kaiser should avoid downtown tomorrow morning."

"What do you mean?" asks the same man.

"You must tell all trusted Germans to stay away from downtown after dawn and before noon—tomorrow, June 14th."

"Why?"

"Start spreading the word now! All will become clear soon enough."

CHAPTER 83

SAWDUST SALOON

T he men look through a window that faces Fifth Avenue and
see St. Patrick's Cathedral across the street. St. Patrick's is
the archbishop's seat of the Roman Catholic Archdiocese of New
York. The Gothic style cathedral with spires that rise up 330 feet is
on Fifth Avenue between 50th and 51st Streets. They have a round
of beer in the 'Irish' tavern that has walls decked with old artwork
and old newspaper articles.

Murphy drains his glass and says, "St. Patrick's has been searched;
no signs of a bomb. Yet, they are making a powerful bomb, one with
enough TNT to knock down the cathedral down to the street."

"Are you convinced that the target is St. Patrick's?" Haughey
asks.

"No. I am convinced we need to know the target. They will kill
many innocent people if we don't find out. The death toll could be
unbearable."

"We need to search for explosives. If not here, then somewhere
in a Manhattan skyscraper," Centori says.

"The PC should order more detectives to work known places that are pro-German. We need to step up surveillance and infiltrate beer and meeting halls too," Murphy replies.

"More men have been assigned to the new bomb squad to identify targets and find dynamite," Grandinetto adds. "Yet, they are not trained for bomb disposal."

"Murphy states, "Let's get men here to search the church again."

"I can call the PC," Haughey announces.

"Good," Murphy replies and thinks, *we are running out of time.*

Haughey goes to the phone at the end of the bar. Murphy turns to Centori and Grandinetto, "Now, about finding Jarvia."

"Sure, if she is not halfway to Germany by now," Centori says.

"No," Murphy says, "She's a murderer and may enjoy watching her destructive plan play out."

"You could be right," Centori replies.

Murphy stands and says, "Let's go."

Outside the bar, the three men stare at the cathedral until Haughey joins them and informs, "The men are on the way."

Less than 20 minutes later, two dozen police cars from several precincts converge at St. Patrick's. Captain Thomas Byrn runs up the steps followed by 25 men in blue. Five men wait at the top of the steps framed by the large entrance.

Murphy flashes his credentials to the captain, "I'm John Murphy and this is Adobe Centori from my office, Jack Haughey and Rocco Grandinetto from the NYPD and this is Rector Egan."

"I'm Captain Byrn. What can we do?"

"We need to search every inch of this building and look for any suspicious items."

"A bomb?"

"Yes. Have half of your men check each pew. Take several men with you and follow Rector Egan. He will show you the inner spaces. We will search the high areas that are not accessible to the public."

The men in blue swarm the pews, startling the worshippers. Byrn and six cops follow Egan. Murphy, Centori, Haughey and Grandinetto ascend to the higher levels.

⚬⚭⚬

The comprehensive four-hour search reveals nothing. They leave the building. A distressed Rector Egan remains behind, fearful that the cathedral will be dynamited and collapse onto Fifth Avenue.

Outside again, Byrn asks Murphy, "Are you satisfied that the building is clear?"

"Captain, if there is a bomb in this building it is well hidden. Will you leave two uniformed men at each entrance for a few days?"

"Yes."

"Good, the NYPD is already watching."

"I know."

"Of course."

Byrn leaves and Centori asks, "What's next?"

"Let's go to Police Headquarters and see if the usual suspects are talking. If not, maybe we can get someone to talk," Murphy answers.

CHAPTER 84

THE THIRD DEGREE

JUNE 13TH 7:30 P.M.

At Police Headquarters, intense interrogations of the usual suspects are ongoing. Deputy Commissioner of Detectives Bingham is in charge of administering what is known, in police parlance, as the third degree.

The strong-arm police procedure has extracted information in the past; Bingham hopes to uncover the time and place of the planned terror attack. This type of examination is conducted in the basement of the headquarters building. Upstairs, Commissioner Waldan, Inspector Cropsey, Deputy Police Commissioner MacKay, three captains, including Captain Byrn, surround the conference table.

Murphy, Centori, Haughey and Grandinetto enter through the front doors of police headquarters and go to the second floor. The same police sergeant stands watch in front of the PC's door. The four men enter the commissioner's office and see New York's top cops.

"Good morning," Waldan says.

Murphy and Centori find seats at the table; Jack and Rocco take seats against the wall.

"I have read your report, Mr. Murphy," Waldan informs. "We have investigated TNT purchases; small amounts of dynamite have been purchased in different places. We found many individual orders. Combined, the orders totaled over 300 sticks."

"That much TNT can destroy any skyscraper," Murphy adds.

"You're right. Oh, good work in finding the papers."

"The four of us found them in Corona together."

"We know that a large amount of TNT has been purchased and could be used for a terror attack on our city. Yet, we do not know the target. Or the day of the intended attack," MacKay states.

"The commissioner has ordered the NYPD to patrol important buildings to help determine the target," Byrn adds.

Waldan nods, "Yes, but I am afraid we do not have enough manpower to patrol every important building. So, we are placing most of our men in the Wall Street area."

"St. Patrick's could be the target," Murphy objects.

"Captain Byrn has uniformed men at each entrance and we have undercover men in the pews," Waldan replies.

"There is a reference to propaganda by deed to the *Kathedrale* in the report," Murphy argues.

"I don't understand you. Should we lock down the cathedral indefinitely? No! We will focus on the Wall Street area. *Kathedrale* could be code for Trinity Church and St. Paul's Church—both are near Wall Street."

A knock on the door stops the conversation, "Come in," Waldan shouts.

The police sergeant enters and says, "I have a message for Mr. Centori."

"I am Centori."

"We received a telephone call from the Knickerbocker Hotel."

Centori stands and waits for more; perhaps the note is from Jarvia.

"There is a sealed note for you at the front desk."

Centori looks at Murphy and says, "There is nothing more I can do here."

"That goes for all of us, "Walden says. "We have a race against time. Let's hope that Bingham is successful before it is too late."

The extent of the third degree is a matter that will be determined by Bingham. He has approval from the PC to conduct the interrogations according to the needs of public safety. Saving the city from a major terror attack is top priority.

Murphy returns to his apartment to re-read the papers; perhaps he has missed something important that would reveal the location of the terror attack. Jack and Rocco go to the armory in case Jarvia returns. It is a long chance, but it is all they have at the moment. Centori returns to the Knickerbocker, walks quickly toward the front desk, "You have a note for me."

"Yes, Mr. Centori," the clerk says while handing him a sealed envelope.

Centori rips it open to find a phone number with a request to call a number at precisely 8:00 p.m. or at 8:00 a.m. Although it is after 8:00 p.m., he goes to a nearby telephone booth and calls anyway: no answer. He considers going to Jarvia's apartment but instead walks through Times Square.

CHAPTER 85

BROADWAY COLOSSAL

JUNE 14TH 3:00 A.M.

All through the night and into the early morning, Spooner and Warren nervously waited for the appointed time. That time is now. Bachmeier is wearing his boater hat and his black rumpled suit. He huddles with Spooner and Warren in Battery Park.

"Are you prepared for the attack and its associated risks?"

"Yes," they both answer, although Warren sounds less enthusiastic.

"You will go to Broadway between Park Place and Barclay Street at 4:00 a.m. You will be met by a wagon, pulled by two black horses. Seiler will be driving; you will accept two large bags from him. Each is filled with 150 sticks of dynamite," Bachmeier informs.

Spooner and Warren look around nervously.

Bachmeier continues, "The detonator is set to engage tomorrow morning precisely at 8:00 a.m. The lobby man and the night watchman on duty will ignore you when you enter the building."

"Are you sure?"

"I told you they were paid enough for their cooperation."

"The elevator operator, a pro-German immigrant, will take you and the bags to the 57th floor observatory."

"Then what?" Spooner quickly asks.

"You will find a canvas covering construction tools and materials under a corner window; hide the two bags under the canvas. Check the timer before leaving."

Disguised as construction workers, Spooner and Warren arrive in front of the building at 4:00 a.m. They hear the clip-clop of the delivery wagon. Seiler drives up and points to his bags containing the explosive devices. They carefully remove the bags from the wagon and set them down.

Warren says, "They are very heavy."

"And suspicious—get the bags inside now," Seiler orders.

The saboteurs enter the marble lobby of the Broadway Colossal under the vaulted ceiling. They walk near the circular reception desk and enter the elevator to the observatory; the lobby man avoids eye contact.

The elevator man looks away as the saboteurs struggle with the heavy bags. They ride the elevator in silence. On the observatory level, they place the suitcases under the canvas s instructed. Spooner checks the detonator timer: 8:00 a.m.

Centori impatiently wanders around Times Square worrying about the message in the note. In the Automat, he buys coffee but refuses to sit down. Ignoring the lively patrons sitting nearby, he wonders how he will react to Jarvia now that things are dramatically different. After two coffees, he continues walking the streets filled with merrymakers.

At 2:00 a.m., he returns to the lobby and calls Police Headquarters to see if new information has been discovered. No news. At 4:00 a.m. he calls again. Bingham is running out of suspects as time is running out. At 6:00 a.m. he waits in the lobby.

CHAPTER 86

MUDDY THE WATER

JUNE 14TH 7:59 A.M.

I n the shadow of the Statue of Liberty, Spooner and Warren look at the skyline of New York from Bedloe's Island; a great explosion is a minute away. An excited Bachmeier waits in Battery Park near the ferry dock.

At 8:00 a.m., Spooner and Warren stare across the harbor, ready to witness their greatest success: nothing happens. They freeze, still hoping for the sky to explode. At 8:05 a.m., nothing happens. They stare at each other in a near panic. At 8:15 a.m., they finally accept that the bomb did not detonate as planned.

A ferry with Spooner and Warren on board arrives at Battery Park. They are greeted by an infuriated Bachmeier.

"Fools! Do you know what they will do to me now?"

"Herr Bachmeier, perhaps the suitcases were discovered."

"You must go back, everything depends on it now," Bachmeier orders.

"No. I will not risk my life again. We could be killed by the bomb or by the police," Spooner protests.

"You will be killed right now, if you do not return," Bachmeier warns.

"But, the suitcases could be gone," Warren pleads.

"For your sake, I hope they are not. If that bomb does not explode this morning, you will be hunted down like dogs!"

"Herr Bachmeier, you want us to risk death for the fatherland, yet you will not go with us?"

"Take your jackets off and return as workers to reset the detonator. This time, I will go with you to ensure success."

CHAPTER 87

GOTHIC CATHEDRAL

At 8:00 a.m., Centori made the telephone call on time and was shocked to hear a woman state, "I am Felicity Brimwell. Please meet me at the Hotel Astor. I will be in the Palm Garden."

The Hotel Astor, on Broadway, is in the heart of Times Square and close to the Knickerbocker. Centori walks a few blocks, crosses Broadway and enters the elaborate French Renaissance hotel. He rides the elevator to the ninth floor.

The Palm Garden was designed as an Italian garden. Centori goes into the room, under a ceiling painted as a Mediterranean sky, and looks for her.

Felicity Brimwell sits at a table next to a Roman column. She wears a black dress similar to the one she wore at Mad Mady's Saloon, the first time he laid eyes on her. This dress flatters her supple body to perfection.

He startles her from behind. "What are you doing in New York?"

"Is that anyway to speak to a lady?"

"Damn you! Where is Jennifer? I must see her now. It is a matter of great urgency!"

"I don't know?"

"Are you sure?"

"Yes."

"Then, what do you want?"

"Please, people are looking at us. Will you sit down?"

"Look, I'm busy. Care to tell me why you disappeared from Valtura—at the same time Jennifer disappeared?"

"You saw me walking on Park Avenue."

"I did."

"Please sit down."

"No. So, you know her and you know about her crimes."

"I am just a close friend."

"You are an accomplice to murder," he accuses. "I can arrest you right now."

"I worked in her doll store, nothing more."

"Nothing more? Was it a coincidence that you were in Valtura? No! You followed her to New Mexico and fooled Mady. I don't know what you want. Tell me why I should not arrest you?"

"Please, I am afraid of her. If she thinks I know things, I could be in danger—I could be killed."

"Do you know about a looming terror attack on this city?"

"No. Nothing important, but *she* may not believe that."

"So you have nothing to deal. Why come to me for anything?"

"I know much about you."

"You don't know much about me at all."

"As Mad Mady's unhappiness about you increased, bitterness built within her and she spoke of little else while you were gone."

"That's none of your affair."

"Perhaps you are right. I felt something when our eyes locked in Mad Mady's Saloon."

"If I wanted to know, I would have asked."

"I thought you did on the day you came into the saloon."

"I would not turn my back on you. Let alone engage in what you are suggesting."

You wanted me, desired me, in New Mexico."

With doubt showing in his eyes, Centori folds his arms. "You have learned certain things from her. Look, I don't have the time for this."

"You can imagine the taste of my kiss; imagine undressing me, stopping to kiss my naked shoulder. We both know that is true," she says.

"Nice try, now where the hell is Jennifer?"

Felicity snaps back, "She is not careless with such information."

Losing time and patience, Centori stands erect and says, "Then what do you have to make a deal?"

"Mady said you are a man who is inclined to help a lady in distress."

Shaking his head he replies, "A *lady* in distress, perhaps."

"I don't blame you for that. I want Jennifer arrested so I can stop living in fear."

His eyes narrow. "Why are you afraid?"

"I believe she is a dangerous woman who is involved with very dangerous people. I have a chance for a job as a typist for the Woolworth Company in the new building. I could become a secretary and have a good life in New York."

"What did you say?"

"I could become a secretary."

"Where?" Centori demands.

"At the new Woolworth building. Why?"

"Something a friend said about that building…" *Charity said it bears a resemblance to a European Gothic Cathedral.*

He stands up quickly. "I have to go."

"What's the matter?"

Without answering, Centori rushes out to Times Square and hails a cab. The driver calls out in a New York accent, "Where to, Mister?"

"Gramercy Park, and step on it!"

CHAPTER 88

CATHEDRAL OF COMMERCE

JUNE 14TH 9:00 A.M.

Centori arrives at Murphy's brownstone and jumps out of the cab. In seconds, he bangs on the front door, "Murph, open up."

Footsteps echo on the hardwood floor on the other side of the door. Murphy yanks the door open, and with equal urgency. "Adobe, what's going on? We were to meet Rocco and Jack at the armory in an hour."

Centori puts his right hand on the door frame and leans forward. "Call them and tell them to get downtown now. I know the target."

Murphy steps back and asks, "What building?"

"It has a cruciform structure."

"What building?" Murphy demands from the other side of the door frame.

Centori takes a deep breath and exhales, "The Woolworth Building."

Murphy raises his right hand to his chin. "Why do you think it's the target?"

"Charity said it looks like a cathedral and that people call it the Cathedral of Commerce!"

"That's not conclusive."

"It's the Woolworth Building," Centori insists clenching his right fist. "I can feel it. What represents capitalism more than a cathedral dedicated to commerce?"

"Come inside and close the door. We need more than your feelings to get the PC to move men away from Wall Street."

"The symbol of U.S. economic power reduced to rubble—there is no better target for American Scream after the Wall Street attack, Centori says. "It is a good target for Germany too. American capitalism provides funds to England and France to finance purchases from U.S. war industries."

"You could be right. The U.S. is inclined to help Germany's enemies by financing the Allies as long as money can be made—and the U.S. would continue to do so when the inevitable war starts."

"Yes, and the Woolworth Building is the ultimate symbol of capitalism. Destroying it will have a great impact; terrorizing everyone in New York—and in America."

"We have nothing to lose by adding the Woolworth Building to the list of potential targets."

"Murph, we need to alert Waldan and get downtown now."

"Okay, let's go. We are wasting time."

"No kidding," Centori responds.

In the basement of Police Headquarters, a series of harsh interrogations failed to uncover any pertinent information about the terror attack. Deputy Commissioner of Detectives Bingham ordered a second wave of suspects be interrogated. This time, the police rounded-up many from the German-American population in Yorkville.

Bingham's men continued to be frustrated until a Yorkville man provided no resistance to the third degree. When questioned, he revealed that June 14th is the day that sometime big will happen in downtown.

Without confirmation, the NYPD is operating on the premise that today is the day of the attack—wherever the location. The day the U.S. adopted the Stars and Stripes during the revolution, June 14th, has become a red flag day for the NYPD.

CHAPTER 89

THE WOOLWORTH BUILDING

J ust as they are leaving the apartment, the telephone rings. Seconds later, Centori asks, "What is it?"

"A break in the case; the police extracted a date from a Yorkville resident."

"What is the date?"

Murphy ignores him and telephones Haughey with an urgent message.

"What is the date?"

Murphy grimly answers, "June 14th."

"Today! What time?"

"We don't know. Jack will alert the NYPD and the bomb squad. We must clear the Woolworth building now."

"If it is not too late."

They enter the black sedan and race downtown; McGillivray's replacement starts the siren. The shrieking causes Centori to look at Murphy, "When did you get that?"

"Welcome to the big city. Jack and Rocco are on their way downtown."

"There may not be enough time to get everyone out of that building."

Murphy glances at Centori. "Let's hope the bomb squad is there." He leans forward to the driver, "Can you go any faster? Beyond the immediate devastation, this attack could shake the American will—at least temporarily but long enough for a German victory in Europe."

At 9:45 a.m. the sedan comes to a screeching halt in front of the Woolworth Building—the tallest building in the world.

Grandinetto has arrived and is waiting; the bomb squad has not. Centori and Murphy jump out and enter the ornate marble lobby with a vaulted ceiling and mezzanine balconies. They confront the man behind the circular reception desk.

"Federal agents," Murphy yells with his badge up. "Get the building manager and let nobody else in the building."

The lobby man freezes, "Now!" Centori says. He looks up at the mezzanine and the murals *Labor* and *Commerce* and flashes on his visit with Charity.

The manager arrives, "This building must be evacuated!" Murphy yells again.

"That is most extraordinary—impossible!"

"We have reason to believe there is a bomb ready to explode in this building. Evacuate now!"

The manager runs to comply. Murphy turns to the lobby man, "Where are the overnight people?"

"They all have gone home after their shift."

"I want the names and addresses of all the overnight people. Jack, get that information from him. If anyone lives nearby, drag them here now."

"Okay."

Police cars respond to the radio dispatch: "Calling all cars, calling all cars, proceed to the Woolworth Building on Broadway between Park Place and Barclay Street. Calling all cars, calling all cars..."

The three saboteurs had returned to the building earlier and remain on the observation deck. Spooner and Warren created a distraction while Bachmeier inspected the suitcases which were still hidden under the canvas. He reset the detonator. Their suspicious behavior attracted attention of a few people.

At 10:00 a.m. the evacuation reached the observation deck causing the saboteurs to be alarmed at the chance of being exposed. They remove their overalls and blend in with the stream of people. In the lobby, Grandinetto and Haughey encourage the office workers to leave quickly as they exit the elevators. The stairway from the mezzanine level to the lobby is jammed with office workers.

From the distant streets, police car sirens start to fill the air around the building. The saboteurs exit on the mezzanine level to join the larger crowds of workers who are walking down the steps. It is 10:15 a.m.; they must evade detection and escape before the explosion. Centori and Murphy are on the mezzanine directing people as fast as possible. Bachmeier is confronted by Centori, this time there is nowhere to run—gunfire and screams erupt.

From a close distance, Bachmeier fires his snub nose revolver and misses. Centori waits for the crowds to clear—then he returns fire and narrowly misses Bachmeier. In seconds, Spooner, Warren and Murphy join the gunfight. Shots ricochet off the marble walls with deafening reverberations. Office workers continue to run down the mezzanine steps and from the building. Centori is hit in the upper arm; the bullet rips his shirt and slashes his flesh.

Grandinetto and Haughey run up the steps. Murphy fires and hits Spooner square in the chest, blowing him over the rail and to the hard stone lobby floor, barely missing the escaping people. Blood runs from his dead body.

Bachmeier sees an elevator door open and runs inside as it closes. Warren throws down his gun and throws up his hands. Centori checks his wound, watches the floor indicator and takes the next car determined to get Bachmeier—this time. Murphy puts his pistol to Warren's head, "ONE CHANCE, WHERE IS THE BOMB?"

"Observation floor...under a construction canvas in two suitcases." Warren eagerly answers.

"When will it detonate?"

"11:00 a.m."

"Damn. What time is it Jack?"

"It's 10:30."

In the elevator, Centori breathes heavily and holds his bloody arm. At the top floor, he bolts from the elevator and sees the sunlight stream through an open door up a short staircase. With gun drawn, he slowly approaches the door—fires to distract, runs on to the roof and finds cover. Bachmeier returns fire, and misses by a wide margin.

"This is the end of the line," Centori yells. "Where is the bomb? You would be wise to disarm it now! Where is the bomb?"

Bachmeier answers with hot lead.

Centori levels his Navy Colt and fires, a near miss. He fire two more rounds that forces the saboteur to backpedal—the motion propels him over the side of the building. His gun falls away as he grasps on to the head of a roof gargoyle, his feet swing for a non-existence foothold. Unconcerned, the frightening gargoyle stares straight ahead looking out over New York and the many police cars that are jamming Broadway below. Centori rushes to the saboteur and reaches over the side with his unhurt arm, "Grab my hand."

Still on the mezzanine, Murphy yells to the crowd, "We need everyone out now! Keep moving faster." He turns to Haughey. "Where the hell is the bomb squad?"

On the roof, the desperate saboteur takes one hand off the gargoyle to reach up and grasp his pursuer's hand. He has one hand on the stone demon, as Centori struggles to pull him up. At the same time, the police arrive and form a perimeter in the front of the building.

"We don't have time to wait, I'll disarm it," Haughey says.

"What do you know about explosives?"

Haughey does not respond.

"We can check the suitcases and see if we can do anything."

"Right, we have no choice. There are people still in the building."

"Rocco wait for the bomb squad in the lobby; tell them we are on the observation floor with a bomb set to explode at 11:00 a.m."

"Are you sure about this?" Grandinetto asks.

"Yes!" Murphy yells before they rush to the elevator.

On the street, more police cars converge on the building from all directions. On the roof, the saboteur clings to the grotesque head, carved to prevent water damage to the building; now it prevents his death. Centori continues to struggle, trying to pull him up with one arm. The gargoyle is unaffected by the screaming sirens from the street.

Murphy and Haughey reach the observatory, throw open the canvas and find the two suitcases.

"Which suitcase has the detonator?" Haughey asks.

"Maybe both. Take this one," Murphy shouts.

Both men carefully open a suitcase and look for a detonator.

On the roof, the saboteur's grasp on the gargoyle is slipping. Centori's grip is slipping too; one arm injured and the other losing strength.

"Help me, I will tell…you everything," Bachmeier pleads holding on for life.

"Where is the bomb?"

"The…observation deck…we have time to disarm…help me…"

At the bomb location, Murphy calls out, "No detonator in this one."

"I have it…"

"We are running out of time!"

Haughey stares down in confusion.

"Jack!"

"I'm not sure…"

Grandinetto and five men burst out of the elevator.

"Stand back," yells the bomb squad leader. After a quick inspection, he orders, "Get this suitcase out of the building!" Then he examines the suitcase with the detonator. It's 10:50 a.m.

The frantic struggle on the roof becomes more desperate. The saboteur's hand slips to the lower jaw of the gargoyle, his other hand is still holding on to Centori.

On the observation deck, the bomb squad leader carefully and deliberately disarms the bomb within a minute of exploding.

Murphy turns to Haughey, "Thank God…Adobe chased the other one to the roof. Let's go."

They take the elevator to the top floor as the last of the workers leave the building and go beyond the police parameter.

Entering the roof, Murphy and Haughey see the situation.

Centori yells back, "The bomb is on the observation deck! Get a rope!"

Haughey turns and runs. Murphy runs to the short wall and grabs Centori around the waist. Then the stone sculpture's jaw rips into the saboteur's hand. Centori's arm fails—the saboteur plummets 790 feet to the street as the gargoyle stares with demonic eyes over New York.

"The bomb," Centori breathlessly says. "It's on the observation deck."

Murphy pulls him up. "We know...we got it. You were right about this building."

CHAPTER 90

DETECTIVES

Two days later, the Woolworth Building remains standing. The leadership of American Scream and of the Kaiser's network in New York does not. The Cathedral of Commerce is back to normal, except for increased security.

Felicity Brimwell did tell all that she knew, including the identification of Riesenfelder as the top German spy. The count escaped New York one step ahead of the authorities and returned to Berlin. Some of the waterfront leaders and the accomplices in the Woolworth plot were arrested. The location of Jarvia Hoffmann remains unknown. Yet, the location of the men who stopped the terror attack is known to Martini the bartender.

Centori, Murphy, Haughey and Grandinetto have a farewell drink at the Knickerbocker. They stand together one more time.

"Gentlemen, it has been an honor to work with you," Centori says while holding his usual drink.

"Here is to all of you," Haughey declares.

"To you all," Grandinetto adds.

"Good luck!" Murphy says.

Looking at Centori and Murphy, Haughey pronounces, "You men are always welcome in New York."

"With your promotion, you can give us a parade!" Murphy jokes.

"Ha-ha, I will try," Haughey replies. "Adobe, if you get homesick or get tired of playing cowboy, there is a job for you with the NYPD."

"Thanks, Detective, and come to the Circle C. We will ride the range, if you can handle a horse! That goes for you too, Detective Grandinetto."

"There is a home-cooked Italian meal the next time you are in New York," says the newly promoted Grandinetto.

Centori smiles and responds, "I would like that very much."

Murphy touches the two NYPD officers on the shoulder, "We worked well together; it was an enterprise of a lifetime."

"I thought we had that already," Centori says.

Haughey looks puzzled. Centori adds, "When you come to New Mexico, I will tell you about it over drinks at Mad Mady's Saloon."

"Mad Mady's what?"

All laugh and raise a glass again. Martini walks over with a tray, "Here's a round on the house for you men!"

"Thank you," they all say.

"To what do we attribute this kindness?" Centori asks.

"You look like you deserve it; may I join you?"

All nod in agreement; Martini lifts his glass, "*Ecco a voi tutti. Buona fortuna.*"

"Good luck," the men repeat.

The time has come. "Detectives, take good care of yourselves and your families," Centori says.

Haughey offers an old Irish toast, "May heaven want you all, but not too soon."

"So long, cowboy," Grandinetto says.

"Hey, Adobe, whatever happened to your hat?" Haughey asks.

"Ha! Remind me not to enter the subway!"

"Jack, Rocco, When I return, the drinks will be on me," Murphy promises.

The two detectives leave the hotel, enter a waiting police car and drive away from Times Square.

In the end, it is Centori and Murphy again. It was a long road together, which started in Cuba.

"So, what will happen back in Valtura?"

"Together with Francisco, we will continue to run the Circle C…"

"I meant Mad Mady," Murphy interrupts.

"As I once told you, only a fool could answer that kind of question."

"You have embraced the wrong woman. Have you resolved things?"

"Every man has a limit to his foolishness. Jarvia may have escaped us, but she cannot escape herself. I suspect she has returned to the fatherland."

Murphy drains his glass, gently places it on the bar and says, "I have to get a train back to Washington."

"Be sure to arrange a drink with TR for us when he regains the White House. Or will you be too big for an old cowboy?"

"How about the inaugural ball; you would look good in white tie or black tie."

A solemn Centori offers a quick smile at his friend. After a moment, he says, "Do me a favor, the next time the world needs saving, don't call me."

"Who else would I call?"

"Ha-ha, okay, Murph."

"Adobe, you didn't ask, but I will tell you anyway."

"Go ahead."

"Jarvia had a profound impact on you. Yet, there is nothing more profound than the way Mady has waited for you, more than any woman would care to do so. Look toward a woman who has a big heart, who is open to you without any other reason except loving you. It's none of my business, but if I had a woman like the one waiting in New Mexico, I would hold on tight and not let go."

"That is quite a speech, Murph."

The two men shake hands and embrace. Then Murphy puts on his hat and says, "Take care of yourself. I hope you find the peace you deserve."

"It has been quite a ride. So long, Pard."

Centori finishes his last New York drink and turns to the area where he first laid eyes on Charity. *It seems so long since she smiled from under her wide-brimmed hat. I could have loved her. Gabriella will journey no further with me. Nothing lasts forever. La Guerrillera will haunt me no longer.*

Part Four

Sweet Home

CHAPTER 91

PATRIOT POWER

One week later, Centori is expected at the Valtura Rail Station. Francisco Greigos waits near the cast iron columns. The American flag whips in the wind. Greigos is on his horse and holds the reins of Patriot. A soaring hawk announces that the train is not far away. "*Kaah, kaah.*" Then, the two horses react to the arriving train. Soon after, Centori steps off the railcar. "Francisco."

"*Amigo!*"

"It is good to see you."

"Welcome back," Greigos says, while reaching to shake his hand.

"Thanks for remembering my hat," Centori smiles, ties his duffel on Patriot and jams his cowboy hat low on his head. He has completed a journey and now the way forward goes through New Mexico.

The train rolls on. Centori mounts up, looks Greigos square in the eye and declares, "Let's ride!"

Centori starts at a full gallop, running flat out. Riding slightly out of the saddle with slack in the reins—exhilarated by the explosion of Patriot's power. Greigos is surprised but follows at equal speed.

The sight of two cowboys charging over the flat desert terrain attracts a band of curious coyotes. The riders show the coyotes speed and skill in handling horses. Riding fast under the big sky, the men create an optimistic and dynamic image on the open range.

After several minutes of fast riding, they slow to a trot. When they cross the invisible boundary line to the Circle C Ranch, Centori yells, "Francisco, it is good to be home."

Given the size of the ranch, a half hour passes before the house comes into view. Then Henry Parker, riding a big bay horse, sees the arriving men. "Mr. Centori," he yells. "Mr. Centori!"

Adobe Centori, waving his big hat, returns the greeting as he returns to the Circle C.

They enter the barn, dismount and slightly loosen the saddles. As they walk the horses around to cool down, Centori says, "Francisco, we should all have a drink later. Please inform the men."

Greigos smiles as they unbridle their horses and take off the saddles and blankets. "We have planned to have much more than drinks."

CHAPTER 92

STEADFAST LOYALTY

That evening, Greigos and the men hold a cowboy cook out. During first drinks, Centori asks the men to gather around. Twenty men raise a glass together. "Here is to A.P. Baker," he chokes up for a moment. "He was a fine man, a great cowboy and a great top hand."

"To A.P. Baker," all heartily agree.

Parker shouts, "And here is to Adobe Centori."

The men drink again.

"So, you boys ever hear of a Delmonico steak?" Centori asks "New Yorkers say they are the best. Well, we have the best steaks right here at the good ol' Circle C."

"That's right, Boss," says one of the wranglers. "Where do those New Yorkers think their steaks come from?"

They cheer in agreement as dozens of steaks cook to perfection over an open fire. Alongside the sizzling steaks are baked beans, cornbread muffins, potatoes and green chile stew.

Centori and Greigos end the evening in the library. They sit across from each other with a drink and a cigar and discuss ranch business.

"The Circle C is in fine shape now. Thank you for handling the ranch and the roundup while I was gone."

"De nada."

"You are a good foreman; the Circle C is lucky to have you."

"We were all worried about your safety in New York."

Centori pauses and then says, "Francisco, it is good to have friends and you are a great one."

"We are all happy that you are back. So, you remember that things start early at the Circle C."

They laugh and shake hands. "That sounds about right. Good night, Francisco."

"Hasta mañana."

Centori is alone again. He puts down his cigar, goes to the Victrola and plays a song from the opera *Clari: Or the Maid of Milan*.

Which seek thro' the world, is ne'er met elsewhere.
Home! Home!
Sweet, sweet home!
There's no place like home.

CHAPTER 93

FABULOUS FLASHES

JULY 4, 1912

Under Title 4 of the U.S. Flag Code, adding stars for a new state that joined the Union shall take effect on the fourth day of July succeeding admission. For New Mexico, July 4, 1912, is that day. The new Santos Square is illuminated for the Independence Day celebration—as well as for the new star addition to the flag.

Close to sundown, Centori takes Patriot for a ride to Valtura. The 'Star Spangled Banner' is playing loudly on the center gazebo. He ties up Patriot in front of his office, wades through the welcoming crowd and enters the crowded Mad Mady's Saloon.

Mady rushes to him, "Adobe!"

"Mady," he says with a hug.

"Welcome back."

"It's good to be back."

"Do you think you will stay a while this time?"

"I think I will."

"I was worried about you. What happened in New York?"

"We will have plenty of time to talk about that."

"Will you stay in New Mexico this time?"

"Yes, now let's watch the fireworks. It's almost sundown."

"Okay, cowboy, let's go."

"What?"

"Let's watch the fireworks together, from the roof."

Minutes later, Adobe and Mady stand behind the parapet and behind the big Mad Mady's Saloon sign. The top of the saloon provides a clear view of the town and the mountains beyond.

At sundown, the fireworks show begins and illuminates the sky. Shells burst in the firmament and fall slowly in rings of red, white and blue stars. Mady turns to him and points to the fabulous flashes, "Those stars are my favorite."

The stars fall for a short distance and erupt again. The skyrocket show continues for 20 minutes before ending in wild cheering and applause.

"That was a great celebration, Adobe. Everyone is waving the new 48-star flag."

"Yes, and this time the flag is official."

Mady holds court at her table with Centori. Greigos and Parker, who arrived during the fireworks, walk from the bar to Mady's table.

Centori stands to greet them as Mady says, "Join the table."

"Thank you, Mady," Greigos says.

"Thanks, Miss Mady," Parker adds.

After several rounds of drinks, Greigos and Parker move to the poker table and leave them alone.

"Mady, things will change in Valtura—they have changed. The *Valtura Journal* needs new ownership and the colonel's house is in question."

"You never talked about Jennifer. What happened to her?"

"I don't know; she disappeared in New York."

"She seems to be good at that sort of thing."

"Okay, Mady, things start early at the Circle C. Don't get those men too drunk tonight."

"I am glad you are back."

"So am I, Mady."

Centori takes his leave, rides out of Valtura and back to the ranch. He has been the quintessence of a romantic man; now his quixotic world view is all but gone. Perhaps the woman he seeks has been near all the time. Perhaps she is sitting at that corner table in Mad Mady's Saloon.

CHAPTER 94

⚬✖⚬

UNCHARTED WATERS

O ne week later at the Circle C Ranch, there is not a breath of wind on the summer night. The cowboys are settled in for the evening. Centori is settled in his *sanctum sanctorum* with a Jameson. One mile from the Circle C, she rides at a steady pace and is expected to arrive soon. She has been anticipating this evening for a long while.

Centori finishes his drink and walks outside into the twilight. The time between sunset and dusk has light that can change the image of distant objects. He watches and paces on the portal. Then, in the distance, a barely visible cloud of dust signals her impending entrance. Coyote cries herald her approach and a few horses in the stable let their existence be known.

She rides up to him and declares, "What a beautiful evening!"

"Welcome to the Circle C," Centori smiles.

"Thank you," she returns the smile and dismounts.

"So this is the grand Circle C Ranch," she states.

"Yes, this is my place."

"It is wonderful. Seeing it for the first time finally puts my imagination to rest."

"I have imagined many things over the years," Centori adds.

"Is that so?"

"Yes."

Mad Mady Blaylock has finally arrived at the Circle C. She wears a pair of old jeans tucked into her boots with a leather belt and turquoise buckle. She has a blue bandana tied around her neck. Her red plaid shirt is slightly unbuttoned.

She looks at him from under her cowboy hat. "This visit is long overdue, Adobe."

"I can't argue with you, Mady."

"Now, that is a change!"

"Nothing in this world is everlasting."

"You are changing," Mady says. As they look up to the mountains and to the sky, she adds, "The universe around us is changing too."

"I may have lost myself over the years."

"Adobe, I have been hard on you, but you kept coming back for more."

"Not so hard."

"Remember the past; she was the world to you."

"Sometimes you just have to let people go. Mady, your saloon has served me drinks for years, so allow me to do the same."

A band of coyotes around the ranch sing their approval. No matter how far a man travels, his destiny ultimately awaits. Adobe Centori and Mady Blaylock enter uncharted waters.

EPILOGUE

⌐◯◯⌐

DOUGHBOYS

The Kaiser's first secret war against the U.S. ended in defeat. German networks of spies and saboteurs would operate in the U.S. again. However, none would stop the transportation of war supplies to the Allies; none would stop the U.S. from entering the war.

The debate among Roosevelt's 'New Nationalism,' Wilson's 'New Freedom' and Eugene Debs' socialism dominated the 1912 presidential campaign. Debs received the largest share of the popular vote ever recorded for a socialist candidate. Although TR enjoyed a positive personal appeal, the campaign was driven by policies, not personality. The democrat Wilson won the presidency.

The Stratford gold strike was significant but did not rise to the level of the California strike. The pursuit of the Stratford raiders was abandoned after an unsuccessful invasion of Mexico by the U.S. Army. A few years later, Zapata was killed in a hail of bullets.

The Revert Document did not end Huerta's presidency as it did for his predecessor, Madero. However, in 1914, after losing the Battle of Zacatecas to Pancho Villa, Huerta resigned the presidency and went into exile. An attempt by Germany to restore him to power ended with his suspicious death. In the same year, Archduke Franz Ferdinand was assassinated by a Serbian nationalist in Sarajevo, starting the Great War.

In 1915, the ocean liner RMS *Lusitania,* on the way to Liverpool from New York, was torpedoed near Ireland by a German submarine. The ship sank quickly killing 1,198 people, including 128 Americans. The passenger ship was carrying war materiel for the British Army. The victims list included the name Jennifer Prower.

After German submarines attacked U.S. shipping, President Wilson and America became motivated to enter the conflict. These attacks, along with Germany's endeavor to turn Mexico against the U.S., led Wilson to ask Congress to declare war.

In 1917, General John 'Black Jack' Pershing and the American Expeditionary Forces arrived in France. The first U.S. infantry troops were met by enthusiastic multitudes when they landed in Saint Nazaire. Four months later, the Army's First Division was in the Allied trenches near Nancy, France. The U.S. soldiers in the trenches included Lieutenant Colonel Aldoloreto Centori and Brigadier General John Murphy.

ACKNOWLEDGMENTS

W ithin this historical fiction, efforts were made to be factually accurate. Yet at times, the story created some inaccuracies. Throughout the process of writing *Water Damage*, people in New Mexico and in New York have taken time to enhance the story and the characters. I am appreciative of their contributions and insights. Dr. Catherine Akel and Dr. Christine Sacco provided significant support for this book. Special thanks to Nancy Maffucci for challenging critiques and constant assistance in the creation of *Water Damage*.

ALSO BY THE AUTHOR

STATEHOOD OF AFFAIRS

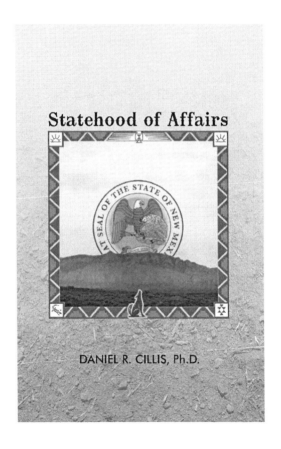

For an excerpt, turn the page.

PROLOGUE

CHACO CANYON

Two columns of horse soldiers cross the vast, high desert landscape toward Chaco Canyon. The mounted men, armed with Brown Bess muskets, flintlock pistols and lances, are creating a legend in the year 1861. As they ride deeper into the broad canyon, the hot, harsh climate increases the challenge of the mission.

Located in northwestern New Mexico Territory, Chaco Canyon sits on the Colorado Plateau, enclosed by the grand Chuska San Juan and San Pedro Mountains. The remote canyon is the site of significant archaeological ruins--Chaco Pueblo. Almost a thousand years ago, this dramatic dwelling was a habitat and cultural center for a population called the Anasazi. These strange soldiers riding strange, large creatures would have appeared extraordinary to the pre-Columbian Anasazi.

Twenty-five hard riders enter Chaco Canyon heading toward Chaco Pueblo. The sky grows darker, and a ghostly strong wind creates a sense of peril. A mystical world unfolds, revealing strange secluded ruins. The riders become increasingly aware of the canyon's spiritual nature. Although hardened by war, they share glances of anxiety.

The men are Mexican cavalry troops commanded by Colonel José Bautista Alvarado. Their colorful uniforms provide a stark contrast to the earthen tones of the desert. They wear cropped, green jackets with yellow turnbacks and piped yellow lapels. Their trousers are grey and their helmets are black, with brass visors and red plumes. It is the first time in Chaco Canyon for the men, but not for Colonel Alvarado.

Resplendent in his uniform and officer's saber, Colonel Alvarado is a tall, forty-four-year-old veteran soldier. Mounted straight and stoic on his stallion, there is nothing in the colonel's bearing except a strong sense of purpose. Yet he has doubts about the number of men required to complete the mission. His force must be big enough for security yet small enough to avoid detection.

The Mexican cavalry is a long way from home and is, in fact, an invader of the United States. If caught in the territory of New Mexico, the soldiers would cause embarrassment, at the least, for Old Mexico. Despite the risk, Alvarado, driven by duty and some sort of instinct, believes that the gravity of the mission outweighs the risk of the border-crossing. Ironically, his assignment is more about foreign policy than war. Alvarado carries an intergovernmental document that could exacerbate Mexico's relationship with the United States and even change history.

The desolate location, appropriate to the clandestine mission, provides a fantastic view into the past. Many of the men marvel over the sacred archeological sites that were homes for an advanced society. Some soldiers wonder why the Ancient Ones abandoned this place. A long drought in the twelfth century was probably the cause, but that is something these men could not have known.

Rain clouds appear and swirls of dust devils develop into huge funnels as the riders get close to Fajada Butte and Pueblo Bonito.

Pueblo Bonito, a complex of 650 rooms, is four stories high. A wall bisects a central plaza that contains a circular ceremonial room—the Great Kiva. The dusty, weary men squint against the remaining sunlight and wonder at the spectacular sight. They slow down and stare opened-mouthed at the ancient masonry dwellings with some carved out of the sandstone—and then continue to Fajada Butte.

At the base of the high-reaching butte, with a gesture of his hand, the colonel halts his columns and in a strong voice, says, "*Capitán Santos, hemos llegado a nuestro destino.*" (Captain Santos, this is our destination.)

Santos answers with an interested look, "*Si Coronel.*"

Alvarado dismounts, opens his saddlebag, and asserts, "*Desde aquí tenemos que seguir a pie, Capitán.*" (We must proceed on foot from here, Captain.)

Captain Antonio Santos shifts uneasily in his saddle. A strong, seasoned soldier in his late twenties and highly trusted by Alvarado, he wonders about the mission. He has some awareness of the Mexican government's long-term strategy, but not of the thinking behind the Chaco Canyon operation. He looks over at Alvarado, a man with whom he plays chess, knowing the game reveals an officer's strategic competence. The colonel is a brilliant chess player, but Santos still wonders.

Alvarado pulls a thin metal box containing a document case from his saddlebag, turns to Santos and asks, "*Capitán, se siente cómodo para cruzar la frontera?*" (Captain, are you comfortable crossing the U.S. border?)

Santos dismounts, takes the colonel's horse, hands the reins of the two horses to the closest soldier and replies, "*Coronel, no hemos cruzado la frontera, la frontera nos ha cruzado!*" (Colonel, we did not cross the border, the border crossed us!)

Alvarado smiles to display his understanding of the sentiment, and then turns his attention to the fine document case with solid brass hardware and a flap-over buckle. The colonel knows about its markedly valuable contents and the momentous implications it holds for Mexico and the United States. The men will not be part of the final journey; he will finish the assignment alone.

The leather case contains a diplomatic pouch with a manuscript copy of the Treaty of Mesilla signed by President Pierce and the recent Article X signed by President Buchanan. The original treaty, which clarifies the boundaries created at the end of the Mexican-American War, has nine publicly-known articles. The tenth, the new Article X, a potentially explosive political agreement, is unknown beyond the walls of government, a secret agreement made between American and Mexican leaders. The version of the treaty ratified by the United States Senate contains only nine articles, omitting Article X, at least publicly.

Should other manuscript copies secured in Old Mexico disappear, there will be a return to Chaco Canyon. The act of hiding a manuscript copy inside the United States is hard for Alvarado to resist. Somehow, the irony seems appropriate to him.

At the last moment, Alvarado ignores orders from the Mexican government to ascend Fajada Butte alone and deliberately says, "*Vamos, Capitán.*" (Let's go, Captain.)

Surprised by the sudden change, Santos replies, "*Si Coronel.*"

Both men go up the prehistoric trail on foot. The climb to the summit is difficult and dangerous. There is only one possible path and Alvarado knows it well. As a boy, he grew up in the north when New Mexico was part of Old Mexico.

Toward the middle of the climb, Santos becomes aware of the geological patterns along the higher cliff bands facing the butte. Noticing signs and symbols etched into the sandstone, he says, "*Este sitio es interesante, mi Coronel. Ya entiendo porqué usted lo escogió para esconder el maletín.*" (This is an interesting place, Colonel. I can see why you chose to protect the case here.)

"*Interesante y seguro.*" (Interesting and secure.) Alvarado pauses for a breath and continues, "*La parte superior del cañón está más de 134 metros por encima de la parte inferior.*" (The top rises over 440 feet above the canyon floor.)

The two officers climb in silence for what seems like a long time. Then Santos stops to examine the strange lines and shapes in the sandstone. These petroglyphs, marking solar and lunar cycles with light and shadows, are a mystery.

"*Mi coronel, ¿qué son estas figuras y marcas tan increíbles?*" (Colonel, what are these amazing pictures and markings?)

At that time, Chaco Canyon had not yet been identified as an observatory. The colonel replies, "*No se.*" (I do not know.)

They continue with unwavering determination. Finally arriving at the summit of the butte, they admire the breathtaking landscape from the high elevation. The commanding views of Chaco Canyon distract them from their purpose, but they refocus on the mission and search for a suitable place.

Scanning the area, they find a large crack in the sandstone that will conceal the leather case. Santos clears away brush. Alvarado places the case deep within the recess, followed by small rocks. He reaches for a knife and carefully scratches a simple yet distinct marking above the opening. The marking blends with the petroglyphs; it is an image of a coyote.

High above the canyon, the summit of the butte becomes a time capsule. The case will stay hidden there until the document becomes politically relevant. They carefully walk back down the summit on the same path. Alvarado descends without looking back, but Santos hesitates and looks back. The officers go down and rejoin the men who are anxiously waiting to leave this unsettling place and return to their side of the border.

No one has seen the activity of the two officers at the summit—no one except a lone coyote. Now the task is to return to Mexico unbeknownst to the Americans.

Alvarado quickly mounts and orders, "*Vamos, Capitán,*" and leads the columns out of the canyon. Suddenly, a distant rumble blends with the noise of fast-moving horses. They cannot see the source of any movement but hear it, a sound that Alvarado and his men take as a warning. Alvarado stops his columns to reconsider their direction. The rumble changes to a loud roar and a wall of large rocks comes crashing down, narrowing the escape route.

The colonel commands what the men already instinctively know. The riders have only one option. They must outrun this deadly rockslide. The troopers desperately kick the flanks of their mounts and gallop away, riding low in the saddle, at breakneck speed, hooves fiercely pounding the earth. Horses and men, breathing heavily, confront violent dust devils whirling wildly. Branches breaking, snapping, and cracking reach a grand crescendo. Then it stops as abruptly as it started.

The colossal rockslide is a force of nature, but Alvarado knows that rockslides are uncommon in the canyon. When water gets into the rocks, they can slide, but Chaco is one of the driest places in the world. Perhaps ancient spirits haunt the canyon and are responsible. The men entered a sacred space as one European-American group in conflict with another European-American group, over land inhabited by native people for thousands of years. In the future, the mystifying vanishing of the Anasazi from Chaco Canyon will connect to the mystifying vanishing of Article X.

With relief, Alvarado and his men continue riding hard through the unforgiving desert, quickly moving away from any powerful presence that may have caused the danger. The colonel senses the rockslide was more spiritual than geological. Alvarado rides on, doubting whether Chaco Canyon is the best hiding place for Article X.

CHAPTER 1
⟨∞⟩
NEW YEAR'S EVE

1910

All three men sitting in the Circle C line shack on the open range had arrived on the strength of their character, having met the physical and emotional challenges of the day. More than two feet of snow covers the range, the result of a blizzard that has blanketed the central New Mexico Territory. The blizzard has exposed cattle to the most severe winter of the new century. Snow-covered grass is beyond reach and time is running out.

When the storm hit the territory, ranchers had found it nearly impossible to help their drifting cattle. Yet the three men of Circle C have led a valiant effort to save many animals and will continue their work at daybreak. Since the three men had arrived at the shack, the temperature had dropped and the wind had worsened.

Exhausted, wet and chilled, they are dressed in heavy coats, with their collars pushed up and their hats pulled down. The small, one-room structure houses an old rough-hewn table, a few bunks and a stone fireplace. The flames dance wildly as the Circle C men sit around the table. Line shacks across the range provide shelter to men protecting invisible boundaries. Tonight the cabins protect against nature's wrath.

Inside, the fire gives the line shack a slight smoky smell. Outside, lingering clouds conceal the sky; the darkness is absolute with no visible moon or stars, and the air is getting colder. Intermittent coyote cries shatter the otherwise complete silence. According to legend, the coyote gave man fire; on this night, the men are especially grateful for the gift of the crackling blaze.

One man offers coffee, cigars and appreciation to the two other men for their courageous and decisive action out on the range. He is Adobe Centori, sole owner of the Circle C Ranch. The vast ranch, with thousands of cattle on thousands of acres, is located near the town of Valtura, in Corona County, New Mexico Territory.

The conjunction of the Sandia Mountains to the east and vast mesas and plains to the west distinguish Valtura, the county seat. Established along the Rio Grande, the high desert town is elevated 4,800 feet above sea level. Although there are many sunny and dry days, the winters here can be unpredictable.

Adobe Centori is forty years old, intelligent, educated and romantic to the extreme. At times, practicality pushes his romantic view of the world to the back of his mind. Today was one of those times. The handsome leader is square-jawed with a slender, square-shouldered build. He wears a long brown coat, a big tan hat and an ivory-handled, silver-plated Navy Colt pistol.

As Centori drinks black coffee, his cool blue eyes see the cigar smoke and fireplace smoke intermingle. His thoughts turn to his responsibility as a New Mexico statehood delegate. He thinks, *Will the economic impact of this winter have an adverse effect on statehood? There always has been some reason that stops the process short.*

The people in Valtura appreciate Centori's integrity of character, expressed by his public-spirited work and his willingness to provide territorial leadership. A rising star in New Mexico politics, he will probably do nothing in the New Year to spoil that promise.

Centori has lived a life encircled by honor and has placed his trust in men based on intuition—experience has confirmed his feelings. Earlier, the other men had displayed their true mettle and clear devotion to the Circle C Ranch.

"Thank you for all you have done," Centori says. "There's no doubt that Circle C men are the best in the territory. This is risky business, yet you came through with skill, confidence and, above all, friendship."

The two other men nod in support of the emotion. Suddenly, the blizzard intensifies, sending a violent wind roaring across the range and slamming the cabin. The strong blast causes the door to crash open; the loud noise and the cold wind rushing through the quarters surprises the men. Centori jumps up, causing his straight-back chair to fall over with a crash. He pushes the door closed and places two heavy pieces of firewood against it as a defense against the howling power of the blizzard.

That night, the stockpiled firewood and stone fireplace shield against raging winds and frigid temperatures. That day, there had been no defense against a blinding snow driven horizontal by high-speed winds. The horses, with steaming breath, had staggered through poor visibility, fighting the deep drifts, with shards of ice flying up as they had struggled for footing. Pressing on, the men had screamed to communicate over the deafening roar of the brutal winter winds.

Sitting directly across from Centori is twenty-one-year-old Henry Anthony Ellison. A strong young man with long, wild hair, he has a devil-may-care attitude. Although he had little ranching experience, Centori had hired him and helped him to learn the job. On the surface, Ellison is loyal, but known to trust the wrong people. Nonetheless, at the Circle C, he has been a good cowboy.

The oldest in the group, A.P. Baker, has gray hair and slit eyes. An honorable person with a general good character, he is friendly and dependable. He drives a hard bargain and takes risks for a good cause. At one time, he was one of the youngest to ride the Chisholm Trail, driving longhorn cattle from Texas to Dodge City's railhead. A dedicated cowboy, he moved herds ten miles a day for bread, beans, bacon, coffee, SOB-stew and $30 a month. Upon his arrival in Valtura, the fast-growing Circle C had needed help. Centori had hired A.P. based on his notable ranching skills and had soon promoted him to line foreman.

It is the first decade of the twentieth century but this is not the first big snow of the century. According to A.P., this snow is similar to the blizzard of 1901, making it one of the worst winters in New Mexico's recorded history. Although the exact snowfall is unknown in Valtura, one thing is obvious: the unrelenting snows had started in December and had created a hard winter.

Although the men had spent the last several days focused on their jobs, they were also aware of the closing of the west. In the last century, men had protected invisible boundaries around the open range. The new century had increasingly called for more fencing, causing sweeping changes in the cattle business. The most significant sign was barbed wire—a stark symbol of the end of an era.

Centori reaches into his pocket to look at his watch while thinking of the doom that had fallen upon many unsuspecting animals. His thoughts return to New Mexico's long struggle in seeking statehood. He draws on his cigar and thinks, *Will this disaster hurt our chances again? We have sought a self-governing state for so many years with so many failed attempts.*

Coyote cries shatter the silence again, jarring Centori from his thoughts. The coyote is an amazingly adaptive animal known for shortcuts; but there are no shortcuts for the cowboys on the open range and there are no shortcuts to statehood.

Americans in New Mexico remain without self-government, a condition that has existed since Mexico ceded the territory in 1848. For centuries, New Mexico had been a Spanish province and then a Mexican territory, with Santa Fe as a significant trading town. Yet New Mexico, a low priority in Washington, was still a territory.

It is 11:58 p.m. Centori turns, pulls out a bottle of whiskey and three dusty old glasses from a not-so-hidden box and considers his role as Corona County statehood delegate. He thinks, *Since the first attempt in 1850, New Mexicans have been continually disappointed, but I am resolute that the territory achieves statehood in the New Year. This year our destiny will be different.*

The latest statehood procedure had started in June with a referendum vote by the people and then a petition to Congress. An enabling act, signed by President Taft, had allowed the territory to hold a convention to create a state constitution in compliance with the U.S. Constitution. Centori and delegates from each county had assembled in Santa Fe where they had drafted and framed a constitution for the proposed new state of New Mexico.

In the New Year, the people will vote on the constitution and, if approved, the territory will be able to seek congressional and presidential support for statehood. Another election can follow for ratification and approval of congressional conditions. If Congress passes a joint resolution accepting the territory, the president can sign the bill for statehood.

Centori and the delegates know the statehood process, but a dormant political time bomb hidden in a time capsule is unknown. The time-sensitive Article X that could awaken with far-reaching repercussions for the United States, Old Mexico and New Mexico is nearing its deadline.

In the middle of a frigid, windswept blizzard, Centori pours, raises his glass and says, "Happy New Year."

"Happy New Year to you too," Ellison says.

A.P. says, "Boss, any wishes for the new year?"

"Same wish as last year, New Mexico statehood."

"Well, with you involved as a delegate, New Mexico will finally become a state."

"Thanks, A.P. but many others have tried before."

"You will do more than try, you will succeed," A.P. insists.

Centori pledges, "I'll do my best for statehood."

A.P. smiles and says, "Happy 1911."

STATEHOOD OF AFFAIRS

Finalist - 2012 New Mexico-Arizona Book Awards, Historical Fiction
- New Mexico-Arizona Book Co-op

In this fun and insight work of historical fiction, *Statehood of Affairs* presents readers with an excursion into a hidden history of New Mexico and its long struggle to achieve statehood. By leading the audience through an international plot surrounding the mysterious Article X of the Treaty of Mesilla, known as the Revert Document, Cillis crafts a story of romance and revenge, with major significance for New Mexico's fate in the Union. Embroiled in this plot is Sheriff Adobe Centori of Valtura, who finds that statehood, as well as life and love, are at stake.

-True West Magazine

Visit
www.statehoodofaffairs.com
www.facebook/statehoodofaffairs

CPSIA information can be obtained
at www.ICGtesting.com
Printed in the USA
FFOW02n2249290415
13063FF

9 781491 756829